Praise for Lori Verni-Fogarsi

"Smart, crisp dialogue and a fast-moving, entertaining plot make this a fun, 5-star read."
~Jan Moran, bestselling author of "Scent of Triumph"

"[Momnesia] is about being a good mom without losing yourself in the process. The author tackles the subject with humor and gets you thinking about a worthwhile subject… yourself!"
~The Boston Globe (Boston.com Moms)

"An unforgettable journey laced with humor and reality."
~Jill Schnake-Roeder

"An entertaining read for moms of all ages!"
*~Jackie Hennessey, author of
"How to Spread Sanity On a Cracker"*

"This summer's hot new read!"
~Heard on the My Carolina Today Show

Lori Verni-Fogarsi's novel, *Momnesia*, earned her recognition in both the **USA Best Book Awards** and the **National Indie Excellence Book Awards** as a finalist.

ALSO BY LORI VERNI-FOGARSI

Momnesia

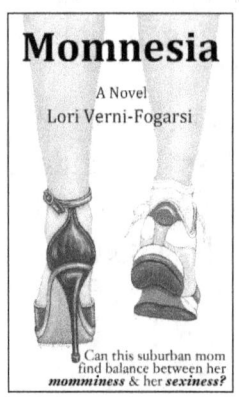

Everything You Need to Know About
House Training Puppies and Adult Dogs

Unexpecting

A Novel

Lori Verni-Fogarsi

Brickstone Publishing
133 Clay Ridge Way, Suite #200
Holly Springs, NC, 27540
www.BrickstonePublishing.com

Library of Congress Control Number: 2013934563
Publisher Cataloging Data:
Verni-Fogarsi, Lori
    Unexpecting: a novel / Lori Verni-Fogarsi.—1st ed.
    p.   cm.
    ISBN: 978-0-9840284-3-6
    1. Mothers—Fiction. 2. Family—Fiction. 3. Love—Fiction. 4. Women—Fiction.
5. Self Discovery—Fiction. I. Title.

BISAC: FIC044000
BISAC: FIC045000
BISAC: FIC027020

Designed by: Lori Verni-Fogarsi
Edited by: Clarice Joos

*Building a solid foundation
for books and their authors.*

To anyone who has ever wondered if it's only *your*

family that is so filled with love, loyalty,

heartbreak, and humor... this is for you.

~Lori Verni-Fogarsi

Chapter 1

It all started on a Tuesday morning. Shelley stood in her kitchen, pouring a cup of coffee and marveling that there was any left in the pot. The house was completely silent; no one else was home and during the busy summer season, that felt like a near miracle.

With three college-aged kids home for their break and a fourth living at home full-time, she and David would often joke that the kids and their friends were like a mathematical phenomenon: They seemed to multiply faster than amoebae, resulting in somewhere around nine teenagers at any given time. Sleeping, running around in bathing suits, asking for a ride, and eating, eating, eating… ceaselessly eating.

So when the doorbell rang, Shelley didn't run to answer it. The UPS man, whose job brought him to their door with astonishing regularity, would ring it whenever he left a package on the porch. And since she wasn't expecting anyone, she saw no need to go to the door in her PJs and reveal to the young-ish, good-looking courier that she was still in a state of undress even though it was after ten o'clock.

Then it rang a second time, which meant that either it was a package she had to sign for, or a neighbor stopping by for some as-yet-unknown favor to ask. Sighing, she set down her mug, still her favorite despite the chip on its rim because it said, *I'm 30… it seems like I should have money by now.* It had been modified with a Sharpie on its ten-year anniversary to read, *I'm 40*, and when she'd reached forty-five she decided not to bother updating it anymore; it was still funny.

As she approached the door she could see through its glass oval that there was a woman standing on the porch. Bracing herself to deal with whatever solicitation it might possibly be, Shelley opened the door and discovered that it wasn't a woman at all. It was a girl-woman. And not just any older girl/younger woman, but one that was hugely pregnant, her glistening face pocked full of acne, and bright blue eyes so watery they reminded her that she'd been meaning to water the hanging flower baskets on the porch.

"Yes?"

"Is this the Morsony household?"

Shelley knew immediately that this was not someone intimately acquainted with the family: She had pronounced Morsony the way most people would, *more-sewn-ee*, when in fact her husband's unusual ancestors had decided to pronounce it *more-sunny*.

"Yes it is. Can I help you?"

"I need to talk to David Morsony."

"He's not here at the moment. May I help you with something?"

The girl blinked. Her first tear fell and she fidgeted with her blonde ponytail. Shelley noticed that her hand was trembling and watched with horror as the girl's lips began to quiver in a fashion that she knew could be a precursor to the bawling, snot-bubbling drama she was very familiar with, having raised two girls of her own.

Averting her eyes, Shelley glanced toward the driveway, noticing that there was a Ford Focus that looked as if its only opportunity to move would be via a tow truck. It was blue, with a dented front fender and two different colors of duct tape hanging off one of the headlights. The windows were open and at first glance it appeared that someone was sitting in the passenger seat. Then she realized that it was a dog; one of those gigantic brindle dogs that made her think of that 1980s movie starring Tom Hanks.

The girl was sniffling and wiping under her eyes while Shelley thought longingly—and selfishly—about her coffee, abandoned on the counter inside. She didn't mean to seem uncaring, it was just that after raising four kids through their teen years, including all the ups and downs with friends, boyfriends, girlfriends and so on, the sight of a crying teenager on the porch seemed like yet another daily drama rather than an actual event.

At the same time, there was a niggling sense of foreboding lurking in the back of her mind. Shelley noted that she didn't appear to be selling anything, yet she had asked for her husband, David. Strange.

Slapping at yet another mosquito and beginning to perspire, Shelley looked at the girl, waiting for her to say something. Neither the bugs nor the heat ever let up during North Carolina summers and they were both out in full-force that morning. The girl leaned up against one of the porch columns, causing Shelley to realize that since she was so uncomfortable, the pregnant young lady must be about ready to collapse.

Mentally relinquishing any hope of enjoying her quiet morning, Shelley gestured toward the rocking chairs and asked if the girl would like to sit down. But either she didn't notice the gesture or chose to ignore it because she said, "That would be amazing," and stepped toward the entry.

Quickly deciding that she didn't meet the qualifications for a dangerous intruder, Shelley held the door open and the girl squeezed past with her big, tight belly leading the way. Walking straight ahead into the kitchen the way all visitors do, she sat at the counter where Shelley's stool was already pulled out from her earlier attempt at solitude.

"Would you like some iced tea?"

"Sweet tea? That would be great!" Disproportionately appreciative, Shelley hoped she realized that this was no home-steeped, prepared-in-the-sun-all-day sweet tea. It was Crystal Light, the former New Yorker's halfhearted attempt at Southern hospitality.

Accepting the glass and a napkin, the girl immediately started mopping the sweat that had beaded up on her forehead.

"So, can I ask why you're wanting to speak to my husband?"

"Oh. Yeah, I guess so. So, you're David's wife?"

"Yes."

"Oh."

A dawning sensation swept over Shelley, bringing pinpricks to her formerly relaxed body as it occurred to her that this girl was not only similar to her own seventeen and nineteen-year-old girls, but she was also not that much younger than her twenty-two and twenty-four-year-old stepsons. And she was pregnant. Very pregnant. Her internal rosary beads started twisting as she understood that they could be in for some seriously bad news. *How many times have I talked to those boys about safe sex?* The anger welled up inside her even though she had no information yet. *I'll kill them!*

The girl fidgeted with her napkin, twisting it into a pointy little cone, then tapping its end with her fingertip. "You're probably going to be surprised," she said, her eyes turned downward.

"I may not be as surprised as you think," Shelley replied, looking pointedly at her stomach.

"I'm David's daughter."

*****

She was right. Shelley was surprised. And that was an understatement. Disappointment washed over her as myriad implications spun through her head: *David lied to me; David has a child he doesn't take care of; David lied to me!*

It just seemed impossible—theirs was a marriage built of trust! A second marriage for each of them, the ten years they were together still felt like a dream come true. Every day. They told each other everything, shared every thought, feeling, nuance of their lives. From day one their philosophy was that they might as well be honest, be themselves, because eventually the truth would come out anyway. Unfathomably, it seemed that day had come.

The girl was watching her, undoubtedly seeing the horror reflect on her face as the betrayal of David's omission coalesced in her stomach. *It just seems impossible,* was all she could think. *David is the most ethical man I've ever met. Or even heard of!* The idea that he had a child he had nothing to do with was preposterous. Yet here she was, sitting in their kitchen.

"He doesn't know."

"What?"

"He doesn't even know I exist. My mother never told him."

Relief and confusion combined so that Shelley didn't know if she felt better or worse.

"Do you mind if I use your bathroom?" The girl indicated her belly with the commiserative expression all pregnant women use when they're talking to another woman who has had children. Shelley tried to ignore the childish, midlife crisis part of herself that resented the assumption that she had kids. *Of course I look like I have kids. I'm a forty-six-year-old woman who has kids!* she admonished herself.

"Sure, it's there in the hall, to the left."

"Thanks."

Shelley picked up her mug and took a sip of the now-tepid coffee, then dumped it down the sink. Pulling the pitcher out of the fridge, she poured herself a glass of iced tea and contemplated what to do. Standing there in the quiet kitchen, a squeaky, high-pitched noise broke through her thought process. Listening carefully, she realized that it didn't sound like the neighborhood toddlers or any other recognizable sound.

Striding toward the front of the house, the bathroom door flung open just as she was passing it, smashing into the top of her foot.

"Omigod, I'm so sorry!"

Shelley rubbed the spot, which she already knew would be yellow and blue by nightfall.

"I'm really sorry, are you okay?"

"Sure, I'll be fine," Shelley looked at her, questioning.

"I was rushing because that's Tiny, making that noise. It's too hot for him to stay in the car and he hates being alone.

"Oh."

"Do you think it would be okay for me to bring him in? Just for a little while? The air-conditioning will make him feel so much better."

Shelley peered through the front door at the enormous animal. A true pet lover, she liked dogs; she would even go so far as to say that she loved dogs. But this was a huge dog, and a dog she didn't know. Her mind's eye went into her living room where there was brand new white furniture—she and David had ordered it when their youngest turned seventeen. The plan was to hurry up and enjoy nice furniture while the kids were older but didn't yet have grandchildren to bring over and destroy it.

Shelley looked at the girl. Her face was filled with hope. She looked again at Tiny (who was anything but). His chin was resting where the car window was wide open, heartbrokenly staring at the house and occasionally making a yelping noise that made him sound... well, tiny.

"How does he do with cats?" Shelley asked, thinking of Frick, their nineteen-year-old cat who had been melancholy ever since losing his buddy, Frack, just six months earlier.

"He's great. He loves cats!" the girl exclaimed in a desperately bright tone.

"Fine," Shelley sighed, hoping that he loved cats as friends rather than as hors d'oeuvres. "But make sure he doesn't chew anything in here."

"Oh, he won't." She smiled, a glimmer of happiness brightening her face for the first time since she'd arrived. "He's a really good dog. You'll see."

The girl went outside to get Tiny while Shelley went into the kitchen and phoned David at work.

"I need you to come home. Yes, now. Right now. And drive carefully. I love you."

Chapter 2

It turned out, her name was Alexandra. Alexandra Johansen, daughter of Patricia "Patty" Johansen. And David. Who didn't know.

Right after he'd gotten divorced seventeen years earlier, David had dated Patty. Twice. Two dates. But apparently he slept with her because here was Alexandra.

She told them the story as she knew it: Patty had gotten pregnant even though she was on the pill. She never told David because she knew they didn't love one another and didn't want to raise a child under those circumstances. She had a decent career as a horticulturist at North Carolina State University and decided to have the baby and raise her herself. And she did.

Until a month before, when Patty passed away in a freak incident of heat stroke while planting flowers on a Saturday afternoon. Poor Alexandra had come home from having a milkshake with a friend and found her mother unconscious in the small, common area garden in front of their apartment complex. By the time the ambulance arrived, it was too late to resuscitate her.

The couple listened to the story in shock, Shelley distracted by the thought that she never even realized you could die from heat stroke unless you were, let's say, stranded in a desert or something.

Alexandra, eight months pregnant and with no other relatives, had stayed with their next-door neighbors until the Department of Child Services caught up with them and informed them that because she was only seventeen she would have to go into foster care. The family showed no signs of wanting to take on the permanent responsibility and planned to drop her off at DCS the next day, and bring Tiny to the animal shelter.

Patty did have a will, in which she left Alexandra everything she owned: The old car that she'd been saving until Alexandra was ready for one of her own, a few pieces of jewelry, household belongings, a meager college savings account, and information about David

Alexandra had packed up their small apartment, and all of it, plus Tiny, had been loaded in the car and sat in their driveway.

*****

David looked at Shelley. Shelley looked at David. Alexandra looked at both of them. They looked at Alexandra. And her belly. They all looked at each other, each trying to figure out what to say, the magnitude of shock at the situation weighing heavily on them like elephants. Elephants in the room. Such a cliché but so irascibly perfect that afternoon.

Trying to grasp the concept that David had a daughter, that she was his *child,* was so unfathomable as to be beyond full comprehension at the moment.

What demanded their attention first and foremost was Alexandra's full, round stomach, so ripe with pregnancy that it seemed like a ticking time bomb. Shelley and David glanced at one another, silently communicating their thoughts: Were they expected to take this girl into their home and raise her and her baby? Even if they weren't expected to, wouldn't that be the *right thing* to do?

Then there was the other thing they were both thinking—one that most people would hate to admit out loud but David and Shelley readily admitted to one another in the privacy of their bedroom, whispering even though they didn't have to, but just because they liked to: They didn't want any more kids. And not by mild standards either. They *really, really* didn't want any more kids, and especially not babies.

This is not to say that they didn't love the kids they already had. They loved them very much and were glad they had them. It was just that they had never wished there were more. They'd discussed babies when they married ten years earlier, when Shelley's girls were seven and nine, and David's boys were twelve and fourteen. Did they want to have another baby? A baby they could raise with the knowledge of hindsight strengthening their parenting skills and their relationship like steel-reinforced beams? Allowing them to do things differently, being parents together, yet remaining a couple who don't forget all that they were before?

The answer was no—unequivocally and with no hesitation on either of their parts. They didn't want any more babies then (David had a vasectomy two months later) and they didn't want any more babies now.

Further, as their kids grew into teenagers, the couple had a multitude of conversations about what a nightmare it would be if one of their own kids got pregnant. Especially Rose or Grace.

They fully acknowledged during the privacy of their talks that it was a double standard—and if Michael or Russell got someone pregnant it certainly would not be a good thing—but the fact was, it would be the girl's parents who would be charged with the day-to-day responsibility. It would be an unfortunate situation, but their responsibilities would be more financial and emotional, rather than the daily task of raising a baby in their home.

If Rose or Grace got pregnant, however, *they* would be the girl's parents, imposed with the daily responsibility. And they really, *really* did not want to raise another baby.

Having analyzed this during many a whisper session, they agreed that it would be a no-win situation.

Would they try to convince them to have an abortion? No. They wouldn't be entirely against it if that's what they wanted, but it was mostly against their beliefs.

Would they refuse to help their own daughter, telling her she had to find somewhere else to live and go take care of a baby on her own? Realistically, no. How would a teenaged girl take care of a baby and all of those responsibilities anyway?

Would they let her live at home, helping out by watching her baby all day and night so she could go to school and work? That sounded equally as unpalatable as throwing her in the street.

In their minds, if Rose or Grace got pregnant, the options were either to let it ruin her life or let it ruin theirs. Which was worse? They hoped to never find out.

Instead they (especially Shelley, as their mom) talked to the kids about safe sex. They talked about how hard life is, how much everything costs, how it's better to wait until you're able to manage your own responsibilities. She utilized brevity when talking with the boys while still emphasizing that, "condoms prevent minivans." She confided to the girls that all men, without exception, would swear that sex with a condom doesn't feel good to them. Which is a lie… it feels a hell of a lot better than not getting laid and if you make that the only option, they'll use one without hesitation.

It was embarrassing, both for Shelley and for the kids. Rose and Grace would roll their eyes and say, "Mo-om, do you think I'm a slut?" But it was all she could think of to do, and the discomfort of discussing it was far better than having their childrens' lives be irrevocably changed and them ending up raising another baby.

*****

Given that David and Shelley had already dissected this to the nth degree and had decided that the only acceptable option was prevention, they had no idea what to do about Alexandra. Not to mention that they hadn't even known about Alexandra herself until an hour earlier!

The silence was voluminous. The only sound was of Tiny's breathing. He was lying on the kitchen floor, resting his enormous head on the cool tiles. His pendulous lips were hanging open and a sizeable puddle of drool was forming.

Shelley was jealous, wishing she could lie on the floor and cool her head, which felt like it would explode from the overabundance of thoughts pulling at its seams. Glancing at David, he looked as if his level of shock would cause him to start drooling as much as the dog at any moment.

Poor Alexandra sat there miserably, her lips formed in a quivering frown as she looked down at her lap where she was picking at her cuticles. Shame washed over Shelley as she thought, *Imagine, being a seventeen-year-old girl, pregnant, with nowhere to go and no family except a stranger.* Their stunned reaction did not exactly impart excitement at meeting her, and that had to be even more painful.

Knowing that she and David needed to talk privately, Shelley suggested that Alexandra go lie down and rest for a while, and she asked if she could take a shower first; she was sweaty from loading up the car. Shelley showed her to their master suite, gave her some towels, and told her to take her time.

They were going to need it.

*****

They talked for two hours. They talked about their personal ethics, about what was the right thing to do. They talked about what they would want someone to do if this happened to their daughter. They talked about the fact that she *is* his daughter.

They went over logistics, which seemed inane in comparison to the overall scenario, but still needed to be sorted out. For example, where would they put another teenager and a newborn baby? Theirs was a three-bedroom house. It was a nice house, but it did have only three bedrooms.

Grace lived in one of them, as she was seventeen and about to start her senior year of high school. Rose, who had just started college the year before, shared the room with her sister when she was home for the summer and during breaks. David and Shelley had the master bedroom. And the third bedroom was the boys' room, currently inhabited by Russell, also home for the summer from Colorado State, and by Michael, who had an apartment near Appalachian State but sometimes came home from grad school to visit.

Actually, it all seemed quite simple when they focused on things like who would use what bedroom. In denial of the bigger issues, the discussion took on the air it had when they invited guests from out of town.

Even when they talked about adding another teenager to the household, the conversation didn't hold much weight—between the kids and their friends, they were already accustomed to scores of them. They'd worked hard to make sure their house was known as the cool one, where kids could be themselves and where potato chips were always in stock.

But when they tried to talk about the baby they were struck dumb. The couple stared at one another, each recalling memories of when their kids were babies. The all night crying. The giant plastic accoutrements that become part of the household décor. The constant diapering, attention needed, the putting of everything in their mouths. The toddler phase, in which they are mobile but don't yet have any common sense. The safety latches that make everything so inconvenient yet are more convenient than trips to the emergency room.

There was a self-centered, yet strongly wishful moment when they talked about the fact that there were programs for girls like this. That she would only be in the system for one year, and that they had group homes for young pregnant girls and their babies.

Then they talked about Shelley's friend Kristen, who grew up in foster homes and had shared some of her stories during moments of strong feminine bonding combined with significant quantities of wine. She had been in five families over the years and only two of them were decent. Another was moderate. The other two? Suffice it to say that she was still in therapy.

Trapped. That's what they were. There was simply no other acceptable option than to take the girl into their home, raise her as their own, and do the right thing. What exactly that was, they weren't absolutely sure. But they did know that turning her away was not something they could live with.

Shelley and David held each other, there on their new white sofa, his heart beating beneath her cheek, the strength of his chest symbolizing the strength they would need together. She wrapped her arms more tightly around his waist, hoping that he too felt some semblance of courage emanating from her soul into his.

Chapter 3

"I can't find any towels!" Rose screeched, "and I have to leave for work in half an hour!"

Shelley walked to the bottom of the stairs. "Did you check the linen closet?"

"No. I was looking in the dishwasher. Of course I checked the linen closet! There's not even one towel in there!"

Knowing that she'd just done laundry the day before, Shelley went upstairs and opened the linen closet. No towels. Rose rolled her eyes.

"Sorry, it just seems strange that there are no towels."

"I kno-ow."

Shelley walked into the hall bathroom and saw that there were the typical towels hanging on the hooks: Grace's favorite and two green ones probably used by the boys. In the master bath the only towels were David's and hers.

"Here, use mine for now. I've only used it once."

Rose looked at her with an expression of disgust that reminded Shelley of how she felt toward her own mother's body when she was Rose's age. Oldness—it just seemed so gross at the time. A small shock went through her core as it occurred to her that to Rose, she was old. She didn't feel old, but apparently she was old enough for her towel to be gross.

"Sorry, it's all I can offer right now."

Sighing, Rose grabbed the towel and stomped off to the bathroom, slamming the door.

"You're welcome!" Shelley shouted in its direction.

*****

The mystery of the missing towels was soon solved. Fancying herself a detective of Nancy Drew proportions, Shelley systematically checked the entire house, working her way from the upstairs bedrooms, through the downstairs living room, kitchen, even the dining room, and eventually outside.

Which is where she found Tiny, blissfully rolling on her (formerly) white towels in the driveway while Alexandra wound up the hose.

"What are you doing?"

"I gave Tiny a bath."

"Didn't you just wash him last week?"

"Yeah but I wanted him to be extra clean."

Extra clean? It seemed that the nesting instinct was taking its toll on Alexandra, and by extension, on Tiny. Shelley looked at her stomach; if she thought it was big when they first met a month before, it was enormous now. "Now" being two days after her due date, and forty weeks after she had sex with Juan, a Mexican guy she met while she'd been on vacation with her mother and had snuck out of the resort's teen program to go to a bar. A bar where they were evidently unconcerned about serving alcohol to a sixteen-year-old American girl, and where guys named Juan hung out hoping to get lucky. (No, she didn't know his last name and yes, her mother had tried to investigate, to no avail.)

"Didn't I ask you not to use the white towels when you wash him?"

"Yeah, but I couldn't find the blue ones from last week."

"I don't remember seeing them when I did the wash yesterday. Where did you put them?"

Alexandra thought for a moment, then froze. Nervously, she said, "I think I left them in the garage."

The two squeezed past Shelley's car (now unable to be driven without moving at least two other vehicles) and found the blue towels piled in a stiff heap.

"Omigod, I'm so sorry!"

Shelley was torn. This was the biggest challenge so far in adding another child to their household: If it was one of their own kids, or possibly even one of their regular-visitor friends, she'd have been yelling about how now they were mildewed and they'd better get their butts into the laundry room and take care of this immediately. If it were a guest, she'd have said it was no problem and would have taken care of it herself.

However, Alexandra was neither one of their own kids nor a guest. Or more accurately, she was one of their own kids but it just didn't feel right to yell at her yet.

She was trying to fit in, but no one was making it easy on her. Rose was too busy with her own life to give her more than a passing glance, while Russell and Michael treated her like she was a temporary houseguest for whom they had to evacuate their room and sleep on the pullout sofa. For the three older kids who were away at college the majority of the time, Alexandra's existence was nearly irrelevant.

Grace was another story. They were within one month of each other age-wise, and Grace's attitude toward both Alexandra and Tiny could be described as nothing short of contemptuous. Shelley noticed that Grace's facial expression when she was around Alexandra was similar to the one she wore when she would scream for David to come kill a bug in her room.

Shelley tried talking to her about it. They went out for lunch, just the two of them, about a week after Alexandra moved in.

Shelley spoke about family, about flexibility, about being charitable toward others who are less fortunate.

Grace spoke about sluttiness, pathetic-ness, and the likelihood of catching a disease from some Mexican guy while on vacation.

Even Tiny, whose sweet, dopey personality grew on everyone else quite quickly, could not get Grace to warm up. "Uccch," she would complain, even though he was gazing at her with pure canine adoration, "Isn't there something you can do about those slime strings?"

(The slime was not Shelley's favorite of Tiny's traits either. But his personality—sweet and calm, and having no clue that he was any larger than a lap dog—quickly won her over. She'd purchased bandanas in a variety of colors, which he wore most days in an attempt to keep his drool under control.)

Now, standing in front of the crunchy, mildewed blue towels, Alexandra said, "Don't worry. I'll wash these. And I'll wash the white ones with bleach too." There was desperation in her voice, making Shelley wonder if Alexandra thought she was a tyrannical stepmom who was going to beat her for messing up some towels.

"It's okay. I'm sure you'll do a great job. Let me know if you have any questions about the washing machine."

Alexandra bent down, gathered the towels clumsily, and started hauling them inside.

"I'll go get Tiny and the white ones," Shelley said.

"Oh, you don't have to do that! I'll do it!" Alexandra dropped the towels right where she stood and started trying to squeeze past. Shelley put a hand on her shoulder, stopping her. "Alexandra, it's okay. I'll get him, I don't mind. Now you just go start with those and we'll be inside in a minute."

*****

That night David and Shelley lay in bed, exhausted as usual but forcing themselves to converse, as it was the only time of the day they could truly connect uninterrupted.

His job as a corporate accountant was extremely busy in the mid-summer months. His company's fiscal year ended in August and he was overloaded with end-of-year statements, training overflow workers, and tax planning for the following year.

Shelley's days were filled with the usual stream of teenagers coming and going, chauffeuring them, searching for lost items, and doing the usual food shopping, cleaning, paying of bills, and other household duties. She had taken Alexandra to the obstetrician that afternoon (she was added to their medical insurance once David's paternity was confirmed), and the doctor assured them that although Alexandra was so uncomfortable, everything was fine with the pregnancy, and the baby was still too high to consider inducing her.

After they gave each other the summary of their day, they agreed that they had to discuss Alexandra's schooling. Shelley had gotten the transcripts from her old high school; she was a good student, with only one C and the rest of her grades higher.

She'd been on her school dance team but had been disappointed when she was told she could no longer participate due to her "health condition." In fact, according to Alexandra her entire school life changed dramatically as soon as her pregnancy began to show. Kids she'd been close with since kindergarten avoided her, her best friend stopped calling, and she'd even overheard two of her favorite teachers whispering behind their hands about what a shame it was for such a nice girl to get "in trouble."

The only friend she still had was Amy, an outcast sort of girl who never seemed to have any friends at all until she befriended Alexandra, sitting alone in the cafeteria one day. "I can't believe it," Alexandra described, "the only person who is still my friend is someone I never even knew before."

Shelley's heart ached for her. It reminded her of years earlier, when she'd gotten divorced from her first husband and all of her neighborhood friends treated her like a pariah—a pariah who was out to steal their husbands. Please. As if their pot-bellied, unhelpful, can't-see-them-as-anything-more-than-a-mommy husbands were any better than the one she'd just gotten rid of.

She too hadn't heard from people she'd considered close friends. Even the vast majority of family members were mysteriously absent. It was a difficult time for her—more because of the faithlessness of friends than because of the divorce itself—and that was without the viciousness that's so rampant amongst teens. Girls *can* be vicious, they knew, and that's why they'd researched all of the options, ranging from having Alexandra attend normal high school to taking online classes.

Alexandra wanted to do it online. David and Shelley suspected that she was afraid to attend school in person and risk rejection from all the girls who would undoubtedly know she was a teenaged mom.

David also wanted her to take online classes; he didn't want Shelley to be left to take care of the baby all day.

As for Shelley, she wished it would all just go away; she didn't want to have to decide. But it wasn't going away, and in fact it was only going to get worse. Very soon. And her logical side, her *unselfish* logical side, couldn't deny her gut, which said that she should attend normal school.

She felt it was the only way Alexandra could have any semblance of a normal life. Her only chance to make friends. The only opportunity to have a period of time each day when she could be a regular girl who giggles about boys and fixes her lipstick in the tiny mirror stuck to the inside of her locker. Shelley knew from experience how easy it was to completely lose your Self in the role of mother, and how priceless it was to have time to just be who you were.

She and David debated this at length, each of them sometimes being the nurturing one, and sometimes playing Devil's advocate.

It was her mistake, not ours. She should have used protection, not snuck out in the first place. You wanna play, you gotta pay.

And yet, she's a young girl with her whole life ahead of her. How can we expect her to become a successful woman, go to college, if we don't try to provide a normal life?

Why should she have a normal life? It is not normal to get pregnant at sixteen and expect to have a normal life.

Everyone makes mistakes. What mistakes have we made over our lifetimes that we each wish we could go back and change?

Then again, no one helped us when we made those mistakes—we had to dig ourselves out of the holes we dug.

On the other hand, didn't we wish someone had helped us? Why didn't they? And would we have turned out better or worse if they had?

It was exhausting, the factors to be considered seemingly infinite, and with no end in sight.

Concurring that they should sleep on it, Shelley reached over and clicked off the bedside lamp. Snuggling up behind her, David's kiss was warm and loving on the back of her neck. It was something they'd agreed upon years earlier, when their focus was on steps they could take to make their marriage work for a lifetime. Ways to stay close even when life stood staunchly in the way.

They'd promised that they would kiss, that they'd be affectionate toward one another, even if only for a moment each day. That they would do so with the understanding that not every sign of affection was an obligation to have sex (although that might be nice too). But they agreed that the kissing was important and had been doing it ever since.

Guiltily thankful that the neck kiss was not accompanied by the butt rub on that particular night, Shelley nestled even closer to David and drifted off to sleep.

*****

It was pitch dark in the room. Confused, Shelley sat up and wondered what had woken her. Then she heard it again. A soft knock, someone at the bedroom door.

Feeling her way along the dresser, she stumbled to open the door and found Alexandra in the hallway on her hands and knees with paper towels, soaking something up from the rug. The hall nightlight lit her face softly as she looked up and said, "My water broke."

Chapter 4

"It's a boy!"

The nurses rushed to take the baby from the doctor's hands as Alexandra strained in their direction, trying to see her child.

This was something Shelley had forgotten: How they get in the way the moment the baby is born, then take them and do all sorts of things to them before you even get to see. She remembered feeling enraged and cheated; she didn't get to hold her child until she was a minute old, while the nurses got to measure her, put stuff in her eyes, and count her fingers and toes.

"Do you want to do the honors?"

"What?" She hadn't realized the doctor was talking to her.

"Would you like to cut the cord?" He extended the surgical scissor toward her.

It wasn't that she didn't care about Alexandra. Or her baby. But she really didn't want to cut the cord either; it was a matter of squeamishness. The very thought caused her to experience nausea not unlike how she felt when she accompanied a friend to get a small tattoo on her hip after she'd begged her to hold her hand during the process.

Then she recalled the resentment she still felt toward Paul, her ex-husband, because he'd declined to cut the cord for either of their babies.

"Sure, that would be an honor," she said. Holding her breath, she lined up the scissors in between the two hemostats and squeezed, trying not to hear the sound of human tissue disconnecting under her touch.

Queasy, she turned to Alexandra and smiled. Better. Better to look at this strong woman—she could not think of her as a child at the moment—this woman who had valiantly survived one of life's most difficult challenges right before her very eyes. Delivering a baby.

"I'm so proud of you, sweetheart. And I know that your mom is watching you from heaven, feeling very proud of you too."

"Thank you, Shelley. Thank you for being there for me and for doing this with me."

So formal! So polite! Disappointment stabbed Shelley's heart as she realized how diminished this experience was for Alexandra, having to do it with her instead of her own mother. It was so inappropriate an exchange to occur between two women who just experienced the miracle of labor and delivery, side-by-side, over the last nine hours.

She wished her real mother were there. It was sad. Very, very sad.

At the same time, the ironic side of her—the side that couldn't help being giddy on such a momentous occasion—quelled the urge to point out that just moments earlier she'd taken a video of Alexandra's crotch with the baby crowning. Instead she said, and truly meant, "It was my pleasure."

*****

It was around 2:00 am when Shelley rubbed Alexandra's shoulder, trying to rouse her from sleep.

"The nurse is here to help you with breastfeeding."

Alexandra rolled over and moaned. "My bottom hurts."

"I know it does, sweetie. Come on, I'll help you sit up. She's brought the baby."

"Uurgh."

Lifting as gently as possible, Shelley pulled her up and plumped some pillows behind her. The nurse stepped closer and placed the baby, wrapped impossibly tightly and wearing a tiny blue and white striped hat, into Alexandra's arms.

He was screaming—as loudly as a just-under-seven-pound baby can scream anyway. He looked surprisingly small to Shelley, paralleling the surprise she'd felt the first time she marveled over the largeness of her own eight-and-a-half and nine-point-three-pound babies when they were born. The innate urgency to comfort him welled up inside her, making her breasts tingle even though it was sixteen years since she'd nursed a baby.

"He's hungry," the nurse said. "Let's see if we can get him to latch on."

"I can't."

"Of course you can, Ms. Alexandra. That's what God made breasts for."

"I don't want to breastfeed, I want to give him a bottle."

"It's normal to be scared, that's why I'm here to help you. Now let me help you with your gown."

"No. I am not breastfeeding!"

Honestly, this had never occurred to Shelley. She had never even thought to discuss it with Alexandra because in her mind, breastfeeding was what one did with a baby. She couldn't imagine why, when the body so miraculously produces the perfect food for a child, a person would prefer to feed them a liquid produced by cows and mixed with oils and God knew what else. Not to mention the inconvenience of bottles: sterilizing them, warming them up, keeping them refrigerated...

"Shelley, will you please tell her that I'm not breastfeeding."

"Well, I..."

"It seems your mamma thinks you should breastfeed too," the nurse pointed out.

"She is *not* my mother and I am *not* breastfeeding!"

*****

Two days later, little baby Patrick came home from the hospital, complete with all the pomp and circumstance that accompanies the occasion: the nurses insisting on bringing Alexandra downstairs in a wheelchair; David bringing the car around and re-checking the car seat for the umpteenth time; Shelley sitting in the front seat and Alexandra in the back next to Patrick, all of them undoubtedly visualizing every lunatic on the road swerving out of control and hitting their car.

Shelley smiled to herself as she recalled a memory from nineteen years earlier when she took her first baby, Rose, out for a walk in the stroller for the very first time. It was a crisp autumn day, with skies impossibly blue, the temperature perfect for taking a walk. She remembered guiding the stroller along the sidewalk and feeling so proud: proud of the baby she'd created, proud of having figured out how to open the stroller whose mechanics were so simple yet so difficult to figure out those first few times; proud of the life she led as a mother, a wife, a business owner, a home owner.

Blissful in her newfound motherliness, and with the soreness of childbirth becoming more of a memory than a current reality, she'd walked slowly, carefully, down the residential street where she lived at the time. Birds were chirping and she could hear the sounds of children playing, punctuated by the exuberant bark of a dog in a nearby yard. Squirrels were scampering, animated as cartoon characters, leaping from branch to branch, busily bringing their loot back to their nests to save up for winter.

And that's when it hit her: *Squirrels* were scampering. *Jumping* from branch to branch *right above* where they were walking! She froze, aghast, staring at her vulnerable newborn who slept, blissfully unaware that at any moment a rodent could fall right into her stroller.

She'd rationalized with herself, *Stop being ridiculous! In your entire life, have you ever seen a squirrel slip and fall? Of course not!*

It didn't matter. Suddenly the world seemed filled with danger. Squirrels slipping, birds pooping, bumps in the sidewalk upending the stroller and sending the baby flying onto the pavement despite the five-point restraint that had her strapped in as if riding on an upside-down roller coaster. It felt like a dangerous world, one in which she could never keep her child safe. In which Shelley, at that moment, vastly preferred to stay safely ensconced in their tidy little ranch home where the most dangerous hazard would be their elderly dog walking by and wagging his tail.

Riding along in the car, recalling that day and looking around at all the "maniacs" on the road, Shelley felt her lip curl upward with ironic mirth and turned around to see how Alexandra was handling it.

She was flipping through a magazine—the latest issue of *Cosmo*—undoubtedly filled with advice for good fashion, good makeup, and good sex (just what a seventeen-year-old girl needs). Shelley's concern about how she'd gotten the magazine was overridden by her surprise that Alexandra seemed entirely unconcerned about taking her son for his first ride in a motorized vehicle. She asked how she was doing.

"Fine. I can't *wait* to get home and take a nap. The nurses brought him into my room at like *six o'clock* in the morning." She rolled her eyes.

A bit alarmed, Shelley recalled that this was covered in the parenting class she'd attended. A program designed for first-time mothers, it had covered everything from how to put on a diaper to handling the late-night waking, as well as all of the other issues inherently routine with newborn babies.

Reminding herself about Alexandra's raging hormones, Shelley decided not to take issue with any of it, and instead reached over to hold David's hand. "Sorry, babe," he said. "I want to keep two hands on the wheel." She looked over at his face, steadfastly trained on the road, and at his hands, white-knuckled on the steering wheel, and took comfort in the like-mindedness that was yet another example of how in sync they were with one another.

*****

"You. Have. Six. New. Messages," said the computerized voice on the answering machine. Grabbing a pen, Shelley prepared to write them down when Russell ran into the kitchen and asked, "Can you drop me off at McDonald's?"

She held up a finger, signaling that she was busy.

"My buddies are already there." There was an exasperated whine in his voice and he pulled out his cell phone to check the time, even though there was a clock right there on the microwave.

Shooing at him and implementing the I Mean It Glare, she tried to block out his voice and concentrate on the messages.

Tiny started barking in earnest—something he indulged in only when there was someone at the door.

Russell didn't move and she had already missed two of the messages. Sighing, she pressed the Save Messages button and went to answer the door.

"Is Grace home?" It was Cassie, Grace's best girlfriend, and as she pointed upstairs toward Grace's room, Shelley vaguely wondered why she bothered ringing the bell at all; she practically lived at their house. Grateful that at least someone had a little manners, she told Russell that she'd drive him in ten minutes and turned a blind eye when he moaned and spun on his heel.

Responsibility pulled her in opposite directions as she contemplated leaving the house so shortly after arriving home with Alexandra and Patrick, versus her obligation to also take care of the other kids. Over the last few days they'd been left to take care of themselves, the house, the pets, and give each other rides to their summer jobs, while she and David were consumed with the birth and hospital visits.

As for David himself, if she thought her life was backed up, it was nothing in comparison to his. She experienced a pang of sympathy as she visualized him back at his office, undoubtedly checking far more than six messages.

Figuring that it would only take a short time and that she'd multitask while she was out, Shelley grabbed the grocery list from the fridge and added a few things to it, used the bathroom, swiped on some fresh lip gloss, checked to see if Tiny's food was getting low (that dog went through as much food as ten truck drivers), and yelled up the stairs to see if Michael could go with her.

His voice came from behind her shoulder, startling her. "I'm staying in the living room now, remember?"

"Oh yeah. Can you come with me to the store? I'd like to spend some time together and I could use your help carrying Tiny's food."

"Sure, let me get my flip flops."

As she waited for Michael, Frick walked into the kitchen, all skinny with his elderly feline gait. Running her hand along his still-silky fur, she felt a crunchy section: dried slime from Tiny licking him. The two had hit it off immediately, with Tiny taking on a role that was almost paternal and Frick resignedly succumbing to it. Grabbing a paper towel and wetting it in the sink, she ran it over Frick's fur to remove the crunchy spot, knowing that it would be replaced with a new one shortly.

Walking out to the driveway, Shelley realized that both Rose's car and Michael's would have to be moved in order to get hers out. "Can we just take yours?" she asked Michael, heading back inside to get Rose's keys while Russell stood there sulking because now it was probably eleven minutes he'd had to wait.

Finally alone in the car together after Russell leaping out without so much as a word of thanks, she studied Michael's profile, noticing for the first time that his light shadow of a beard no longer had the look of a fuzzy adolescent, but rather the wiry texture of a man. His jawbone pulsed, reminding her that he was David's son, the clenching movement being David's signature habit when under pressure. She asked Michael how school was going.

"Okay, I guess."

"You guess? Is something not going well?"

"No, it's fine. I mean, I'm doing fine in my classes."

"So then what's making it only 'fine' instead of 'great?'"

"I don't know… I guess college was more fun than grad school is."

"What's the difference?"

"The kids are all so *serious*. No one wants to go out anymore and everyone's always either studying or working. Including me."

Shelley thought that his use of the term "kids" was ironic. When she was in her twenties, they considered themselves men and women. Regardless, she understood what he meant; she too had always felt that life is far more work than books or movies—or even parents—make it out to be.

She and David had agreed that they would pay for each of the kids' four-year degrees. But grad school, doctorates, or any other advanced degrees were to be paid for by them. Not only would it have been impossible for them to afford it, but they also felt that the kids needed to take some responsibility for their own futures. Plus, they didn't want to end up like their friends, Claire and Brian, whose son accomplished a Masters in Social Work that cost them forty-thousand dollars a year at an Ivy-league school, only to pursue a career in the social security office at a salary frighteningly near the poverty level.

"I know what you mean. Life is exhausting."

"I'm just starting to wonder whether it's even worth it. You go to school so you can get a good job, so you can make a lot of money, and for what? So you can buy a bigger house, have a nicer car, go on a better vacation? Then you just have to keep working harder and harder to get more things."

"Well, you don't *have* to do that. You could choose to work a moderate amount and live in a more moderate house, keep more moderate bills."

"So then what's the point of doing all this?"

"It's hard to say," she mused, realizing she'd asked herself this question thousands of times.

Her cell phone rang but she ignored it, figuring she'd check the voice mail at a more opportune moment. "I think it's nice to have choices. For it to be your *option* to do what you want, rather than being limited to what you *can* do."

"I guess." He didn't sound sure at all.

Her phone rang again, too soon for the previous caller to have left a message.

"Excuse me a minute, sorry." She swiped to answer the phone. "Hello?"

"Shelley, they are waking up Patrick!" It was Alexandra, sobbing as if the world were coming to an end.

"Who is?"

"Grace and her friend!"

"What are they doing?"

"They have music on in her room and it's so loud, it woke him up!"

"Did you ask her to lower it?"

"I did, but she said it's the middle of the afternoon and there's no reason she shouldn't listen to music."

Grace did have a point. Shelley had always been of the mindset that you can't expect to maintain a silent household just because babies are around. She'd always vacuumed, listened to music, and carried on normal activities during the day when her kids were babies. In fact she was glad if they were awake, figuring it would increase the odds of them sleeping at night.

Although she did feel for Alexandra being that they'd *just* gotten home from the hospital.

"Okay, so he's awake. It is daytime. Maybe it would be nice to go sit out on the screened porch with him for a while? Get some fresh air?"

"I don't *want* fresh air. I just want him to go back to sleep!"

Shelley could hear Patrick crying in the background, the mother in her recognizing that since he just woke up, he would need a diaper change and a feeding—not to mention a little snuggling being a good idea too.

The call waiting beeped on her phone. "Hold on a minute."

It was Grace, calling to complain that Patrick was crying and that she and her friend "can't even hear themselves think." What was she, a little old lady? Telling her to try and ignore it and that she'd be home in half an hour, Shelley clicked back over to Alexandra, where now she could hear Patrick wailing, obviously still not attended to.

"Alexandra, babies almost never do what we want when we want. It sounds like you need to change him and feed him, then maybe just hold him for a while."

"Ugh!" Her typical teenaged response was punctuated by her hanging up, which was not at all typical in their household. Or at least not tolerated: the rest of the kids had done it no more than once each and it was obvious that now she'd have to address this with Alexandra too.

Silence filled the car as she and Michael absorbed the blatant disrespect of the phone hang up, both of them fully aware of the impending consequences. As he navigated into a parking spot at the pet supply store, they looked at one another, their lives so astronomically different, yet surprisingly the same.

"You see? It doesn't matter whether you're in school, at work, or at home. Life is just way too much work," Shelley sighed.

"Yeah, I guess it is."

Chapter 5

Alexandra sat in her room with the curtains drawn, the only light coming from the flicker of the small, ancient, black and white TV she'd brought from her mom's house. It was ridiculous, the stupid thing, with tin foil scrunched around the old-fashioned rabbit ears that were not removable even though it was hooked up to cable and they weren't doing anything.

I should at least take off the tin foil, she thought. But she was so exhausted. And the noise might wake up Patrick who was sleeping *right there* in the bassinet. It seemed like he never slept and she'd gotten to the point where she'd do anything to avoid waking him up during the tiny breaks from his constant needs.

It had been a week since he was born and honestly, she felt like crap. Nothing was what she'd expected. Not that she had any idea what to expect once her mom died. But before that, she was excited about the baby and her mom was too.

They had cleaned out and painted the extra room in the apartment they lived in, and although his room was small, at least it was a separate room. She remembered laughing with her mom when they were painting together; they'd both turned at the same time and gotten paint in each other's hair. Eyes filling with tears at the memory, Alexandra's stomach felt as if it were being pulled downward by the weight of missing her mother.

Lying back on the bed, ever so slowly in her effort to be as quiet as possible, Alexandra heard the distant sounds of people talking and laughing. It sounded like it was coming from the driveway and it took her a moment to remember that even though her room was so dark, it was the middle of the day.

With a pang of regret, she recalled sitting at the breakfast table that morning when Rose mentioned that she and a friend were going to the mall and asked if anyone else wanted to go. Grace had squealed, "Oh yeeeah!" in that annoying, cheerleader-type voice of hers and immediately started texting her friends. Rose, who was looking for something in the pantry threw over her shoulder, "What about you?" and Alexandra had mumbled "No thanks."

Who were they kidding anyway? She knew they were only including her because they felt obligated to, and besides, what would she do at the mall with no money, still wearing maternity clothes, and no friend to invite?

Tears threatening at the back of her eyes, she rolled onto her side and was reminded of yet another thing in her miserable life: her stomach. It still felt almost as huge as when Patrick was still in there. She couldn't believe it! She knew it wouldn't be quite as flat and toned as it was before she was pregnant, but she was completely unprepared for it to still be very round in shape and all mushy, like a deflated balloon. He was a week old and she still couldn't even remotely consider putting on her pre-pregnancy clothes, or even ones she'd worn in the early months.

With tears streaming steadily now, the only thing she could hear was the sound of Patrick's breathing. In, out. In, out. Every now and then he would make a little sound that brought a bolt of fear to her heart, thinking that he was waking up. It seemed like he was *always* up. And not only that, but it seemed like he *needed* something every minute when he was up.

She knew babies cried a lot and you had to change their diaper and stuff. She'd read books and even took that stupid new mom class that Shelley had signed her up for at the hospital. But still, it was all just so different than she'd imagined. Whenever she had pictured what it would be like, she'd visualized pushing an adorable toddler in a swing at the playground, or even a cute infant, crawling around the living room like you see on diaper commercials. But all Patrick did was sleep, eat, poop, and cry. Not much else. He didn't even smile yet but he sure made it known that he wanted to be carried around, like, *all* the time.

And Shelley wasn't much help either. Sure, she watched Patrick for a couple of hours every day and would make suggestions like why doesn't she take Tiny for a walk or call her old friend Amy from her mom's neighborhood and invite her over. *Yeah, right.* As if she would want to spend her only free time exercising when she was already so tired, or would want to invite an old friend over when she looked like this! She knew Shelley was just trying to be nice but couldn't help feeling like everything would have been so much better if her real mom were there.

In her mind's eye, she always felt normal—not exhausted—when visualizing what it would have been like to have Patrick with her mom around. Her mom wouldn't act like it was mainly Alexandra's job to take care of him; he would have been *their* baby. And her mom wouldn't have that underlying attitude of disapproval like everyone had around here. She'd had Alexandra as a single woman after all, so it wasn't such a big deal to her like it was to the Morsonys.

Alexandra struggled to deny the truth that lurked in her subconscious: That her mom had, in fact, been very upset about her getting pregnant. That she'd spent weeks encouraging Alexandra to "really, seriously think about what you want to do," and talked about how much it was going to change her life. She'd never come right out and said that Alexandra should have an abortion, but she had made it clear that it was an option to be considered, and had talked extensively about how hard it would be to have a baby while still in high school, and what about college, and all that crap that moms say.

Nonetheless, somehow Alexandra just knew that everything would have been better with her mom around. And besides, if her mom didn't help her it would be because she was at work. Not like Shelley who didn't even work but still expected Alexandra to, like, wash bottles, and do laundry and stuff.

There was a light knock at her bedroom door and Alexandra's head whipped around to see if it woke Patrick. He was still asleep. Thank God! She tiptoed to the door, wiping her tears quickly with her index fingers before cracking it open. It was Shelley.

She whispered, "I'm taking Tiny for a little walk. You want to come?"

"No thanks."

"Are you sure? David's home so he can keep an ear out for Patrick. It might be nice to get outside a bit."

Alexandra noted the look of hopefulness in Shelley's face and the sound of encouragement in her tone. "No thanks," she replied dully.

"Oh. Okay then. We'll see you later." Shelley turned to walk back downstairs and Alexandra felt a stab of… something. Happiness that she'd made Shelley sad? Regret that she'd made her sad? She didn't know what she felt but she did know that it kind of hurt, either way.

Chapter 6

Two weeks later, David and Shelley talked while snuggled up in their luxurious, pillow-laden king-sized bed. The romantic master bedroom was quickly reverting to the oasis they'd originally designed it to be, back when all of the kids were younger. They'd decorated it together, taking their inspiration from the sumptuous bed and breakfast where they'd gotten married, their goal being to create a quiet, adult space in a house that was otherwise as hectic as Disneyland.

Over the years they'd come to take the room for granted, but after twenty-one sleepless nights with a crying newborn, a crying teenager, other door-slamming, loudly-groaning teenagers and young adults, and a dog who thought the middle of the night would be a great time for a walk since everyone was up, their bedroom had reclaimed its status as a tranquil, French country retreat.

After giving one another the rundown of their day, the conversation turned once again to the kids and what to do about them. A discussion they'd had many times before, they rehashed the dilemma of where to draw the line: They'd always agreed that they couldn't make an issue over every hormonal eye-roll, but there was also a fine line between being understanding, accepting parents, and being pushovers who tolerated disrespectful behavior.

Earlier that day, Shelley had intervened in yet another clash between Grace and Alexandra, when Grace discovered the *Cosmo* magazine in Alexandra's room. Accusations flew from both of them—toward each other and Shelley—about unequal rules, trespassing, too-long showers, baby noise, music noise, and dog slobber, as well as a multitude of other complaints. It went without saying that there was plenty of eye rolling, door slamming, and even some name-calling.

Then there was the matter of Russell, who constantly emitted an air of entitlement, somehow under the impression that Shelley was put on the earth to wait on him and his friends, cooking, driving, and accommodating their every desire even though he was nasty most of the time, not to mention old enough to do most of those things for himself. And Michael, who was conspicuously quiet and appeared to be neither socializing with his local friends nor staying in touch with his school friends.

Rose was, at the moment, the only one who seemed to be having no particular problem, although her snotty aloofness was still annoying.

Overriding all of that was the issue of Alexandra's parenting. Or more accurately, the lack thereof. It had been three weeks since they came home from the hospital—weeks that consisted of Alexandra staying holed up in her room with Patrick all day and night, coming out only when he was crying and she hoped someone else would take over.

Recalling how stressful it was when her own kids were newborns, Shelley sometimes took the baby, freeing Alexandra to take a shower, play with Tiny, or just have some alone time. Other times, Shelley would go in to help her, only to find that she wasn't interested in learning techniques for managing things on her own—the moment she realized Shelley was only helping and not taking over, Alexandra reverted to her disdainful, bordering-on-neglectful attitude. Which Shelley found even more peculiar, given that prior to Patrick's birth, Alexandra's attitude would have been more accurately described as formal, polite, and conscientious, almost to a fault.

David felt that Shelley should let her tough it out; that she'd eventually get the hang of things on her own.

Shelley agreed to some extent, but also shared that that was easier said than done since it involved her listening to the baby cry for hours, knowing that his mother was there but ignoring him. David sympathized: they'd all been woken multiple times every night to the sound of Patrick crying punctuated by Alexandra's frustrated huffing and puffing, and her refusal to accept either of their advice.

Theirs was not a household where any child, of any age, ever went unattended. As they talked, David's hand soothing hers with the autogenic stroke of his thumb, Shelley's mind sifted through dozens of mental snapshots: Singing songs when the girls' friends couldn't warm up during a play date, putting Band-Aids and kisses on *everybody's* boo-boos, holding her colicky niece when she cried for five hours straight while her sister-in-law attended a wedding.

There were more mature memories too: Comforting her daughters' friends when they cried over "lost loves," breaking up fights between teenaged boys over whose turn it was to play Guitar Hero, letting a friend live at their house for two weeks so he wouldn't miss school while his parents took a younger sibling to Sloan Kettering for treatment.

No, theirs was not a household where children were left to cry unattended. Made to feel un-cared for. Wore dirty diapers. Or anything else of that nature.

Yet it was also not a household where people got away with shirking their responsibilities and leaving others to take care of them, which is what it felt like whenever Shelley "helped" Alexandra.

On the third hand (David and Shelley often referred to themselves as octopuses during these conversations), allowing a baby to be neglected under their own roof was not the same as refusing to clean up someone's muddy shoes, letting them suffer their own consequences the next time they went to wear them.

On the fourth "tentacle," Shelley had dedicated the past twenty years of her life to being the best mom she could be. At each phase of their lives, she had done all that she could for all of her kids, emotionally, physically, and financially. She had enjoyed each phase of being their mom, from when they were newborns right through their current ages of being almost-adults. But she also had no urge to reset the clock way back to square one by accepting one hundred percent responsibility for Patrick.

Deciding on a three-pronged approach, they concluded the discussion and settled into their favorite cuddle position: Shelley with her head on David's shoulder, her hand strewn across his chest, and he with his arm wrapped protectively around her waist.

Relaxing together, their minds winding down to rest, Shelley noticed that David's body wasn't winding down at all. A familiar tingle of excitement rippled through her as she recognized that his chest muscles remained firm beneath her cheek rather than slackening toward the softness of sleep, his hand stroking her waist in a rhythm she recognized as more than just habitual.

Tilting her mouth toward his, their bodies followed suit, facing one another in their routine yet intoxicating cadence; two bodies harmonizing together like magnetic puzzle pieces that couldn't possibly move any way other than together.

*****

The next morning, Part I of the three-pronged David and Shelley Family Improvement Program began. Starting with a family meeting at 10:00 am—much to the chagrin of all who thought they'd be sleeping 'til noon (except Alexandra who was smug because she knew she'd be up anyway)—each of the five kids were given their task list for the week.

Moaning and complaining earned additional tasks. Swearing gained them two. Rational objections such as, "This is a two-person job!" were met with suggestions of how they might help one another out, working as a team to accomplish things faster.

Russell's comment of "This is like boot camp," was addressed by David showing him what real boot camp would be like, complete with one hundred push-ups and one hundred sit-ups.

Once the shock of understanding that they were expected to behave like respectful, helpful family members rather than spoiled brats wore off, they were presented with their reward lists, which included things like being given a ride, earning ten bucks, an afternoon off from chores, and other such treats that were formerly taken for granted.

They'd done something similar a few years earlier and it had worked like a charm. Fingers crossed, the couple hoped that adding Alexandra, Patrick, and Tiny to the mix would enhance rather than hinder the results.

*****

Later that afternoon when most of the kids were lazing around doing nothing—apparently in denial, thinking that they wouldn't dare enforce their vows to not drive them, cook for them, or allow any friends over—Shelley went into Alexandra's room to discuss Phase II.

Shelley had found a program for teen mothers and their babies. Chicks With Chicks (Shelley couldn't decide whether she loved or hated the name) was geared toward helping girls find a way to be well-balanced young ladies, yet also responsible parents, and was run by a clinical social worker, with the meetings held in the hospital basement.

Shelley handed Alexandra the flyer she'd printed from their website and said, "I think you and Patrick might enjoy this."

She took the flyer, gave it the barest of glances, tossed it on the floor and said, "I am not going."

"Maybe you're misunderstanding me," Shelley asserted. "I said you might enjoy it… I did not say it was optional."

"What do you think I am, crazy?" Alexandra shrieked.

"Of course not. What makes you think that?"

"This is run by, like, a therapist!" Spoken as if therapist were a dirty word.

Ahh, if only I had time for the luxury of therapy, Shelley thought. Then joked with herself, *And if only she used that tone when she spoke an* actual *cuss word.*

Aloud Shelley said, "The idea of the group is to help young mothers make friends they have something in common with, and maybe to work through some of the upsetting things you have to deal with, being a teen mom."

"See? Therapy."

"Regardless of what you choose to call it, I think it's a good idea. At the very least, it will get you and Patrick out of the house, and that's got to be worth something."

"Oh, great. So I'm supposed to *bring* him?" Again with the outraged expression, as if Shelley had suggested that she walk to the moon.

"Of course. He's your baby and you'll need to get used to taking him places."

She just glared at her, as if Shelley were ruining her life.

You think I'm ruining your life, sweetheart? Well let me tell you… Shelley stopped her thoughts before she ended up speaking them aloud, instead saying, "Make sure you and Patrick are dressed and ready to leave by five o'clock. And I recommend taking a shower."

*****

That evening, Phase III was implemented (neither of them ever having been procrastinators), which consisted of David and Shelley having a romantic evening out, just the two of them.

Of course, this was complicated by the fact that they had to simultaneously enforce Phases I and II on the same evening.

First there was the uproarious reaction from Russell, who was extremely upset about not being driven to the movies after he'd used an online gift certificate to purchase nonrefundable tickets because he didn't believe they really wouldn't drive him even though he'd completely disregarded his task list.

Then there was Rose, who accomplished most of her list for the day and was outraged that she had to cancel her date with her boyfriend, rationalizing that she'd had to work from noon until four and then also "had to" spend another hour at Walgreen's buying new makeup, thus leaving her with no time to finish. This one did leave David and Shelley with some guilt, but they knew they had to be consistent, and really, it doesn't take that long to do a load of laundry.

The whole project was further exacerbated by Alexandra and Patrick, who were nowhere near ready at five o'clock, resulting in Shelley bathing and dressing Patrick herself while warning Alexandra that they were leaving at five thirty, even if Shelley had to drag her out of there naked. Offsetting some of this stress was David's compliment of her foresight, having told Alexandra to be ready at five when she secretly knew the meeting didn't begin until six.

Then there was Michael, who'd completed his task list and could do whatever he wanted, yet chose to do nothing. Which brought its own level of worry.

And Grace, who haphazardly completed her final chore for the day, then asked to be dropped at a friend's for a sleepover. Which they knew she thought would get her out of tomorrow's list—but that was an issue to be dealt with tomorrow.

Finally, with the entire dog and pony show corralled, David and Shelley—practically gasping for air, and she with a spit-up stain on her dress—strolled into *Las Tres Señoritas*, hand-in-hand, and ordered a pitcher of sangria… stat.

Chapter 7

Bash, bash, bash! "Mo-om! Get her out of there!"

It was six in the morning. Grace was screeching at the top of her lungs and there was a banging that sounded as if the fire department were breaking in with axes.

What the hell was that? Shelley sprang out of bed and rushed down the hall, using her hand to shield her eyes from the hall light.

Grace was standing there grimacing, with one foot lifted, rubbing her toe.

"What's going on here?" she squinted at Grace just as the bathroom door cracked open and Alexandra, her face red and tear-streaked, peeked out.

"Would you tell her to stop pounding? I'm trying to get ready and she's going to wake up Patrick!"

Shelley turned to Grace, who was still rubbing her foot. "That was you pounding?"

Alexandra went on, "Yes! She is *kicking* the door while I'm trying to get ready!"

"Well if she would just get out of there I wouldn't have to. I need to get ready too!"

Apparently, there's a phenomenon wherein two seventeen-year-old girls getting ready on the first morning of school somehow requires more bathrooms than people. Or more specifically, *because* the girls were Grace and Alexandra—who refused to so much as brush their teeth in the same vicinity, yet whose stuff was in the same bathroom—to say there was drama would be an understatement.

"How long have you been in there, Alexandra?"

"Ten minutes!" "Thirty minutes!" Came their simultaneous objections.

"All right, girls. Listen to me. Alexandra, you have five minutes to finish up and then it's Grace's turn."

"Five minutes! I can't be done in that time!"

"Just do your bathroom stuff and then you can finish getting ready in your room."

"But that will wake up Patrick!"

"Oh, so what am I supposed to do?" Grace snarled. "Not get ready just because you have a baby?"

Shelley interrupted before things got any worse. "All right, all right. Let's do this: Grace, go in there now and get whatever you need. You can get ready in my bathroom just for today and then tonight we'll figure out a better plan for the mornings."

Grace sighed, long and exasperated at the injustice, then grumbled an acrimonious "Fine-uh." She pushed past Alexandra and came out with various toiletries, then stomped her way into her mom's room.

*****

Once they finally left for the bus stop at 6:40 am (teary-eyed and far-from-bushy-tailed), Shelley took a moment to just breathe. The house felt empty. *Pleasantly* empty.

Michael had driven back to his apartment in Boone near Appalachian State two weeks earlier, saying that he wanted to get in some hours at work and stockpile some cash before classes resumed.

Russell had flown back to Colorado State, barely sparing a goodbye glance as he strode through airport security.

Rose was staying on campus at UNC Chapel Hill even though it was only thirty minutes from home. They had said their goodbyes three days earlier, David giving her bicycle, propped amongst others in the long rack in front of the dorm, a sturdy pat as if *it* was the one he was going to miss.

Walking through the rooms of her now quiet house, Shelley tried enjoy the solitude instead of feeling overwhelmed by the many things she needed to catch up on… namely, everything she'd left undone over the summer months in favor of family fun, combined with her promise to herself that she would not suffocate the kids with her neatnik tendencies.

The kitchen was cluttered with half-eaten bags of chips, fastened with so many bag clips she was amazed that they even had that many. Tiny's area had a grimy oval around the perimeter of his raised food and water holder, streaks of slobber-water and little crumbs stuck to the wall behind it.

There was mild relief in the dining room where everything looked fine except for her houseplants, which showed their tiredness at not having been watered. Astounded that they were still alive, she went and got the small plastic watering can that she liked better because of its broken spout: it made faster work of a task that she disliked for no logical reason.

Filling it at the sink while lamenting the empty bird feeders that hung in the back yard, she heard Patrick's whimper over the baby monitor. A sinking dread came over her, surprising herself with the intensity of her own reaction.

Turning off the faucet, listening to his squeaky sounds, it dawned on her that it wasn't Patrick himself that she dreaded. Rather, it was her habitual anticipation that Alexandra wouldn't pick him up in what she considered a reasonable time span. But Alexandra wasn't home; the baby was her responsibility that day.

School days.

She washed her hands with soap, then dried them on her jeans on the way up the stairs. As she ascended, his muffled cries from the monitor became real-time cries, and she felt her step quicken in an almost ill sort of relief, knowing that comforting him was imminent.

Amazed at how rapidly he escalated into full-fledged shrieking, she rushed to the plain, box-like bassinet—Alexandra had stripped it of its white gossamer shirring, saying that it was too feminine. The baby's tiny fists were clenched, his face scrunched and reddened with effort. Scooping him up, she held him against her body, expecting his cries to ebb. Instead, he stiffened further, arched his back, and wailed even harder.

Rubbing his back, barely larger than her hand, she began rocking him in that rhythmic, side-to-side motion of parents. Her mind flashed to being in David's arms, dancing at a charity benefit—an inane thought considering the predominate number of hours she'd spent rocking babies.

It wasn't making a difference. Patrick's tiny head bobbled as he flailed in her arms and continued to cry, his legs wedged stiffly against her stomach.

She carried him to the changing table and lay him down, a chill hitting her stomach the moment their bodies separated. The front of her shirt was wet—saturated really—and when she turned on the little lamp she could see that he was soaked from his diaper to his neckline.

Did she actually get up and go to school without even changing him? Shelley had heard him crying at around 6:30 and she'd knocked to see if Alexandra needed any help but she'd said no and he'd quieted after a few minutes; she figured she must have changed him and put him back down. Glancing at the clock, she saw that it was only 7:12. *There's no way he could be this wet in less than an hour, could he?*

Undoing the mile-long row of miniscule snaps on his blue one-piece sleeper, thinking that it was too hot for him to have been wearing it in the first place, she discovered that Patrick's skin underneath was clammy—definitely from urine, and possibly from being overheated.

Pulling off his diaper and placing a cloth over his penis, she felt herself smirk, remembering how David had laughed at her the first time he saw her change Patrick. He'd reached over to grab a burp cloth from the stack while informing her that with boys, you're a sitting duck if he isn't covered. By the time he stood up, a surprisingly strong stream arched from the baby, right onto David's arm. He'd laughed and said, "See? Boys will get you every time."

Noticing a little rash on his bottom and wanting to let him dry completely and get some air on his skin, she tried to calm Patrick with the age-old tactic of letting him suck on her pinky. His crying subsided immediately and the significant suction he applied left no question that he was overdue for a bottle.

Two seconds later he was hysterical, enraged at being tricked, quickly escalating back into full-fledged hysteria. Shelley tucked a fresh diaper under his otherwise naked body, slung him onto her shoulder, and looked around for his soft receiving blanket, which she found on the floor, mixed in with Alexandra's clothes.

Heading downstairs, she went to the fridge where she found that, of course, Alexandra hadn't prepared any bottles. This was something she'd suggested to her on many occasions: that it's much easier to soothe a hungry baby by feeding him quickly, rather than making him wait while you prepare a bottle each time.

She didn't care. In the typical fashion of teenage procrastination and rebellion, she refused to do it, despite admitting (when it was done for her) that it was a better system and really did make things easier.

Trying to hold Patrick, still crying, his tonsils displayed in starved outrage, she set about getting the bottles out of the dishwasher and the formula from the cabinet.

Tiny, alarmed at the baby's distress, came loping into the kitchen, slumped himself onto the floor, and put his gargantuan head on her foot, his droopy eyes watching her with worry.

As she stood there waiting for the bottle to heat in the microwave, she tried for the thousandth time to suppress her disagreement with Alexandra's decision not to breastfeed. As much as she tried to convince herself that she'd come to terms with the bottles themselves, the concept of feeding a newborn a *powdered* mix that had to be heated through *radiation* was still beyond comprehension to her.

The truth was, she secretly attributed most of Patrick's fussiness to one of two things: Alexandra's inattention, or being fed formula instead of breast milk. Either way.

Finally ready, she shook the bottle, sighed when she saw all the air bubbles it caused, tested it on her wrist, and carried the baby outside to the screened porch with Tiny following closely behind.

*****

They sat on the big, comfy chair; it was a splurge she'd invested in two years earlier—expensive, plush. The early morning air was comfortably cool, or at least cool in comparison to how hot it would get later in the afternoon.

By the time she held the bottle to his lips, Patrick was so frenzied that he couldn't even notice it. Arching his back in the signature silent-scream of babies, which somehow seems louder than actual screaming, he was beyond hysterical.

Shelley suddenly felt inept. Intimidated. Completely at a loss for what to do. Of course she'd fed him plenty of bottles before, but this time he was so distraught that he was turning his face this way and that, not recognizing when she would touch the nipple to his lips.

Despite raising two children of her own, she'd never been faced with a situation in which her child was in such bad shape: covered in urine, developing a rash, starving, and so hysterical they couldn't even drink.

Think, Shelley, think!

She remembered how her girls would instinctively curl around her belly, knowing the breast was near. The books had said they could identify the scent of their mother, understood that milk was nearby. In desperation, she laid Patrick across her lap near her breasts the way she had when she'd nursed her girls and squeezed the bottle nipple so that some formula dripped into his mouth.

"Shhh," she whispered. "Shhh, baby Patrick." She squeezed another drop.

He paused. She saw his throat move and prayed he was swallowing a taste. Struggling to angle the bottle toward him, another drop landed on his cheek just as his faced crumpled, back in the direction of crying again.

"Shhh, shhh, shhh." She squeezed another drop into his mouth, and then quickly pushed the bottle in while he was swallowing, hoping he'd get a good taste.

He did. So much so that he started coughing, choking on the big gulp. She quickly sat him up, patting his back so he could catch his breath, then laid him right back down and got the bottle between his lips before he could start crying again.

He started sucking. Too fast at first, gulping and swallowing lumps of air, streams of formula leaking out the sides of his mouth and down into the folds of his neck.

She let him go at it for a few minutes, then took the bottle out of his mouth, sat him up and burped him, leaning him forward on her lap, his little chin resting on her hand. He let out a huge air bubble—the kind she'd always referred to as a "truck driver burp," exactly the kind that prevents gassiness in babies—then situated him along her belly again and placed the bottle back into his mouth.

Calm now, his drinking took on the rhythm of drawing in and swallowing, sounding almost like sighs. Suck, swallow-sigh. Suck, swallow-sigh. His breathing slowed, his hysteria replaced with contentment.

Nestled against her body, the cool morning air glancing across them, his soft blankie loosely covering his naked legs for coziness, Shelley listened to his swallow-sighs, kept her face turned away from the empty bird feeders, and tried to relax.

*****

The rest of the day progressed uneventfully. After the bottle, she took Patrick upstairs and gave him a bath, then dressed him in a summer jumper of lightweight cotton: white, with little green frogs smiling in a repeating pattern.

With a full belly, a clean body, and plenty of powder on his bottom, he was content to be carried around the house, keeping her company while she straightened the mudroom and dusted the living room, watching her from his little seat with the grey-eyed stare of newborns; the one that makes you wonder whether they can actually see you or if they're just following the sound of you.

When he fussed, she picked him up and carried him in her arms for a while. When he started dozing, she talked to him, tickling his little old man chin to keep him awake. After two hours had passed, it was obvious he needed a nap so she fixed another small bottle, fed him half of it, changed his diaper in between to keep him awake, fed him the other half, then put him down in his bassinet.

He slept for two-and-a-half hours, during which she filled the bird feeders, straightened out the car washing supplies in the garage, took a shower, made some phone calls, and caught up on e-mails. When he woke up, she changed him and carried him downstairs to the sunny living room where she fed him one of the dozen bottles she'd also prepared during his nap.

Uneventful. It was a quiet day and rather productive, all things considered. She'd saved her errands for late afternoon when Alexandra would be home, and once 2:30 rolled around she set up Patrick's seat on the kitchen island so he could keep her company while she made her list: she had to get to the dry cleaner, supermarket, post office, and drug store.

Immersed in her usual state of anal retentive organization, figuring out the order in which the errands should be done to maximize her time while also ensuring the food wouldn't have to sit in her car and spoil, she thought she heard the front door slam, but when she looked up, no one was walking into the kitchen. Instead, she heard the sound of stomping on the stairs.

Chapter 8

Lifting Patrick out of his little seat, Shelley called up the stairs. "Hell-oo. Anyone home?"

The front door opened and Grace strolled in, the sight of her making Shelley marvel once again that her characteristics were tantamount to her name. Even after being at school all day, Grace's dark blonde hair shimmered down her back in a silken sheet, bringing attention to her impossibly small, taut-as-a-drum waistline, further emphasized by her low-rise jeans—jeans that had to be purchased at a specific—and very expensive—store where sizing was available in Extra Slim.

"Hi sweetie. How was the first day?"

"Fine." She swung her backpack off her shoulder, letting it thunk to the floor as if filled with bricks, and strode past, straight to the kitchen pantry.

"Does everything seem right with your schedule?"

"Not really."

"What do you mean? Didn't they put you in honors math?"

"No, Ma. My *academics* are all fine, don't worry." She huffed as she pulled out some frosted Pop Tarts and tossed them in the microwave. Shelley refrained from pointing out that she should use a paper towel.

"So then what's wrong with your schedule?"

"My electives. Can you believe they gave me ECD? My requests were dance, pottery, or Internet marketing!"

"What's ECD?"

"Early Childhood Development." She challenged her mom with her eyes, silently daring her to utter a platitude.

"Oh."

"Yeah, 'oh.' And guess what baby mamma up there got?" She jerked her chin toward the stairs.

"What?"

"Dance."

"Oh." There was nothing she could say aloud about this. The mom in her was relieved that Grace's academics were fine, and she was even slightly pleased about Alexandra getting dance; she knew that she'd enjoyed it at her old school. She also couldn't help silently appreciating the irony of Grace, the new auntie who was so unsympathetic to Alexandra, receiving her assigned elective.

On the other hand, the teenager in her, whom she tried to nurture and maintain in the interest of having good relationships with her kids, understood that this felt like a severe injustice to a seventeen-year-old girl who recently had a "competitor" and a newborn move into her home.

Trying to find a positive, Shelley said, "At least you'll still be on the dance team even if you don't have it as an elective."

"Speaking of team! You know what else?" She turned to get the Pop Tarts out of the microwave, using a fork to fling them—crumbs flying, too hot—onto a paper plate.

"What?"

"She signed up for tryouts, too!"

Shelley's heart sank. Grace had performed on her school dance teams since seventh grade, preferring to organize her extracurricular activities around her school day. Now that she was a senior, they would perform at football games and other events that were reserved for the older kids, the better dancers.

She knew Alexandra had been on the team at her previous school too; she remembered her talking about how disappointed she was about being excluded once her pregnancy became evident.

She also knew that Grace wanted *nothing* to do with Alexandra—not inside the home and especially not out. As for social situations—and particularly the dance team, where Grace was accustomed to being the ever-popular leader of the pack—she shuddered to imagine how this would play out.

Grace broke off a piece of her Pop Tart, blew on it, then stuck it in her mouth, its brown sugar aroma filling the kitchen.

Shelley set Patrick in his little seat, still atop the counter, while pondering, *Does he suddenly seem heavier because Alexandra wants to do dance team, which means I'll have to either watch him more or tell her no? And if I do say no, won't it seem as if I'm doing it for Grace, and not only for myself? Would there be any truth to that?*

After clicking the baby's safety strap, she walked over to Grace and put her arm around her shoulders. "Let me have a piece of that thing, will you?"

*****

Thirty minutes later, Alexandra still hadn't come downstairs.

Initially, Shelley appreciated having the time to chat with Grace. Then she figured she'd give her a few minutes to relax, use the bathroom, whatever. But once it became evident that she wasn't coming down, she carried Patrick upstairs and knocked on her door.

No answer.

She knocked again.

Still no answer.

Finally, after banging loudly in the style she employed when she was relatively certain the occupant has their iPod in their ears, Alexandra came to the door.

"What?"

"What do you mean, 'what?' I came to see how your first day was and I brought Patrick so you can say hello to him."

"Oh. Okay." She strode into the room, flung herself onto the bed, and glared at her impatiently.

"So, how was the first day?" Shelley sat on the bed with her legs crisscrossed and propped Patrick in her lap, facing Alexandra.

"Fine."

"How did it go, finding your way around the school?'

"Fine."

"And your schedule?"

"It's fine."

"Can I have some sort of answer besides 'fine?'"

"What do you want me to say?"

"There's nothing in particular I want you to say. It's just that I'm asking about your day and you're acting as if I'm bothering you."

"Everything was fine, all right? I didn't get lost, I went to my classes. What else do you want from me?"

Tiny ambled into the room, his gait quickening as he trotted over to Alexandra and thrust his head into her lap. "Hi Tiny! How's my sweetie,

weetie, baby dog?" she gushed, ruffling his ears in both hands, smiling and leaning over to kiss the top of his head.

Observing this was like watching a scene in a science fiction movie—in which the rabid werewolf transforms into a docile housewife.

"Actually, there is something I would have expected from you. How about asking about your son? Asking how things went on the first day you were apart from him all day? Maybe apologizing for not feeding or changing him before you left?"

Alexandra looked at her dully. "How did it go?"

"It went well! We sat outside for a while and then I gave him a bath. He really liked it!" Shelley cringed at the forced brightness in her tone, recognizing that she was trying to get her interested the way she thought she should be. "Doesn't he look so cute in his little froggy outfit?"

"Yup."

"Grandma Morsony sent this one."

"Yeah, I know. *Don't worry*, I sent a thank-you note."

"That wasn't what I was trying to say, Alex. I was just saying that he looks so cute, that's all."

Alexandra just sat there staring at her, obviously waiting for her to leave her alone. Well that was fine. Just fine!

"All right then. I have some things to do so I'll just leave you two to get caught up on your day." She set Patrick onto Alexandra's lap and stalked out of their room, experiencing a guilty satisfaction at the surprised look on her face.

*****

Shelley shouted up the stairs, "Grace, I'm going to do some errands. Want to come?"

"No, but can you get me a deodorant? The lavender kind."

Grabbing her list and snatching her purse from the counter, Shelley recognized that she was angrier than was reasonable, given the circumstances. In general, this was something David and she had come to terms with years earlier: Kids, especially teenagers, are ungrateful little snots.

Still, as she backed out of the driveway (her car's new permanent residence, having decided that keeping Alexandra's hunk of junk in the garage until she got her license and a job was easier than having to move it every day), she couldn't help feeling resentful toward their new seventeen-year-old snot who treated her like crap after she watched her baby all day. Not to mention her original seventeen-year-old snot who may not have been quite as nasty at the moment, but was surely no more appreciative.

Pulling up at the post office, she flipped the visor down to do her habitual once-over. Horrified, she realized that although she'd showered, she'd completely forgotten about her makeup, and was still wearing leggings and a tattered tee-shirt—things she'd deign to wear even for yard work, never mind out in public.

Sighing, she grabbed her papers and went inside. She was browsing the funny postcards while waiting in line and wondering why post offices always have only one teller working while three others are just sitting around, when she heard, "Shelley?"

It was Claire Whitman. Of all people. Elegantly turned out in her crisp slacks and medium-heeled shoes from Barney's New York where she made bi-annual shopping trips, insisting that you can't find any decent clothing in North Carolina.

"Hi Claire."

"How *are* you?" Her averted gaze spoke loudly that she noticed her non-couture.

"Fine, thanks. Just a little hectic today, you know, always running. And you?"

"Well, I am simply exhausted." She looked far from exhausted. "I have been meeting with the Women's Club, preparing for the luncheon. It will take place in a fortnight, you remember." Her inflection was a strange blend of Southern charm and Bostonian wasp; particularly strange because Shelley knew that she was from New Jersey. She tried not to roll her eyes at Claire's habit of using words that are uncharacteristic for American conversation as she went on, "You will be joining us at the club, of course?"

"Of course." *Damn!* She'd completely forgotten about the luncheon and it was in just two weeks. Her mind started scrolling through possibilities: see if David can take a long lunch to watch Patrick, try to keep Patrick awake all morning and hope he naps in his stroller at the luncheon, cancel her attendance, make Alexandra stay home from school...

"Next in line, please."

As she handed the postal clerk her envelopes and ordered an extra sheet of stamps, Shelley could feel Claire's eyes burning at her back, no doubt wondering if she had the flu, for surely there could be no other reason why any forty-six-year-old "lady who lunches" would leave the house looking that way.

Chapter 9

They made it through the rest of the week with Grace and Alexandra using a system of even and odd days to determine who used the bathroom first in the morning, and Patrick getting onto a better schedule with Shelley changing him and feeding him first thing.

It was a dilemma. *Everything* was a dilemma—for Shelley at least—her mixed feelings causing her to never feel fully okay with any of the infinite decisions to be made. Take the mornings for example. A huge part of her felt that Patrick was Alexandra's baby and that she should get up and take care of changing and feeding him first thing. And because of that, it would only make sense for Grace to use the bathroom during that time.

On the other hand, she didn't want it to seem as if she were favoring Grace, and she did feel for Alexandra, understanding that in addition to having a baby, her mom just died, she moved in with a new family, and started at a new high school.

On the third hand, Shelley was not a morning person. And she did not sign up to have another baby. She'd already put in her years of getting up at the crack of dawn, barely able to pee—forget about coffee—before taking care of someone else. In addition, she and David had a tradition of sitting together for fifteen minutes in the morning, just relaxing in one another's presence before launching into their day. It felt as if she hadn't seen him all week.

So by the time Friday rolled around, she was feeling excited about the weekend. She took Patrick to the supermarket, and once she spent twenty minutes—with her sweating and him crying while she figured out how to get his rear-facing car seat carrier out of its base—it actually went okay. She bought ingredients to make a huge lasagna with the plan that they could eat it just about all weekend without her having to cook as many meals.

One thing she had forgotten about was how, when you have an infant, strangers feel compelled to talk to you, and even try to touch your baby. And the commentary! One woman, a young mother, come over to coo over Patrick, sitting wide-eyed in his little seat, which Shelley had set down inside the wagon.

"He's so cute! Are you a nervous type of Grandma?" the girl smiled sympathetically, "Because you can mount his seat up top to give yourself more room in the wagon." Her smile imparted that she thought Shelley was an adorable old lady, perhaps just as cute as Patrick himself. *Ugh!*

Another woman, who appeared to be in her mid-forties like Shelley, stopped with her toddler to say, "It's so nice to see other mothers in the same situation as me. People just don't understand how wonderful it is to finally have a baby after years of trying! We thought about adoption too, but finally the in-vitro worked."

Shelley tried to just smile politely and keep walking but the woman continued, her commiserative smile indicating that they must be soul sisters. "Do you have any other children?"

"Yes." Shelley hoped that her brevity would convey that she was not interested in sharing their life stories.

"How wonderful! I don't have any others. How old are yours?"

Do I really owe this woman a whole explanation?

"Seventeen, nineteen, twenty-two, and twenty-four."

"Wow! You don't look old enough to have kids that old!"

Okay, maybe she's not that bad after all.

"So, you just decided to adopt a baby after all this time?"

Wow! Some people! Although she could understand the woman assuming Patrick was adopted because of his dark, Hispanic features, she could not imagine asking all these questions of a perfect stranger!

"He's not adopted," she stated, focusing on putting onions into a bag, and moving along hurriedly.

"So I guess this one must be an 'oops?'" the woman went on, now approaching stalker status as far as Shelley was concerned.

"Something like that." *Really? Who does this woman think she is?*

"Well, we'd better get going," Shelley said with a tone of finality, deftly steering her wagon around the woman's toddler who was lining up potatoes on the floor. "Have a nice day."

"You too! Maybe we'll see you again some time!"

Shelley hoped that would never happen.

*****

After school, Grace came breezing into the house, straight to the pantry as usual, talking a mile a minute.

"I'm going to sleep over Cassie's tonight, okay?" she bubbled as she put her daily Pop Tart into the microwave, this time using a paper towel. "We're working on the first dance for team."

"Fantastic! So I guess you got the tryout results and made it!"

She looked at her mom as if she were crazy. Rolling her eyes, she said, "Duh. I'd have to be pretty bad to not get in at this point, don't ya think?"

"That's true, but still, it's nice to know for sure."

She just sighed and blew on her Pop Tart (Shelley had given up long ago trying to tell her that if she put it in for less time it wouldn't be so hot).

"Aaagh!" Shelley heard a scream, apparently Alexandra, followed by her stomping up the stairs and slamming her door so hard you could feel the whole house rattle.

"Oh my God! I hope she's okay!" She'd been holding Patrick and now placed him into his little seat and buckled the strap.

"She's just mad because she didn't make it," Grace said, not bothering to mask her spitefulness. "I can't believe she thought she'd get on anyway. She sucks."

"I can heeear youu!" Alexandra screamed, her vocal chords sounding guttural, vibrating at top volume.

"Grace!" Shelley admonished. "You're being very unkind. I'm sure she doesn't suck and she must be very disappointed, just like you would be!"

She rolled her eyes.

"I'm going upstairs to talk to her. Please keep an eye on Patrick for a few minutes."

Grace looked at him, sitting docilely in his seat, then glared at her. "What am I supposed to do with him?"

"Nothing in particular. Just watch him 'til I get back."

"What if he starts crying or something?"

"Then talk to him, or bounce his seat a little. It wouldn't kill you to be nice to him, you know."

"I'm not the one who decided to have a baby!"

"Neither am I. But I'm nice to him anyway. It's not his fault! Just watch him for a few minutes, for goodness' sake!"

"Fine-uh."

*****

Upstairs, Shelley knocked on Alexandra's door and there was no answer. She knocked again. "Whaat?!" came a sob.

"Can I come in?"

"Why?"

"I'd like to talk to you."

"You don't even care anyway! Don't even bother!"

"Yes I do care Alexandra. But I don't want to keep talking to you through the door. I'm coming in."

She turned the knob, surprised to find that it wasn't locked, experience telling her that she never wanted to keep her out in the first place.

The room was dark—blinds drawn and curtains closed, lights off. Alexandra was sprawled on the bed, still wearing her backpack, lying on top of it. Her tear-streaked face and puffy eyes left no doubt that she was not just being dramatic; She really was upset and had obviously been crying for a long time.

Shelley walked over to part the curtains and began lifting the blinds. "I know you're disappointed about not making the dance team," she said factually.

No response. Alexandra flung her arm across her face as the sunshine and a light breeze streamed in through the window she'd opened.

"But you did get dance as an elective, so at least that's a good thing, right?"

No response. Shelley could hear Patrick beginning to fuss downstairs and wondered whether Grace was paying any attention to him.

Sighing, she said, "You know, I care very much about you being so upset, but it's pretty difficult to be there for you if you're just going to ignore me."

"I just can't believe it!" she finally moaned. "I used to be such a great dancer and then at the audition, I *fell!*"

"Oh man, that stinks. Did you get hurt?"

"No." She rolled her eyes.

"Grace has been dancing a long time; I'm pretty familiar with these things. Girls sometimes fall. Is that all that happened?"

"I couldn't even, like, *move!* I'm like, *too fat* now! And everyone laughed!"

"Wow, that's pretty rough. I'm sorry it went that way."

Eyes widened, she sat up and said, "Are you agreeing that I'm fat?"

"No. I was saying that the whole thing sounds pretty rough. I don't think you're fat. But I do think you just had a baby and some of your muscles may not be used to moving the way they did before."

"That's disgusting! So what am I, like, supposed to be *fat* and, like, *old,* from now on!"

"No. I think a young girl like you can easily get back in shape. It's just going to take some work, that's all."

"Just what I need. More work." She sighed and picked up the remote for the TV.

What kind of a person turns on the TV in the middle of a conversation like this? Shelley thought.

Suddenly it occurred to her. *A child, that's who.* Like a slap in the face, it suddenly clicked into her consciousness that Alexandra was, herself, a child. A little girl beginning to come into her own, just like Grace. Just like Rose had been a few years earlier, and to some extent, still was.

She realized that maybe she'd left too much up to her, that she'd expected her to handle things like an older young woman would. It was as if she had been looking at her through the wrong lens, an adult lens.

Alexandra had shown up at their door, pregnant. Like an adult. She'd packed up her entire life, possessions, and dog. She'd found a way to locate David, navigate to their house without even having a driver's license, and handled her early integration into their household like a polite, responsible adult.

But she's so impolite now! she thought. Then, *Of course! Just like* all *kids, who are extraordinarily polite to their teachers and when out visiting, but act like... kids, at home!*

It occurred to her that maybe she'd been doing Alexandra an injustice by treating her in too adult a fashion, rather than the same as she would one of her own girls. She comprehended that her first impression of Alexandra as incredibly resourceful had made her forget that teenagers often needed to be reminded what to do, even when they really knew.

"I hate to point this out, Alexandra, but you haven't been working that hard."

"What!" She stared at her, aghast. "I have Patrick!"

"Yes, you do have Patrick, but as long as we're being honest, it's me who's been doing most of his caretaking. And I'm getting pretty sick of you acting like you don't care about him."

She just stared at her, apparently shocked, unused to Shelley's tell-it-like-it-is persona. Which, now that she thought about it, Shelley realized she had also been curbing due to the newness of their relationship.

"I do care about him," Alexandra murmured, almost inaudibly.

Shelley sat down next to her and put her hand on her shoulder. "Sweetie, I know it's hard. But it's really upsetting when you come home from school and don't even stop into the kitchen to say hello to him. Or me."

"I'm just so *tired*. I just want to *relax* for a while."

"I understand that. But after watching him all day, I could use some time to myself, too. I know it's hard to imagine, but I used to have a life before all of this too, you know?"

"Sure. Doing what? Going to your little lunch meetings and reading books all day?"

Her snideness was really getting old.

"As a matter of fact, yes! I've already raised my kids, and what I choose to do with my free time is up to me. Fortunately for you, I've chosen to use my time to take care of *your* baby! And before you say anything else, let me point out that I do love him, and don't mind doing it, but I *do mind* you being so unappreciative and treating us both like crap!"

Pulling away, Alexandra just sighed and clicked on the TV.

Shelley stood, walked over to the television, and turned it off. "Come downstairs. You can take Patrick for a walk in the stroller."

"I don't want to."

"At this point, Alexandra, I really don't care what you want. You could use the exercise, and you could both use the fresh air. I expect you downstairs in five minutes, with sneakers on, ready to go. I'll get Patrick ready."

"What are you, trying to like, *make* me?"

"I don't have to 'like' make you," Shelley stated, actually making finger quotes in the air. "I'm the mom of this house and you'll do as I say. Downstairs. Five minutes. Or consequences."

Shelley stalked out of the room, leaving Alexandra looking equally as stupefied as she felt.

Chapter 10

Later that evening, Grace was in her room chatting with Cassie on Skype while she got ready to go sleep over. They were deciding on a movie to watch and Cassie suggested *The Backup Plan*.

"Ugh, isn't that one where the girl is preggers or something?"

"I think so, something like that. It's supposed to be really good. It's with Jennifer Lopez."

"Let's pick something else."

"Well, I already have it because my mom rented it and it doesn't have to be returned 'til tomorrow."

"Fine. Whatever," Grace sighed, almost moaning.

"What's the matter?"

"I am just so sick of all this baby crap around here! It's Patrick this and Alexandra that. It's like my mom doesn't do anything but worry about them all the time."

"Doesn't your mom, like, watch him all day?"

"Yeah. That's my point! And then at night she's all worried about Alexandra and stuff. I'm so sick of that bitch."

"Who? Your mom?"

"No! Not my mom. Alexandra! Well, I guess my mom too but it's not really her fault. She's just trying to 'help out those less fortunate,'" she mocked.

"Well, just come over and forget about them for a while," Cassie said. "My mom said we can order a pizza, and I just made a big pitcher of pink lemonade."

"Fine. I'll see if my mom can drive me in a few minutes. If she's not *too busy* for me!"

"Okay, text me."

"Yup. See you soon."

*****

After a quiet evening at home on Friday night, with Grace situated at Cassie's, and having told Alexandra that she was solely in charge of Patrick, Shelley and David fell into bed emotionally and physically exhausted, and caught up on some sleep.

On Saturday morning they had a sit-down with Alexandra, having decided that they couldn't just wait around for her to magically become a good mom on her own. Keeping in mind the realization that Alexandra was, in fact, just a kid herself, they outlined exactly what their expectations were, including her taking care of Patrick when she wasn't at school, and assigning tasks in the hope that they would become habits after a while: Prepare the bottles ahead of time, do a load of laundry, give the baby a bath, take him for a walk in the stroller each day, spend twenty minutes in the yard playing ball with Tiny, etc.

While Patrick was hopefully well taken care of, David and Shelley spent a tranquil Saturday afternoon strolling through Peakton Village, a quaint mini-town that consisted of a gourmet deli where they had lunch, a cozy bookstore where they browsed at leisure, and a kitschy garden center where they bought a planter shaped like an antique wheelbarrow.

In the evening they fixed a platter of cheese, fruit, and chocolate, grabbed a bottle of wine, told the kids to fend for themselves (the lasagna she'd prepared was in the fridge), then locked themselves in their bedroom for an at-home date night.

Reminiscent of the early years of their marriage, conversation quickly became consumed with talking about the kids. They'd had a number of rough years back then, combining families and trying to find the right balance of fairness between his kids and hers. They would talk and talk about them for hours, dissecting every intricacy of every interaction, their minds spinning with all of the variables and their myriad complications.

It was a heart-wrenching time, and their marriage quickly became smothered beneath their anxiety for the children's happiness.

What they hadn't realized at first was that the timing of their marriage coincided with his boys becoming teenagers, followed shortly by her girls becoming teenagers. This amounted to them always worrying because this one or that one seemed miserable—which they were, but as it turns out, not because their parents had gotten married, but because they were adolescents.

In any event, after almost two years of overanalyzing, pining, discussing, and stressing, they'd finally realized that *they* were the ones who were *actually* miserable. They eventually determined that *they* needed to change; to accept that it was unrealistic to think that the kids were going to act happy all of the time, or even most of the time. That they could teach them to behave respectfully, but it wasn't going to make them be genuinely okay with every decision they made, no matter what.

The couple determined that the best thing for everyone would be for them to focus on their marriage and not allow every nuance with the kids to take over. Yes, they cared about them and yes, they still discussed them when necessary, but they drew the line at becoming consumed with the spinning cycle of never-ending analysis that was dooming them to endless frustration.

Now that Alexandra and Patrick were in the mix, however, they easily reverted to the in-depth discussion they'd sworn off years before. They agreed that it was inevitable, given that the circumstances demanded a certain level of thought and decision-making. Nonetheless, it made their date night feel more like a counseling session than a night of romantic reconnecting.

At some point, Tiny came tapping at the bedroom door to join them, sitting next to the bed with his chin resting upon it, staring at them sadly, since they were not giving him any cheese and it was a terrible injustice that Frick was on the bed, nestled among the pillows. They tried playing music to set the mood, but it was interspersed with the sound of Patrick crying down the hall and Alexandra stomping repeatedly past their bedroom door, huffing and sighing loudly.

Grace—who'd gone to a party where they had confirmed that there was parental supervision—called for a No Questions Asked pickup, an agreement they had with all their kids in the event that they ever found themselves faced with an unsafe situation, such as a friend who was supposed to drive them but then ended up drinking. Michael called just to say hello because he was bored. On a Saturday night at college? Kind of alarming.

Shelley ran out to pick up Grace, taking Patrick with her in the hope that the movement of the car would help him fall asleep, while David chatted on the phone with Michael. By the time she got back, David was sound asleep and Tiny had snuck onto the bed, raising his head and looking at her guiltily when she came into the room.

Bemoaning her freshly shaven legs and accepting that tonight was not going to be the passionate night of reconnecting she'd fantasized about, Shelley pretended that she didn't see Tiny, slid quietly into the little space left on her bed, and picked up her book with the hope that a little reading would help to quell her longing.

Chapter 11

The date of the Spring Valley Women's Club Luncheon came along and with no other viable option, Shelley prepared to take Patrick with her. She'd started days in advance, working on having him stay awake in the morning, take a long nap in the afternoon, then having Alexandra keep him up and moving with only a short nap in the evening so that he would hopefully start sleeping through the night.

It needed to be done anyway and had worked like a charm with both her babies when they were infants. Ever since she'd come to terms with the fact that Alexandra wasn't going to do a whole lot of in-depth parenting—in fact, had no idea how to and was so preoccupied with being a teenager that she resisted every opportunity to learn—Shelley had relaxed a bit more into her role with Patrick. What exactly that was, she couldn't really define, but in any event she'd decided that since she was his full-time caretaker she needed to do her best.

At almost two months old, he was already wearing size three-to-six months clothing, his roly poly face and body becoming more olive as the pigment of his half-Hispanic heritage developed. His eyes too had lost their newborn greyness and were a sparkly brown color, framed with thick, dark lashes that matched the cap of hair on his head.

She selected a soft outfit for him to wear, with long pants but short sleeves, hoping to keep him as comfortable as possible in the warm autumn weather. The pants were beige, giving the appearance of slacks despite their flexible cotton fabric. His "little man" button-down shirt was baby blue with pinstripes of beige and she smiled as she stretched his tiny matching blue socks onto his feet, knowing that he would have them off in no time in favor of sucking on his own toes. She couldn't blame him; they were adorable and she too enjoyed nibbling them on occasion.

With Patrick ready, she brought him into the bathroom with her, strapping him into his bouncy seat so that she could make sure he stayed awake while she showered and dressed. Stripping out of her PJs and stepping into the shower quickly, she admonished myself for feeling so self-conscious in front of the baby. *Is it because he's a boy baby?* she wondered. *Or is it just that I'm unaccustomed to moving about in the nude in front of anyone other than David?*

Years earlier she'd resigned herself to the fact that her body was never going to be like it was before she had children. She'd spent her late twenties and a good portion of her thirties agonizing over her physique, mourning the flat stomach she used to have, which had become the disgruntled home of what she not at all fondly referred to as her Chicken Belly Flap Thing.

By the time she reached her late thirties, she'd had enough of yearning for something that could never be. With significant relief, she came to accept that she may not be perfect but her choices were either to embrace the things about herself that were still attractive—right now, at this moment in time—or spend the rest of her life "waiting" to get her sexy back. With some effort, she had chosen the former, and had set about buying clothes that fit properly, that enhanced her strengths and disguised her weaknesses. She vowed not to torture herself with pointless comparisons to women who were either not her age, had never borne children, or were airbrushed magazine models.

Over the past ten years she'd done a pretty good job of accepting her current self even with the permanent existence of the Chicken Belly Flap Thing, but strangely, she found that now that she was Patrick's grandmother she was feeling out of sorts again. Her wardrobe, developed during the years when her children were no longer babies, was not really suitable for zipping around town with an infant. Fitted jackets didn't lay right when carrying him in his baby seat, along with her purse and the diaper bag. Not to mention that she was sweating like a drinking glass on a hot summer day the majority of the time, whether from the exertion or pre-menopause or both.

Concurrently, she had zero inclination to re-purchase the "young mom" wardrobe of jeans and tee-shirts, which had become, to her, what one wears to do yard work or housecleaning. She enjoyed her extensive variety of high-heeled sandals and didn't want to abandon them for sneakers. Yet the pain in her feet and lower back by the end of each day indicated that jetting around town in heels was neither practical nor comfortable when doing it with a baby.

Sighing, she wrapped herself in a towel and stepped out of the shower, noticing that Patrick was looking sleepy. She talked to him while she dressed and did her makeup, telling him all about the fabulous bottle he was going to have in just a little while. Determined to keep him awake, she tickled his toes in between applying her lipstick and selecting shoes that were entirely impractical but would look nice at the luncheon.

Finally ready, she lifted him out of his bouncer and brought him downstairs, carrying her matching suit jacket instead of putting it on just yet. As they headed through the foyer she caught a glance of herself in the mirror and stopped, taken aback in surprise.

There she was, in her fitted, plum-colored skirt with a crisp, cream-colored blouse and matching cream pumps. Her hair was fully done and her makeup immaculate, a state that used to be a daily norm for her but was now, she realized, something she'd let slip in recent months, replaced by quick touchups and barely a swipe of lip gloss.

If you didn't notice the baby she was carrying, it was as if she were seeing Herself again. The Self she hadn't seen in two months. Or longer, really, when you added the summer months during which she annually set aside her own needs in favor of maintaining a laid-back household that the older kids could enjoy coming home to.

Patrick, growing ever more tired, lay his head on her shoulder, his thumb finding its way into his mouth. Sighing at the sight of the two sides of herself that she couldn't begin to reconcile as one, she stepped away from the mirror, grabbed a bottle, and tried to mentally prepare herself for the afternoon ahead.

*****

Overall, the Women's Club Luncheon went well. Shelley's plan for Patrick to nap went off without a hitch, resulting in her being able to behave almost as if it were a normal luncheon. With a fresh diaper and a full belly, he fell asleep during the short car ride over. She'd (now expertly) lifted his car seat out of its base, snapped it into his stroller, and extended its canopy to keep the bright sunshine from waking him up.

Entering the lush country club via its handicapped ramp, the concierge held the heavy oak door and nodded formally as she wheeled the stroller inside. Grateful that she'd decided to nix the matching jacket altogether, she walked into the luncheon with as much grace as possible, easily locating her seating assignment among the miniature placards.

She knew everyone and was greeted warmly, with all of the ladies cooing and sneaking peeks at the sleeping baby. She wasn't sure who told them or what they knew (she was pretty sure Claire had spread the word), but no one asked about the unusual circumstances surrounding her becoming an instant full-time grandmother at the age of forty-six.

Of course, with her being one of the youngest in the first place and many of the other women already being "regular" grandparents, there were many exclamations about what a *joy* it is and how it's *so different* being a grandma.

The problem was, she wasn't finding it different at all. In fact, she was finding it exactly the same as when she raised her own children, except for the fact that she was not as energetic as she used to be and was no longer in the mindset to sing nursery rhymes and play on the floor.

The truth was, as much as she loved Patrick, her grandparenting experience had thus far been quite different than their realities—in which they'd visit for a few hours and then return home to their calm and tidy townhouses. Frankly, she was finding it to be more like life on a hamster wheel—running and running with no end in sight, and with the claustrophobia of still being caged in, even if she were to slow down.

However, since life experience had taught her that to verbalize all of this would be pointless, she just smiled and nodded pleasantly, and tried to enjoy the fact that she was sitting in a chair and being served a meal that was prepared by someone other than her.

*****

By that point in her adult life, Shelley had already gone through various stages regarding her women friends, and figured that she would likely go through many more until she was an old, old lady… an *actual* old lady.

There was the phase of reckoning during her twenties, in which she discovered that the friends who were so fun in high school may not be quite the same people you chose to spend time with as an adult. She didn't doubt that their feelings toward her were mutual—for whatever each of their reasons were—and she'd continued to maintain friendships with only a handful over the years.

In her early thirties, she'd gone through the struggles of developing friendships with other women while they all had young children, almost always doing things with the kids and doing their best to *accept* one another's parenting strategies without *judgment*. Ahem.

Then there was her late thirties when she'd divorced her first husband and dealt with the extra sting of no support from friends or neighbors, resulting in her exchanging little more than a passing nod with any of them ever since.

After a few years of choosing not to spend much time with friends at all—during which she met David, fell in love, and confided only in those far and few long-term friends that she'd known since forever—she reached her mid-forties. At that point she came to the conclusion that she really didn't care if people were "real friends" or not. She cherished the few she had, and found that she could enjoy people's company for the thing they had in common at the moment, and that not every friendship had to be deep and meaningful.

Which all meant that, while she knew all of the women at the luncheon, she expected little to nothing from them along the lines of support. She didn't resent them not calling or offering to help out because she was never under the impression that they were close friends in the first place.

Their underhanded comments of, "How is that new daughter of yours doing?... Bless her heart!" didn't annoy her because she was cynical enough not to expect anything else. When conversation turned to the big golf outing/fundraiser event and who they thought would be the committee chair, she was relieved to hear them say, in their sugary Southern accents, "I'm sure Shelley has already got her hands full as could be," thus superseding the need for her to say it herself.

Shelley chalked it up as a successful afternoon out. Patrick slept practically the whole time, waking up fifteen minutes before the end, and sat in her arms contentedly drinking his bottle and looking around wide-eyed while everyone finished dessert.

*****

That was how most things went during those months when Patrick was an infant. He wasn't very fussy, and as long as he was kept fed, changed, and he had his nap, he was generally pretty happy.

For the most part, Shelley was able to keep up with things around the house and when she took him out with her, a little planning went a long way toward being able to accomplish her goal, whether it was to do the food shopping or to meet with David near his office for an impromptu lunch.

It wasn't until he got a bit older and was no longer content to stay in his little seat and take two-and-a-half-hour naps that things became more challenging.

Chapter 12

While Shelley felt that she took care of Patrick almost exclusively, Alexandra felt like *she* was his sole caregiver. She felt like she had no life, between getting up at the crack of dawn every day for school, then coming home and taking care of Patrick every night and on weekends, plus all the homework and projects.

Spring Valley High School was so different from her old school. Most of the kids came from good homes and lived in nice houses. Not that her mom's place had been in a bad neighborhood or anything; it was just that parents weren't *so involved* and the school didn't expect you to do *so much* on your own at home. And now that she was a senior, there were all these programs and meetings and stuff about applying to college and preparing for college. They were, like, shoving college down her throat! The weird thing was, it seemed like everyone else thought it was fine and they were all planning on going. At her old school, not everyone went to college. Most kids either went to trade school or just got jobs or got married or something.

Even when they had the open house, she was mortified when both Shelley and David insisted on coming and meeting all the teachers. They brought Patrick, of course, and everyone had fawned over him. She'd spent the whole time fluctuating between praying they wouldn't tell everyone the baby was hers, and being angry that they didn't.

Oh sure, David had talked to her before they went and asked how she wanted to handle it. He'd come into her room, after knocking and saying "Hey Kiddo, can I come in?" So annoying! For some reason, Shelley and David always felt like they had to *talk* about everything. They always wanted to make sure everyone was *okay* and not upset about anything.

"I'm looking forward to meeting your teachers tonight," David had said.

"Yeah."

"I wanted to find out what your thoughts are about Patrick. I didn't know whether you've mentioned that you have a baby, or if you don't want anyone to know, or what."

She'd just stared at him, not knowing what to say. What was she going to do, come right out and say that she didn't want people to know? For some reason that just seemed... wrong.

After a few moments of her silence, David said, "If you're undecided, we don't have to say anything one way or another. Chances are people will just assume he's ours unless you say anything different."

Why was he making this her *responsibility to decide?* She didn't want to have to decide, as both saying and not saying that Patrick was her baby just felt uncomfortable, either way.

Again, he waited a few seconds, then said, "Okay then. We'll be leaving in thirty minutes. Please make sure he's got a fresh diaper and a light jacket on."

He'd walked out of her room and left the door open. *So annoying!* They knew she always liked to keep it closed! Yet they were constantly "suggesting" that she leave it open. "Let the air flow" through the room and "be a part of the family." *Ugh!*

For some reason, she felt hot with anger and when she got up to close the door, she couldn't help kicking it shut a little too hard and making it slam.

*****

In any case, Alexandra felt like she had no life, either inside or outside of school. Most of the kids at school were such goody-goodies, and all everyone talked about was college and football games and the stupid dance team that she wasn't on. Most of them had been going to school together for years—some since kindergarten—and even though everyone was pretty nice to her, she just felt like she had nothing in common with them.

Plus, with watching Patrick every night, she had no time for all the nonsense most girls did. It would be Wednesday and they'd all be in front of the mirrors in the bathroom, already talking about the weekend and the mall, and some stupid movie they were planning on seeing.

David and Shelley had told her lots of times that if she wanted to do something on weekends she should let them know and they'd watch

Patrick. But where was she going to go? It wasn't like she had any friends or anything! In order to make friends, you had to, like, go to all this after school stuff or be in a club or something. Impossible!

The only friends she did have were a few kids who walked off campus during lunch. Like her, none of them had cars, and so they would just hang out at the pizza place up at the corner, then go around back and smoke. Even though she knew they were losers, she hung around with them anyway; there was nothing else to do and it felt like lunch was her only social time all week. Plus, they didn't ask questions like most people did, trying to make conversation about stupid crap all the time. Mostly, they just sat around, each listening to their iPods or talking about bands and stuff.

Once in a while, one of the guys would light up a joint. At first she didn't try it but then one day she decided, *fuck it, why not?* She only took two tokes but it was enough to make her feel really… different. It wasn't necessarily great or terrible but for some reason it just felt good to not feel the same as she always felt. Which was mostly bad.

Ever since that first time, she started to say "yes" whenever they had some.

Chapter 13

The house became filled with plastic. A baby swing in the living room, a highchair in the dining room, an Exer-Saucer in the kitchen, each of them built of sturdy, primary-colored plastic. There was a huge, blue Rubbermaid bin, filled with trucks, stuffed animals, blocks, and board books—seemingly all of them musical.

Unlike the toys Shelley's girls had when they were small, these musical toys required little to no interaction to set them off. Motion activated, even the vibration of Tiny walking past was enough to send them into mechanical peals of "The Wheels on The Bus."

Patrick loved them. At six months old, he was no longer the sedate newborn who sat in his little seat, staring contentedly while Shelley got things done. He no longer slept in his stroller during her Women's Club luncheons. In fact, she was eventually confronted by Hope Winston, one of the club's leaders, who pulled her aside and suggested that she make other arrangements for Patrick, as his excited squeals and all the ladies cooing over him was a disruption to the planning of the gala. Ten years older than Shelley—with grandchildren borne by adult kids who owned their own homes—she even went so far as to point out that, "I enjoy visiting with my grandchildren but I don't *bring them* everywhere with me." As if she had a choice! *Bitch.*

Alexandra was settling into more of a routine—initially enforced by her and David. She went to school during the day, took care of Patrick after school, did her homework and had some free time in the evening while David watched the baby for a few hours; then she went to bed so she could be ready to do it all again the next day.

The walking Shelley insisted on her doing, taking Patrick in his stroller up and down the hills in their neighborhood, had paid off in the form of her getting back into shape and, surprisingly, making some new friends. Alexandra had told her that, after seeing her pass by several times, a group of girls from a few blocks over had chatted with her, and had even invited her to a birthday party where they did manicures and put cucumbers on their eyes, and watched "The Scary Movie" series during the sleepover.

It had been a bit of a dilemma for Shelley, as she didn't know the girls or the parents, and when she phoned to introduce herself she'd had to leave a message. But Alexandra was so excited that she didn't have the heart to not let her go until she spoke to them, which was her usual rule. She didn't want to stop her from doing the only "normal" thing that had come along so far, so she and David had decided to let her go, and when she came home the next morning she'd said that she had a great time.

*****

Patrick was adorable, in that cute baby stage of sitting up, trying all the new flavors of baby food, and laughing with a rolling giggle when Tiny would lick the stickiness off his arms and legs, his tongue easily covering half the baby with each swoop.

It was Shelley, *herself*, who was having a problem. It seemed that nowhere was just right for her anymore. After the confrontation with Hope at the Women's Club, she decided that she would look into other ways to spend some of her time during the day with Patrick. Besides, he was getting too big to spend all day at home, despite the plethora of toys at his disposal.

Figuring that she would try some of the things that had worked for her before, she signed them up for a Mommy and Me class at the library. There they all sat in a circle for story time, then sang the "Itsy Bitsy Spider" and other nursery rhymes, followed by letting the babies crawl around on the colorful rug while the moms sat around to chat.

The first day had been okay, although with all of the sitting on the floor it was evident that her normal wardrobe of slacks and a nice blouse was not going to work for these events. The young moms, not knowing one another yet, were immersed in impressing one another with their outstanding parenting skills: "Darling, we don't put things in our mouth, do we?" they'd announce in a singsong cadence with a quick glance to make sure everyone could hear.

Even the presence of that woman from the supermarket—the one who was closer to Shelley's age, who had assumed she'd adopted Patrick, then assumed again that he'd been an "oops," so to speak—

didn't seem that bad at first. She'd smiled and gushed at how nice it was to see them and waited until the second class to tell everyone how Shelley had *so many* kids and wasn't it *so wonderful* that she still did this with her youngest. Which basically forced Shelley to have to explain to the group that Patrick really wasn't *her* baby, and that no, she wasn't his babysitter, she was his grandmother.

There was a pause of contemplation at that point, after which each and every twenty-and-thirty-something mom felt compelled to say something like, "Wow, you don't look that old," or "You must've had your own kids really young." Which was nearly as complimentary as being at a bar and having a cute guy come over and say, "You're pretty hot, for an old chick."

This newfound information instantly led to her being perceived as the older, wiser, all-knowing adviser to the new moms, who would ask her questions about everything from stain removal to getting their babies to sleep through the night. *Okay, fine.*

After several weeks, though, the girls became more comfortable with one another and their conversations became more intimate. Namely, bitching about their husbands.

"Yeah, he's off on another business trip and I'm stuck home by myself, *again,*" sighed a pretty blonde named Brittany, as she smoothed her perfectly coiffed hair aside, her hand adorned by a clump of diamonds.

"He always wants to have sex," complained another. "I mean, I really think once or twice a month should be fine."

"I know what you mean," Brittany agreed, "after being alone all week, he assumes I want to get it on? Please!"

Shelley would just quietly play with Patrick, sitting on the rug and going over the colors: "Do you see blue?" It was one of his favorite games. Nobody believed her that although he couldn't talk yet, he could identify colors, even if his hand-eye coordination wasn't perfect when he flung his arm in the general direction of the blue bird on the rug.

"What about you, Shelley? You must have some experience with this whole husband thing," said Brittany, winking.

"I'm not sure I really look at things from the same perspective," she said.

"What do you mean?"

"Being on my second husband I just look at things a bit differently."

"Like how?"

Should I really continue full on with this? Shelley speculated. She knew that her tendency to tell it like it is, was a trait people either loved or hated about her, and she'd always struggled with deciding when to bring it out and when to suppress the urge.

"Have you ever thought about things from your husband's point of view? Maybe he's not thrilled to be on a business trip either; it's not as though he's on vacation."

Shocked, Brittany's demeanor instantly became defensive. "But he hardly even calls me and when he does it's at, like, the worst time to talk."

"Why do you think he calls so little?"

"He says it's because he's in meetings all day, and then at business dinners in the evening. And then it's a different time there. The other day when he called me it was 3:00 am there!"

"Mm hm." Shelley looked at her pointedly.

"What?"

"Do you think it's possible that he had to set his alarm to get up in the middle of the night just so he could call you?"

"No, I didn't think that. I just figured he was up."

"Really? Is he normally up making phone calls at 3:00 am?"

"Well no, but…"

Shelley waited. Brittany just stared at her. The other women were watching both of them.

"I just think I look at things differently, with the knowledge of hindsight," Shelley said. "When I was your age it did feel almost like my husband was the enemy most of the time."

They all nodded.

"But what about the sex," murmured Supermarket Mom commiseratively. "I'm sure you must have some good ideas how to get out of it."

"Why would I want to get out of it? I love having sex with my husband."

"Really?" She sounded shocked. Apparently it never occurred to her that "old people,"—like she and Shelley—would have an active sex life. What with being forty-six and all.

Shelley stayed silent, hoping to put an end to the conversation.

They were all still staring at her, waiting for her to say more.

Oh God. Now I'm all in, Shelley regretted.

"But I'm just so *tired*," Brittany whined. "And I just want to go out and get the things done that I can't do all week when he's away."

Shelley didn't say anything.

The younger woman went on. "You know what I mean, right? How am I supposed to be in a sexy mood when I have so much to do!" The other girls were all nodding in agreement.

"I understand how you feel, and I've felt exactly the same in the past, but I just don't agree anymore," Shelley said, standing and grabbing her diaper bag.

Brittany kept pushing. "I'm just not in the mood when I know I have so much to do."

Now aggravated, Shelley said, "So what you're saying is that catching up on your food shopping is more important than maintaining a good sex life with your husband?"

"Well no, but…"

"Whatever. It's none of my business. I was just saying, because you asked."

Other people started arriving: the next class consisted of preschool-aged children who came running into the children's area, stepping over the babies. Shelley scooped Patrick into her arms and said, "Come on, sweetie. Let's get you changed so you'll be ready for your nap." She turned in the direction of the restroom.

"You're going to change him in there? On the *public* changing table?" said Supermarket Mom incredulously.

"Yes, of course. Chances are he'll fall asleep in the car and then I can just transfer him into his crib for nap time."

"Oh, I would never use a public table. Unless it was an emergency, of course. She falls asleep in the car but once I get her home and change her she's wide-awake. I *wish* she would take a nap."

Shelley couldn't help it; she had to roll her eyes.

Chapter 14

Shelley missed David. David missed Shelley. Of course, they were both still there every day, but it seemed like they never really saw each other anymore. Their morning routine of having coffee together had been abandoned once she started taking care of Patrick on all of the school mornings and he took one of the weekend mornings so that Alexandra and Shelley could both sleep in.

Despite their mutual awareness about the dangers of losing oneself under the overwhelming task of parenting (um, grandparenting?), evenings were frequently spent separately, especially as Patrick grew more active, because Shelley would run around catching up on chores and errands, unable to have gotten much done while watching him all day. With David volunteering to take the baby for a few hours each night so that Alexandra could shower and get her schoolwork done, evenings when they were together would consist of them sitting on the living room floor, entertaining Patrick with musical toys and sturdy board books. Basically, it was the way things always are for parents of young babies.

Except that they weren't his parents.

Yet they weren't really his grandparents either; at least not the way they'd always envisioned grandparenthood. They'd joked for years about how someday when their kids had children, they'd come to visit, bringing a drum set and a tray of brownies, play with them, and then leave. There would be no rules from their end, and they'd simply get them riled up to their hearts' content, then go home to their peace and quiet.

They hadn't counted on this situation, in which they were not really parents but didn't have the freedom to simply be fun-loving grandparents either.

Complicating things even further was David's attempt at developing a father-daughter relationship with Alexandra. When she'd first arrived they were all in shock, focused on the birth of the baby and getting the basics settled into a routine.

More recently it had occurred to David that *he had a daughter*. A daughter he hadn't known about! One who was raised her entire life with no paternal influence and no siblings. An adolescent child who was suddenly a mother, a daughter, and a sister.

Fortunately, Patty, Alexandra's mother, had always maintained that her father didn't know about her and emphasized that it was by her own choice. She'd said that she didn't know him very well but she knew him well enough to be certain that he would have wanted to be involved in Alexandra's life. As Alexandra matured, Patty had explained that it was this positive trait in her father that had made her specifically not want to tell him: She didn't want to be in a relationship, and as time passed she didn't want their solitary lives to be interfered with either.

Over the years, Alexandra had complained to Patty and said she wanted to meet her father, that it wasn't fair. And she was right, it wasn't fair. But Patty, in her warped sense of self-preservation, had refused, saying that she would give Alexandra the information on her eighteenth birthday and that if she wanted to contact him then, she could do so on her own.

As circumstances went, it didn't take until she turned eighteen. Yet that didn't make it any easier for the two to get to know one another. Being that this was real life, David and Alexandra didn't instantly connect, watching hockey together or having heart-to-heart talks the way they would have if they were in a movie. Instead, conversation was often stilted, not to mention constantly interrupted, with Patrick and Tiny in the mix.

Speaking of Tiny, that was one area where Alexandra and David did connect and he decided to build on that. Several times a week they would head out, taking turns walking Tiny and pushing Patrick's stroller, and they'd go all the way to the dog park, about two miles away. Tiny loved it there, although David had to swallow his pride a bit when Tiny, despite his elephantine physique, was afraid of the big, rambunctious dogs and preferred to play with the small ones more similar in size to Frick.

Along the way they'd chat, mostly about inane topics but sometimes about Alexandra's childhood, things she liked or didn't like, and so on. David, riddled with guilt, shied away from talking about his boys' or Shelley's girls' childhoods, instead sharing stories of his time in the Air

Force, places he'd traveled for work, and other things he'd deemed interesting, yet safe.

Upon their return, Alexandra would head up to shower, while David and Shelley would give Patrick his bath in the kitchen sink, going over the play-by-play of what they'd talked about, analyzing whether or not they were developing a closer relationship, and how each family member was doing with the whole situation. It was their "new normal": the cyclic scrutinizing of every microscopic detail.

Furthering their time apart was the issue of Shelley trying to fit in some one-on-one time with Grace, who was usually still at dance team practice during those evening walk times. As a result, she and Grace spent their time together later in the evenings or on weekends, trying to do the things they did before, like shopping or an occasional game of bowling, an activity Grace secretly enjoyed but would never admit to her friends.

Over time, Grace's attitude toward Tiny became one of acceptance, and she even started to be somewhat nice to Patrick, understanding that he really was just an innocent in the whole scheme of things. As for her parents, she seemed to feel sorry for them, an interesting turn of events because they hadn't realized she even noticed that they were human before, never mind being concerned about the sacrifices they made.

The only area in which Grace's attitude hadn't improved at all was toward Alexandra herself. To say that she was contemptuous would be putting it kindly, and her modus operandi was to either pretend she didn't see her at all, or to sigh loudly in disgust when they would pass in the hall.

Even during family dinners when they were all sitting around the table, Grace would direct her conversation toward David and Shelley, as if Alexandra wasn't even there. Alexandra, who'd never really tried to earn Grace's friendship, deemed her a "spoiled snot" anyway, and seemed perfectly fine with being ignored. The only time Grace could get a rise out of her was in defense of Tiny, when Grace would complain about him staring at her or sitting on her foot and Alexandra would say, "Oh, get over it-tuh."

*****

They hadn't seen their friends in ages and so when Claire Whitman called to see if they wanted to go out to dinner, Shelley evaluated their exhaustion (emotional, physical, and financial), and decided that even though Claire drove her a little crazy, yes, they would go.

"After happening across you that day at the post office and then you being so preoccupied during the Women's Club luncheons, I have wondered how you have been," Claire said, her strange Southern/Bostonian accent irritating Shelley immediately, even over the phone. "It appears that you have not been at meetings for months." She cleared her throat.

"I've been busy, and since Patrick's become so much more active, it's easier to do more baby-friendly activities," Shelley said, biting her tongue so as not to get into gossiping about Hope Winston and how she'd basically asked her to leave.

"Oh, really?" Claire replied, her overly exaggerated tone leaving no doubt that she already knew about their run-in and was looking for more kindling to stoke the fires of gossip at next Wednesday's meeting.

"And you? How have you been, Claire? Is all well with you and Brian, and with Jacob?"

"Oh yes, dear. Brian and I are fine and Jacob is still working at social security, living in his rundown little studio." She sighed. "I do wish he would get a nicer place but I suppose on the salary he has chosen…" She sighed again.

Shelley knew that Claire and Brian were disappointed that Jacob had "wasted" his Ivy League education by choosing a low-paying social work job, and if she were to be honest, she would feel similarly—although privately. But looking at the big picture, things could be much worse. He'd graduated with a 3.8 average, was living independently, enjoyed his career, and had chosen his apartment for its downtown Raleigh location, preferring to live within walking distance to work rather than having a car.

Trying to keep things more positive she said, "I'm glad to hear everyone has been well."

"Oh yes, yes. That is why I was calling. To see if you and David would like to join Brian and myself for dinner? Washington Duke?"

One of the priciest restaurants known to mankind. Also involving formal attire and either refraining from drinking or the utilization of a car service, as it was forty-five minutes away.

"We'd prefer to stay a little closer to home. How about Maverick's?" The small, yet upscale steakhouse offered some of the finest meals in the area with a more casual atmosphere.

"Oh dear. You don't want to go to the Duke?" Claire's tone was that of a woman used to manipulating circumstances to her satisfaction.

Staying firm, and at this point having decided that Maverick's sounded like a great idea even if David and she went alone, Shelley said, "If you really have your heart set, we can just make it another time."

"No no. I suppose Maverick's will be fine," she semi-sighed. "See you Saturday at eight? I will have Brian make the reservation."

"See you then."

*****

David was pleased about them having dinner plans for Saturday, as Brian Whitman was unquestionably the more enjoyable half of the couple. Their week took on the air it used to have back when the kids were younger and they would hold on tightly to one another, looking forward to their free weekends when the children would all go with their other parents.

By choosing not to have children together, those weekends were often the reprieve that kept them sane, providing the couple with an oasis of romance, or at least peace, offsetting their regular daily mayhem. However, now that Patrick had joined their family there was no weekend reprieve; just as if they'd had a baby together he was always there—there was no "other" household of parents for him to go to every-other weekend.

On Thursday, Alexandra asked if she could speak with her about something; strangely polite, Shelley knew that she was about to ask a favor.

"Guess who called me?" she said a bit breathlessly.

"Who?"

"Amy!"

Shelley was confused for a minute, mentally scrolling through the names of the few friends she'd made and not coming across an Amy.

"Ya know, my friend from my old school. By my mom's house?"

Ah yes. The one girl who had befriended Alexandra after all of her friends had ditched her upon finding out that she was pregnant.

"That's great! It's always nice to hear from an old friend. How is she?"

"Great, great!" she chirped.

Okay, any minute she'll get around to asking what she wants to ask.

"Actually, she's having a big party this Saturday night. It's at a hotel and everything! With a DJ!"

Saturday night. The one night David and she were looking forward to and already had plans for.

"What kind of a party is it?"

"Well, it's kind of a sweet sixteen, even though she's seventeen-and-a-half already. She didn't want to have one but she's made a bunch of new friends, so her parents are letting her have a party now."

"Wow." Shelley didn't know what to say. It sounded like this was really important to Alexandra, but getting out for an adult night with friends was really important to her and David too.

"So can I go? I would need you to watch Patrick and it's an overnight thing so you'd need to watch him in the morning, and I'm not sure what I would wear so I might need a dress because even though I've lost some weight my old dresses probably won't fit yet. But I can do my nails myself and I can wear my hair the way I used to wear it when I was taking head shots for dance team..."

Shelley had never seen Alexandra so excited. Gone was the sullen, woe-is-she persona of late, as well as the overly adult facade she'd attempted at first. She was a normal teenager, excited about a party. An important party.

"Your dad and I have plans to go out Saturday night with friends." She was crestfallen. "But I'll see if I can change it to Friday or something."

"Oh. Okay." Alexandra's eyes welled with tears. "Thanks."

*****

A quick call to Claire revealed that they weren't available on Friday. Ironically, they'd promised to babysit for their next-door neighbors. Figuring she'd chat about it with David later that night and probably end up canceling, Shelley went to pick up Grace from dance team practice.

On the drive home they chatted about Grace's plans for the weekend, which included a movie Friday night and helping a friend on Sunday afternoon with a fundraiser she was organizing as part of her Girl Scout Gold Award activities.

"I wonder why I haven't heard from the Millers lately for babysitting," Grace said. "I barely have enough for the movie and won't even be able to buy popcorn."

"Hmm." Shelley's mind was instantly flooded with ideas of how Alexandra could go to her party, David and she could keep their plans, and Grace could make some money. Simultaneously, she was also filled with hesitation, as she couldn't imagine paying one family member to watch another, money was tight, and it was hard to visualize Grace being all that nice to Patrick, despite her recently reduced scorn toward him.

"What?"

"I don't know," Shelley hesitated. "I have a dilemma for Saturday but I don't know if it could work out."

"What is it?"

"David and I have plans to go out that we'd really prefer not to cancel, but Alexandra was invited to a party that's really important to her."

"So you're thinking I could babysit Patrick?"

"Maybe. I'm not sure."

"Why not?"

"You've been far from thrilled about Patrick and at the stage he's in, he is quite a bit of work."

"So what are you saying, that I'd be mean to him?" Grace was clearly horrified that she would think such a thing.

"No, of course I know you wouldn't be *mean* to him. It's just not something I thought you'd be interested in."

"Well, a cute baby is a cute baby, even if he is Alexandra's," she said, shocking her mom with the revelation that she even noticed he was cute. "Besides, I could really use the money."

"That's the other thing. I don't feel it's appropriate to pay one family member to watch another, and even if I did, we really don't have the budget to pay the eight dollars an hour that the Millers pay you."

"Oh."

They rode along in silence for a while, undoubtedly each internalizing about how this might or might not work for everyone.

"Well, I guess…"

"I guess I could…"

They laughed, having both started saying the same thing at the same time. Shelley went first.

"I was going to say that I guess we could pay you some, but not eight dollars an hour."

"And I was going to say that I know Alexandra has no money, but maybe you could pay me a little and I could, like, get her to do some of my chores or something."

"That would be fair," Shelley agreed, trying to hide her surprise that Grace would consider having anything to do with Alexandra whatsoever. "Why don't we all talk about it when we get home."

*****

By the time Saturday rolled around, everything was in place. Setting aside her astonishment about Alexandra and Grace actually communicating with one another and coming to an agreement without any doors being slammed or tears being shed, Shelley focused on her own responsibilities.

She took Alexandra to a local consignment store that was well known for offering a large assortment of formalwear. She found a really nice dress in a deep purple color that fit well and only cost twenty-one dollars. While they were there, she also found a black and red Kate Spade purse in brand-new condition marked down to thirty dollars, which they purchased as Amy's present.

Alexandra was thrilled and Shelley thought it went well too. It was the first time they'd done something together that wasn't fraught with tension. Even Patrick seemed to understand that it was a special day, sitting in his stroller quietly, looking around and smiling at the ladies rather than fussing about being contained.

On the car ride home, the two chatted, Shelley enjoying that for the first time ever, their interactions felt… normal. She forced herself not to say more than a sentence or two about the No Questions Asked Pickup Policy of their family, but she did make sure that it was understood.

She had phoned Amy's mom to introduce herself and confirm the time and location, as well as the fact that only girls were invited for the overnight portion and that there would be parental supervision at all times. There was a part of her that was uncomfortable not knowing the parents better, but the other mom seemed to be very like-minded. She forced herself to push aside her cynicism about Alexandra's previous error in judgment, figuring she'd learned her lesson and must have developed greater wisdom by now.

By the time they pulled out of the driveway Saturday night, leaving a freshly bathed and pajama clad Patrick in the care of Grace, who was sitting on the floor making block towers for him to knock over, all was well and good.

They dropped Alexandra off at the party, where the concierge was gallantly escorting the guests to the ballroom and they had the opportunity to briefly meet Amy's mom, Gail, who was hanging around the arrival circle, making herself available to greet parents.

Pulling away, right on schedule to meet Claire and Brian at Maverick's, Shelley enjoyed David's slight smile and noticed that for the first time in a long time, she didn't see his jaw working in its clenching beat of stress.

Chapter 15

Maverick's was delicious as usual. Shelley ordered the roasted duck breast because, well, if you're going to order duck, Maverick's is the place to do it.

Interestingly, Claire was not as annoying to be out with in public as she was when interacting privately. She was too engrossed in her inner world of ensuring that she gave off the right appearance: her signature waspish/Southern style that in reality served to make her appear old and stodgy, rather than chic and elegant the way she thought.

Regardless, Claire being in her own world meant that David, Brian, and she could chat freely and intelligently, their laughter increasing throughout the evening, much to Claire's disdain. It didn't matter. It was a pleasant time of good food, good wine, and interesting conversation, and as David opened the car door for her, he swung her into his arms and looked into her face, his chocolate eyes shining with love, and said, "It's so nice to have been *with* you tonight!"

Shelley knew exactly what he meant.

*****

Arriving home, the couple—downright giddy after their evening out—tiptoed into the house, praying that it would be quiet. They paused in the kitchen, each tentatively looking toward the stairs and holding their breath to see whether they heard anything.

Not a peep.

She texted Grace, figuring that if she was awake she'd come downstairs and if not, no harm done: she always kept her phone on vibrate.

No reply. Which meant that not only was Patrick sleeping, but Grace was too!

Giggling at their good fortune, Shelley started rifling through the fridge to find the apple butter while David started making toast. It was their ritual whenever they went out; they'd come home and have toast with apple butter. It was something she'd always done when she was single, and when they discovered that David liked it too, it became a habit they enjoyed together.

She swiped their crumbs onto their paper plates while David prepared the coffee for the morning. When she went to fill up Frick's food bowl, she found a sticky note from Grace that said CAT 8. Rotten beast! He was slinking back and forth meowing like a starving stray, trying to trick them into feeding him again.

Smiling together with David, both of them relishing the fact that finally, *finally,* their kids were all responsible adults or semi-adults who would actually do things like feeding the cat not because they told them to but simply because it needed to be done, they ascended the stairs hand-in-hand.

Walking into their bedroom, they each went to their side of the bed and started getting undressed.

"I'm really in the mood to watch The Weather Channel, are you?" David asked.

Shelley laughed. "I've been thinking about it all night!"

The custom had developed years earlier. When they wanted to make love and not worry about the kids hearing any "sounds of Mommy and Daddy doing their exercises," they would put on The Weather Channel for background noise. It was perfect, as it sounded to the kids as if they were watching "boring news," while for them it wasn't a distraction the way it would have been if they were to put on something like The Comedy Channel.

Making sure that Frick and Tiny were already inside the room so as not to be interrupted by them wanting in, David shut and locked the door carefully, keeping the handle turned so as not to make it click.

Sliding into bed together, their bodies naked, his arm automatically slipping under her head and their lips naturally finding one another, she could feel that they were both instantly ready. It seemed like it had been forever since they were together like that—although if she'd thought about it, it was technically only a few weeks. Still, too long.

Maybe it wasn't so much that they hadn't made love, it was more that they hadn't made love *like that.* Not exhausted. Not stressed. Not feeling like it was more of a physical release than an emotional one.

As she tried to roll on top of David, wanting the pleasure of his fullness inside her, he put his hand on her shoulder, stopping her, encouraging her to lie back.

"Not yet," he whispered, sliding down her body. His lips traveled over her collarbone, between her breasts, down her stomach, his eyes locked on hers as he worked his way lower and lower. A thrill shot through her as she recognized the leisurely, loving look in his eyes that meant she should settle in and enjoy herself. "Not just yet, Sweet Shelley Bean. I've been wanting to do this all night."

*****

They slept soundly; their legs twined together, the wine and lovemaking providing the perfect foundation for a restful night. Patrick's baby monitor stood next to the bed but they didn't hear a sound until 7:45 am.

Going into his room, Shelley could see that although he hadn't called for them until now, he had been up for a while. He'd been playing with his toys in his crib and now stood, smiling, cruising back and forth along the rail, his one white tooth sparkling proudly in contrast to his rich coffee-colored skin.

As she approached, Patrick stretched his chubby little arms up toward her, then got a comical look of horror when he realized that he was standing up but not holding on, and promptly fell back on his bottom. Giggling, he climbed back up and reached for her with only one arm. Smart little guy.

Lifting him out, the weight of his ten-month-old body against hers, he put his arms around her neck and lay his head on her shoulder. It was part of their morning routine, one of the best times of the day. Feeling him relax, allowing his weight to fully slacken in her arms, she felt honored—and awed—at the complete trust a baby will impart unto those with whom they feel safe. She enjoyed this moment each morning, as it was one of the rare and few waking moments when Patrick was not in motion. Knowing that it would be over shortly, she felt his little muscles prepare for the next part of their routine.

"Paaaaaah!" He flung his head back, laughing at her "surprised" expression, enjoying his version of peekaboo. Then he lay his head down on her shoulder again.

"Paaaaaah!" Pretend-surprised again, she tickled his belly. "Hey you! Stop scaring me!" His rolling laugh tumbled out of him as they did it over and over again.

Continuing on, she brought him over to the changing table and quickly handed him his stuffed llama, keeping him busy gumming on it while she changed his diaper and dressed him in one of his comfy play outfits. So different from the lace-trimmed pink things and coordinating ribbons when her girls were little, she enjoyed his little jumpers that depicted dinosaurs, trucks, and the like. This one, while a soft one-piece, was designed to look as if it were overalls, complete with "tools" embroidered on the waist area.

"Bah, bah, bah, bah..." Patrick babbled as she carried him downstairs, yet again blowing her mind at how close he was to talking. Morning bottle time was his favorite, and he would sit in her arms and guzzle it noisily while watching Tiny, who, excited that everyone was awake, would traverse the living room, bringing his rope toys, bones, and squeaky things, piling them on their legs. Frick, in his elderly cat way, would slink over resignedly, curl up next to them on the couch, and seemingly roll his eyes at the dog.

David came downstairs and Patrick, hearing him in the kitchen, immediately stopped drinking and strained to look in that direction. A minute later David came into the living room and set her coffee down on the side table where she could reach it but Patrick could not. Leaning down, he said, "Morning you two," and pecked a quick kiss on each of their cheeks.

"What time are we supposed to pick up Alexandra?"

"She said that it should be eleven o'clock, but if it was different she would call."

"I thought I might go to the hardware store and get some things for the yard work. Do you want me to take Patrick, or are you?"

"I'll take him," she said. "He'll be excited to see his mom."

Smiling at her knowingly, David shook his head almost imperceptibly. *Wishful thinking*, he imparted. She smiled back at him wryly. *I know.*

*****

Arriving at the hotel just a few minutes before eleven, Shelley parked and walked to the entrance, carrying Patrick on her hip, over to where Gail was standing.

"Hi!" she exclaimed, immediately cooing at Patrick, who was already charming her with his one-toothed baby grin.

"Hi. Looks like you held up well last night!" Shelley said, gesturing to the gaggle of girls just inside the hotel lobby with their piles of sleeping bags and pillows, waiting for their parents.

"Yeah, they were up pretty late, but they're a good bunch," she said. "I didn't know Alexandra had a baby brother. He's so cute!"

"Oh. Um. Thanks." *Should I say that Patrick is Alexandra's son, not brother? And how is it possible that she doesn't already know?*

"Did Alexandra forget something?" Gail asked, interrupting Shelley's internal dilemma before she could decide.

"I hope not," she said. "But I'm sure we'll know shortly once we get home and she unpacks," she laughed.

"What?"

"You know these girls. She's sure to discover some hairbrush or something she left behind."

"She didn't unpack last night?"

"What?"

The two of them stood there, looking at one another, equally confused. Suddenly, Gail's expression changed, awash with horror.

"She said she wasn't feeling well last night and that she wanted to go home. She told me she called you and that you were picking her up."

"What? No. She didn't call us."

"I arranged for the concierge to phone the room to confirm that she'd been picked up. It was just before midnight."

"We didn't pick her up. She didn't call us at all."

Pulling out her phone, Shelley checked to see if there were any voicemails or missed calls. There were none. There was, however, a text message, sent at 10:45 am saying that she should come at 11:45 instead of 11:00. She must have missed it because she was driving, and already almost there.

"I'm so sorry. It never occurred to me to make sure she was with you. She told me she had a stomach ache and that she called you, and I believed her."

"It's not your fault," Shelley said, mortification beginning to set in over the fact that not only was Alexandra unexplainably missing *since last night*, but had also lied to her friend's mom and put her in this position. "You could never have known she would do this. Shit, *I* never would have thought she'd do this either!"

She could see Gail recoil a bit at her use of foul language, especially in front of Patrick, but Gail just as quickly recovered as it occurred to her that she, as the responsible party, could be in for some serious trouble.

"Is there anything you want me to do? What do you think we should do?"

"I see here that she texted me, asking me to pick her up later, apparently thinking everyone else would be gone by then. I think I'm just going to call my husband and wait. I'm assuming she plans to get here by then."

Gail walked over to her own pile of stuff and shuffled through her purse a bit, coming up with a business card and pen. Scribbling on it, she said, "Please, keep me posted! I'm absolutely mortified that this happened while she was on my watch!" She handed Shelley the card, where she'd added her cell phone number to the back.

"Okay, thanks," Shelley said. "And don't worry, I don't hold you responsible. You could never have known she was lying." Although there was a part of her that thought she should have checked. But then again, would she have? Or would she have done the same thing, assuming that they were dealing with a bunch of high school seniors—and nice girls at that. She tried to imagine if it were Grace and her friends and concluded that no, she wouldn't have demanded to personally speak to the mother either. Probably not, anyway.

Walking back to the car, Patrick now becoming heavy, she contemplated what to do. Settling the baby into his car seat, she gave him his little container of Cheerios while she called David to figure out a plan.

Chapter 16

At precisely 11:45, Alexandra came walking out of the hotel lobby looking appropriately exhausted, hauling her duffle, sleeping bag, and pillow. All of the rest of the girls had been picked up earlier, and Amy's mom had walked over to where Shelley was waiting in her car, to say goodbye—still apologizing profusely—about thirty minutes earlier.

"Hey sweetie," Shelley greeted her, trying to sound as normal as possible. "How was the sleepover?"

"Great. I'm just really tired." Alexandra piled her stuff into the back seat, barely giving Patrick a glance, then hopped in the front.

"Yeah, I bet you girls were up late last night."

"Late? We were up *all* night," she smiled tiredly.

"So, what did you guys do?"

"Oh, you know. The usual."

"The usual? That's weird. Wasn't it a semi-formal party with a DJ and everything?"

"Oh. Yeah. Um. It was good. Yup, lots of dancing. Then we hung out in the rooms after."

"Really? Which girls were in your room?"

"Oh. I don't really remember their names." She paused and thought a minute. "But I was in Amy's room."

"That's nice. I guess she didn't want you to feel left out being that you didn't already know all the girls."

"Yeah, I guess so."

"So, did you watch any movies?"

"Yeah."

"What movie?"

"Um." Long pause. "I don't remember the name."

"Well, what was it about?"

"I'm just really tired. Do you mind if we don't talk for a while?"

"Sure."

Steering toward home, trying to cover her seething anger, Shelley put on Patrick's "The Wiggles" CD and turned the volume way up. Alexandra glared at her, horrified, and sighed.

*****

Pulling into the driveway, David came out to greet them, his eyes questioning Shelley's, wondering whether she'd confronted her. She shook her head slightly, letting him know that she hadn't.

"How was the party?" he asked Alexandra, unbuckling Patrick from his car seat.

"Good, but I'm really tired," she said.

"Yes, it sounds like it was quite a night," Shelley said. "Alexandra was just telling me about all the dancing they did and movies they watched."

"Really?" he emphasized, carrying the baby inside and setting him on the living room floor in front of his blocks. "That's strange, because I just got off the phone with Amy's mom who called here to apologize again for not knowing that you lied to her when you said we picked you up last night."

Alexandra froze, her mouth dropping and eyes opening wider.

"So let's cut the bullshit and tell us where you really were last night," David said.

"Out."

"Out? Yes, obviously you were *out*," he said, his baritone voice becoming louder. "But since you weren't where you were supposed to be, I'm asking you again, where were you?"

"With a friend."

"What friend?"

"My boyfriend, okay?" she mumbled.

Boyfriend? I didn't know she had a boyfriend! Shelley thought.

"No, it is *not* okay!" he yelled.

"Oh, so what do you think, I'm never going to have a boyfriend or something?"

"Never going to have a boyfriend! What the fuck, Alex? Do you even know what we're talking about here?" Now he was screaming full throttle, red in the face and with the vein on his forehead looking like it was going to pop through his skin.

Trying to bring the conversation back to a calmer level, Shelley said, "Alexandra, the issue here is not you having a boyfriend. It's you telling us that you were at Amy's party when really you weren't. And staying out all night with a boy we didn't even know existed."

"He's not a boy, he's a man," Alexandra said smugly.

"A man!" David yelled. "What the *fuck* are you talking about?"

"He's twenty-five. I was at his place, okay?"

"Twenty-five!" David and Shelley yelled simultaneously.

Where and when would a seventeen-year-old high school girl who has a baby at home even meet *a twenty-five-year-old guy?* Shelley thought to herself.

"Who is this guy?" David demanded. "I want to speak with him immediately. Does he know you're seventeen?"

Alexandra just stared at her feet.

"Well?"

Still no answer. They could see that they weren't going to get any further at this juncture.

"Alexandra, go up to your room and get your thoughts straightened out so we can talk more about this later," Shelley said. "While you're up there, I expect you to clean up and get your chore list done. I'll call you when we're ready to talk."

"Fine-uh." She spun on her heel, walking right past Patrick who was sitting there, bewildered at the whole exchange, and started stomping toward the stairs.

"And take your son with you!" David yelled. "It wouldn't kill you to spend some time with him, you know!"

Sighing, she stooped down, picked him up like a sack of potatoes, and started marching toward the stairs.

Vacillating, Shelley fought with herself: *Do I really want Patrick spending time with her when she's like this? Then again, he is her son! But I don't want him to feel her tension and she's sure to ignore him. On the other hand, David and I need to talk and we're sure to be emitting stress too. But at least we wouldn't ignore him...*

Interrupting her thoughts, David said, "C'mon babe, let's go for a walk."

*****

Tiny, thrilled as dogs always are when they're going for a walk, was oblivious to the tension that weighed so heavily on the couple as they walked and talked for over an hour. Gleefully sniffing bushes and peeing on fire hydrants, he trotted along happily like a goofy pony on a leash.

They dissected the many aspects of the dilemma with Alexandra, irresolutely trying to figure out what sort of punishment fit the crimes of lying, staying out all night with a boy—who was actually a secret twenty-five-year-old boyfriend—and ignoring her son on a regular basis.

Their positions swung like a pendulum from one extreme to the other. First they decided to ground her, remove all of her privileges, and return them one-by-one as she regained their trust. A minute later, they countered that it was her life and she could screw it up if she wanted to. Then they would return to the fact that it wasn't just her life—it was *their* lives, and *Patrick's* life—that she was messing with too.

Although she was new to the family, Alexandra *was* their daughter and they felt that they should punish her to the same extent they would any of their other kids. However, they'd never had anything quite this severe happen with any of the other kids. Their agitation mounted as they acknowledged the frustration of feeling as if they were cleaning up her mom, Patty's, mess, and that if they had raised her, none of this would ever have occurred in the first place.

Realistically, they knew none of that was true: It could just have easily have happened to them. *Right?* Who knew? There was Patty, taking her daughter on a wonderful vacation in Mexico, staying at a four star resort she probably had to save for years to pay for, and her daughter sneaks out of the top-notch teen program to go drink at a bar, and ends up getting pregnant.

When push came to shove, it really didn't matter. The fact was, Alexandra and Patrick were with them now, this was the situation, and they had to figure out what to do. In the end, they decided on the removal of all privileges with her having to earn back their trust, just like they did several years earlier when Russell took the car out on his own when he only had his permit but no license. He'd dented a neighbor's car when he backed out of the driveway. They'd had to pay cash to fix it in order to avoid legal ramifications that could have affected his driving record and their insurance premiums for years.

Now only a block from home, David turned to her and put his hands on either side of her face. "Thank you, babe. I'm sorry you're having to deal with all of this."

"I'm sorry too, love. I'm sure it will all be okay."

They gazed at one another an extra beat, each of them knowing that they'd been apologizing this way for years. During their time as a combined family, they each felt like the other "had to deal with" their kids and their problems, although they both knew that they really never resented any of it and always felt like they were all "their kids" anyway.

Tiny, never one to miss out on a good snuggle, leaned up against their legs, making a big slobber spot on Shelley's thigh.

"Let's go, Sweet Shelley Bean. It's getting hot out here."

Hand in hand, they walked the rest of the way home to dole out the consequences, content in the knowledge that they stood firm together in understanding and accepting the grueling realities of raising kids.

Chapter 17

A few weeks later, Shelley was stumbling in the door carrying Patrick, his diaper bag, her pocketbook, and a cake for Michael's birthday when she heard the phone ringing. Lugging everything to the counter, the machine picked up just as her back was starting to get that scary twinge indicating that it was considering going out altogether.

She set Patrick down and he ran (ran!) straight to the dog's water bowl, where he started splashing. Exhausted and wondering how he could possibly have any mischievous energy left after their morning at the playground, she told him no, explained that this water is for Tiny to drink, not to play in, then dried his pudgy little hands on a kitchen towel.

Carrying the wriggling toddler straight upstairs before he could execute any further shenanigans, she changed his diaper, then closed the blinds in his and Alexandra's room and read him his favorite naptime story, a pop-up board book with various textures to experience. As she turned the pages, giving him plenty of time to feel the scales on the fish and the fur on the kitten, she tried to quell her growing tension. She was quickly becoming overwhelmed with the feeling that she had *so much* to do, and she just wanted to get through the story so Patrick would go down for his nap and give her two hours of peace and quiet.

Patrick was actually a great baby… a pretty good listener and a fantastic napper. But a toddler was still a toddler, with enough stamina and mischief to put even the most energetic young mother into a stupor. And she was not an energetic young mother.

Heading downstairs to deal with the pile of stuff she'd dumped on the counter, Shelley pressed Play on the answering machine. She listened to the messages while she washed her hands in the kitchen sink, amazed at how much brown was coming off her hands and silently ruing her broken, unpolished nails that used to be so elegant.

"You. Have. Four. New. Messages," said the mechanical voice. As she dried her hands and put the cake into the fridge, she heard that the first message was from the pharmacy, reminding her that her cholesterol medicine was ready to be picked up. *Great,* she thought. *Another thing I forgot to do while I was out.*

Next was David. "Hey Sweet Shelley Bean. I'm really sorry to miss dinner tonight, but I have a mandatory dinner meeting, so I won't be home 'til nine." Okay, so maybe she'd give herself a break and make something like pancakes and bacon for dinner instead of the chicken she'd been stressing about having forgotten to defrost.

"Hi Shelley, it's Pam from Prime Vacations. I'm calling to touch base about your trip. There are some really good flights right now for advance booking. Call me!" *Ugh.* Shelley's heart sank as she thought about the dream vacation they were planning. They'd been saving three hundred dollars a month for five years, as well as all of their airline miles and David's vacation time to go on the very luxurious, very adult, very far away trip to Bora Bora. For a month. They already had reservations for a premier, over-water bungalow at the Four Seasons, complete with glass-bottomed floor set over a coral reef. Still a year away, their plan was to take the trip after Grace graduated and was settled well into her first year of college, when they could go knowing that all four of their kids were adults who would be fine for the month without them.

Now that there were five—six including Patrick—they had to consider them too. Alexandra would be the same age as Grace, but fine for a month without them? The thought of leaving her unsupervised with Patrick for an entire month was unsettling to say the least. Plus, even though graduation was only a few weeks away, Alexandra hadn't made any plans for college yet. They hoped she would go, at least to the local community college. But if she did, who would watch Patrick when she was at classes? And if she didn't go, she would need to at least work and do *something.* Either way, college or work, Patrick would be with her and she would need someone to watch him.

Shelley's thoughts were interrupted by the fourth message, another mechanical voice: "This is a message from. Spring Valley. High School. Your child. Alexandra. Johansen. Was absent today. Upon returning, please send a signed note explaining why your child. Alexandra. Johansen. Was absent today. Thank you."

Absent! What the heck? Fatigue hitting her harder than ever, her brain and body both feeling like they were going to collapse, she decided to use Patrick's naptime to take a nap herself.

Settling on the still-should-be-darn-white new sofa, she tried not to notice the strip of grey along its edge where Patrick's clammy hands and Tiny's slobbery mouth had left the smudges of life in their wake. She pulled the soft blanket from the corner of the couch, threw it over herself and was out cold before she could think another thought.

*****

"Mom! Mo-om!" Shelley heard Grace's voice, sounding very far away as she struggled to wake up.

"Mom?" she opened one eye to see Grace standing there. Her hip was killing her. Trying to sit up, she realized why: Frick was sleeping on top of the blanket on top of her hip, somehow feeling like he weighed fifty pounds even though he was only a skinny ten-pound cat.

"Are you okay?"

"Sure, why?"

"Because you're sleeping in the middle of the day. Are you sick?"

"No. Just tired."

"Oh. Okay." She walked off toward the kitchen, and soon there was the familiar sound of her preparing her daily Pop Tart. Shelley listened carefully and glanced at the baby monitor to see if its lights were indicating noise. No action from Patrick yet. *Goodness! What time is it?*

She walked into the kitchen and saw the time on the microwave, noting that it was only two thirty. Normal time for Grace and Alexandra to come home. Reminded of the message from school, she asked Grace if Alexandra was already upstairs.

"Nope."

Was it her imagination, or did Grace seem nervous?

"She wasn't on the bus?"

"I'm not sure," Grace said carefully.

"What do you mean you're not sure? You don't notice your own sister on the bus?"

She just stared at her, like deer in headlights. Deciding to let her off the hook, secretly feeling a tiny iota of relief that Grace finally had some semblance of a relationship with Alexandra—at least to the point where she didn't want to be her whistleblower, she said, "Aw, forget it," and pulled out the step stool to search the top of the pantry for the birthday-themed paper plates they'd need for Michael's cake the next day.

Shooting her a worried glance, Grace stood there eating her Pop Tart mutely and Shelley winked at her, imparting that she knew something was up, but that she wasn't going to make her tell.

"So, what's going on with you?" Shelley asked, knowing that this would kick off a chatty conversation with Grace, who loved to share the details and dramas of her life.

As she listened to the updates about the flips they were working on in dance team and the fight her best friend Cassie had with her boyfriend, she located the purple and black birthday plates that were left over from Grace and Alexandra's eighteenth birthdays a few weeks earlier and handed them down to her, taking comfort in the normalcy of the conversation as well as the knowledge that Michael wouldn't care that the plates were purple.

*****

Blub blub blub blub blub blub. Fifteen minutes later, as she was heading upstairs to get Patrick from his crib, Shelley heard the unmistakable sound of a motorcycle. *Loud pipes save lives*, she thought, the refrain having stuck with her from a Harley Davidson advertising campaign back when she was a kid. Walking over to the window, she looked out and saw the bike motoring away from the house, its adult male, tattooed rider's long hair flying behind him. Alexandra was coming up the front walk, backpack slung over her shoulder, with her signature scornful expression already on her face.

Greeaat. Cutting school wasn't enough. Having a baby at seventeen wasn't enough. *Oh no, not enough at all.* She had to have a way-too-old-for-her biker boyfriend on top of it all. She assumed he was the very same twenty-five-year-old boyfriend she'd been forbidden to see after the staying-out-all-night incident. The incident which resulted in her being grounded, having her phone taken away, being driven over to Amy's to personally apologize to her mother, and having to gradually regain privileges, such as being allowed to go anywhere for an hour or two.

Not enough of a punishment. Apparently.

Sighing, she turned to Patrick who, smiling from ear to ear, was ready for the second half of his action-packed toddler day. He was holding on to the top rail of his crib, jumping up and down as if on a trampoline. He was in a super playful mood, giggling and running to the other side of the crib every time she tried to lift him out.

"Come on, sweetie. Grandma's tired." He stopped for a moment, gave her a mischievous grin, then ran to the other side anyway, still giggling his rolling laugh.

Not in the mood, she sat down on Alexandra's bed and crossed her arms, knowing that to a more mature audience, she'd look more petulant than his actual teenaged mother. "Fine. If you're not going to let me get you, you'll have to stay in there."

Coming to the edge of the crib, he put his arms in the air, indicating that he wanted to come out. "Ub, ub, ub!" he said, his way of saying "up."

"Okay, but *no* running!" She wasn't yelling, but her tone clearly indicated that she was not playing around. His face falling serious, she could see a slight quiver in his bottom lip. *Nice, Shelley! Now you're making the baby sad? Great move!* she chastised herself.

Trying to calm down, she forced a smile on her face and made his stuffed llama tickle his belly while she changed his diaper yet again, then carried him downstairs.

*****

The confrontation with Alexandra was basically identical to the one that occurred when she was supposed to be at Amy's party: First she lied, carrying on a conversation about how her school day was, then got angry when she realized that she was already busted.

The evening progressed the way all "there's a teenager in the house who is in big trouble" evenings do, with dinner conversation over pancakes strained, and extra sighing from Alexandra when she was told to clean up her son's sticky high chair.

Not knowing what else to do and exhausted beyond measure, Shelley went to bed early, leaving it up to Alexandra to give Patrick his bath, read him his story, and tuck him in. Curling up in bed with a pile of electronics on her nightstand—now consisting of not only her own charging phone but also Alexandra's phone and iPod—she passed out, incoherent.

Several hours later, she felt David curl up behind her the way he always did when he got into bed after coming in from an extra late night at work. Snuggling up, she enjoyed the way his breath felt on her ear as he whispered, "Long day?"

"That's an understatement." She hadn't called him to tell him what had gone on. What would have been the point? He was working super hard, all day and night, and she figured telling him about it another time would be soon enough.

"Anything in particular?" As he nuzzled in closely, his body flush behind hers and his mouth against her neck, she could feel the unmistakable evidence that he was in the mood for more than a snuggle. Guiltily, her mind raced between the options: Tell him about Alexandra now and ruin the mood? Or indulge in one another and save the discussion for another time?

Allowing her body to rock against him, secure in the comfort that she didn't *always* have to be the most energetic lover, she murmured, "Nothing that can't wait 'til morning."

Chapter 18

The next day, David planned to work from home after having put in such a long day the day before. As usual, Shelley went into Patrick and Alexandra's room bright and early in the morning to take care of the baby while Alexandra and Grace got ready for school.

What was not usual, however, was the fact that poor Patrick hadn't been changed, bathed, or anything else the night before. Thinking back, recalling her very concise instructions, she was astounded that Alexandra—even after getting in so much trouble—still hadn't given him a bath, read him a story, or done anything else to take care of him before putting him down for the night. Still in yesterday's clothes, his diaper was so full that it had expanded to a painfully tight point, actually leaving red marks on his hips when she took it off. His poor little bottom was all red and the urine had leaked up the front of his diaper and into the fabric of his shirt, all the way to his neckline.

She was so livid, she could barely look at Alexandra. Not to mention that 6:00 am was not exactly her favorite time of day in the first place. Knowing that the girls had to get off to school on time, she made it clear that there would be a family discussion that evening, that she would be checking with the school to make sure she was there for every class, and that she was disappointed in the way everything was going.

Grace, also getting ready at that hour, simply rolled her eyes, apparently unsurprised by anything Alexandra would do or not do. Thanking her lucky stars that she seemed to be doing well in school, dance, and at home, Shelley's mind raced through the muck and mire of her preoccupation to try and remember what was going on for Grace that was important. "Good luck on that math exam," she said. "I know you've been studying hard."

Grace stopped, looked at her sideways and said, "That test was yesterday."

"Oh God, I'm so sorry. I've been so exhausted, I lost track of the days. How do you think it went?"

"Fine. I think I did pretty good."

"That's good."

They looked at each other, sharing an unspoken conversation in which they communicated to one another: *I'm sorry; I understand; I care.*

"Well, I've gotta go. Don't want to miss the bus."

"Okay. Love you."

"Love you too, Mom."

*****

After giving Patrick a nice warm bath, Shelley let him play naked for a while to give his skin a chance to dry fully and heal from all the urine exposure while she spent a few minutes cleaning up their room. Should she have to? No. Did she want to? No. But she couldn't allow Alexandra's neglect to affect Patrick so extensively. His crib sheets needed to be changed, the diaper pail was making the room stink, and there was no sign of his llama, which she saw that he'd slept without the night before, causing her heart to break a little at the thought of him having to fall asleep without his comfort animal.

She opened the window and gathered all of the clothes that were strewn on the floor, over the chair, and on Alexandra's bed. All of them were hers; more evidence that Shelley was Patrick's primary, if not only, caregiver, since all of his clothes were neatly stowed in his little baby hamper to be washed separately with his baby laundry detergent.

As was her habit, she checked all of the pockets before tossing Alexandra's clothes into the hamper, not wanting to end up with things like gum or tissues cycled through the washing machine. Picking up yesterday's jeans, she pulled something out, initially thinking to herself, *See, gum.* Upon closer inspection, however, she realized that the foil was not a gum wrapper at all. It was an actual piece of aluminum foil, folded multiple times to create a sturdy square. On one side was some sort of whitish-brownish substance, and on the other the unmistakable black film caused by a lighter, like when you light a candle and accidentally get that annoying shadow on the inside of the candle holder.

Stunned, she stood there holding the thing by its edges, not wanting to get the substance on her fingers. She knew Alexandra was doing naughty stuff: cutting school, lying about her whereabouts, being neglectful of her responsibilities to Patrick. But drugs? It hadn't even occurred to her that she would do something so stupid.

Shelley had never been one to beat around the bush with her kids—Alexandra included—about the fact that she understood that some experimenting is normal. She wasn't naive: she realized that they'd have the opportunity to try alcohol and pot, and that they'd be offered other things too. Her mantra was that she didn't think they should do any of it, but that there were certain drugs that should be off-limits no matter what: Drugs that could be instantly addictive and end up ruining your life permanently, even if you only intended to try them once. In her mind, and in her mini-lectures, those included crack, crystal meth, and heroin.

Any of which could be the stuff on the foil square. To her knowledge, all three were substances that druggies might use these melting squares for, and in her mind, they were all equally as dangerous. She certainly had never heard of anyone using something like this for pot.

Fear surged through her as she made sure the baby gate was closed at the top of the stairs and went to the hall bathroom to wash her hands. Setting the poisonous little square on the counter, she wrapped it carefully in tissues, went back and dressed Patrick, then headed downstairs to find David.

*****

It felt like it must be at least noon, yet in reality it was still only 7:00 am. David and Shelley sat at the dining room table drinking their coffee, with Patrick in his high chair next to them. He had already finished his scrambled egg, and was happily eating his Cheerios and clumsily drinking milk from his sippy cup, a new skill he was working on.

After filling David in on the previous day's events and the morning's disturbing narcotic discovery, they spent a few minutes quietly absorbing it all, each of their minds racing through the various options, ramifications, and potential actions they should or shouldn't take.

Hating to do it, but having no other option, she also filled him in on the other current dilemmas, including the fact that they were going to have to figure out what to do about the Bora Bora trip. She needed to return the travel agent's call, and if they were not going to take the trip, they needed to decide soon: They'd booked it two years in advance and paid for the hotel bill in full in order to receive a twenty percent discount on the extremely pricey, five-star resort. The caveat for this deal was that if you canceled with less than nine months notice, you lost half of your deposit, which amounted to nine thousand dollars. They had about one month left to decide.

In addition, Shelley was just overwhelmed in general. She felt like she had no time for the other kids anymore and confided in him how guilty she felt about not realizing that Grace's exam was yesterday, not today. She hadn't visited Rose at school in two months, finding that bringing Patrick to her dorm was an impossible task,, and on the one weekend that Rose did come home, Shelley ended up preoccupied with the baby because he had a fever that resulted in a trip to urgent care, two visits to the pharmacy, and many hours of just holding him because he didn't feel good. They never made it out to go shopping, which had been the plan, and while Rose did seem understanding about it, Shelley still felt guilty.

To add to the crises, Russell, away at school in Colorado, had sent an e-mail letting them know that he was getting a D in his physics class. His message had an unmistakable undertone of preparing them that "even though he's not out partying all the time, it's a hard class and he thinks he might fail it and need to retake it." At thirty-six thousand dollars a year, this was not good news.

To top it all off, there was Michael, who would be home tonight to visit for the weekend and celebrate his birthday. Whom she felt guilty about because she had no time to go to the party store for plates that were not purple, and had bought a cake instead of making one, as she usually did for each of the kids. But beyond that, Shelley was concerned about his utter lack of enthusiasm about everything at a time of his life that should be one of the most exciting.

In just two weeks, Rose and Russell would be home again for the summer, and Grace and Alexandra would be graduating high school. Shelley was so overextended already, she hadn't made any arrangements for any of this.

She could feel herself ranting, her hysteria just beneath the surface, barely held in check and even then only because Patrick was sitting right there with them. David, with dark circles under his eyes and a weary expression on his face looked like he could hardly take any more.

"It sounds like you need to get out a bit, babe," he said.

Really? That's what he has to say after all this?

"Yeah, right," she harrumphed. "Like that's about to happen."

"Why don't we plan a time for me to watch Patrick so you can do something with your girlfriends?" he offered.

"My girlfriends! What girlfriends? I guess you haven't noticed, but I don't have friends anymore."

"What are you talking about? What about all of your friends from the Women's Club?"

"Apparently, they never were my friends. Real friends wouldn't ditch you the way they have. Not that I ever thought they were 'real friends' in the first place! As soon as Patrick got big enough to be disruptive, it was made clear that I'm no longer welcome at the meetings, and once I stopped volunteering to organize all of the fund raisers, I haven't heard from anyone!"

"What about the moms from that library thing you go to? They have little ones. Maybe you could do something with them?"

"I just don't enjoy their company."

"Why not? At least you have the babies in common."

"Do you *hear* yourself? Babies in common! If you haven't noticed, Patrick is not my baby! He's my grandson! And being around those girls is like being around a bunch of kids. They're all young and stupid, making the same mistakes we all made at their age. I have no patience for it… it's bad enough I have to be with them at Mommy and Me, I am not getting together with them elsewhere!"

Frustrated, David glared at her. "What do you expect me to do about this?"

"I'm not asking you to do anything. I just want you to understand!"

"I do understand," he sighed. "What I understand is that you're miserable and it's because of my daughter."

"What?!" Now she was outraged. In their entire marriage, they'd never delineated between his kids and hers. Yes, his kids were originally his and hers were originally hers. But they'd always felt that they were all "their kids," and that they were equally responsible for all of them. Alexandra, and by extension Patrick, were no different.

"Well what the fuck, Shelley! What the *fuck* do you want me to do about all of this?" Now he was yelling and she hated it when he yelled.

"Stop talking like that in front of the baby!"

"Fuuuck!"

"No, fuck *you*. I'm going in the living room until you get a hold of yourself and stop yelling at me like that. I'll go sit on our filthy, ruined couch in our plastic-filled living room!"

Grabbing her coffee, she marched into the living room where she found Tiny stretched out across the entire (formerly white) sofa, with Frick snuggled up in the curve of his belly.

Adorable. Just freakin' adorable.

Chapter 19

David sat for a moment, frustrated, trying to absorb it all. Everything was going wrong at once and he couldn't begin to imagine what he was supposed to do about any of it. David was by nature a cool, calm and collected problem-solver… a trait that had helped him rocket up the corporate ladder. But thorny corporate accounting problems seemed like playtime to him, compared to what was happening in his family.

He walked into the kitchen, wetting a paper towel at the sink and wringing it out so that he could use it to clean Patrick's face and hands. Shelley had stomped up the stairs and now he could hear that she'd turned on the shower. A moment of panic struck him as he thought about the report he needed to be working on. A report that he was expected to present via Powerpoint in just under two hours. He had all the information but still needed to prepare a few slides and practice his timing. It was an important meeting; the statistics would be used when the company did their quarterly announcement to the shareholders.

Reminding himself that she would be back in under half an hour, he unbuckled Patrick and brought him into the living room to play with toys. Sitting on the floor, David started building a block tower but instead of knocking it over or showing any interest at all, Patrick ran into the other room. Listening carefully, David couldn't tell what he was doing.

"Patrick! Paaatrick! Come on back and play with Grandpa!"

He didn't return.

Getting to his feet, David went to see what he was doing and found Patrick in the half bath, splashing in the toilet water.

"No! No Patrick, that's yucky!"

The baby froze, unused to hearing his grandpa sound so stern. His face crumpled, instantly brought to tears.

"Aw, don't cry. Grandpa just doesn't want you to get sick."

He lifted Patrick into his arms, cringing when he felt his wet hands on his own shoulders as the baby cried, hiccupping, while he carried him upstairs.

He hated to do it, but he really had to turn on the bath water so he could clean Patrick up. Guiltily—guilt being the new flavor of his life— he turned on the tap, hoping it wouldn't take too much heat or water pressure from Shelley's shower.

Patrick, once naked and seated in bath bubbles, quickly went from crying to smiling as he played with his plastic boats. Giving him a few minutes to play before beginning to wash him, David sat on the bathroom floor and leaned back against the wall.

His mind whirled, abounding with dilemmas, all of which he felt nearly powerless to do anything about. Powerlessness was not a feeling he was accustomed to or comfortable with, and at home, with the people he loved the most, it sometimes brought out the worst in him. Bile shoved its way into his throat as his mind spun with all the stress. Recognizing this, he reminded himself to take a deep breath and attack each problem individually.

Russell possibly failing a class? No biggie; he would just remind him that they were paying for four years of college and that's it. They would not be paying for retaking failed classes, so if that's what happened it would be up to him to take out loans to finish.

Michael not being "happy enough" and Shelley worrying about the color of the birthday plates? Check that one off: the least of his worries was one of their kids not having any problems at all, and he knew that boys don't care about plate colors, so long as there's cake.

Starting to feel slightly less pressure in his chest, he continued to attack more issues in his methodical, effective way.

Rose and Grace not getting enough attention from their mom? He knew it would be fine in just a few weeks when everyone was home for the summer and they all had more free time. He was pretty sure this was more an issue of Shelley feeling unnecessarily guilty than the girls being upset anyhow.

The Bora Bora trip? With a month left to decide, he didn't find this as imminently important as Shelley did.

Knowing that he was putting off the big ones for last, he absently started shampooing Patrick's hair with his baby shampoo while his mind started tackling the bigger issues. Namely, Alexandra and Shelley. And by extension, Patrick too.

When he thought about the issue of Alexandra not taking care of Patrick the way she should, he was torn. Truth be told, he was a lot more concerned about it before they found out about the drugs and cutting school. Now that there were those issues to contend with, it seemed relatively minor in the scheme of things.

But not really. Because that brought up what he considered the most important issue: Shelley. Just thinking of her brought a pain that could only be described as *heartbreak*. It reminded him of his Grandma Ella, who at ninety years of age had imparted her lifelong wisdom when he and Shelley got married.

Shelley, new to the family, had politely asked, "So, Grandma Ella, after seventy-two years of marriage, what is your advice for making a marriage work?"

Much to everyone's dismay, Grandma had said, "For the wife, my dear, it is to always keep your husband happy in the bedroom."

Remembering the exchange, David smiled to himself as he recalled how he'd almost snorted coffee out of his nose. Grandma Ella had continued, "And for the husband, it is to always make sure your wife feels appreciated."

His smile vanished. He knew Shelley wasn't feeling very appreciated but he felt powerless to do anything about it. There was only so far his acknowledgment could go, especially when counteracted by Alexandra's consistent disregard for everyone and everything around her.

Drugs. Jesus Christ! He couldn't begin to fathom what would happen if, as they suspected, it turned out that she was doing serious drugs. Which he was pretty sure was the case, given the tinfoil thing Shelley had found.

He was trying to wrap his mind around it, trying to formulate a plan of how he would address this when his phone, in its holder on his waist, twittered with a reminder. He quickly dried one hand on a towel and glanced at the phone: It was his one-hour reminder for his meeting coming up.

Trying to suppress the mounting agitation about his project and the guilt he felt about Shelley, he quickly rinsed Patrick off, wrapped him in his towel, and went to find her so he could get into his office.

Chapter 20

Later that morning, Shelley looked at herself in the mirror while blow-drying her hair, recalling the first time she found out that she was a "cougar" and not a "MILF." She and David were out for cocktails together at an upscale lounge and they were chatting with a bunch of people about various places to go. Telling David about a new wine lounge that just opened, a man had said, "You and your wife would probably fit right in." He winked. "There are lots of hot cougars; the view is great!"

She recalled feeling shocked that he referred to her as a cougar, which in her mind always held the negative connotation of an older woman pathetically trying to hold on to her youth, attempting to hook young men.

This was quite different than years earlier when someone had jokingly referred to her as a MILF. She didn't even know what it meant, so she'd looked it up on Urban Dictionary when she got home and found, MILF: Acronym for Mom I'd Like to Fuck. Slightly offensive, but in her mind also an indirect compliment, as it implied that even though she was a mom, she was still desirable—a status that can be hard to maintain when in the throes of mommy-hood.

Back then, she'd gone through a time when she recognized that she'd become so overrun by her responsibilities to her family that she'd completely forgotten about her Self. She even gave it an official definition:

Momnesia (mahm-nee-zhuh) -noun-
Loss of the memory of who you *used to be*.
Caused by pregnancy, play dates, and trying to keep the house cleaner than the Joneses.

After "diagnosing" herself as a bonafide momnesiac, she'd taken active steps to find balance between "momminess" and "sexiness," striving to find a way to be a supermom and an actual person with her own interests at the same time. And she'd done a pretty decent job of it.

Now, years later, it seemed that she was going through another version of Momnesia, although at a different stage of her life:

Gramnesia (gram-nee-zhuh) -noun-
In which a woman is so busy trying to be all things to all people, she doesn't fit into any particular category; She may be a grandmother, mother, wife, and friend, but doesn't truly belong anywhere.

Now that she was immersed in being Patrick's grandmother and full-time caretaker, she felt like she was in a category all her own. A one-person category in a world full of groups.

She didn't fit in with the grandmothers whose homes were nice and tidy, who attended their knitting clubs during the day and visited their grandchildren on weekends, with the pleasure of being able to spoil them and then go home. She didn't have that luxury, as not only did Patrick and all of his accoutrements live at her house, but as his full-time caretaker, she couldn't very well go around spoiling him and leaving disciplinary issues to someone else, the way a regular grandmother could. Plus, at forty-six, she wasn't ready for the knitting club anyway.

She also didn't fit in with the young moms in their twenties and thirties who were experiencing parenthood and marriage for the first time and were making the mistakes they all made during that time in their lives. She just didn't have the patience for it. Or the energy. Been there, done that.

Likewise, she no longer fit in with the moms of older kids—her former friends who she used to spend time with, all of their children older and mostly self-sufficient. They would work together on booster club fundraisers, Rotary events, and see one another at the occasional high school theater or dance performance. They all had time to take care of themselves, having abandoned the young mom uniform of stained tee-shirts, jeans, and a ponytail in favor of tailored slacks, nice blouses, and professional manicures. None of them had babies and their cars were no longer filled with car seats, phonics CDs, or Cheerio crumbs.

Now that she had Patrick (although she didn't actually *have* Patrick, did she?), there was nowhere she truly felt right. When they were out and about, she wasn't comfortable dressing in the playground attire she'd abandoned years earlier, yet she also found it decidedly uncomfortable to go to the playground dressed in her "adult mom" clothes. She had no time for manicures, hadn't had a professional haircut in months, and was so exhausted all the time that her idea of a fun weekend brought visions of napping and being caught up on laundry.

Patrick himself created so many mixed feelings that it was a dilemma all its own. A sweet, adorable baby, she couldn't help loving him, just the way she'd loved her own kids when they were little. His chubby little arms reaching for her, the amazement of watching him soak up the world and learn about each little thing, whether the rustle of a leaf or the way dry sand doesn't hold its shape the same as wet sand does. She wanted the best for him and made sure that his life was as safe, enriching, and loving as he—an innocent baby with his whole life ahead of him—deserved it to be.

On the other hand, there was the undeniable truth that she felt resentful about the entire situation. The fact was, she and David had taken definitive steps to ensure that they wouldn't have another baby. They had each enjoyed their babies back when they had them and they'd never felt the need to do it again. She'd dedicated the last nineteen years of her life to raising her two children, and did her best with all four after combining their families. She'd put in her time, so to speak, and had been ready to move on to the next phase of life: The phase in which she and David had time to travel, to be adults. To make love in a room other than their bedroom. To have nice things that didn't get destroyed within a week of entering their home.

Maybe it would have been different if Alexandra took more of an interest in Patrick. If Shelley felt like she were helping *her*, as opposed to the reality that everything involving the baby was her job with Alexandra helping on occasion. When she was forced to.

Her head and heart spun constantly: *How much should I help her? And how could I not? Should I try to leave Patrick's caretaking up to her with the expectation that she will do it? Maybe if I don't do it, she will. But he's just an innocent baby and the fact is, she doesn't do the things he needs! Can I sit by and watch as she neglects to bathe him and change his diaper? Wait until he gets a rash and the doctor has to tell her what to do? No! Or yes! I know that as long as I keep doing it, she'll never do it. Would it be fair to Patrick for me to step aside and have him go through whatever trials and tribulations he's sure to experience with an eighteen-year-old, uninterested mother? On the other hand, would it be fair for me not to "train her," so to speak, so that she continues to be unprepared to take care of him? And what if she's a drug addict? What will we do then?*

Practically frothing at the mouth from the stress of these spinning thoughts, she'd eventually screech to a halt with the big question: *What will happen if Alexandra never matures into a mother than can give Patrick a proper life? Are David and I prepared to raise him ourselves forever?*

The thought of this was so mind-boggling, she'd have to stop there, unable to think any further.

At times like these, the thought of being "a cougar whose presence makes the view very pleasant," would start seeming like not such a bad thing. If only she had the energy. Rowl.

*****

Deciding to take David's advice and do something for herself, Shelley did a little straightening up around the house, played with Patrick and Tiny out in the yard for a while, and then, when it was naptime, she went and set up what she called a full-fledged bubble bath. Even though she'd already showered in the morning, she hadn't shaved her legs and besides, the main point was for it to be relaxing. While waiting for the tub to fill, pleased at the sight of the Sensual Amber scented bubbles frothing higher, she lit a candle, turned on some soft jazz music, set her tall iced coffee on the edge of the tub, then gingerly stepped into the scalding water inch by inch.

Trying to relax for what seemed like the first time in months, she lay back with her head on a rolled up towel and sipped her drink. Then she sat up, feeling like she should *do* something. She told herself that there was no rush; David was working from home and if Patrick woke up he would get him from his crib.

But then again, David was supposed to be working. Even though he'd told her that his important meeting was finished, how could she expect him to get any work done if he was watching a baby in the middle of the day?

On the other hand, a few hours here and there wouldn't exactly kill his career.

Yet, she always tried to put herself in David's shoes—she had an awesome respect for him as the family provider, with the financial pressures of having to earn enough money to pay for everything. And there was *a lot* to pay for.

She reminded herself that it was David who suggested she go relax and had offered to watch Patrick.

It didn't matter.

Figuring that maybe she'd be able to calm down if she got business taken care of first, she grabbed her razor and started carefully shaving her legs, reminding herself to go slowly, that she wasn't in any rush.

It didn't help.

She still felt an underlying sense of panic, like she needed to hurry up and get done. Her mind wouldn't stop racing with all she had to do: Michael and Rose would both be home later in the afternoon to spend the weekend and celebrate his birthday; they still had to confront Alexandra about the drug paraphernalia; Patrick still needed all the attention a baby needs; Frick's prescription refill needed to be picked up from the vet, and while she was at it, she figured she might as well bring Tiny, who had been shaking his head a lot, which she knew was a sign of a possible ear infection—not to mention the thrilling side-effect of him splattering drool even more widely every time he did it.

Aaaaagh! This spin-cycle thought process reminded Shelley of years earlier, when she and David had recently combined families, and constantly analyzed who was happy, who was not, what they should do, etc. It had extended to extreme anxiety about all things, and she'd actually taken an anti-anxiety medication for a few years, which, combined with some therapy and coming to terms with the fact that they can't "make" all the kids happy all the time, had helped immensely.

She'd stopped taking the medication several years before, as she no longer had such extreme worries and felt much more able to deal with the ups and downs of normal daily life with their blended family.

Shelley knew that she was overreacting; that everyone has rough days. Or even weeks or months. But recognizing that she was starting to have these mind-reeling thoughts day-in and day-out was still an unsettling concept.

Reminding herself to look at the good things, she thought about her relationship with David. She knew they were solid, as close to one another as ever. They'd always worked well as a team and, despite their early morning argument, she knew that they were on the same page and would get through all of this.

Sure, their sex life had waned significantly now that they were always exhausted and there was always a baby around. But when they did make love it was still good and she had her trusty Wascally Wabbit, the vibrator of all vibrators, to take the edge off in between. Not that she'd recently been in the mood for that, either. But that wasn't the point.

Having talked herself off the ledge, she felt a little more calm and decided that she didn't need to force herself to stay in the bath. Clearly, it was not good timing and she was finding it more stressful to try and relax than to simply get out of the tub and get on with her day.

Relieved, her mind ticking off the order of her To-Do List in her head, she started toweling off, feeling a bit better already.

*****

The afternoon went smoothly, even if typically exhausting. Shelley took Patrick with her, having a talk with him before they left, during which she made it clear that he was going to have to stay in his stroller during the errands. She knew some people thought she was crazy when she did this—having a "discussion" with a just-under-one-year-old who stares back at her with rounded eyes. However, she had found that babies understand far more than most give them credit for, and she did experience far less resistance during the many times she had to strap him in.

They went to the vet and it turned out that yes, Tiny did have an ear infection. Twenty minutes and $326. later, they walked out with an antibiotic and a special ear wash for Tiny, and Frick's prescription refill.

Next stop was the wine store, where they went to get some red for Michael, which she knew he preferred over the pinot grigio she and David always drank. While they were there, she found some vastly overpriced blue paper plates, which she bought anyway, laughing at herself for caring so much about the plate color when she knew that Michael himself couldn't care less.

When they came out of the wine store, Tiny, with his gargantuan head out the open window of the car, had drawn a crowd. Two teenaged girls and a guy were gathered around, petting and cooing over him. So much for any sort of protection. As they walked up he was nuzzling his head against one of the girls, trying to get her to scratch his ear just right.

"Oh, hi Mrs. Morsony!" said the other girl.

Shelley looked at her, trying to place who she was. "Hi," she said, although she knew she wasn't doing a good job covering up that she didn't recognize her.

"It's Amanda? You know, from the dance team?"

Oh yeah, it finally clicked. It was one of the girls from Grace's dance team. She'd known the girl since she was little. As Shelley looked at her, she was reminded of just how *not little* these girls were anymore.

"I didn't know you had a baby!" Amanda said.

Shelley, knowing darn well that Amanda knew it was not her baby replied, "This is Patrick, Alexandra's son."

"Oh yeah. Right," Amanda said awkwardly. Shelley noticed the other two kids glance at one another, gossip confirmed.

Amanda continued, "Right, I think I remember Grace saying something about a baby in the family."

Shelley shuddered to imagine what that statement might have been.

Obviously catching on that this conversation was making Shelley uncomfortable, Amanda bubbled, "Wow, it looks like you have a lot of party stuff!"

"Yup. It's Michael's birthday and we're having cake tonight."

Amanda turned to Tiny and gushed, "Aren't you such a lucky doggie, getting to go on errands to the party store! Yes you are! Yes you are!"

Shelley had taken Patrick out of the stroller, and had him on her hip as she was placing the bags in the car. When Amanda saw that she was getting ready to close the stroller with one hand, she said, "He is sooo cute! Can I hold him?"

Looking at Patrick, Shelley noted that he was hamming it up, grinning at the girl and kicking his chubby little legs in excitement.

"Sure, but be careful, he's pretty wiggly."

"Oh, don't worry Mrs. Morsony. I've been babysitting for years. I just love babies!"

She expertly took him from her arms and started playing peekaboo using the collar from her polo shirt. Patrick loved it, giggling his rolling laugh and kicking his legs even more, making him bounce up and down in her arms.

"Omigod! He is just the cutest thing! Alexandra is sooo lucky!"

What do I say to this? Shelley thought. *Yes, Alexandra is lucky to have such a wonderful son, as well as a stepmother who takes care of him all the time? Or, be careful what you wish for, honey, you're way too young?*

"Thank you," she said, putting the stroller in the car. "He is a very sweet boy."

"I know Alexandra probably doesn't need any help because she's got you, but if she ever needs a babysitter, here's my card." She handed her a light pink business card that said Amanda's Anytime Babysitting. In one quick glance, Shelley noted that the card included her cell phone number, e-mail address, and mother's name and phone number to speak with. Red Cross Certified Babysitter was written across the bottom in red.

Impressive.

"I know it says anytime, but I'm not actually available *any*time, just when I'm not in school." She blushed a little. "I needed to think of something that goes with Amanda."

"I understand. This is a very nice card. I'll definitely hold onto it."

"But I am available anytime I'm not in school. Evenings, weekends, summer, school breaks. I'm trying to save up for my own car," she chattered on. "Not that I'm expensive or anything…"

"I understand. This all looks great, Amanda. I'm very impressed. I will definitely call you if we need someone to watch Patrick."

"Or if Alexandra does."

Oh yeah. Alexandra.

*****

The rest of the afternoon went smoothly, with Patrick and Shelley swinging by the house to drop off Tiny, then zipping back out to the grocery store to get a few things that were the older kids' favorites since Michael and Rose would be home for the weekend.

She was excited to see them, but she couldn't help feeling a little melancholy after her conversation with Amanda. *Why couldn't Alexandra be more like that?* She knew it wasn't fair to compare the freewheeling lifestyle of a seventeen-year-old girl whose only responsibility was to go to high school, and who took on childcare for pay, with one who had a baby at too young an age, but really, it had been Alexandra's own decision to keep the baby. She'd seemed so responsible in the beginning, when she'd first come to them. Would it have been too much to ask for her to be even one-tenth as interested in her own son as Amanda was?

Pulling into the driveway, her heart sank with guilt when she saw that Michael's car was already there. *Damn!* She chastised herself. *I wasn't even here when they got home!* Reminding herself that they weren't supposed to be there for another hour and she should just be happy to see them didn't outweigh the guilt she felt over not being home to welcome them. It was ridiculous, she knew. But still.

Rose came running out of the house. "Surprise! Aren't we so devious? Michael and I planned it to get here early and surprise you!"

"Wow! I certainly am surprised! I'm sorry I wasn't home when you got here." Shelley drank in the sight of her daughter, feeling a jolt of surprise at how much she'd changed in the past few months. Her thick, dark hair was swept up in a messy bun, imparting a certain... sensuality that she'd never seen in her before. Her skin was smooth and unblemished, all signs of the acne she'd had since puberty completely gone. Could it be that Ramen Noodles are actually better for one's complexion than home-cooked meals?

"You look beautiful, Rose!" Shelley exclaimed, hugging her. "I'm so happy you're home."

Michael came loping out of the house, his casual gait and suppressed smile looking the same as ever.

"Hi," he said, giving her a loose hug like one would give to a stranger. Shelley knew he didn't mean it that way, it's just that by the time his dad and she married, he was already too old to develop a snuggly relationship.

"Hey, handsome. What a nice surprise!"

"Me, me, me, me, me!" they heard from the car. Apparently Patrick had had enough of waiting to be noticed. Laughing, Shelley unbuckled him from his car seat—a place he'd spent way too much time that day.

She knew he'd be raring to go and she couldn't blame him. It would be perfect for visiting with his older aunts and uncle.

"Wow! Look how big he's gotten!" Rose extended her arms to take Patrick while Michael started grabbing bags of groceries to bring inside.

"I hope you didn't peek in the fridge," Shelley said to Michael.

"Don't worry. I grabbed a soda but didn't see any cake," he winked.

Feeling lighter than she had in a long time, Shelley headed inside where she found that David had been part of their scheme and had done a bunch of things to get the house ready.

"Hey, Sweet Shelley Bean," he held her in his arms for a quick moment. "Looks like it's going to be a good night."

*****

Half an hour later, Grace arrived home from school, she and Rose screaming when they saw each other like… well, a couple of teenaged girls.

Shelley stood at the counter cutting vegetables that they'd use for shish kebabs later, listening to their chatter in the background as they caught up on what was going on with school, "men," dance team, and technology club. Over the years she had found eavesdropping on those two to be a very effective way of getting caught up on their lives. She had to laugh to herself when she overheard Rose telling Grace, "I figured out the greatest way to get rid of acne! I learned it in my human anatomy class, about the pores and stuff. I clean my face every morning and every night with this mild benzoyl peroxide stuff and it's like a miracle!" Shelley shook her head at the irony of how you can tell your kids this same information for years, but they wouldn't listen until they figured it out on their own.

David and Michael were in the living room, sitting on the floor while Patrick toddled around. They'd set up an elaborate Hot Wheels track, which was way too complicated a toy for Patrick at this time but David was so excited to buy one, Shelley figured it was a great toy for *him*. They were teaching Patrick how to place the car at the top of the hill and let it go, where gravity would take it racing through the course. Tiny stood there with his dopey face, looking very confused and a little scared every time the little metal car zoomed past him.

Music was playing, at a low enough volume to still converse but loudly enough to bring a festive feeling to the air. David had set it on a playlist they'd put together a few years earlier, called A February Party. They'd created it when they had a house party one February, and it had songs from every genre each of the family members enjoyed, ranging from classic rock to top forty, country to heavy metal, and everything in between.

After about fifteen minutes, it occurred to Shelley that Alexandra still wasn't home. She asked Grace if she saw her on the bus and once again received that deer-in-the-headlights look, which she took to mean "no." Not wanting to ruin the moment, she pulled David aside and pointed out that she should have been home by now. Sighing, he tried calling her phone and texting her, but got no response. They decided to go on with their evening, enjoying the other kids, and worry about her later. There was nothing else they could do at the moment anyway, and there was no sense letting her ruin the night.

Shelley went back to the kitchen counter, now stringing vegetables and shrimp onto skewers, and trying not to worry. *She's probably just with the boyfriend,* she told herself. *That's supposed to make me feel better?* her "other hand" argued. *Stop, just stop,* she chastised herself. *Just try and have a good time. How bad could it be anyway?*

She was not convinced.

It turned out, her other hand was right.

Chapter 21

"Well isn't this just fuckin' cozy!" Alexandra shouted. They were all sitting around the dining room table, finishing up cake, with half-sipped glasses of milk in front of them, when she came stumbling in after 8:00.

David stood up. "Alex, where the hell have you been?"

"Where the hell have you been?" she mimicked. "What do you fucking care? You're all so worried that you're sitting around eating fucking cake!"

"Watch your mouth," he said, already using his No Bullshit Voice. "And lower your volume. Patrick is already in bed."

"Patrick schmatrick. I'm so fucking sick of hearing about Patrick!" She started swaying toward the table but misjudged and tripped, landing half in Michael's lap and half on the table.

"Whoa, are you okay?" Michael said.

"Are you okay?" she mimicked some more. "Daddy's little boy, home from college. Aren't you so fucking amazing?!"

Horrified, they all just stared at her. All you could hear was her breath, which was coming so fast it sounded as though she just finished running a marathon rather than simply walking into the house.

"Come with me." David took her firmly by the arm, his voice extremely low now… a volume they all knew was far more ominous than his louder one. Leading her toward his study, Shelley heard him growl, "Enough is enough. This is too much!"

The other kids, still at the table, were all looking down at their blue paper plates full of cake crumbs.

"Omigod. She must be drunk!" Grace whispered.

Michael and Rose glanced at each other knowingly, then averted their eyes.

"What?" Grace said. "You don't think she's drunk?"

"I think she may have been drinking some," Michael said, "but I think she's on more than just alcohol."

Shelley saw Rose nod in agreement, although she was still looking away.

"Well, what do you two think it is?" Shelley asked, in a tone which they knew meant she wouldn't give up until she got an answer.

"Crystal," they both mumbled.

Crystal! Oh God! Not only was I right that Alexandra's probably doing it, but my other kids refer to it by a nickname!

Trying not to flip out, she forced herself to sound calm, "What makes you so sure?"

Michael, always level-headed and full of information explained, "You can tell from the way she's all speedy and hopped up. The wide-open eyes, the fast breathing. And she has those marks on her face."

"What marks? I thought that was just acne."

"That's an easy mistake to make," he explained as if she were a child. "But I can tell some of it is from picking at her face, like meth heads tend to do."

Meth heads!

"How do you know so much about all of this?" she asked.

"Mo-om," Rose piped up. "We're in college now?"

As if that explained it all.

Meanwhile, Grace was sitting there with a look of horror on her face, apparently affected exactly the way Shelley wanted her to be after all the years of her talking about how there are three things you don't even try, "crystal" being one of them.

They could hear muffled yelling coming from David's office: both his voice and Alexandra's. Excusing herself, Shelley walked through the kitchen to join them, leaving the other kids to clean up the cake.

It only took about two minutes for she and David to conclude that there was no point in trying to talk to Alexandra then. Obviously, she was so high that there would be no progress made, as all she had to say was, "You think you're so fucking perfect... what do you, shit rainbows?"

"Yes, I'm a unicorn," David had replied.

They sent her up to her room, confiscating her pocketbook, jacket, and phone before she went up. Although David felt she was overreacting, Shelley also insisted on rolling Patrick's crib out of Alexandra's room into theirs, as she didn't want him left alone with her like this. Miraculously, he slept right through the process of being rolled down the hall, even when the crib had to be jammed through the doorways. Even while Alexandra paced the hallway, arms crossed, mimicking them loudly as David and Shelley whisper-planned their maneuvers.

Back downstairs, the other kids had cleaned up the cake plates and cups, and were all sitting around in the living room with Michael flipping through the channels on TV. Rose was playing rope toy with Tiny, who was gleefully pulling on it and growling, trying to sound like a vicious dog. Grace was curled up in the corner of the sofa with Frick on her lap while she scrolled through something on her iPhone.

"Thanks for taking care of the cleanup, guys," David said, pointedly ignoring the sounds of Alexandra stomping around in her room upstairs. It sounded like she was pacing back and forth, intermittently opening and then slamming the door to express her agitation.

"No prob," Michael replied, clicking off the TV.

"So," David said, "let's try to go on with our evening. Everyone want to do 'the update?'"

It was something they'd started years earlier, when all of the kids become teens who, with the exception of Grace, generally didn't share the details of their lives on a moment-by-moment basis. Each family member would take a minute or two to give a summary of what was going on with them, both good and bad, and they'd found it an effective way to stay posted without having to "interrogate" each child individually and be frustrated by their single-word responses.

"Sure," Michael said, actually looking happy about it. The girls just nodded.

"Great! I'll go first," Shelley said, knowing that none of the kids were going to volunteer. Grace set down her phone and Rose, much to Tiny's disappointment, stopped pulling on the rope.

"For me, on the good side, things have been going very well with Patrick. He's a sweet baby and even though he's a lot of work, he really is a good boy." She paused, noting that they were all looking at her with skepticism, surely aware that not everything had to be going well for her. "Another good thing is that all the running around with him has gotten me into better shape!" Everyone chuckled.

"On the bad side, I've been having a hard time finding any time for myself, and obviously, things with Alexandra have been super stressful." To this they all nodded, not surprised, but appreciative of her honesty. She and David had never been ones to sugarcoat things—they believed in being forthcoming for the most part, so their kids would also feel free to open up, and so that they would be better prepared for real life, including the good, the bad, and the ugly.

"I'll go next!" Grace piped up. The others rolled their eyes in preparation. "Dance team is going great! I've been learning to do all of these really cool flips and there's been great weather at most of the games this year! Coach wrote me a really good recommendation that I sent with my college applications too. Also, my hair is really long, which I've been working toward for *years*, and my classes have been really easy because I got my hard stuff done already," she paused for a breath, then launched on. "Oh, and I don't have a boyfriend but that's because I don't want one but there is this one cute guy who asked me to the prom and I said yes because I do like him but Cassie doesn't think I should go out with him because he's not friends with her boyfriend, but I don't think it matters, even though it would be cool if our boyfriends were friends, so I'm going with him and Cassie will just have to get over it."

"Wow, that's great," David interjected. "Any other *summary* of good stuff going on?"

A little embarrassed, she said, "No, not really, that's most of it."

"And what about bad stuff?" he asked, just as they heard more stomping sounds coming from Alexandra's room upstairs.

Grace glanced up at the ceiling, and then said, "Well, I guess it's the same as Mom said. It's just that Alexandra is kind of hard to deal with. And Patrick is cute and all, but it's really different having a baby around all the time. Last week at my game, he cried for like *five* minutes, and I felt like everyone *knew!"*

"Knew what?" Michael asked.

"You know. That I have this, like, *sister*, who like, had a *baby* and stuff. It's so embarrassing! And sometimes people think he's Mom's baby, which is just as bad! I mean, whose mother goes around having a baby at *her* age?"

My age. Niice. Shelley thought ruefully.

"Well I don't care what other people think," Rose said. "I mean, we all know what is or isn't the truth, so who cares what other people think? I think Mom is doing a nice thing by watching Patrick all the time. And anyhow, what was she supposed to do, just throw them in the street?"

"No, I'm just saying," Grace defended. "It's just embarrassing, is all."

"That's okay," Shelley intervened, before it turned into an argument. "Each person is entitled to feel however they feel, so it's fine. Everyone's different." She looked at Rose pointedly, as this was an issue the sisters had always grappled with. They were very different, which sometimes made them get along better, but more often had caused clashes over the years.

Ready for a change of subject, Shelley said, "Who wants to go next?"

No one said anything.

"Rose," David said, "What's been up with you?"

Irritated at being "called on," she sighed. "Fine, I'll go. My classes are really hard but I'm getting pretty much As and Bs in everything. I really like my English literature class but the historic one is a pain. I was nominated as a team leader in technology club for the convention in June, which is a college recruitment thing, so I've been figuring out how to set up the booth and stuff." She crossed her arms and sat back, apparently feeling she'd satisfied her obligation to share.

"That's all good stuff," David said. "Nice job! Any bad stuff?"

She thought a minute, then said, "Oh yeah, my bicycle got stolen, but I got it back. Some jerk must've clipped my lock and used it to ride one building over, which is where I found it."

"Ugh, that sucks," Grace said. "Something like that happened to my friend, only it was a long board instead of a bicycle. He left it outside the Starbucks for like, one minute, and then…"

"I got a new lock. It's fine," Rose interrupted before she could go on.

David and Shelley both laughed, his hand automatically reaching for hers where they sat together on the living room floor. Their fingers twined together as they both enjoyed a moment of happiness, with things feeling somewhat… normal, for the first time in months.

"Michael?" David asked.

"I'd like to go last, if you don't mind."

"Okay, then I'll go. Work has been good, and I got a promotion and a raise a few months ago because of a project I did last year that earned me some recognition. Which is good because things have gotten even more expensive around here lately," he chuckled. "I'm very proud of all my kids and the things you're all doing with school and jobs and clubs…" the kids looked at him dubiously, surely thinking of Alexandra. He continued, "…even though there are a lot of problems with

Alexandra, we're all doing our best, especially my Sweet Shelley Bean, who has been doing most of the caretaking with Patrick."

Collective eye rolling from all, emphasized by a gagging sound from Grace, all of the kids good-naturedly loving to tease them about their use of pet names for each other all the time.

"Thanks, Mr. My Love," Shelley said.

More eye-rolling and some laughs.

"Well, I guess it's the moment of truth," Michael said.

Moment of truth?

"Everything has been going fine with grad school and work and everything, so you don't have to look so worried. It's nothing terrible."

Okaay.

"But I've been thinking a lot about how much money I'm spending on being at grad school at Appalachian, and I'm racking up these huge loans that are going to take forever to pay off."

"Understandable," David said. "But remember that once you're working, you'll be able to chunk away at them."

"I know, I know, but it will take at least ten years to pay them all, even if I have a great job and live in a really cheap place. Probably more like twenty."

Rose and Grace, both still under financial care from their parents, appeared appropriately horrified.

"So," Michael went on, looking at Shelley, "I was planning on talking to you and Dad about the possibility of moving home." Before they could say anything, he quickly added, "I do want to finish my degree but I've looked into online courses, which would be so much cheaper, plus I wouldn't have the expenses of my apartment and food and stuff. I could even get rid of my car."

Move home and *get rid of his car?* Shelley's mind filled with undesirable images of her driving her twenty-four-year-old son to and from the movies like she did ten years earlier.

David, rescuing her from her speechlessness said, "It certainly sounds like you've give this quite a bit of thought. Shelley and I will have to do some talking and together we'll all figure out what's best."

Michael, looking surprised that they didn't all start jumping up and down with joy and an immediate yes, just said, "Oh. Okay."

"It's not that we wouldn't love to have you around," David said, "but it is already quite crowded around here so we'd have to come up with some creative maneuvering."

"I know, I know," Michael said, holding his hands up in deference. "Just so you know, I did talk to Mom, but she said it wouldn't work moving into her place because she just bought one of those new condos in downtown Raleigh and it's only a studio. She's got her house on the market and will be moving in a few months."

David, unsurprised that his self-absorbed ex-wife would live her life with complete disregard for what the kids might need—like she always had—reassured Michael, "It's okay. We wouldn't mind having you here, we just need a little time to discuss it."

"I understand."

I'm glad he understands because I feel like I can't figure out even one more dilemma, Shelley thought.

They all just kind of looked at one another, each involved in their own thoughts. There was only one thing Shelley could think of to say.

"Anyone for more cake?"

Chapter 22

Endless hours of discussion over that weekend brought David and Shelley only marginally closer to reducing the cacophony of dilemmas that were constantly screaming through their heads.

She'd done some research online about crystal meth and no matter which site she visited, the messages were all the same: It's a highly addictive drug that frequently causes users to become hooked after only one or two times. Extremely hard to kick, it was a habit that most often destroyed people's lives permanently, and even the most extensive treatment programs were generally unsuccessful at securing long-term results.

Alexandra's apparent drug problem once again forced the couple to sacrifice time with the other kids, as they spent hours that weekend discussing what to do about it. Put her in a residential treatment program? They worried that she'd be exposed to even worse drug addicts. Enroll her in an outpatient program? Sure, but would it be enough? And what would be the long-term plan with Patrick if she never got her act together? They couldn't even think that far ahead.

Then there was the new situation with Michael. This brought up issues they had always struggled with due to differences between their generation and their children's generation. When they were teenagers, you couldn't wait to get a car and enjoy all of its associated freedoms. When you turned eighteen, you moved out of your parents' house, never to return other than as a visitor. If you went to college, you went, and when you graduated, you got an apartment and a job. Again, their generation, for the most part, didn't return to reside at their parents' homes unless there was a catastrophic emergency.

Not so with Generation Y, as they are referred to. They'd first started to notice the gap when their oldest—Michael—became of driving age. Not interested. They'd been astounded that, even at sixteen, when he could have had a full-fledged license, he was entirely uninterested. Also at seventeen. It wasn't until he turned eighteen and they pretty much forced him by refusing to chauffer him and his friends everywhere that he finally got a license and a small part-time job to cover his insurance so he could drive their cars.

This was in stark contrast to the way David and she were as teenagers: They'd gotten jobs as soon as they were old enough and even before then made a little money here and there, he mowing lawns and she babysitting. Even though they'd grown up in different regions of the country, all of their friends had done the same, too. They all worked and saved as much as possible with the goal of having their own cars as soon as humanly possible. The only exceptions had been the very wealthy kids whose parents had promised cars for their sixteenth birthdays.

This phenomenon about driving—or the lack thereof—extended throughout all their kids. Grace had been the only one to show an interest in driving by the age of seventeen, without waiting until eighteen to be forced. Incidentally, their home state of North Carolina allowed for a permit at the age of fourteen-and-a-half. Even after four kids, they still found this astonishing.

Much dialogue had gone on between David and Shelley over the years as they tried to accept the differences and understand their kids' choices. To some extent it made sense that more kids stayed living at home into their twenties, since attending college had become more of the norm, whereas in their generation, not as much. So far, Michael and Russell had both chosen colleges far away, and Rose, whose school was half an hour from their home, had also chosen to live on campus. But what if they'd wanted to attend a local school and live at home? Of course they would support them, although unlike some of their friends' kids, they did expect them to move out once they graduated and not stay living with them into their adult years.

Which all meant that of course they would welcome Michael to come live at home while he finished his master's degree. The problem was, they couldn't figure out where to put him! Now that they had Alexandra and Patrick, there wasn't an empty bedroom in the house. Were they supposed to have him stay in the living room like a guest? Obviously not. Likewise, they couldn't have him share Grace's room, as it just wouldn't be right to have an eighteen-year-old girl and a twenty-four-year-old boy share a bedroom that was too small to be sectioned by a room divider. Install a bunk bed? Still, not right. Plus, Rose would still need somewhere to stay during summer and school breaks.

They briefly discussed the other areas of the house. Give him the study? They couldn't do that, as David did sometimes work from home and Shelley's computer was in there too. Plus, "study" was a generous term for the tiny six by ten room, which was more like a closet. Finish the attic? That was a possibility, but they'd priced it years earlier and discovered that it would cost at least ten thousand dollars, plus they'd have no storage area left anywhere in the house. Additionally, it would take several months to accomplish, and they just plain couldn't afford it with all of the new expenses they had with Alexandra and Patrick, not to mention the impending likelihood of having to pay for some sort of drug treatment program.

Close off the living room? There would be nowhere for Patrick to play or for any family members to relax and watch TV or have friends over.

David suggested the dining room. They could close it off by adding double doors on one side and a single door on the other. It would make a nice-sized room for Michael; they could put their china cabinet and dining table and chairs in the attic, and use the kitchen nook for all eating. They discussed that they wouldn't be able to seat all of them, plus Patrick's highchair at the tiny café table for four in the kitchen, and figured they could get a different table—one of those that has the sides that flip up to become larger when you're eating but doesn't take up as much space when you're not.

Shelley tried to visualize meals with her, David, Grace, Alexandra, Michael, and Patrick, all eating in the tiny space two or three times a day. It would be extremely crowded and she'd have to pass the food over the kitchen counter because there wouldn't even be enough room to walk past the table. Imagining Russell and Rose being home was farfetched. A holiday like Thanksgiving or Christmas with other family? Entirely unimaginable.

There was no other choice. The least of all unpalatable options, they figured the two thousand dollars they'd need to spend and the inconvenience it would cause, would be worth it to make sure they provided for all of their kids, their goal always being to provide them with the best start in life they could possibly manage. David agreed to go to Home Depot with Michael the next day and Shelley agreed to look on Craigslist for a suitable table.

*****

Part of the plan that weekend had been to take Rose shopping for some new clothes. That had also been their plan two months earlier when she'd come home, but they'd never gone because Patrick had been sick and Shelley couldn't count on Alexandra to take care of him properly even in the best of health. Now, once again faced with a quandary surrounding Alexandra and Patrick, she was determined to find a way not to have to sacrifice the time she craved with her other daughters due to the major difficulties with her newest daughter.

Easier said than done. David and she had agreed that Alexandra was to be supervised every minute, and also that for the time being, they didn't want Patrick left alone with her. He and Michael had begun working on transforming the dining room into Michael's bedroom, so it was understood that Shelley would be taking Patrick with them when she, Rose, and Grace went shopping. But Alexandra? Shelley couldn't imagine taking her on a fun girls' day out, never mind buying her things and rewarding her after her recent behavior. Yet she knew that David's hands were full and there was a part of her that secretly hoped that spending time with them would set a good example for Alexandra, and would hopefully show her how nice "good clean fun" could be. She opted to take her with them.

The morning was a bit hectic, with everyone trying to get showered and out of the house all at the same time. Once the guys left for Home Depot, Shelley had individual discussions with each of the girls, explaining to Rose and Grace that they were going to do their best to include Alexandra and hopefully teach her something. To Alexandra, she made it clear that she expected her to behave like a human being, and not ruin the day for everyone.

Piling into the car with Shelley driving and Rose in the front seat next to her, and Alexandra and Grace squished into the back with Patrick's car seat in the middle, they drove to the mall uneventfully. Rose chatted animatedly about what items she was looking for, while Grace was uncharacteristically quiet and they all tried to ignore Alexandra's sighing and bouncing her knee the entire time.

Miraculously, they found a parking spot close to the main entrance. Walking to the back of the car, Shelley tried not to be irritated as Alexandra just stood there. She made not one motion to help as Shelley opened the stroller and lifted the baby out of his car seat, making sure he had all of his little toys close at hand. Stowing all of their purses in the storage section of the stroller, Grace, Rose, and Shelley were ready to rock and roll, while Alexandra stood with her arms folded.

"Let's go," Shelley said, using her body language to indicate that they were going to walk toward the entrance.

"Oh, so I'm like, supposed to *push* this thing with like, all *your* stuff in it?" Alexandra said, sarcasm dripping like blood from a vampire's mouth.

"Yes, Alex," Shelley sighed. "That's what people do with strollers. And if it hasn't occurred to you, that's *your* son who is riding in the stroller and *your* diaper bag that has all his stuff in it too."

"I can't believe this! I don't even have a pocketbook because you *stole* mine, and I shouldn't…"

Shelley had had it. Clearly, she was going to need to cross over into the Let Me Slap You Into Reality side of things. "Shut the hell up and start walking," she growled. "Now!"

Apparently this provided enough shock value to get Alexandra moving. They all walked into the mall, Alexandra pushing the stroller with a puzzled expression on her face, and Grace and Rose both trying to suppress their smirks.

*****

Against all odds, it ended up being a surprisingly pleasant day. Once Alexandra got the gist that as long as she acted rotten, they were all going to ignore her and not let her ruin their good time, she went through a quiet but not nasty phase, and by lunch time, she was actually participating in conversation, apparently much more able to behave normally once her jitters wore off. Or maybe it was that her nastiness wasn't getting her anywhere. Who knew?

Either way, it went far better than Shelley had braced herself for, and there was a festive air mixed with underlying relief as they rode home, munching on hot pretzels and chatting about the day's purchases while

Patrick, out cold in his car seat, slept soundly after his stimulation-filled day.

Rose had gotten what basically amounted to a new summer wardrobe, being that the weather was getting hotter and the last time she'd gotten anything new was before school had started in the fall. Grace, not needing much, still got two new bathing suits, a pair of shorts, and couple of fresh camis.

At first, Alexandra just stood by, leaning on the stroller with bored petulance on her face, and not looking at any merchandise, which was fine with Shelley. However, throughout the afternoon Alexandra's attitude improved dramatically, and she even said something nice a few times when the other girls came out of a dressing room to model their choices.

Finally, when they were in a store that Shelley knew had a lot of the styles Alexandra liked and noticed her gazing longingly toward the racks, she said, "Go ahead, Alex. See what you can find."

Alexandra turned to her, eyes pricked with tears and said, "Thanks, Shelley. A lot."

*****

The weekend continued without further drama. Michael and David did a great job on the dining room renovation, with the doors all closing smoothly and no damage done to the hardwood floors—nor to the dining set that they'd carried up two flights of stairs into the attic.

Standing in the driveway, waving goodbye to Michael and Rose as they headed back for the last few weeks of school, Shelley shook her head in amazement. Before leaving, Michael had told her and David that he'd already met with his guidance counselor, and had notified both his landlord and his job *before* coming home to speak with them, so certain had he been that he'd be able to move home.

Chapter 23

Research.

Shelley, being a detail kind of gal, rather enjoyed research. Things like finding the best deals on flights for a trip or rustling up a new restaurant to try were things that, while some other people (like David) found tedious, she found kind of fun. However, she quickly discovered that it is decidedly un-fun when researching which drug treatment program would be best for your child.

She was further disgusted to find out that, while you may have medical insurance that you pay an arm and a leg for, it is still likely to cost thousands of dollars a month and you'd better hope it works the first time because it will never be covered again. "Covered" being a loosely used term.

Having narrowed down the choices via the Internet and hours of telephone discussion with seemingly every unknowledgeable person at their insurance company, David and Shelley, dragging Alexandra along with them, met with directors at two different drug treatment programs. They had to jam both visits into the same afternoon when there was a half-day of school, so that Grace could watch Patrick and Alexandra wouldn't miss any more classes.

Each of the programs took place seven days per week, from eight in the morning until seven in the evening and Alexandra would need to be driven and picked up every day.

At the first place, Fresh Start, which was only fifteen minutes from the house and (after insurance) would cost eighteen hundred dollars a month, they were also informed that family participation was required every Monday, Wednesday, and Saturday from five to seven, with Alexandra being the person to decide which family members' attendance would be required each time.

"We have found that family dynamics often play a significant role in driving the user to turn to drugs," explained the director. The young woman sat behind her polished mahogany desk in a business suit that looked like it would be far more appropriate for a banker, her pixie-like frame and perfectly styled hair giving the impression that she was a little girl dressed up for Take Your Daughter to Work Day.

"Excuse me?" David said, his jawbone pulsing as he fought to maintain decorum. "What about placing responsibility with the person who chose to make these poor decisions?" He indicated Alexandra, who was sitting there, arms crossed, looking pleased at the implication that it must be their fault.

"Certainly, Mr. Morsony, there is some responsibility on the part of the user. But it has been our experience that family dynamics often play a significant role in driving the user to turn to drugs," the girl repeated, reminding Shelley of one of those telemarketers who are trained to read from a script and never deviate.

The second program, New Beginnings, was forty-five minutes from the house and would run them twenty-one hundred dollars per month.

Again, they sat across from the director, this time looking past piles of disorganized papers scattered amongst coffee cups and an ashtray on a desk that looked like it had been purchased secondhand from an old elementary school. Standing at only about 5'4", the eccentric man had given them the tour of the facilities, his untucked Hawaiian shirt flowing, as he explained that since it was almost June, they were preparing for their summer luau theme. David and Shelley looked at one another, thinking the same thing: *Are we sending her on vacation or to a drug program?* Not to mention Shelley's more extensive inner sarcasm: *And we know what happened the last time she went on a tropical vacation!*

New Beginning's philosophies, however, were a bit different. The director explained that although family may be invited to attend occasionally, the main work was done with the "client" (Shelley was distracted for a few minutes as she pondered what might have been a better term. Patient? Resident? Student?), helping them take ownership of the problem and learn how to live their lives without the need for artificial substances to hide from real issues.

Euphemisms aside, Shelley was a lot more comfortable with this philosophy and she knew that David would be too. Alexandra, of course, had an angry expression on her face, making it clear that she disagreed.

After shaking hands with the director, they gathered the papers he'd given them and walked out to the car. Sitting there in the stifling North

Carolina heat, they were each lost in their own thoughts, going over the options and their myriad differences.

Finally David turned on the ignition, the blast of hot air coming out of the vents still better than nothing. He turned to Alexandra. "I just can't believe this, Alex!"

"Neither can I-uh," she said, glaring out the window. "I don't even need to go to a program like this and you're like, making everything worse!"

"Worse!" he roared, instantly ratcheted up to his full-fledged, pulse-pounding anger level. "What could be worse than you doing crystal meth, cutting school, and neglecting your son!"

"Maybe I should just move out," she stated, crossing her arms and still staring out the window.

"Move out! Where the hell are you going to go? You don't even have a job and we're hoping you'll even graduate next week after all the absences you've had!"

"I'll move in with Tyler."

"Tyler? I assume you're talking about your twenty-five-year-old boyfriend, who is probably a drug addict too!"

"Actually, he turned twenty-six. It was his birthday last week. And he doesn't do drugs. *And* I'm not an addict."

"Oh, so I suppose this very responsible, twenty-six-year-old man is going to want to take on a girlfriend who has a baby, no job, and a drug problem? Fat chance." David threw the car into gear and started pulling out of the parking lot a little too fast.

"He loves me! Not like you people who make me feel like I'm some sort of monster in your perfect little family!"

Shelley interjected quickly, as she knew David was ready to really blow his top. "Alex, come on now." While her tone indicated that this line of discussion was silly, she sensed that this outburst had been coming for some time. "We've never treated you like a monster or even thought you were a monster. We've always welcomed you into our family from the first day you came."

"Yeah, right."

"I mean it! I'm not going to tell you it wasn't a shock for us, but we love you and have done our best to welcome you and Tiny, and Patrick into the family. I can't imagine what more you think we should have done!"

"You could at least give me a chance before trying to toss me into some sort of drug addict program!"

"Alexandra," Shelley sighed deeply, trying to maintain her composure. "Believe me, the last thing we want is to be here doing this either. But after the past two weeks, it's clear that you're not stopping on your own! We're trying to help you before it gets so bad that your entire life is ruined!"

"Hmmph." Alexandra just sat there, arms crossed, her expression contemptuous.

"Fine. Why don't we just ride quietly for a while, then try and talk about this more calmly over a burger or something," Shelley said. Before she could help herself she added, "And then you can tell us, Alexandra, exactly what else you think we possibly could have done to help you!"

Alexandra just continued to stare out her window, her face clouded over with anger, its petulance and oily sheen reminding Shelley that with all of her adult problems, she was still just a teenager. A teenager who should be visiting colleges instead of drug treatment programs.

"Fine," David growled, accelerating even harder on the twisty country road.

Woop woop! Blue lights bounced around the car and David slammed his fist against the dashboard as they realized that they were being pulled over.

Greeat.

*****

Thirty minutes and a hundred twenty-five dollar speeding ticket later, they pulled into an IHOP and were seated right away. Looking over the book-length menu, Shelley tried to concentrate on what she wanted to eat as her mind raced through the many issues that needed to be sorted out. Alexandra, taking her pocketbook with her, went to the restroom, leading Shelley to wonder whether she had her period or was doing drugs in there.

David was staring at her, shaking his head but not saying anything.

"What?"

"I'm sorry babe. I'm just so sorry you have to deal with all of this."

"I'm sorry too. For both of us having to deal with it. Actually, for *all* of us to have to deal with it."

"What do you mean?"

"I mean, this affects everyone, beyond just us as parents, and Alexandra and Patrick. Mainly Grace. She's graduating next week and I've hardly been able to pay attention to any of the things going on with school and friends and parties. She didn't even *ask* if she could have a party and you know that's not like Grace."

"Well what the fuck do you want me to do?" he semi-yelled, causing people at nearby tables to glance their way.

"Lower your voice!" she whispered. He knew she hated it when he raised his voice in public, although she understood that the magnitude of the problem and his inability to solve it had worn him down. "I'm not saying you should do anything about it. All I'm saying is that it sucks and the problems are not limited to just us!"

"Fine." He slammed his water glass down, causing some to splash onto the table.

"What the heck, David?"

He opened his menu, obviously ignoring her and pretending to look at the choices when they both knew that he always ordered the cheeseburger deluxe whenever they went to IHOP.

"Where the hell is Alexandra anyway?" he grumbled.

"I'll go check."

*****

Walking toward the restrooms, Shelley thought she heard Alexandra's voice but when she turned the corner, she was just walking out of the vestibule that contained the restroom entrances and a pay phone.

"You okay?" she asked.

"Yeah, fine. Why?" Alexandra said, her eyes darting toward the pay phone for a split second.

"Were you on the phone?"

"What makes you think that?"

Shelley noticed the lack of a true answer and that she'd employed the tactic of answering a question with a question.

"I thought I heard you talking."

"Huh." She shrugged and started walking toward the table as Shelley followed behind, studying her gait and hoping that she wouldn't see any signs of her being high.

Back at the table, David, his hair sticking up from rubbing his head in frustration, scowled and told Alexandra to sit down.

"Decide what you want, Alex," Shelley said wearily.

"What's the problem?"

"Wow, that's a loaded question!" David nearly shouted.

Shelley shot him a look and tried to calm the situation with her tone. "You were gone for a really long time. Just decide what you're having please."

The waitress took their order quickly and moved on, understandably relieved to depart from the Table of Tension. The three of them sat there staring at each other, each wondering where to begin.

"Okay, I'll start," Shelley said. "I think the better of the two programs is the second one and that Alexandra should begin attending right after graduation next week."

"I don't need a program," Alexandra objected.

"So what you're saying is that you aren't going to be doing any more drugs and you feel you'll have no problem quitting?" Shelley asked.

"I didn't say I'm not going to party. I just don't think it's a problem. I have it under control."

"Oh, so you think it's fine to do crystal meth?" David gasped.

"It's not like I'm one of those drug addicts who are like, crazed with it or something. I just like it."

"Alexandra, I'm glad that you're not a full-fledged junkie, lying in the street. But it is entirely possible—and even likely—that that could happen if you don't quit," Shelley said, fighting the urge to shake her head in disbelief that they were even having this conversation.

"I'm fine-uh."

"I don't think you're anywhere near fine!" David rumbled. "You've been neglecting Patrick, cutting school, not coming home when you're supposed to, and making a ridiculous scene on your brother's birthday!"

"I'm eighteen. I can do whatever I want."

"No, Alex. You can't," Shelley said. "Yes, you're eighteen, but that doesn't mean doing those things is right!"

"I don't have to answer to you. I don't have to answer to anyone anymore."

"When you live in our house you do!" David whisper-roared.

"Well then maybe I shouldn't live in your house," she said, and then sat back, childishly crossing her arms and staring at him.

Trying to bring some reason back into the discussion Shelley went on, "Alex, even when you're an adult, there are common courtesies you extend to the people you live with. Even if we were roommates and not your parents, it's common courtesy to let the people you live with know if you're not going to be home, and make sure you show up for things when you said you would."

"I never said I was showing up for Michael's stupid birthday."

The waitress came, halting their conversation as she set down their platters of burgers, fries, and onion rings.

Once she left Shelley continued, "I wish you'd explain what problem you have with Michael. Or any of us, for that matter."

"I don't have a problem. It's you people that have a problem."

"Oh really?" David said. "And what problem is that?"

"You all think you're just so fucking perfect and you're not!"

Shelley sighed at the typical teenage angst that was so much less tolerable when accompanied by drug abuse and child neglect. "Alex, we don't think we're perfect. No one in the universe is perfect. We're just a family of regular people doing our best. Trying to make good choices, be good people, do the right thing. And that's all we're asking of you, too."

"I think we're getting off track here," David said. "The issue we need to deal with right now is which program Alex should attend."

"I think I should just move out," Alexandra said.

"We already went over this…" David began.

Shelley quickly interrupted. "Alex, why don't you tell us how you think that would work out."

"I can live with Tyler. He loves me."

"Jesus Christ!..." David began.

Shelley held up her hand, stopping him before he could continue. "Hold up here," she said, trying to communicate in a way Alexandra might relate to. "I'm not saying he doesn't love you. What I am saying is that you don't have a job, you've been doing drugs, and I don't think you're ready to take care of Patrick on your own."

"I don't need a job. Tyler can take care of me."

"Let's assume that's true. There's still the fact that you've been doing crystal meth! And you've done very little taking care of Patrick. So what makes you think that once you're out on your own you're suddenly going to start doing all of his caretaking and not doing drugs?"

"I didn't say I'm not gonna party."

Shelley, ready to pull her hair out, gritted her teeth and said, "Alex, partying is one thing. Crystal meth is another!"

"I'm fine-uh."

"No you're not," David said. "Not fine at all!"

"Oh yeeah, baby. I think she's reeally fiiine," came a raspy masculine voice.

Shelley looked up and there stood a man she could only assume was Tyler. Motorcycle helmet in hand, he stood beside their table in all of his twenty-six-year-old biker guy glory, complete with leather chaps, Harley Davidson boots, and a sleeveless black tee-shirt that afforded them a view of the snake tattoo that wound its way down his arm and onto his hand which was currently extended toward David for a shake.

"I'm Tyler," he rasped.

Jeez, how much does this guy smoke to have a voice like that?

"You must be David." He smiled, revealing a missing gap of top teeth on one side.

"*Mr.* Morsony," David said, sliding out of the booth and standing up. He shook Tyler's hand, a little too firmly.

"Hey dude, sorry," Tyler laughed, holding his hands up in a defensive pose. "I come in peace."

Alex, suddenly the hostess of this little get-together, provided introductions. "Shelley, this is Tyler; Tyler this is Shelley."

"*Mrs.* Morsony," David emphasized.

"Nice to meet you, Mrs. Morsony," Tyler said. Shelley couldn't determine whether he was being sarcastic or not.

"So apparently you *were* on the phone," she said to Alexandra.

"I never said I wasn't!"

Speechless, Shelley just nodded at Tyler.

"Come! Sit down!" Alex said, continuing in her hostess role. "Do you want to order something?"

"I got no cash right now, baby," he said, sliding into the booth next to her.

"Oh," she said, looking pointedly at David, apparently expecting him to offer to buy the guy dinner.

David shook his head nearly imperceptibly and said, "Maybe you'd like something to drink?" He figured a soda would be nice gesture while a full meal would imply that they agreed with this relationship.

"Sure man. That would be great," Tyler said, then raised his arm and his voice, "Waitress!"

She came over, her eyes leaving no doubt that she was dying to know how this little soiree had developed.

"Lemme get a beer. Budweiser."

He's ordering a beer? At an IHOP the first time he meets his girlfriend's parents? And didn't he arrive by motorcycle? Shelley and David looked at each other, equally troubled by the circumstances.

"I'm sorry sir, but we don't carry alcoholic beverages."

"No beer!" Tyler exclaimed. "What kinda joint is this place?" He chuckled at his own joke while Shelley and David were deadpan.

Alex's facial expression could only be described as rapt. She gazed at Tyler the way a normal teenaged girl might if Zac Efron himself had sat at their table.

Shelley felt like she was going to throw up from the stress of the whole situation and the reek of stale cigarettes that clung to Tyler. David looked equally as pale as she felt.

"So Tyler," Shelley tried, once the waitress left with his order for a milkshake. "Why don't you tell us a bit about yourself."

"What do you wanna know?"

"I don't know, whatever. Where do you live? Where do you work? That kind of thing."

"Whoa! What is this, like, the Italian inquisition or something?" he laughed.

Shelley tried not to smirk while David clearly did not think his error was funny at all. They waited for him to answer.

"Well, uh, I do welding and stuff."

"That's great. Where do you do that?" she asked.

"Well, I'm not really working right now. I'm kind of in between jobs."

"I see."

They all just sat there, the silence speaking more than any words could say.

Alexandra chimed in, "But I can still move in with you, right baby?" She snuggled herself up against him, his snake-decorated arm draped over her shoulder a little too intimately to be sitting across from her parents.

"Yeah. That's right."

"You realize Alexandra doesn't have a job, right?" David asked. "And that she's still in high school? And has a baby?"

Tyler laughed. "Yeah, yeah, I know. But she can stay with me anytime."

"Really?" David snarled, his anger barely held in check. "And what about Patrick?"

"Who's Patrick?" He sounded genuinely confused.

"Her son! That's who!"

"Oh yeah, the kid. Sure, that's fine."

"The kid?" David repeated. "Alexandra, are you seriously telling us that you want to move in with a man who is eight years older than you, has no job, and refers to your son as *the kid?"*

"Whoa, whoa. Don't get insulted, man. I think rugrats are cute. What is he, like four or something? I can take him for rides on my bike and shit."

"First of all, he is not four, he's almost one. He's a little baby!" David turned his attention to Alexandra. "Haven't you even told him anything about Patrick? This love of your life that he supposedly is?" He looked back toward Tyler. "And second of all, he is not going on any motorcycles."

"What do you got against bikes, man? Bikes are cool."

This whole scene was just unbelievable to Shelley. She began to get a Twilight Zone feeling, as if she were somehow living inside a very bad "B" movie, complete with its stereotypical lame characters. Except it was real.

"Let's try to get back on track here," she said. "Are you aware that Alexandra has been doing drugs?"

"Yeah, but man, a little partying never hurt no one."

"She's been doing more than a little partying," David said. "She's been doing crystal meth. I suppose you do it too?"

"Naw man. That shit'll kill ya. I don't do that. Just smoke a little herb and drink my beers, you know?"

David certainly *didn't* know.

"Well Alexandra has been doing it. What do you think about that?" David asked, evidently hoping Tyler would suddenly become responsible and be aghast at this information.

"I don't personally like that shit. But when Alex is on it, man is she a real firecracker!"

He actually *winked* at David!

David slammed his coffee cup down on the table and said, "Excuse me." Stalking toward the front door Shelley saw him stop at the vending machine and buy cigarettes.

Greeat. He hasn't smoked in seven years.

With no other option, she decided to wrap things up.

"Tyler, you seem like a decent guy," she said, hoping to appeal to any smidge of responsibility that might exist within him. "Here is our concern. Alexandra is only eighteen years old, hasn't even graduated high school, and has a baby. She's been cutting classes, neglecting her son, and making scenes at family events. We feel she should attend a drug treatment program to get into the right direction, and take some college classes. Don't you agree that that would be a better way for her to be living her life?"

"College? I never went to college and look at me! I even gotta Harley." He patted his helmet for emphasis.

Shelley signaled to the waitress, who brought the check, then scurried away at Tyler's lecherous grin.

"Anyhow, I think she should do whatever she wants," Tyler said, pulling Alexandra in closer to him. "And she don't have to go to no program if she doesn't want to." Alexandra smiled up at him, then turned to Shelley, smug in her agreement.

"Well, it seems that we'll have to agree to disagree on that one," Shelley said, setting some cash on the table for the tip and taking the check to bring to the register. "It was nice to meet you Tyler. We have to get going now."

Walking toward the register, she realized that Alexandra and Tyler hadn't left the table. After paying, she called over, "Come on Alex. We're leaving."

The two of them walked over to her, his snake arm draped over her—still.

"Tyler's going to give me a ride. I'll be home later."

"No, Alex. You need to come home now. Patrick will need your attention and we need to figure out what we're going to do from here."

"I don't *have* anything else to figure out. I'm an adult and I'll come home when I come home. You can't *make me* do anything."

Stumped, she stood there, speechless. *What do you even say to this?*

"Alexandra, do you really feel that the way you're acting is the right thing to do?"

While she awaited an answer she glanced back toward their table and saw that the cash she'd left for the waitress was missing.

"I'm sick of doing the 'right thing,'" Alexandra said snidely, actually making air quotes. "I'm just going to do what I want, which is ride home with Tyler."

"Do you even have another helmet for her to wear?" she addressed Tyler. At this point, Shelley was praying for the bare minimum.

"Course! I keep my baby's helmet strapped to my bitch bar for whenever we need it."

Well that's a relief. He keeps it attached to his bitch *bar. Lovely.*

Chapter 24

David made a brief call to their attorney who confirmed that to a great extent, Alexandra was right. Since she was over eighteen, they couldn't force her to do anything. If she were to attend a treatment program, she would have to sign herself in and would have the freedom to sign herself out at any time. If they didn't agree with the way she behaved in their household, they could ask her to move out, but they couldn't technically make her follow their rules.

David and Shelley thought this entire concept was one hugely ridiculous irony after another. By law, even at over eighteen, none of their kids could get their own college loans without using *their* tax returns. They were also expected to keep providing all of their medical insurance. These aspects, in their opinion, meant that they were still children and their responsibility. Yet the law provided that they were adults. Adults whose grades and medical records were kept private even though their parents were paying the bills. Adults who could "live their lives how they want," even when they were supported entirely by them.

According to the attorney, the only recourse they could potentially have would be to file a complaint with Child Protective Services and try to have Alexandra declared an unfit mother. However, there would be no guarantee that Patrick would stay with them, and a very strong likelihood that he would be placed in foster care with strangers, even if temporarily. It would likely involve a lengthy, expensive court battle, and by the attorney's advice they would lose anyhow because her behavior wasn't "bad enough" that the court would judge in their favor.

They both agreed that Alexandra wasn't bad enough that they wanted to take her parental rights away. Yet they also couldn't see letting her continue to live in their home and behave like this. Nor could they imagine that making her move out would be a good thing, as surely it would result in her and Patrick living with Tyler.

Should they suggest she go live with Tyler and leave Patrick with them? Would she agree to that? And even if she did, is that what they wanted and thought was right? While it might be best for Patrick, it would also lead to his mother being free to become a full-fledged street junkie with nothing holding her back. Not to mention that David couldn't bear the idea of putting Shelley in a position to have to do any more than she was already doing. And it could mean that they were taking on the permanent, full-time responsibility of raising another child.

No, what they wanted was for Alexandra to get back on track. How they were going to do that, they had no idea, but none of the other options seemed right either.

Unable to think, talk, hem, and haw about it any longer, the couple reluctantly decided to set it aside for the short term so they could focus on the festivities surrounding graduation.

*****

The next few weeks passed in a blur of activity. Grace and Alexandra both graduated high school, one with good grades and the other by the skin of her teeth, having brought up her grade point average by doing community service and retaking some tests.

Michael moved into his new room, jamming it with furniture from his apartment in an attempt to turn the former dining room into a bedroom, living room, and office all in one. Russell, home from school for the summer, was pissed about Michael having his own room while he had to stay on the living room pullout.

Rose, having to empty her dorm room for the summer months, came home with all of her worldly possessions. Shelley picked her up, they loaded the car to the hilt with all of her stuff, and during the drive home Rose broached the subject of an exchange program trip she wanted to go on in the fall.

"It will be so amazing," she said, excitement glowing from her like a halo. "It's two months long and I'd get to stay with three different families: one in London, one in Paris, and one in Rome. And in between I can take trips to other countries too, on weekends. You know, how they have the train system that goes all around Europe? And I'll get all sorts of credits in literary culture and the arts…"

She chatted on, filled with all of the energy and hopefulness that's the essence of being a twenty-year-old girl with her whole life ahead of her, while Shelley's mind spun into a lather of thoughts. *Oh God! How much is this going to cost? What an opportunity, I would never want her to miss this! But we just don't have any more money; I can't imagine how we could pull it off. But how could we* not *make sure she can go?*

"Mom? Hello? Earth to Mom!" Rose was looking at her and smiling, a mature understanding in her eyes that Shelley had never seen before.

"Sorry honey, I'm listening. It sounds like a great opportunity." She cringed at the hesitancy she heard in her own voice.

"You must be wondering how much it's going to cost," Rose said. "But I have it all figured out."

"Really? Okay, let's hear it."

"Well, the actual cost is four thousand dollars more than the normal credits would be. But since I'd be away for two months, I was thinking it wouldn't make sense to have the dorm room because I wouldn't be there to use it the whole time anyway. So if I lived at home for the year—well, except for the two months—the money you would save on the dorm room and meal plan would make up for the four thousand."

Shelley nodded, stunned—and impressed—that she'd thought this all out.

"And of course I'll need spending money, but I can work a lot this summer and save it all so I would have that, and I'd need to get my car back on the road so I can drive to school the rest of the year and pay for gas and stuff."

"Wow Rose, I'm really impressed! It sounds like you've given this quite a bit of thought."

"Yeah, well, I really, really want to do this so I figured it would be much easier to get you guys to agree if I already had a plan."

"Smart girl you are," Shelley smiled at her and gave her knee a little squeeze. "I'm proud of you for figuring all of that out ahead of time."

"So? Can I do it?"

"I'll have to discuss it with David, but I would like for you to be able to go. It is a once-in-a-lifetime opportunity."

Crestfallen, Rose said, "What else is there to figure out? I mean, if it's going to cost you the same and everything."

"Listen sweetie, I didn't say you can't go, so don't look so sad. It's just that we've got a pretty full house. Did you know that Grace has decided to live at home and go to NC State?"

"Yeah but I figured we could just share our room like we always have."

"That's true, and I don't object to you doing that. But it's going to take some adjustment and I can't just give you a full-out yes without discussing it with your stepdad first."

"Oh. Okay. I understand."

"So, what else has been going on? Any cute guys to speak of?"

Rose chatted on, telling her about this and that, as Shelley navigated them back toward the house they all called home.

✳✳✳✳✳

"Maymaw!" Patrick ran toward Shelley excitedly, his pudgy arms extended for a hug, his tippy toes propelling him as fast as they could. She quickly put down the armload of stuff she was carrying and turned toward him just as he tripped and fell over the pile of shoes in the foyer. His little face registered surprise, then crumpled into tears. She scooped him up and he wrapped his arms around her neck, crying and hiccupping even as he smiled because he was so happy to see her.

Glancing down in wonderment at the shoes that covered just about every inch of the foyer, Shelley noted that there was pretty much one pair belonging to each family member that was home: six pair and Rose and she hadn't even taken theirs off yet. She sighed, vowing that they'd have to come up with a better system, then she gave Patrick's juicy cheeks a bunch of kisses and set him down.

The other kids all came over to say hi to Rose, the crowd eventually working their way into the kitchen. With a festive feeling in the air, bags of chips and bowls of salsa were set out, soda cans popped, and everyone was talking at once. Michael had Patrick on his hip and was laughing at the funny face he made when he tasted the medium-spicy salsa.

David, with his arm around her waist, looked happy and relaxed for the first time in ages. It was a party; an atmosphere that had been absent with all the stress in their house lately. Shelley knew—could feel it emanating from him—that David was experiencing the pride—the payoff—of being the provider for all of their kids, who were developing into nice young adults, with their college careers underway, high school finished, and goals in progress. Even Russell seemed to have lost the snottiness that had still been in effect when they'd seen him at Christmas, his arrogance having morphed into a more manly, quiet confidence.

The only one missing was Alexandra. There was no sign of her and so Shelley, not wanting to dampen the fun, quietly slipped away and went up to her room.

She knocked on the door and heard shuffling around in there as Alexandra shouted, "Just a minute!" She waited a bit, wondering at the sound of the scurrying, and was just about to knock again when the door cracked open.

"What?" Alexandra said, clearly annoyed.

"What are you doing up here?" She asked, pushing the door open and stepping in to the room. There was a strong odor of just-sprayed Febreze with an underlying sweet, smoky smell. Strangely, the window was open.

"Nothing. Why?"

"First of all, everyone is downstairs. Rose just got home and we're all visiting."

She rolled her eyes.

"Secondly, it stinks in here. What were you doing, smoking drugs in our house?

"Oh nice!" Alexandra shouted, immediately at full volume. "You're coming in here and accusing me now?!"

Trying not to participate in the yelling, Shelley replied, "Accusing you? No. I'm stating fact. Obviously you were smoking something in here. It stinks like crap and you have the window open. You never open the window."

Alexandra was pacing the room, frenetically fixing and un-fixing her ponytail, moving with a jerky speed that was not normal. Not normal at all.

"I can't believe this, Alex! Everyone is downstairs having a nice time and instead of coming down, you're up here doing drugs in your room. Which, by the way, is also Patrick's room!"

"He's fine. Obviously. He's down there with you all."

"That's not the point! Are you smoking things when he's up here too?" Shelley could feel herself starting to panic and heard it in her own voice.

"Ucch. You're so fuckin' lame."

"*I'm lame?* What the heck Alex! He's a little baby! If he breathes even just a tiny bit of that he could get really sick. Or addicted to the stuff!"

"This is so fucked up." She was stomping around the room stuffing things into her pocketbook: her phone, iPod, hairbrush, and lipstick.

"Yes it is. It's very fucked up. *You* are being fucked up and I'm sick of it!"

"Maybe I should just leave."

"Really? And where are you going to go? I suppose it's your plan to just leave Patrick altogether and do what... go live with your unemployed boyfriend and do drugs?"

Shelley heard David coming up the stairs and her heart sank at the knowledge that this was going to ruin his good mood.

"What's going on in here?" he said. Then, "What the... it stinks in here. What the hell is going on?"

"Apparently, Alexandra has been up here doing drugs by herself instead of coming down to be with the family."

"I gotta get outta here," Alexandra said, grabbing her pocketbook and stalking toward the door.

David stood in the doorway, blocking her. "You're not going anywhere young lady. You are going to come downstairs and take care of your son, and be a part of this family!"

"No I'm not. I'm leaving. Move."

"Move? Who the hell do you think you're talking to?" David roared.

Alexandra backed up against the far wall of the room and said, "If you don't move, I'm breaking through." Then she ran, full-bore, apparently planning on tackling David to get him out of the doorway.

He stepped aside at the last second and she went crashing into the railing and tumbled halfway down the steps. The contents of her pocketbook spilled out, including not only the normal stuff but also a glass pipe, a pile of folded tin foil squares, and a lighter that was actually one of those miniature blowtorches.

"Jesus Christ, Alex!" David shouted. The other kids had come running to the bottom of the stairs and were now watching this whole scene in horror.

David picked up her drug paraphernalia and just stared at it. "What the fuck? What the FUCK!"

Gathering the rest of her stuff with a crazed, glazed over look in her eyes, Alex screamed, "You threw me down the stairs! I should call the police!" Her face was flushed with anger and there was already a bump forming on her forehead.

"Go ahead. Call the police! I'm sure they'll be very interested in this crap that just fell out of your purse!"

"Give me my shit. I'm outta here."

"I'm not giving you anything. This is going in the trash. And obviously you need help Alex. More help than we can give you here." David's face drained like a bathtub, going from flaming red to deathly pale in a matter of seconds.

"I don't need any help and I'm not going to any of those drug addict programs you're trying to sign me up for!" Having gathered her other things, she continued down the stairs where the other kids stood, flabbergasted. Patrick was crying and Michael was bouncing him up and down trying to calm him. "What are you all staring at?" she screamed at the top of her lungs. "Move!" She pushed past Rose roughly, stormed out the front door, and slammed it behind her.

In the stunned silence of the foyer, all you could hear was the sound of Patrick whimpering.

Chapter 25

Three weeks later Alexandra still wasn't home. All of their calls and texts to her cell phone went unanswered, and contacting the few friends she had yielded no results. The police informed them that because she was over eighteen and had left of her own accord, she wasn't considered "missing." If they wanted, they could report her to Child Services for abandoning her child, but that would likely result in Patrick being removed from their home and placed in foster care until things were sorted out, which could take months. The cop had pulled David aside and advised in hushed tones that they were better off just waiting it out to see what would happen.

Meanwhile, the other kids were all busy with their summer activities: Friends coming and going, cars being shuffled in the driveway like hands of blackjack, food being consumed at a volume that could compete with a cruise ship, and the house bursting at the seams with people living in every square inch, including not only the bedrooms, but also the dining room and living room. They were having fun as adult kids their age should, with beach trips, going to the pool, summer jobs, concerts, and dating.

Patrick, thrilled at all the attention he got from the older kids, lived as if every moment were a party, which it kind of was. At any given time there was music playing, snacks being eaten, and the older kids' friends cooing over him. Michael had gotten into the habit of taking Patrick to the playground almost daily, pushing him on the swings to scary heights and bringing him home satisfyingly exhausted.

For Shelley, crazy as it was, it was a bit of a break. Not only did she have tons of help with the baby but there was also a sense of relief—guilty though it made her feel—about Alexandra being gone. She was worried about her, but at least she wasn't worried that she was doing drugs in the house. Her absence made it so that her not taking care of Patrick made sense—It eliminated the constant conflict over how much she should "help her" and how much she should "make her" do. This made her feel like a terrible person, but the horrible truth was, she felt less terrible than she had when Alexandra was there.

Faced with the deadline for the Bora Bora trip, she and David had decided to cancel, not only because they still had Patrick and Alexandra was gone, but also because of all the increased expenses of the various kids living at home, the overwhelming expense of all of their college payments, and—at this point they hoped—paying for Alexandra to receive treatment at some point. They were disappointed about the trip but at that juncture neither of them had the strength to be overly concerned about it.

David seemed to be having the hardest time handling all of it. He was quieter than normal and had stopped exercising, saying that he was too exhausted at the end of the day. He didn't even like taking Tiny to the dog park anymore because it reminded him too sharply that his daughter was gone and, for all he knew, dead in the streets from an overdose. His skin took on a permanent pallor and tension, and he seemed to be just going through the motions of daily life, unable to truly enjoy the social summer atmosphere that should have brought some pleasure.

Shelley did what she could to try and make things nicer for him, implementing small indulgences whenever she could, like making his favorite meals, sending him an occasional e-card while he was at work, and treating him to his favorite ministrations in the bedroom even more frequently than usual. None of it seemed to help but she kept trying, figuring that maybe he would be even more miserable if she didn't.

*****

As Patrick's first birthday approached, Shelley could see the hope in David that maybe Alexandra would show up. It was kind of an unspoken thing that they *all* hoped she would. They planned a small party with just family, a few of the kids' closest friends, and Patrick's one little friend, Annabelle, whom he played with during his outings at the park with Michael.

It was the easiest party she ever threw. Rose took Patrick to the party store and came home with a slew of Thomas the Train decorations complete with plates, cups, party hats and the like. She even found a Thomas the Train bandana for Tiny to wear. Grace and her friend Cassie made a chocolate cake with blue frosting, train decorations, and a big, yellow number one. Russell, who was not very baby-oriented, did his part by going to the supermarket and hauling in all the sodas, juice, water bottles, and bags of ice.

Michael and Shelley did the decorating; he was tall enough to hang even the highest streamers without needing a stepladder. She cleaned the house a bit but not too much, having finally learned after forty-seven years of experience to save her energy for the after-party cleanup.

David spent the morning giving Patrick his bath and getting him dressed into his comfy Thomas the Train jumper. Noticing that David kept looking out the windows and front door, surely hoping Alexandra would show up, Shelley slipped her arms around him and reminded him how loved he was, but it didn't make a difference. He shrugged her off and went to check the mailbox *again*, obviously wishing there would at least be a card.

At four o'clock sharp (the party was after nap time), the guests began to arrive. Russell had invited his "summer girlfriend," Rose's friend from work came, and of course Cassie, Grace's best friend was there. Shelley had invited Claire and Brian hoping that it would be worth it for her to have to put up with Claire if there was any possibility that Brian could cheer up or at least distract David.

At ten after four, Michael bolted out to the driveway and came back carrying a living doll. Little Annabelle and her mom Lanie had arrived and Michael became more animated than any of them had ever seen him. Shelley smiled as she watched him introduce them to the family as if royalty had just arrived at their home. Annabelle, in her frilly yellow dress with white ruffles, alternated between smiling widely and burying her face in Michael's shoulder with a familiarity that seemed unusual for a baby who just arrived at a party full of strangers. Lanie, apparently confident with Annabelle in Michael's arms, stood by his side and greeted everyone politely.

Both mother and daughter had blonde hair with soft waves and bright green eyes that shone in happy comfort. Lanie, svelte in a way that only the rare twenty-something mom could pull off, had curves in all the right places, while Annabelle, plump as a little cherub, had the roly-poly look of a healthy toddler whose cheeks begged to be pinched.

Obviously there was more to Michael and Patrick's daily playground outings than had met the eye.

154

*****

The party was a huge success. Patrick received all sorts of gifts, ranging from Little People to big, chunky puzzles to adorable outfits. By seven o'clock, he and Annabelle were grimy and sticky and happily exhausted, a perfect day in the lives of one-year-olds. Even Claire was bearable, having braced herself for the baby party by adorning herself in what she considered play clothes: designer jeans and a jersey cotton Prada blouse, telling everyone that she didn't normally dress that way but had to "adapt to the occasion."

After the guests left and Patrick was tucked in, the older kids called David and Shelley into the living room for a family meeting. Thinking that this was strange and hoping there was no bad news coming to ruin the day, they sat on the loveseat as instructed.

Rose and Grace held court, standing in front of the television, trying not to step on all the toys that were still strewn across the floor.

"We have something to tell you," Grace announced with a sneaky smirk on her face. "Even though it's Patrick's birthday, we all chipped in to get a present for you guys."

Rose took her hand from behind her back to reveal an envelope.

"A present for us?" Shelley asked. "Wow. That's really nice. To what do we owe this honor?"

"We just feel like you guys have been doing so much and so much has been going on, the four of us decided to get you this." Rose handed David the envelope.

"Yeah, we figured after all the years of us torturing you…" Russell joked.

With a confused smile, David ran his thumb under the thick, cream-colored flap and pulled it open. He slid out the paper and Shelley looked over his shoulder to see what it was. It was a homemade gift certificate with a picture of a mountain lodge and a poem.

> *"It's time for you to go, go, go…*
> *and you cannot say no, no, no.*
> *Your room is all paid, including wine and beer…*
> *and we will take care of everything here.*
> *So go and have fun, relax and sleep late…*

all weekend long it will be a special date."

Shelley was speechless and when she looked at David she saw that he had tears in his eyes. Michael piped in, "It's a bed and breakfast in Boone and it's supposed to be really nice!"

Finding her voice but still hearing it break, Shelley said, "I'm sure it will be. This is really over the top you guys! I know this had to be expensive!"

"Well, with four of us it wasn't bad," Russell said, in his new man-voice.

David cleared his throat, but it still wasn't enough to prevent his emotions causing a little crack. "This is very nice and I'm very proud of you all. Thank you."

*****

That night when David and Shelley made love, it was with an atmosphere she'd never experienced with him before. With more physical release than emotional connection, she could feel his anger and disappointment as he pumped into her with a force that would have been a turn on if not for the negativity emanating from him. Disappointed that he wasn't able to set aside his distress over Alexandra, she participated with as much enthusiasm as she could muster, then held him in her arms until he fell asleep, pretending not to notice that he was crying.

Chapter 26

Their weekend in Boone began fantastically but lost its momentum rather quickly. Or, it might be more accurate to say that it came to a screeching halt. Two screeching halts… followed by a flaming wreck.

After saying goodbye to the kids—who, miraculously, had organized their schedules on their own so that someone was always available for Patrick—the couple hit the road nice and early, stopping only for gas and fresh coffee on the way up. It was a sparkling summer day, one of those that reminds you of where the phrase "Carolina Blue Skies" comes from, and as the car rose into the mountains, the lush, green foliage became thicker and thicker, the air offering a crispness that made you feel fresh, inside and out.

The bed and breakfast was nice enough, with clean sheets on the full-sized bed in their tiny room, and a charming claw-footed tub in the bathroom they shared with three other guest rooms. Relieved that the kids hadn't spent as much as they'd anticipated, they enjoyed the accommodations for what they were: a really nice gift arranged by their children.

Having arrived just before lunchtime, they chose to have it delivered to their room, where they ate the little tea sandwiches and chocolate-dipped strawberries on their bed while looking out the window at the view of the rolling hills. They chatted about what they were going to do the rest of the weekend, looking through the brochures that included options such as climbing Grandfather Mountain, driving the Blue Ridge Parkway, visiting a local winery, and other tourist attractions. After narrowing down the choices, they took a nap, and then headed out in the early evening to walk the downtown area in Boone, which was about three blocks long and mainly consisted of bars filled with college kids.

A few drinks and a nice dinner at a steakhouse later, they strolled back to their room holding hands. Shelley had planned ahead by ordering a bottle of wine and leaving it to chill in an ice bucket while they were out. David was looking considerably more relaxed than of late, and she felt the pleasant hum of having enjoyed a relaxing evening beside her best friend.

They chatted about their plans for the next day, about how they were going to head to Blowing Rock, the next town over, where they could visit the Bob Timberlake Art Gallery, a wine shop, do some antique browsing, and the like. Stepping into the bathroom, Shelley locked the other three doors but only closed their door partway so they could still chat while she slipped into something more comfortable.

David was talking about the historic town square as she slid her nightie over her head. A chocolate brown silk with elegant cream lace trim, she knew it was his favorite, sure to get a "rise" out of him any time she wore it. This was a no-holds-barred attempt to cheer him up and she'd done her best to think of every detail.

Quickly unlocking the other three doors, then making a run for it into their room, she giggled as she charged toward David, fully expecting him to be smiling just as she'd heard in his voice moments earlier. Which is why she was so taken aback when his face dropped into a sad expression the minute he saw her.

"What's the matter?"

"Nothing."

"Do I have something on me?" she asked nervously. "Like a stain or something?" She walked over to the small mirror on the back of their room door but didn't see anything wrong. Her hair was fine, pinned up with a few tendrils coming down in a kind of sexy way. She looked fresh and clean—no toothpaste on her lingerie—she even noted that her nipples were hard, creating quite a fetching image if she might say so herself.

"No. Nothing. You look great."

Walking back over to where he was sitting on the bed she said, "So what's wrong?"

He just shook his head and looked sadder than she'd ever seen him.

"Babe, talk to me. What happened? We were just chatting and now you look so sad!"

"I just can't do this. I can't do this anymore." He continued to shake his head.

"Can't do what? What's wrong?"

"I want a divorce."

*****

"A divorce! What are you talking about?" Appalled, she knew she had to have heard wrong.

"I just can't do this anymore."

"Do what anymore? Are you telling me you've been secretly unhappy in our marriage?"

"I can't take all the stress. It's too much." He continued to shake his head.

"And you think the stress is going to go away by divorcing me? The stress has been coming from the kids, David, not from me!"

"I'm really tired. I'm going to sleep." He went to his side of the bed, took off his shirt and jeans, and got under the covers.

"Going to sleep!" She could hear the hysteria in her voice. "You can't just say something like that and then turn over and go to sleep!"

"Yes I can."

"No, you can't!" She walked over and perched on the edge of the bed next to him, noting that he didn't scooch over like he normally would.

Trying to calm her shaking voice and sound soothing she said, "Babe, I know you're under a lot of stress. We both are. But surely you don't actually want to get divorced?"

"It's all I ever think about."

"All you ever think about?" She was utterly stupefied. "David, we don't even fight! I thought we were happy. Just a few minutes ago we were out to dinner and holding hands!"

"I know."

"You can't possibly mean this. Are you having a nervous breakdown or something?"

He sighed heavily, as if she were an annoying toddler who kept asking Why.

"I just want to go to sleep, Shelley. Good night."

"David, our marriage has been like a dream come true for both of us. We have the best relationship I could imagine! Surely you don't think you're going to hit me with something like this and then just roll over and go to sleep?"

He sighed again and pulled the blanket further up to his neck.

"Are you having an affair?"

"No."

"Well then what is it? I don't understand!"

"We can talk about it tomorrow. I just want to go to sleep now. Leave me alone."

All at once her adrenaline surged so that she felt tingly in her arms and legs. Her throat thickened and tears streamed out of her like a faucet had been turned on. She simply couldn't fathom any of this. Not that he wanted a divorce. Not that he would spring this on her and then go to sleep. None of it.

"You're hurting me so much David," she sobbed. "How can you be like this?"

He just ignored her.

Hating the pathetic whine in her voice and the snot bubbling from her nose, she kept at it for a while, thinking that this was not the man she'd been married to for more than ten years and that there must be some logical explanation for this. What that could possibly be, she had no idea, but this… situation, was completely beyond the sphere of reality.

David shot up into a sitting position and roared at the top of his lungs, "Shelley! Just leave me the fuck alone so I can go to sleep!"

"Do you hear yourself? Why are you talking to me like this? What the hell is going on here?" she ranted.

There was a knock at the door and a stern masculine voice, "Is everything okay in there?" It was Thad, the owner of the bed and breakfast.

Shelley went to the door and cracked it open. "Yes, we're fine. I'm sorry, we'll be sure to quiet down."

She could see the pity in his eyes as he said, "Are you okay, ma'am? Just want to make sure everyone is safe and sound?"

Greeat. Now we have the hosts thinking my husband must beat me or something.

"We're fine. I'm sorry for the outburst. Just a little lover's quarrel is all."

"Okay then. Good night."

"Thank you," she said, closing the door gently.

"See? Look what you did," David said. "Now you've disturbed everyone."

"I've disturbed everyone!" she whispered angrily. "You're the one screaming your head off and acting like an alien!"

"Are you happy now? You've kept me up *and* made a scene. I'm going to sleep."

Frustrated beyond measure, confused like she'd never been before, her heart breaking and her mind racing, she knew there was no point in trying to continue with this tonight. "Fine David. If you're able to go to sleep, have at it."

He didn't say anything. Just hunkered down in the bed and was snoring within minutes.

Shelley spent the night pacing the room like a caged animal, alternately screaming into a pillow, reminding herself to breathe, and having dry heaves in the bathroom. The thought of getting into the bed with David was unimaginable. Plus, she wasn't the least bit tired, and there was simply nowhere else to go in the tiny little room. She thought she was going to go insane.

Finally, her throat raw and her stomach sore from heaving, she lay on the very edge of the small bed as far away from David as possible. The last thing she remembered was noticing that the sun was coming up and that it would probably be beautiful if her life wasn't coming to an end.

*****

Shelley woke to the sound of David opening the door to receive room service. He'd ordered coffee and muffins like they always did on vacation, and he was already showered and fully dressed.

Disoriented for a moment, she experienced a surge of pleasure at the sight of him, then became consumed with anger as the night before came rushing into her consciousness.

"I ordered coffee," he said unnecessarily.

"I see."

"Do you want some?"

"Sure." No matter how angry she was, yes she did want coffee. She always wanted coffee.

She watched him fix her mug exactly the way she liked it. The way only the person who knows you better than anyone can fix your coffee and get it just right.

Taking the steaming mug from his hands, she said "Thanks."

He sat on the end of the bed and was rifling through the brochures of the things they'd planned on doing that day, while she sat there staring at him as if he were a zoo animal. Rage surged through her veins as she fought the urge to toss the coffee at him, scream, and rip at his hair. Gone was the sniveling mess she'd been the night before, replaced by the "old her"… the one who didn't put up with any shit from any guy and was happy to show him the door if that was the way it needed to be.

"Too bad we won't get to do any of that stuff," she snarled.

"Actually I was thinking that as long as we're here we might as well go," he said.

"Were we both in this same room last night?" she said in disbelief. "Because last I heard, people in the middle of a divorce don't generally go antiquing and art gallery browsing together."

"I was hoping we'd just make the best of it."

"So you meant what you said last night? That you actually want a divorce? Out of the clear blue sky?"

"Can't we just have a nice day and talk about this later?"

"Uh, no! I'm pretty sure there's no way I'm having a nice day after last night!"

He sighed deeply, as if she were the difficult one.

David had always been perfect for her. Back when they'd first started dating it was immediately apparent that—for both of them—this was a relationship like no other. In those days they'd both had a hard time letting go of the armor we all wear in relationships, and they'd worked hard to set aside those protective habits, to trust one another fully; to allow the other to see their vulnerability, the depth of their love.

This morning, she felt heavily iron-coated, unable and unwilling to let him see that side of her. Reminding herself that this was David, that it was too late to hide how much she loved him, she forced herself to try and communicate with him rationally.

"Did you mean what you said last night?"

He just looked at her, a strange expression on his face as his jaw pulsed and his eyes flickered away from hers.

"The cat is out of the bag, David. If you did mean it I need to know and if you didn't, I need to know what in the world would make you say that."

"I did mean it."

162

Thinking that surely that was impossible, she said, "Do you remember what you said? Are you telling me you really meant it when you said that you want a divorce?" She'd spent the night trying to think of how much he'd had to drink and kept coming up with a blank. Sure, they'd had a few cocktails, but by no means were they drunk or wasted. And truthfully, even if they had been, it still wouldn't explain him saying that.

He shook his head sadly. "Yes, I did mean it. I didn't mean to say anything so early in the trip, but it just slipped out."

"So you *planned* this? That you were, what, going to tell me on the drive home or something, after a weekend of fun and sex?"

"I really don't want to spend the day going over and over this. The kids saved up their money to buy us this trip and I just want to try and have a nice weekend."

"A nice weekend," she parroted. *He wants to have a nice weekend.*

"Yes. I'd like to make the best of it."

"I am having a hard time seeing any way of making the best of it," she said, hearing defeat in her tone.

He picked up a brochure. "I was thinking that we'd drive into Blowing Rock and start at the south end of the main street and work our way up."

*****

Not knowing what else to do, and frankly concerned that maybe David was having some kind of a mental breakdown and she should take him to a hospital, Shelley went through the day in a surreal daze, amazed at how he could behave so normally when the worst crisis of their life was at hand.

She tried to go with the flow, but her head was a swirling typhoon. When he reached out to hold her hand while they were walking, her mind was filled with conflict: *Should I let him hold my hand? Maybe he really didn't mean it. Whether he meant it or not, I still don't want to hold his hand. Maybe I should let him; what if he is having a nervous breakdown? What if he's not? He'd better be! No, no, I don't want that either!*

Suppressing the bile that was threatening at the base of her throat all day, she watched, stunned, when he excitedly purchased a print she'd always wanted from the Bob Timberlake Gallery. She was rendered mute when they went to a wine tasting and he chatted amiably with the host about how they'd tasted wine with a similar bouquet during a trip to Napa Valley years before.

Seemingly relaxed as though they were on a normal vacation and the night before had never happened, he collected menus from various restaurants throughout the day, then selected a romantic one for dinner, where he ordered an expensive bottle of wine and made suggestions about the choices on the menu that were her favorites.

Filled with an anxiety that left her unable to function properly, she let him order for both of them and watched as he smelled the cork. Once the waiter left, their wine bottle opened and sitting in an elegant silver stand filled with ice, she took a sip of her wine and choked out one word. "David?"

His smile fell with disappointment. Apparently he'd been enjoying himself and now she was ruining it.

"Did you mean it?"

"I don't know, Shelley, but I really don't want to talk about it now," he said, with dismissive finality.

Her phone vibrated in her pocket and when she took it out she saw that it was from their home number. The kids calling. Not wanting to answer it in the restaurant, she clicked "ignore," and figured she'd go into the ladies' room and call them back in a few minutes.

Within seconds, it vibrated again, signaling a voice mail. Then again with a text message. And another, and another. Alarmed, she excused herself and, seeing a line outside the ladies' room, went out the front door of the restaurant to return the call.

Swiping her phone, she viewed the message summary.

Grace: Where are you? Call!

Rose: 911! Emergency! Call home!

Missed call: Russell Cell.

Not bothering to listen to the voice mail, she immediately called the house and Rose answered on the first ring.

"Mom!"

"What happened? What's going on?"

"Alexandra showed up and we didn't know what to do! And we called the police but they said there's nothing they can do, and..." she could hear the other kids shouting in the background, "Tell her this, tell her that."

"Okay. Calm down and tell me exactly what happened. Is Patrick okay? Tell me what happened."

"Okay, okay. Everyone be quiet!" Rose shouted. The background noise stopped and Shelley heard her take a deep breath.

"We were eating dinner and Alexandra showed up. She just walked into the house with the key and was just suddenly there! And she was like, all skinny and stuff, and she said she was here to pick up her son!"

Shelley's heart plummeted into her stomach. "Go on," she encouraged.

"So we told her that she can't just walk in here and take him after being gone for so long. And she started screaming, like all crazy, and her eyes were all big, and she said it's her son and we can't stop her. So Russell called the police and they came over, but they said that because she's over eighteen and Patrick is her son, there's nothing they can do to stop her."

"Did she seem like she was on drugs? I can't believe the police would think that's okay.

"That's what we said, but they said that she's 'coherent,' and there's nothing they can do. And that we could get in trouble if we don't let her have her son!"

Unbelievable! "Then what happened?"

"Well, Patrick was crying and she went in the kitchen and took some of those big black garbage bags and said she was taking their stuff! And she went upstairs and filled them up…"

"Tell her I went upstairs and watched her!" Russell yelled in the background.

"And Russell watched her and she took mostly her clothes and stuff, and hardly anything for Patrick. And then she took a bunch of shampoo and stuff from the bathroom, and all of his baby snacks from the kitchen."

A group of people came out of the restaurant, laughing and talking. Shelley covered one ear with her finger and moved over to the side.

"And then Michael was asking her where they were going and she said it was none of our business! She was screaming and yelling about how you guys turned her phone off and that you don't deserve to know anything about her!"

"How did she leave with all that stuff?" Shelley asked.

"Her boyfriend was outside with a friend who had a truck. She brought all the bags out and threw them in the back, and then when she took Patrick, he was crying and clinging to Michael. She was being so scary!" Rose was sobbing now, barely able to get the words out.

"And that was it? They just left?" Terror pulsed through her at the thought that she'd taken Patrick and they had no idea where they went.

Hysterically, Rose went on. "Yes, they left, but Michael followed them so he can try to find out where they're going. He hasn't called yet or anything. And they didn't even have a car seat, so we tried to get the police to stop them because of that but then she said that it was *her* car seat in Michael's car and the police made him give it to her! And then they took a report just for records but said they can't interfere with her taking her own child, and that if we felt he was in danger we would need to file a report with Child Services."

The other kids were shouting in the background again, trying to fill in with more details, but Shelley had heard enough, and poor Rose was understandably distraught. "Sweetie, it sounds like you guys did the best you could. There's nothing we can do right now this minute, so just try to calm down. If Michael calls with any info, let me know. David and I will head home and be there in about five hours."

Rose cleared her throat and Shelley could tell she was trying to be brave. "You did a great job, sweetie. You did everything you could."

"I know, but still," Rose sniffled.

"Let me talk to Russell a minute."

"Hello?" Shelley was stricken by how his pitch was exactly the same as his dad's.

"Russell, can you text me the police report number and the phone number?"

"Sure. I have it right here."

"It sounds like you all did the best you could. I'm proud of you."

"Thanks."

"Okay, we'll see you in a few hours."

*****

Dread pulled at her stomach as Shelley stood outside the restaurant knowing that she was going to have to return to the table and relay this news to David. Other diners who were finished with their meals trickled past her, their laughter seeming incongruous at a time like this.

Taking a deep breath, she pulled the door open and walked to the table where she saw that David looked annoyed, as their food had been delivered and was sitting there getting cold. Irritated at having to deal with even the look on his face, Shelley felt unreasonably angry at the waiter for having brought it when she was not seated in the first place.

She sat down and averted her eyes, wondering how she should start. Deciding on a straightforward approach she said, "That was the kids. We're going to need to head back now."

He dropped his fork angrily, its metallic clatter seeming very loud in the refined restaurant. "Why? What's going on?"

Thinking it was strange that he'd react with anger rather than concern, she filled him in on what had happened. As she told the story, she watched the color drain from his face, back to the pallor it had over the last month.

"Michael is following them and I told the kids to call if they find anything out," she said, rising to stand next to the table and grabbing her purse as she signaled for the waiter.

He just stared at her with a strange look of disbelief on his face. She understood; she couldn't believe the whole thing either.

She opened her purse, trying to find her wallet.

He was still staring at her.

"What?"

"What are you doing?"

"Getting ready to pay the bill," she said.

He just shook his head.

"Why? Did you want to stay here and eat?" She forced a businesslike tone to her voice, "You know, I've got to tell you David, I'm really losing patience with your attitude."

He made a disgusted sound, as if *she* were the one who had ruined their lives right when they needed to hold it together.

The waiter arrived at the table and Shelley asked for their check. Alarmed, he glanced at their untouched dinners and asked, "Was there a problem with your food?"

Accustomed to David assuming the more assertive role, she didn't say anything until she realized that David hadn't replied. She told the waiter that everything was fine, they had a family emergency, and she'd appreciate if he would just wrap the food to go and bring the check.

"Yes, ma'am."

Even though people had been doing it for years, she still hated being called ma'am. It made her feel so old—even though she was old enough that it made perfect sense. But still.

Actually, it would be safe to say that at that point she hated everything.

*****

The ride home was horrendous. Trying to be supportive—despite their marital crisis—Shelley took the wheel while David sat in the passenger seat, staring blindly out the window in a near stupor of stress.

Trees flew past them in a monotonous blur as she set the cruise control for just slightly over the speed limit. Her emotions fluctuated between being so angry at David that she had to fight the urge to scream and claw at his face, and being so heartbroken that her tears streamed freely as she drove. She felt strangely calm about the situation with Alexandra and Patrick; she knew Michael had followed them and it was out of their hands for the moment. But her marriage hung by a thread in the silent car with them, and so it consumed her.

In contrast, David was completely apathetic to her. Each time Shelley tried to talk to him, he refused, brushing her off rather the way someone would wave off an annoying fly, as if she was a horrible person for wanting to talk about their marriage when they had so much else going on. He saw that she was hysterically crying. He heard when she was occasionally unable to swallow a sob. He didn't care... his only concern was for Alexandra and Patrick.

A huge part of her agony was that this behavior was entirely uncharacteristic of David. Their relationship had been built on communication, both of them agreeing from the start that it was always better to address things as they came along—big or small—rather than to allow resentment to fester and kill the relationship over time. Yet there he was, refusing to communicate.

Has he been accumulating secret resentments and I've been coasting along unaware? Is it possible that he is having an affair? Have I been some sort of oblivious moron, thinking we have a fantastic marriage when secretly he thought it was terrible?

She drove along, analyzing and questioning every interaction with him. Sure, there had been a lot of stress in the household lately with all of the various kid scenarios. But they still talked, still made love. Still laughed together in the privacy of their bedroom to the extent that just the other day the kids were teasing them about how they must have their own personal stand-up comic in there.

She just couldn't grasp any of it and so with no other option, she continued to drive, managing the occasional phone call from the kids, and being completely shut out by David.

*****

When they arrived home the house was strangely silent and dark. No music was playing, no toys were strewn across the living room. Even Tiny seemed out of sorts, greeting them at the door somberly rather than like the goofball he normally was. Frick, looking like he just woke up, also hobbled to the door and Tiny gave him one of his giant, slobbery, head-to-tail licks, nearly knocking him over. So okay, at least something was normal.

"Hello?" Shelley shouted. "Where is everyone?"

"We're in bed," came Russell's voice from the living room. "It's late."

Oh yeah. All hopped up from anxiety, it felt like the middle of the day to her although in reality it was after midnight. Still early for everyone to be in bed, but considering the circumstances she couldn't blame them.

David carried their overnight bags in from the car and set them at the bottom of the stairs while she wandered into the kitchen and looked over the police report the kids had left on the counter. There was nothing new. Just as they'd said, it offered no solace whatsoever about Patrick's wellbeing or their ability to do anything about it.

She looked at David. David looked at her. She couldn't think of a thing to say and since he'd been ignoring her for several hours, apparently he couldn't either. She'd spoken to the kids numerous times during the drive home, had received the information from Michael about where he'd followed them to, and there was nothing additional that could be done at the moment.

Psychologically exhausted and emotionally defeated she said, "I guess I'll just say goodnight to everyone and go to bed."

David nodded and walked toward the stairs.

*****

The room was pitch dark and Shelley was in one of those exhausted sleeps where you feel heavy and sore, as though you'd been run over by a truck, when she felt David's hand shaking her arm.

"Shell?" she thought she heard his voice. "Shell?"

Becoming coherent, her first thought was a surge of relief that he finally wanted to talk. Even if he *was* waking her up in the middle of the night to do it. Stranger things have happened, as she'd learned over the past twenty-four hours.

"I'm up."

"I think…" his voice sounded thready. "I'm having a heart attack."

Chapter 27

The next morning, the sun filtered into David's hospital room through blinds so dusty that Shelley wondered how they could be in a hospital.

She stood to stretch, her back and neck aching from spending the night sitting up in a recliner (*why do they call them recliners even when they don't recline?*). Trying to be quiet, she tiptoed into the bathroom, peed, and splashed some water on her face. After patting it dry with a paper towel, she glanced into the little mirror above the sink and did a double take: she'd never looked so crappy in her entire life. Literally.

Her hair looked like it hadn't been washed in days (which it hadn't), and she had dark circles under her eyes that looked as if she'd been swimming and rubbing her eyes while wearing non-waterproof mascara. Wrinkles showed in places she never even knew she had them, and her nose was red and chapped from crying so much over the past two days.

Carefully twisting the doorknob so it wouldn't make a sound, she stole past David's bed and out to the hallway to try and hunt down some coffee. New nurses were at the station, but they pointed her in the direction of the family lounge, where there was free coffee that was—once she overlooked the powdered creamer—not as terrible as she'd expected it to be.

Debating whether she should get some for David too, she slipped into what had become her new normal—namely, questioning every miniscule detail of every single thing before deciding. It was not pretty. *Should I bring him coffee? I'm sure he would like coffee. But are you supposed to bring coffee to a heart patient? Wait, he's not a heart patient! What if there's some other reason the doctors don't want him to have it? Yet they didn't say he couldn't. But I didn't ask. Fuck it, he's a dick, I don't want to bring him coffee anyway. Stop it! How terrible! I do love him, I'm just mad. But how can I be mad at a time like this?!*

Ugh. Deciding that she could always come back for another coffee, she returned to his room, stopping every few feet to take a sip of the scalding liquid. As she entered, she saw that the side lamp was on and David was sitting up in bed. She stopped in her tracks and a little coffee sloshed onto her hand, burning.

"Good morning, Sweet Shelley Bean," he said pleasantly.

What the?...

"Good morning. How are you feeling?"

"Much better," he said, and she noticed a blush of embarrassment creeping up into his cheeks.

"I'm glad."

She walked into the room and set her coffee on the side table. Not knowing what else to say, she stuck with logistics. "The nurses said the doctor is doing rounds and will be stopping by in a few minutes."

"Oh. Okay. Good."

"Would you like some water or something?"

"Yes, please. Water would be great, thank you."

Knowing that both of them felt the awkwardness of their overly polite exchange, she poured a cup of water from the pitcher next to the bed and handed it to him.

"Thanks, babe."

"You're welcome."

Shelley looked at him a moment, knowing that her eyes were questioning but not wanting to ask what they both knew had been consuming her since he'd said the words: *Does he really not love me anymore and want a divorce?* Yet she felt that to push the discussion now was inappropriate, given that he'd been rushed to the hospital the night before, thinking he was having a heart attack.

Feeling her throat tighten and her now ever-present tears begin to well up, she turned away and started tittering around the room. She straightened the little pile of brochures about stress management, folded David's shirt that was draped over the chair, and then, not knowing what else to do, she sat down and started sifting through her handbag as if she were looking for something.

Humiliation surged through her, bringing an unaccustomed heat to her veins. Before David, she'd always been very strong in relationships; probably too strong. She'd been married before and had two other long-term relationships. There were men she'd loved. Deeply. Yet she'd never felt like this in any of those relationships.

Maybe it was because whenever a previous love had come to an end, it was by mutual decision. Situations where the relationship had gone bad, they'd tried everything to work things out, and she was able to end things knowing in her heart of hearts that it was the right thing to do. Which was *so* not the case now.

She felt foolish and abandoned. She'd thought David was her best friend, that their marriage was as close to perfect as a couple could get. They never fought and rarely even argued or disagreed. They made love. A lot. They talked a lot. They dated one another—even if at home with snacks and wine in the bedroom—a lot. Or at least a lot more than any other couple she knew of.

Unlike most of their friends, they didn't jab at one another or participate in the standard jokes people make about wives being shrews and husbands being lazy. They complimented one another regularly and meant it. They each appreciated every considerate thing the other did, and had always been conscious to express that appreciation rather than to assume the other knew.

It was as if she'd been meandering along in a serene field of wildflowers, and was suddenly flattened by an eighteen-wheeler that just appeared out of nowhere.

Shelley could feel David watching her, and when she stole a glance, she recognized a look of pity on his face that she'd only ever seen on him when they visited the animal shelter and felt heartbroken that they couldn't adopt all of the animals. It made her feel disgusting. Dirty somehow, and not herself.

Just as she was fluctuating between humiliation and anger, Dr. Rajan breezed into the room.

"Good morning, Mr. Morsony! And how are we feeling today?" she asked, picking up the clipboard that was mounted to the wall and looking over his information.

"Much better, thanks," David said.

"Your vitals are looking very good here," she said, in the perfectly annunciated English of a person for whom it's their second language, her Indian accent barely detectable. "If you are feeling up to it, you may go home today."

"Okay."

"How about you, Mrs. Morsony? How did you manage throughout the night here?"

"I'm fine, thank you."

"Oh my, you look worse than my patient!" she joked upon noticing Shelley's ragged, tear-streaked appearance. "You do remember that he is not dying, true?"

"Yes." Mortified, Shelley attempted to blot under her eyes with the already balled-up tissue she'd been holding.

Dr. Rajan turned to David, who was blushing red as a beet.

"I know that you may be feeling embarrassed, but really there is no need," she said. "Panic attacks are very serious and are often mistaken for heart attacks. It is always better to be safe than to be sorry."

He nodded.

"The good news is, we have done all of your testing and your heart is as healthy as can be." She whipped a pen out of her lab jacket pocket. "Before I set up your discharge papers, I need to ask you some questions. Would you like your wife to be present or do you prefer privacy?"

Shelley leapt out of her seat, not wanting to interfere if David wanted to speak with the doctor alone.

"No, she can stay," he said to the doctor. Then he put his hand on her arm and squeezed, "Please stay, Shelley Bean."

"Um, okay." She stood beside the bed.

"Wonderful, let us begin then."

The doctor rattled through a series of questions that you might expect if you'd been rushed to the hospital in an ambulance for an anxiety attack: Have you ever attempted suicide? Have you ever thought of suicide? Had unexpected bursts of anger? Incidences of domestic violence? And so on.

David answered calmly with a series of "No" responses, and he reached over to place his hand on Shelley's, stroking the back of her hand with his thumb, speaking to her silently, asking her not to say what he knew was on her mind: *Yes, he is crazy! He just revealed that he secretly wants a divorce! He probably needs a lobotomy!*

Shelley pulled her hand away angrily but did suppress her urge to shout that at the doctor, and before she knew it she was snapped out of her private ruminating by Dr. Rajan saying, "Mrs. Morsony?"

"I'm sorry, what did you say?"

"I was just explaining to your husband that I have prescribed two medications. One is for anxiety, which should be extremely helpful but will take about three weeks before it is fully effective. In the interim, he

174

may also take the Diazepam as prescribed to manage feelings of panic. I am also recommending counseling and I have written a few names of recommended psychiatrists whom I have worked with." She handed Shelley the papers.

"Okay, thank you."

"You will see to it that he follows up with my recommended treatment?"

"Yes, of course."

"Well then, I am off to see other patients!" She signed his chart and put it back in the holder on the wall, then started walking toward the door. Calling over her shoulder, her dark ponytail swinging as she turned, she laughed before she started her own joke: "I am glad you are not dying, Mr. Morsony!"

Hilarious. Absolutely hilarious.

Chapter 28

Time went on like it always does… at warp speed. For everyone but Shelley, that is. She felt like a slug, observing it all from a bed of mud in the yard.

The house was filled with people at all times, living in every nook and cranny, lending an atmosphere of being at sleep-away camp, complete with air mattresses, stuff everywhere, and clothes drying over the rail of the front porch.

She recognized that she should be experiencing a certain kind of joy that summer; celebrating life through the eyes of her four kids. Who, after all the trials and tribulations of growing up, were developing into respectable young adults who had their whole lives ahead of them and every opportunity to relish it. Sure, there were a few spats here and there—mostly due to the close quarters and insufficient number of bathrooms—but overall, they were just doing their thing. Zipping through their days like hummingbirds visiting one succulent flower after another.

Rose was making all of her plans for her trip to Europe, practicing with her language books and getting to know her hosts through Skype. Like extended family, everyone recognized one another when they saw them on her monitor and they would wave and shout "hello" as they passed through. That is, everyone else would wave and shout hello. Shelley mostly just wiggled her fingers as she shuffled along on her way to force herself through another chore.

Not that she was doing many chores. It seemed that she'd arrived—for the first time in her life—at a place where she didn't care about anything. She didn't care that if you walked around barefoot you could feel that the floors were both sticky and gritty. She didn't care that there was always a mountain of shoes strewn by the front door; the very same shoes she'd vowed to set up a system for just weeks before. Laundry was done to the bare minimum and she ordered dinners that were delivered in grease-stained boxes more frequently than she had even when she was a single gal, back in her twenties herself.

David, after keeping up with his "I want a divorce and it's all I ever think about" syndrome for three weeks, had come home one day from his session with his new therapist and said, "I'm sorry. I didn't mean it."

"You didn't mean it," she repeated, not feeling the slightest bit better as a result of him having said this.

"No, I didn't," he said. "I do love you and I do want to be married to you."

"Then why would you say you didn't?"

"I don't know. Sometimes when I'm upset I say things I don't mean." He stated this as though it were perfectly reasonable.

Shelley was glad that at a minimum, she at least had the presence of mind to argue this point. "Saying something you don't mean, to me, is when you say something in the heat of the moment. Like in the middle of a big argument." This was not entirely truthful, as they both knew that she didn't ever say things she didn't mean—not even in the heat of the moment, and certainly not something as serious as threatening a divorce.

"Well this was different."

"Yes, it was different David. It was different because it wasn't said in the heat of the moment… it was said perfectly calmly while we were in the middle of a romantic getaway. It's different because you maintained—for three weeks!—that yes, in fact, you did mean it, and that it's 'all you ever think about!'"

"Look, I said I'm sorry. It was a mistake and I didn't mean it."

"Wow, you really sound sincere." Her tone was so dull that she sounded more pathetic than sarcastic. Which she really didn't care about anymore. Just like everything else.

He sighed and said that he was going for a drive. Which meant that he was going to ride past Alexandra's house to see if he could get a glimpse of her and Patrick. Again.

*****

When David said, "Alexandra's house," he meant Tyler's rickety old singlewide in a trailer park on the not-so-nice side of town. David had been driving past it on what he admitted was a several-times-per-week basis, although it was probably more. He had gathered that there appeared to be at least four different men living there, if you were to go by the number of trucks repeatedly seen in the driveway. Er, gravel pit.

He'd never seen a toy in the yard, a stroller propped up outside, or any sign that a toddler lived in the house. Patrick's car seat was still mounted in Tyler's friend's truck, and one time, David had gotten out and rung the doorbell. A man had answered—scruffy looking, with a long beard, no shirt, and dirt on his chest—and said that Alexandra wasn't home. When he asked about Patrick, the guy scratched his belly thoughtfully and said, "The kid? Nah. He goes wherever she goes." David wasn't sure whether this made him feel better or worse.

He had also gotten rather friendly with the police. Uncharacteristically, he'd taken to stopping in to the precinct once or twice a week to inquire as to what could be done, apparently hoping for a different answer. It had gotten to the point where he didn't ask anymore, but did stop in and have coffee with a few of the cops he'd become friendly with, one of whom was Joe Slade, the officer that had come to the house when the kids had called.

He felt like a private investigator. An *incompetent* private investigator who couldn't find any answers, that is. It seemed that everywhere he turned, he was losing. Losing Alexandra to drugs. Losing Patrick to Alexandra. Losing Shelley to his own stupidity. Losing the older kids by simple virtue of them growing up, which he'd thought he was fine with until the gain and loss of Alexandra and Patrick happened.

He couldn't shake the feeling of being an utter failure; inept in every area of family life and just barely holding it together as a provider, with all of the increased expenses lately. Even the dream vacation they'd planned for years was off the table, and although Shelley *seemed* to be perfectly okay with it—and in fact it was her idea to call it off—he couldn't help feeling inadequate.

David wore his anxiety like a bulletproof vest. Strong, heavy, protective. Sometimes it worked as a shield to protect his subconscious self from heartbreak: *"It can be hard to accept that someone loves you so much that they will stick by you through a time like this,"* his therapist postulated when he would lament about having pushed Shelley away.

At other times, his anxiety was what kept him going through the day, energizing him to work harder on projects at the firm, do more around the house in the evenings, try harder to get Shelley to believe in him again.

In yet other instances, it felt like a cinderblock weighing him down, making him both thankful and wistful that he wasn't in an actual river being dragged under and suffocating for real, rather than just in his emotions.

Chapter 29

Russell, Rose, and Grace spent the majority of their time working at their summer jobs and filled the rest of the hours with their varied social interests. Russell spoke of a different girlfriend every other week and appeared to be taking them to see every movie that passed through town. Grace, in that gap between high school and college, spent her free time meeting up with friends at Adventure Zone, mostly hanging around at the ice cream shop area where there was a guy she had a crush on, and sometimes playing a game of miniature golf or go karts.

Michael, on the other hand, was quite different than the previous summer when they'd been so concerned about him not doing any socializing. Except that his new favorite form of socializing brought its own worries... he was seemingly obsessed with Lanie and Annabelle, and spent every minute he wasn't at work either being with them, talking about them, or dreamily thinking of them.

David and Shelley liked Lanie. She owned her own home: a small, sensible ranch in a family-oriented neighborhood. She drove a responsible car, wore elegant clothing, and had a rising career as a real estate attorney. She was pleasant to be around, but although she was only two years older than Michael, she seemed much more mature—whether it was because of the demands of motherhood and her career, or the actual two-year age difference, they weren't really sure.

They were happy for Michael, as he seemed to be genuinely in love. Lanie too, obviously had strong feelings for him. It was Annabelle that concerned them: The little cherub had grown very attached to Michael, who, at only twenty-five, surely wasn't ready to settle down and become an instant family man.

*****

In any case, while the kids were all living their rich, fulfilling lives, and David continued in his preoccupation with Alexandra, Shelley trudged along in her own private, solitary existence. Just her, Tiny, and Frick. With no other friends she felt close enough to turn to, she turned to the pets for companionship.

If you could call it companionship. It would be more accurate to admit that she just couldn't stop crying over David, and didn't want to come out of the bedroom and have the kids see her with puffy eyes and a red nose all the time. She'd taken to staying in bed late into the mornings, curled up with Frick by her side, who, elderly as he was, didn't need any more action than that.

Once the coast was clear, with everyone gone either to work or to their various activities, she'd leave the bedroom and head downstairs, where she would relocate to the couch. Tiny would sit beside the sofa, his face at eye-level, and keep her company, his droopy eyes filled with concern. Shelley would stroke his silken ears and just cry and cry. Her head, nearly always filled with congestion about the same density as concrete, was constantly pounding, her nose and lips chapped from all the tissues.

Occasionally, she'd mentally smack herself, get up from the couch, and walk around the house, noticing all that needed to be done. Stacks of mail that needed to be dealt with. Plants that needed watering. No food in the pantry, the kids having taken to stopping off to buy bags of chips with their own money, knowing there wouldn't be any in the house… yet weirdly, never asking why.

Finally, around three o'clock each day, she'd wander up to the bedroom, turn on the water, and take a long, steamy shower, trying to clear her congestion. She'd do her hair and makeup to near-perfection, and put on one of her classy, pre-Patrick outfits, in an attempt to give the appearance that everything was normal.

It was not. It was definitely not normal at all.

*****

One afternoon, as she sat on the couch trying to actually *do* something— namely, at least flip through the television channels—the doorbell rang. Figuring that it must be the UPS guy since she wasn't expecting anyone, she didn't get up. Tiny ran to the door, barking and wiggling as usual.

The delivery man had a custom of leaving a treat for the neighborhood dogs whenever he brought a package (smart guy!) and Tiny loved him so much, he had even jumped into his truck one time when they were outside during the delivery.

A moment later, Tiny was still spinning and barking, and she heard the bell ring again. Resigning herself to the reality that she would have to go to the door in her ratty sweatpants with her hair like a nest and her face all red, she shuffled over to the foyer and pulled the door open.

There, standing on her porch, was Claire. Of all people! Beautifully turned out as always, she looked like a commercial for a more expensive version of the L.L. Bean catalog. She was holding a small shopping bag from *Le Pâtisserie*, an expensive French bakery, and smiling kindly in a way that seemed uncharacteristic of her.

Mortified, and unable to think of a thing to say, Shelley just stood there dumbly. Tiny, apparently having decided that he was just as overjoyed about Claire as he would have been about a dog treat, danced around them, one of his slime strings sticking to the leg of Shelley's sweats as he nudged her.

"Well, are you going to let me in?" Claire said, reaching for the screen door handle.

"Um, yeah. Sorry. Come on in."

Breezing through the foyer and pointedly ignoring the mess, Claire strode straight through the hall into the kitchen and began opening cabinets in search of plates and mugs. Speechless, Shelley just stood there and watched, unable to believe her eyes. She had never seen this woman so much as help clean up after a dinner party, never mind go through her cabinets and start setting out croissants.

Claire chattered on, ignoring her muteness. "I've brought some pastries too, and coffee. I didn't know how you like it so I just got American and had them give me all of the creamers and sweeteners on the side." She poured each of the coffees from their to-go containers into the mugs, then opened the cabinet under the sink and tossed the cups into the trash. Shelley couldn't believe Claire even knew where the trash was in her house.

"Oh, okay. Thanks." She self-consciously smoothed her hand over her hair, wincing at the understanding that nothing was going to cover up the condition she was in.

"Come. Let's sit." Claire brought the plates over to the kitchen table and set out the condiments as if they were at a hotel and she was the room service waitress.

Picking at a croissant, Claire asked about the kids and what they'd been doing. Pushing past her shock, Shelley heard herself answering listlessly, replying to the inquiries but without elucidating the way she normally would.

Claire nodded, although they both knew she was not really interested. There was an underlying sense that she was waiting for the opportunity to say something, and Shelley was mildly anxious to find out what it was. She didn't have to wait for long.

"Well, enough of this small talk!" Claire said, setting down her coffee mug with a clunk.

Diverting her eyes out the French doors that led to the screened porch, she continued, "I want to tell you about something. I don't know if it will help." She hesitated, straightening her spoon upon its napkin before revealing, "About five years ago, Brian had an affair."

Shelley tried not to gasp. *Brian?* He was so straight-laced, she couldn't imagine him being sexual *at all*, never mind running around cheating on his wife!

"It almost killed me," she went on. "I have never been so humiliated in my entire life. Not before and not since."

"Oh my God, Claire. I'm so sorry," Shelley said, meaning it.

"It was horrible. It was with a woman from his firm and they started fooling around whenever they were out of town on business trips."

"Oh my God!" *Jeez, Shelley, try and think of something else to say!*

"How did you find out?" she asked.

"That was the worst part. I mean, it would have been bad enough if he were simply having a sleazy affair. But it turned out to be much worse than that."

Shelley nodded, indicating that she was listening.

"The way I found out was that he sat me down one day to tell me that he was in love with her. That he still cared for me the way one cares for their favorite *Teddy bear* they've had since childhood, but that he was in love with her in an *exciting* kind of way."

Astonished, she just listened, feeling an ache deep in her chest even though it hadn't happened to her.

"He said he didn't want a divorce, that he would stay married to me, but that he thought I should know. He was *tired,* he said, of having to sneak around, and wanted my *blessing* so that he could be with her openly."

"He said that?!"

"Well, not in those exact words but that was the gist of it."

"What did you do? Did you confront her?"

"Shelley, I didn't know what to do. What would have been the point in confronting her? Was she going to say, 'Gee, you're right. Sorry, I'll stop fucking your husband now?'"

Shelley was a little taken aback by the fact that Claire, normally so proper, had just said "fuck."

"So what *did* you do?"

"I became depressed. I couldn't eat, I couldn't sleep. I cried so much that I became constipated from dehydration."

"Oh my God!"

"You might remember that there was one year when I wasn't involved in the annual golf tournament for the Women's Club?"

She nodded.

"That was the year."

"Oh," Shelley replied, filled with regret. "I didn't know. I thought you just needed a break after being the main coordinator for so many years."

"No one knew. I didn't tell anyone. I couldn't! I was so humiliated, I couldn't even bring myself to leave the house."

"Did Brian go around openly dating her?" The very notion was horrifying.

"No. Once he realized the enormity of how much he hurt me, he kept on with the affair for only a few more weeks, then ended it."

Shelley picked up her mug and took a sip, nodding that she should continue.

"He came to me and said he was sorry, that it was a mistake, that he loves me and was sorry to have done it."

Shelley was so angry with Brian, it was almost unreasonable. Okay, it actually *was* unreasonable, being that he wasn't her husband. But she could imagine Claire's pain—the abandonment and the trust that was destroyed when something like this occurred in a marriage. Kind of like how she felt toward David.

"It took me a really long time to get over it," Claire said. "And truthfully, there will always be a little part of me that will never feel exactly the same as I felt before."

Frick walked into the kitchen, a momentary distraction as he stood beside Shelley's chair, wanting to be picked up. She lifted him into her lap and felt his motorboat purring begin immediately.

"You're probably wondering why I'm telling you all of this," Claire said.

"Not really. I mean, come to think of it, yeah, now I am wondering why. But I guess I was so caught up in the story that no, I hadn't yet wondered why you were telling me."

"I'm telling you because I know that you must be going through the same thing." She paused. "Oh, maybe not the exact same circumstance," she said, waving her hand as if the difference were inconsequential, "but something serious must be going on with you and David."

Shelley just looked down at Frick, tears instantly springing to her eyes. Humiliation burned up her neck and into her cheeks at the realization that David must have told them; that people were talking about her and her pathetic situation behind her back.

"I'm not saying you have to tell me what's going on. Unless you want to, of course." She reached across the table and rested her hand gently on Shelley's arm. "The reason I told you is because I want to share with you how I got past it."

Shelley couldn't imagine getting past it. Not Claire and Brian. Not her and David. It was like the shifting of the plates of the earth after an earthquake… you could never close that jagged split and make everything whole again.

Picking up her napkin, she dabbed at her eyes and said, "How?"

"I realized that I had a choice: I could either hate him for the one extremely horrible thing he did, or I could love him for all of the many wonderful things he's always done."

A jolt went through her. This was a perspective that would never have occurred to her in the wildest stretch of her imagination.

Claire continued, "I looked at our marriage as a whole. We'd been together for eighteen years at the time. Eighteen years during which we were very happy. Both of us. And I thought, 'Am I willing to do without this man? To start my life over without him because of this one terrible incident?' For me, the answer was no."

"But you would have been okay," Shelley unnecessarily defended. "I mean, starting over is hard, but I'm sure you could have done it!"

"You're right. I could have. But in my heart of hearts, I didn't want to. I love Brian and I know that deep down, he loves me too."

"But it's just so horrible! I don't mean to sound like a troublemaker, Claire, but I don't know how I would ever feel comfortable again when he leaves the house. I'd always be wondering if he was cheating on me!"

"That's true. I have wondered. But in evaluating our entire marriage, including all of the ups and downs and things we've been through over the years, this was the one and only time he ever did anything other than make me feel loved and cherished. It was awful. It was disrespectful. But it was a mistake. And in the end, I decided that I needed to find a way to forgive him for the one bad thing rather than to disregard the years and years during which he was an ideal husband and my very best friend."

Shelley thought about it. Could she do that with David? Things had always been good between them. Not even just good. Stellar. Yet she didn't know how she could ever go through her daily life, wondering whether he was secretly staying with her only because he was an ethical man, or whether he really wanted to be there. Every time he told her he loves her, held her hand, made love to her. Would she ever be able to believe in his love again, deep in her soul the way she had before? Or would there always be doubt, a separateness, a part of her that could never fully believe again?

"I don't know if you're able to do this," Claire said. "Or even if you feel the whole rest of your marriage has been that great—unfortunately I don't know you as well as I'd like. But I hoped that if I shared this with you, that perhaps you wouldn't have to suffer quite as long as I did before coming to terms with things."

"What did David tell you?" Shelley asked, aching with embarrassment. She had visions of him going over to their house and asking for their help with his mess of a wife who couldn't just forget it and move on.

"David didn't tell me anything," she explained. "He and Brian went out for a beer one night last week and all he said was that he'd done something horrible, that you were miserable, and that he loves you so much but doesn't know how to make things right."

"He said this to Brian?" She tried to visualize two men out for a beer, having this openhearted confessional of a conversation. It seemed like a stretch.

"Brian said he seemed pretty desperate. I guess he figured there was nothing left to lose." She looked at her pointedly and went on, "Listen, Shelley, I'm not saying that what worked for me will definitely work for you. I just figured maybe it would help. That at the very least, hopefully you won't feel so alone, the way I did."

"Thank you, Claire." Shelley looked her in the eye, surprising herself as she realized that she hadn't made direct eye contact with anyone in... well, a very long time. Weeks. "It means a lot to me. I know it had to be hard for you to tell me all of this and I appreciate you putting yourself out there."

"You're welcome."

They both just sat there a moment, each engrossed in their own thoughts. Then Claire stood up from the table, brushed her hands together as if wiping them free of the emotionally charged conversation and said, "Now, let's get this place into shape!"

Chapter 30

Summer drew to a close and with it, the atmosphere around the house changed dramatically. After two trips to the airport—one to drop off Russell who was heading back to Colorado State and one to drop off Rose for her two months in Europe (Europe! Their little girl!), the volume of people, noise, and action in the house dropped like the silence after a tornado has passed through town.

Grace began classes at NC State and between school, work, and social engagements, she was almost never at home.

Michael, still living in the dining room, was always either holed up in there studying, or was at Lanie's house, where he'd taken to eating dinner almost every night. He often slept over, driving Annabelle to daycare so Lanie could have an extra half hour to herself in the morning. She'd gotten him a good job doing the billing for the law firm, with the additional benefit of being able to do the majority of his work from home.

With no word from Alexandra, David and Shelley suddenly found themselves with an abundance of free time that they'd never had before. The house was easier to maintain, and Patrick's toys had been stowed upstairs in what used to be his room, no longer spread out across their living room like a Fisher Price showcase.

David's busy season at work had ended, and they began having their coffee together in the mornings like they used to—sitting out on the screened porch watching the birds visit their feeders, still marveling at the miraculous tininess of each and every hummingbird, no matter how many times they saw them.

Things were more formal between them. More polite. She still carried an underlying sorrow, which they generally didn't speak of, although they both knew that it was there.

Shelley often dealt with a level of anger that David certainly wasn't aware of. She sometimes became so overcome with rage that, for days, the sight of him made her nauseous and the sound of his breathing made her want to scratch his eyes out. She found herself attracted to other men, regretting the fact that she'd gotten remarried and that now she was stuck with this man who may or may not love her like she'd believed he did.

In spite of what Claire had told her, she couldn't fathom how he could ruin the special thing they had. He'd damaged them permanently, and she knew in her heart that they may get past this, but their love would never be full, brimming, complete, quite the way it was before.

They had talked and talked about it, *ad nauseum*—over morning coffee, in bed at night, and once, together with his therapist. He always ruefully referred to it as "a mistake," justifying that he'd been under duress, that he was having an anxiety attack or a nervous breakdown. But to Shelley it felt like an "accident" that could have been entirely avoided with better judgment. Like if someone chose to run while carrying your favorite antique vase and broke it; they should never have taken such a risk with something so valuable in the first place.

She was trying, and so was he. She to get back to believing in their love, and he to show her in any way he could that it was true.

Shelley had taken Claire's advice to heart as though it were a mantra, although it was a lot easier to believe it intellectually than it was to put into practice emotionally. Yet what other option was there? She didn't want to let him go. She didn't want a different life. She wanted David. *Her* David. She doubted that she would ever fully feel the same about him as she did before. Yet, like Claire, she knew with absolute certainty that she wasn't willing to do without him.

Over time, she came to believe that maybe having a "big horrible incident" was appurtenant to every marriage. It almost made her want to go around interviewing couples to find out.

*****

Socially, Shelley was still in a state of flux. For the last several years she'd spent small bits of time with various acquaintances, enjoying each for whatever it was they had in common at the moment. There was her cooking friend with whom she'd take jaunts to a little greenhouse farm and buy fresh herbs, her walking friend, her book discussion friends, her community friends from the Women's Club, etc.

They were pleasant. Fun was had. She hadn't done much with any of them since Patrick had come into the picture but she wasn't in the state of mind to call them now either. She did have a few close friends she'd known since forever, all residing very far away, their lives having gone in many different directions since high school. She stayed in touch with them via Facebook, but it was not the same as being able to spend time together in person.

Her "best friend" was David: her real friend in a world full of acquaintances. He was the one she could tell anything to. The one who thought the same as her, did most things the same way, and didn't drive her crazy with the minutiae that normally cause friction in relationships.

But because he was her best friend, she felt she had nowhere to turn. You can't talk to your best friend about how your best friend has screwed you over when they are one and the same person.

She was also struggling with the loss of Patrick—another thing she didn't feel she could discuss with David, knowing that he himself was so distraught. The baby had become such a part of her daily life, it was like she didn't know what to do with herself without him. She missed his chubby little arms around her neck; his peekaboo games. She wondered how he was. Worried about whether he was okay. It was excruciating.

Now that so much had gone on, she no longer had the patience for those other acquaintances. There were so many monumentally important things on her mind, she had zero patience for shallow conversation or for people's incessant complaints about minor problems that were usually self-imposed anyway.

The only person she felt differently about was Claire, ever since the day she showed up at her house and helped pull her out of her slump. But that didn't change the other things about them that were so different it would have been nearly impossible to fully connect. That afternoon was a like one-time anomaly that led to a better understanding between a zebra and a horse, but still didn't make them become the same animal.

So Shelley focused on other things, like getting the house back in shape, catching up on her reading list, reorganizing the kitchen cabinets, and exercising regularly. Her social time was spent with David and even then there was a sense of everything not being just right. A certain reserve now existed within her that kept him at arm's length, unable to fully trust and enjoy his companionship because it felt so diminished from the way things used to be.

*****

Throughout that autumn, Shelley pursued all sorts of things she'd never had time for. During the week when David was at work, she experimented with various art media, like clay, acrylic paints on canvas, and making her own wooden bird feeder, which she painted with a country cottage theme. The birds looked adorable when they would come to get their seeds, sitting beside the white picket fence and finding extra treats under the miniature rocking chairs.

She became more familiar with her camera, and often spent her days walking through the nature preserve, enjoying the outdoors and getting excited when the opportunity for a great photograph presented itself. They weren't professional but she did get some beautiful shots that included a fresh stream, a rabbit poised upon a small rock in a field, and a few magnificent sunsets, each one different with their streaks of grey, pink, or bluish purple.

She enjoyed these outings and hobbies, and they brought her the opportunity to reflect. Certainly, she'd been to the nature preserve many times before, but it was different now, and at first it was intangible to her as to what was in such contrast with her previous visits.

It took a few weeks of speculation before she came up with an answer: It was the first time she'd done these things when there was no stress involved. Sure, there were many nice memories of going there with the kids at their various ages, but when push comes to shove, taking children anywhere is a lot of work. At any given time, someone is complaining about the bugs or the heat, or keeps wandering off. Even as they'd gotten older and things like repeated restroom visits were no longer an issue, teenage drama would be in play. ("I can't believe you're making me be here! My friends are all online!")

While enjoying these activities on her own, Shelley would smile to herself thinking about the times she'd done them with the children. Out on the screened porch with her clay—sloppy, drippy, and far too much of a mess for her to want to do it again—she thought fondly of when Grace was six and she hosted a Princesses Who Like to Play Play-Doh birthday party. The parents had thought she was nuts: "You're having a party *in your house* and are going to let eight kids play with that in here?" they'd marveled.

Yes she was. She also colored Easter eggs with them each spring and had the stains on her hardwood floors to prove it. As the kids matured, she'd hosted innumerable other parties, like an Amazing Race Party ("You're going to let *all those kids* run in and out of your house?!"), and a dance party when Rose turned thirteen, complete with letting them blast the surround sound stereo, dance in the pitch dark with glow necklaces, and a contest where they had to eat doughnuts while blindfolded.

Just that summer, Grace's friend Cassie had confided that some of her favorite memories were at their house, on the many occasions when she and David had allowed each of the four kids to invite a friend to sleep over. "Every time I eat pancakes and bacon, I think of you!" she'd exclaimed. Shelley took this as a sincere compliment.

They were nice memories. Reflecting on them brought a fondness and a sense of pride, feeling good about the mom she was to her kids as they were growing up. She'd enjoyed it. But at the same time, she was also enjoying not doing it anymore. Although she struggled with worrying about Patrick, she began relishing the freedom to come and go as she pleased, no longer carrying the perpetual underlying knowledge that she needed to be somewhere, cook something, or drive someone.

*****

Weekends were different too. David and Shelley slept in, cooked whatever *they* wanted for breakfast, then headed out to do things they'd never really had a chance to enjoy before.

Sure, they'd each been to all of the area museums, but they were always chaperoning field trips when they'd visited before. It was quite different to stroll along enjoying the exhibits at their own pace, reading each information placard and not having to worry about the seven students they were supposed to be keeping an eye on.

On the way home, they'd stop at the grocery store and pick up whatever they felt like eating for dinner. Then they would leisurely enjoy their evening drinking wine and preparing the food together, often not actually eating until ten or eleven o'clock at night, which was what *they* liked.

For the first time, there was an aspect of spontaneity and self-indulgence borne from not having to consider the needs and wants of four or six or eight other people. It occurred to her that they didn't need to be in Bora Bora for this to happen. Sure, the trip would have been nice, a fantasy come true, but in the end their new, more carefree lifestyle, allowed them to embrace this freedom that felt almost like a vacation—but without having to spend thirty thousand dollars.

The entire fall season continued in this vein. David even started taking Tiny to the dog park again, and while they were gone Shelley would relax on the sofa with Frick and read more books than she used to have time to read in a year. Even when Rose returned from Europe the household didn't change much. Just like Grace, she was nearly never home, and when she was she mostly took care of her own things, not needing much more than some good leftovers in the fridge and to not run out of toiletries.

It wasn't until Thanksgiving that the tides turned dramatically once again, with Michael announcing that he'd decided on an entirely different life plan.

Chapter 31

"It's not that we don't like Lanie," David argued. "We do. It's just that you seem a bit young for so much responsibility and I very much disagree with you not finishing your Master's."

Michael sighed. "I know Dad, but I really think this is the right thing to do. I love Lanie and Annabelle, and it will be so nice to be able to just stay with Anna during the day and not have to keep her in daycare."

Shelley interjected. "Michael, we're not saying you shouldn't marry her. I mean, we do think you're a bit young but if it's what you really want we wish you the best. But quitting college to stay home and watch the baby? That seems unnecessary. I really think you should finish your degree!"

"I know you don't see it this way, but Lanie makes a lot of money and I make decent money doing the billing too. Between that and not having to pay daycare, we'll be way ahead. We can pay off our school loans and everything."

"I see what you're saying, Son, but why not just finish your degree? You're doing it online anyway and you only have about a year left." It was taking every ounce of strength for David to force the restraint in his tone.

"I just don't want to Dad. I'm sick of school and this is what I really want to do." Michael averted his eyes, knowing this was not going to go over well with David.

His patience drastically waning, David went on, "Life is filled with having to complete responsibilities we may not be overjoyed about, but it will be so much harder to try and pick up and finish it later!"

"Why would I want to finish it later? I'm never going to need it."

David looked like his head was going to explode. Shelley jumped in.

"Michael, things change over time. What if the firm no longer needs you to do the billing? Or if you two decide to have more kids of your own and Lanie wants to stay at home? How would you provide for the family?"

He sighed, almost a moan. "Not everyone is old-fashioned like you guys. We're a different generation and there's nothing wrong with the man being the one to stay at home."

"I'm not saying that!" she objected. "Even if you were the woman I'd be saying that you should finish your degree before getting married and deciding to stay at home with a child!"

"I don't see why you can't just finish," David argued. "I mean, if you're doing it from home anyway, what's the big deal to finish your studies? You're so close to being done!"

"I just don't want to," Michael said with an adult finality that they'd never heard him use before. "I'm the one paying for it and I just think it's unnecessary for my lifestyle with Lanie and Annabelle."

"I disagree," Shelley said. She debated the wisdom of pointing out that marriages don't always work. That life often throws changes your way and it's best to be prepared rather than caught off guard.

"Disagree?! That's putting it mildly!" David shouted.

Having formulated what she was going to say, Shelley started, "Michael, over the course of many years, life…"

He interrupted, holding one hand up like a stop sign. "We've already made our decision, so I hope you guys will get on board with it." He rose from the table, wiped the crumbs from the bagel he'd been eating onto his paper plate, dropped it into the trash, and strode into his room/the dining room, shutting the door firmly.

The couple sat there in silence for a few minutes. Then David stood, walked over and knocked on Michael's door and when he opened it asked, "Would you like me to help you shop for a ring?"

*****

Within weeks, plans were underway and as Christmas approached and all of the other kids came home for their break, the atmosphere in the house was in the full throes of festivity. Never having enjoyed the commercialism of Christmas, Shelley finally purchased the tree she'd always wanted: a two-foot-tall tabletop tree that was a small token of the season, rather than the mammoth, forest-like encumbrance that had made her living room feel the size of a shoe box for the past twenty Christmases.

They'd planned a small engagement party for Michael and Lanie, to take place on the Saturday night between Christmas and New Year's. Rose and Grace, who both liked Lanie a lot, took charge by decorating the house with strands of silvery cords that by the end of the day seemed to be draped from every light fixture, doorway, and a good portion of the ceilings. Shelley had anticipated that it would look tacky but the end result was actually quite elegant.

Once again, Grace and her friend Cassie took charge of the cake, as they'd done for Patrick's first birthday. This time they practiced for weeks, resulting in the purchase of several hundred dollars' worth of baking and decorating supplies, as well as many discarded attempts (and as many failed efforts eaten by Michael and Russell). In the end, they created a beautiful, edible work of art that not only held up throughout the evening on display, but also tasted delicious.

Guests began arriving at six o'clock, carrying packages mostly wrapped in crisp, cream paper and setting them on the kitchen table, which they'd pushed against the wall to allow for the gifts. One or two came wrapped in Christmas paper, bringing laughter from the group as they all agreed that during the busyness of the season, it's so easy to forget details like engagement wrapping paper.

Wine was poured and hors d'oeuvres were eaten as everyone milled around the kitchen, while the wait staff they'd splurged on finished setting up the rented tables, chairs, and fine china in the living room. With their house now having no dining room, the plan was to use the living room for everything and have the assistance of Miriam and Andrej to set up, serve, and clean.

Shelley had gotten to know Lanie's mom Jacqueline a bit, mostly over e-mail and phone, and during a luncheon the kids set up to introduce the parents (she'd fluttered her wrist elegantly and said, "Oh please, I go by Jackie."). She'd offered to host the party at their home, an historic townhouse in Washington D.C. She and her husband, Brad, had only lived there for three months and would have liked to show off their new place, but in the end they all agreed that with it being located five hours away from the majority of the guests, it would have been a burden for everyone to have to travel, particularly during the holiday season.

David, out on the screened porch, was enjoying a celebratory cigar with Brad and a few of the men, including colleagues from Lanie and Michael's law firm and two close friends of her parents.

Shelley smirked to herself in amazement over why men consider smoking the stinky things to be a form of celebration. She mentally shrugged, figuring men had been doing it for years, and likely continued simply to maintain tradition. Sometimes tradition is nice, even if stinky.

Noticing that a few of their glasses were getting low, she took a wine bottle and went outside to offer refills. As she stepped out, she noted the seriousness on David's face and overheard the reason why.

"I thought Lanie mentioned that you have another daughter?" Brad inquired. "And a grandson?"

David just nodded.

"Are they running late? I hope you didn't think they should be excluded because of the baby," he asked. "After all, our little Anna-Doll is here!" His voice boomed as he laughed, revealing the beginning signs of intoxication.

David's discomfort was palpable as he averted his eyes and took a sip from his wine glass, stalling while he formulated an answer.

Apparently having decided on brevity, he tried to suppress the flush creeping up his neck and said, "No, they won't be here."

"Well why not, man?" Brad said, thumping David on the back. "I thought they live locally."

"They do."

The other gentlemen, having noticed that something was amiss, stepped back into the main house, leaving just David, Brad, and Shelley on the porch.

She interjected. "There have been some problems with Alexandra and we unfortunately haven't heard from her in quite some time."

"Well what about the baby?" Brad continued, oblivious to David's and her discomfort. "Couldn't you just pick him up?"

Poor David looked like he wanted to sink through the floor and disappear under the deck.

"Unfortunately, no," she said firmly. Then, "Oh, look at the time! I do believe it's time for us to head back inside for dinner!"

With Brad confused and David relieved, they followed her in, where she suggested that they all be seated.

*****

The meal went smoothly, with Shelley feeling very grateful and self-indulgent about having decided to hire help for the evening. She was actually able to sit with her guests and eat, while Andrej and Miriam saw to it that everyone's glasses were full and needs were met.

Jackie helped get conversation going by starting a sort of game where each person around the table introduces themself and tells a bit about who they are, what they do, etc. It was a great, informal way to get to know one another's parents, siblings, and close family friends during a party where you might otherwise only get to chat with each person for a moment or two.

The table was just about cleared, with everyone sitting in more relaxed positions talking about how good everything was and how stuffed they all were. Feeling proud about how smoothly the party at her home was turning out, Shelley's ear detected the sound of coffee percolating in the kitchen; right on schedule.

At the encouragement of everyone clinking their glasses with their forks, Michael and Lanie kissed and then everyone agreed that it would be fun for them to open their gifts. Jackie and Shelley set about bringing them all in from the kitchen, piling them up next to Michael and Lanie, while David got his camera ready to take a few shots of the festivities.

With an armload of gifts, Shelley was walking through the hallway when the doorbell rang.

"Just a minute!" she shouted in the direction of the door.

"I'll get it," said Jackie. She was carrying only one gift bag and reached out to pull the door open as Shelley began setting down the pile she'd been balancing.

"Oh, hello," she heard Jackie say pleasantly. "It looks like we have another…"

"Who the fuck are you?" someone spat.

Alexandra had chosen that moment to return home.

Chapter 32

The only sound that could be heard was of Jackie's heels clicking on the hardwood floors as she made a hasty retreat from the doorway. The rest of the guests, understandably aghast, were so shocked that they weren't even whispering. Yet.

David, instantly paling, stood and joined Shelley at the front door where they saw Alexandra—or whom they assumed was Alexandra—standing on the porch. She was nearly unrecognizable, so skeletally thin that her clothes hung off her like a little girl playing dress-up. Except that she didn't look like a little girl. Her face appeared to have aged at least ten to fifteen years, her skin a combination of sallow greyness and red pockmarks.

"Well isn't this nice," Alexandra slur-shouted before they even opened the screen door. "Looks like I got here just in time for a party!"

David stepped outside and Shelley followed, pulling the house door closed behind her in the hope that it would prevent their guests from overhearing what was sure to be another of Alexandra's crazed confrontations. Any hope she'd secretly harbored about her getting her act together on her own had evaporated the moment she laid eyes on her.

"Alexandra…" David said.

"That's my name, don't wear it out!" she shouted, laughing maniacally.

Shelley couldn't help staring at her—her appearance was so alarming. Not knowing what to say, she averted her eyes toward the driveway, curious as to how she'd arrived. There was no vehicle in sight and she couldn't imagine how she got there.

"What's a matter, *Shelley?*" Alexandra snarled, somehow managing to make her name sound like a dirty word. "You lookin' for something?"

"Actually, I was wondering if Patrick is with you." She cringed at how nervous she sounded. But really, she didn't have a lot of experience conversing with strung out drug addicts, which it appeared was exactly what Alexandra had become. Not to mention the house full of elegantly decked-out guests that were inside her home for an engagement party! She couldn't help wondering what was going on in there. Did they just continue with the party and pretend there was nothing amiss? Or were they huddled at the living room window right this very moment, straining to hear every word?

Alexandra started laughing—a cackling laugh, which quickly turned into a phlegmy coughing fit.

"How is Patrick?" David asked.

Swiping her arm across her mouth to mop up the spittle, she thumbed in the direction of the many cars in the driveway and said, "Why don't you ask him? He's right over there."

"Oh my God, Patrick!" Shelley ran over to the driveway, her stilettos and silk pantsuit not exactly cut out for a marathon, but making it to the other side of the row of cars in a split second.

There in his stroller, with his legs bent up to huddle from the cold, was Patrick. He looked so different, she couldn't believe it had only been five months since she'd last seen him. Gone was the adorable "little man" haircut she'd gotten him when he'd needed his first trim, replaced by a shaggy top of thick, dark hair that clearly hadn't been trimmed—or possibly even brushed—since the last time she'd done it.

He was sitting there, empty-handed with no toys or anything, looking around in a bored glaze as if he were accustomed to just sitting in the filthy stroller and waiting.

She overheard Alexandra mimicking her snidely, "Ohh Patrick!" and David saying, "What the hell is wrong with you, Alex?"

Trying not to startle him, Shelley quietly said, "Patrick?"

He turned his head in her direction but his expression didn't change.

She approached the stroller slowly and bent down so he could see her face in the dark driveway, the only light coming from the streetlamp two houses down.

"Hi Patrick. It's Grandma," she said.

He sat up in the stroller and looked at her, leaning forward as if trying to see better.

"Remember Grandma? Maymaw?"

He turned his face shyly, then began peeking back at her. She put her hand on his arm. "Come. You want to come out of the stroller and say hi to Maymaw?"

He nodded and held onto her hand as she helped him climb out, as he was kind of big now for her to lift and he wasn't strapped in anyway. She could hear the raucous sounds of Alexandra and David fighting, but it was like background noise to her; she was only interested in looking the baby over and seeing if he was okay.

Although it was immediately apparent that "baby" was no longer an appropriate description for Patrick. It seemed he'd grown a foot since she last saw him, and his chubby rolls of baby fat were gone, his limbs lean, his appearance much more like a "tyke" or a "preschooler." Except for his eyes. And his diaper. Which were both at unsettling extremes.

His eyes held a wisdom that made her heart sink. It was not a good wisdom; it was a look that somehow revealed that he'd been exposed to things that no one-and-a-half-year-old should be exposed to.

His diaper, which looked out of place on his tall body, was loaded so heavily with urine that it caused his pants to sag way down, despite the fact that they were way too small. As were the rest of his clothes. She recognized them as ones he'd worn the previous winter—when he was six months old!—and the shirt was so short that his belly was exposed on the chilly winter night, while his jacket sleeves looked as if it were a three-quarter-sleeve jacket.

Not wanting to scare him, she stayed crouched down in front of him and opened her arms. He looked at her tentatively, then stepped into her embrace and curled his face into her neck just like he always had.

*****

With Patrick clinging to her like a koala bear, she stood and walked over to where David and Alexandra were still going at it.

"So what's the story, you guys?" she asked.

"The story?" David said, aggravated. "The story is that Alexandra here seems to think she's going to show up all strung out and be invited inside so she can make a scene in front of the guests!"

"How the fuck was I supposed to know you were having a party?" she argued. "Anyhow, what's a matter? I'm not *good enough* for your *stupid* party?" She turned on a whiney, mocking voice, "What happened to 'It's all about *faamily* this and *faamily* that?'"

Shelley stood there observing this, fighting the urge to cover Patrick's ears with her hands and realizing that, sadly, he'd surely heard plenty of this sort of thing over the past months.

"Look at the way you're behaving, Alex!" David roared. "Do you expect us to invite you inside with a house full of people while you're acting like this?"

Alexandra threw her gigantic, overstuffed pocketbook onto the porch steps and plopped down beside it. "I have nowhere else to fucking go. Believe me, if there was I wouldn't show up at your lame-o house."

Shelley vaguely wondered where Alexandra had picked up this outdated jargon. *Lame-o? That's my name don't wear it out? Who says those things anymore?* Then she realized it was highly likely that Alexandra was hanging out with older people; drug addicts who were from a different generation and didn't see anything wrong with including "the youngster" in their midst.

Trying to set aside her anxiety about the houseful of people and put things into perspective, Shelley set Patrick down on his feet and sat down next to Alexandra on the step. Forcing calm into her voice, she asked, "Are you ready for help, Alex? To stop doing drugs and get your life on track?"

David, shaking his head, lifted Patrick into his arms and walked away to get the stroller.

"My *life* is just fucking *fine*, thank you!"

"Really? Because it sounds to me like you have no place to live, and looking at you it appears you have gotten yourself quite far in over your head with the drugs."

Surprising her by not shooting a comeback, Alexandra just looked down into her lap where she was picking at her already scabby cuticles, and didn't say a word.

Shelley put her hand on her back and stroked, trying not to react in alarm when she felt the bony nubs of her spine. "Listen, Alex. Everyone makes mistakes. Everyone needs a do-over once in a while. There's no shame in admitting that you need help and letting us help you."

She turned to her, her eyes filled with tears and said, "I already had my do-over back when I first came to live with you, and I screwed it up."

"Okay. So maybe you did screw up. But you're a young girl. There's still plenty of time to make a fresh start and put all of this behind you."

"But I *like* partying."

"Do you? I mean, I know you probably liked it in the beginning, but can you really say it's fun anymore?"

Surprise registered in her expression, probably shocked that Shelley would ever understand that she may have enjoyed it at all.

"I guess. Not as much anymore, but…" she trailed off.

"Correct me if I'm wrong, Alex, but at this point it's become more of a need to get by, rather than a fun thing."

"Yeah, I guess."

"Our offer to attend a program still stands, you know."

She just sat there, staring into the distance.

Shelley went on, "Sweetie, I know this is a tough decision to make and we don't have to get every detail sorted out right this minute. Do you think you can come inside and not make a scene? Michael got engaged and it really is unfair for their party to be entirely ruined."

Like a switch was flipped, Alexandra leapt up, instantly defensive.

"Oh, so what are you saying? That I'm going to *ruin* your stupid party?"

David walked up dragging the stroller behind him, one of its wheels turning crazily like a broken shopping wagon at the supermarket, causing Shelley to wonder how it was possible for Alexandra to have pushed it anywhere with Patrick in it.

David let out a heavy sigh. "Alex, you already *have* ruined the party. Don't make it worse. You and Patrick can come inside and shower, and then you can stay upstairs. I'm sure it's past Patrick's bedtime anyway."

"Oh, so what? I'm supposed to stay upstairs like some monster in the attic or something?" She screamed at such a volume that Shelley cringed knowing that not only their guests, but surely everyone in all of North Carolina must have heard her.

"If the shoe fits!" David roared. "I'm sick of your crap. Here are the choices: Either you go upstairs and you'll have a place to stay, or you can leave now and Patrick stays with us."

"You can't do that! You can't take him. I'm his mother!"

"Well then start acting like it," he said. "I'm pretty sure that if I call the police you'll be arrested for whatever contraband you surely have in that bag. Maybe that's what I should do anyway… then at least we'll be sure you'll get help!"

"You wouldn't," she snapped confidently. "They'd put Patrick in foster care and you wouldn't want that to happen to your *precious* little grandson would you?"

"Come on, Patrick. Grandpa will take you inside," David said, carrying him toward the door. Then, as he pulled the screen door open he surprised them both when he looked back over his shoulder and said calmly, "It's okay if he goes into foster care. I'm already pre-registered in the system as an authorized foster."

Chapter 33

Over the next few weeks Shelley felt like she and David were on one of those rickety old roller coasters at the State Fair. One minute they were zooming along with joy at the knowledge that Patrick was (mostly) okay, and the next they were chugging along bumpily, feeling like they were going to fall off the track. Their trust level was about the same too: They wanted to welcome Alexandra back into the family just like you wanted to trust that the roller coaster was put together correctly. But then you remember that it was assembled by a bunch of slick carnies who hustle people, which was approximately how trustworthy Alexandra was at the moment.

The night of Michael's party, they'd brought her in and had her go straight upstairs and into the shower. David searched through her pocketbook and removed all the drugs and paraphernalia he could find which consisted of some pills, a little plastic baggie containing a light brown substance, numerous tin foil squares, and a glass pipe. He put them all in a gallon-sized Ziploc bag and hid it in the top of his closet behind some old sweaters.

Shelley had taken Patrick into the master bathroom and given him a quick bath, dressed him in the smallest of Grace's shirts she could find and a fresh diaper they got from Lanie, then put him to sleep, exhausted, in David's and her bed.

Thankfully, their guests were gracious enough not to ask what was going on, and Miriam and Andrej had taken care of serving the coffee and cake, even taking a few snapshots of Lanie and Michael opening gifts, capturing their forced smiles as they tried to make the best of the awkward situation.

They had no idea what to do about Alexandra, and her mood swings were so extreme that you never knew what to expect from her. One minute she would be trying to behave responsibly, cooking hot dogs and macaroni and cheese for Patrick, even offering some to the rest of them.

The next minute, she'd be nasty and foul-mouthed as soon as the slightest thing didn't go her way.

It was typical drug addict behavior, complete with stealing items from family members (they had to install locks on all of the bedroom doors because of her, causing significant inconvenience to everyone else) and doing things like saying she's going to the store for diapers, then not returning home for two days.

David and Shelley trudged along, trying to just take things one day at a time, but as they approached the three week mark one thing became clear: Something had to be done and this was not working.

*****

They sat at the dining room table—their old table, which Michael and David had hauled back down from the attic one week after the engagement party, when Michael moved into Lanie's house. With the doors still attached it still didn't feel like a proper dining room, but that could be dealt with in time.

What needed attention at the moment was the situation with Alexandra. David had asked Joe Slade, the cop he'd become friendly with, if he wouldn't mind coming by to give them some advice, and so it was that they sat at the table with scones and coffee, and the Ziploc bag with Alexandra's drug stuff in it.

"Yes, that does look like crystal meth," Joe said. "Although you didn't hear it from me because I didn't see it. If I had seen it, I would have to arrest someone," he said uncomfortably.

"Thanks, man," David said, taking the bag and stashing it out of sight in the nearby pantry for the moment. "We didn't know what to do with it and we wanted to find out exactly what we're dealing with."

"Listen you guys, it's like this…" Joe paused a moment as if he were deciding whether or not he should be entirely truthful. "I looked on the computer back at the station and found out that Alexandra has warrants."

"Warrants!" David banged his fist on the table. "What the hell does she have warrants for?"

Shelley held her breath in anticipation, hoping it was nothing too terrible.

"Possession of an illegal substance and disorderly conduct. She never showed up for her court date."

"What does this all mean?" she asked carefully. Shelley understood that this was a bit of a predicament for Joe: he wanted to help them out as friends but still had duties as a police officer that he was expected to uphold.

"What it means is that she could be arrested and sent to jail."

Shelley felt sick visualizing Alexandra in an orange jumpsuit, locked in jail. And trying *not* to imagine the things that could happen to a pretty young girl in jail.

David, forcing a level-headed tone asked, "How long would she be in for?"

"Being that she doesn't have a previous criminal record, I'd say probably only six to nine months."

"*Only* six to nine months! That sounds like a long time to me!" Shelley said.

"It's possible that it could be shorter if the court were to send her to a drug treatment program."

The couple sat there, letting this information sink in. They wanted her to get treatment, but in jail?

"Look, you two," Joe went on gruffly, his tone indicating that he was not beating around the bush anymore. "Here's the deal. I know the idea of jail or a court-appointed drug treatment program is not something you ever imagined for one of your family members." He shook his head. "It never is. But I've been a cop almost twenty years now and I can tell you that this meth crap is no bullshit. She is not going to quit on her own; they can't, it's just too hard. And push comes to shove, she is going to have to face these charges at some point anyway."

The two sat there listening and nodding as they absorbed all the implications of what he was saying.

"You asked me over here for my advice, and I'm telling you—both as a friend and a cop—that your best bet is to let the court force her into treatment."

"It's just hard to imagine turning our own daughter in to the police," David said, his voice nearly breaking.

"I know. But the up-side is that she can't sign herself out the way she could if she went to a non court-appointed program and like I said, the day will come that she has to face these charges anyway."

Shelley felt David's hand reach for hers under the table and squeeze.

"I need to be careful not to cross a line here," Joe went on. "So I'm just going to say this and then I need to get going. I didn't see any paraphernalia while I was here at your house, *visiting as a friend,* and I don't know anything about anything. *If* you were to call me, as a good samaritan, to let me know where she is and *if* I were to approach her as a cop on duty and discover that she has a warrant, she would have the best chance of putting this all behind her. *Hopefully* she would not have any additional contraband on her person at the time of her arrest." He winked at them, then said, *"Capiche?"*

David rose from his seat and extended his hand toward Joe for a hearty man-shake. *"Capiche.* We understand."

Shelley stood and came around to the other side of the table. "Thanks Joe. We really appreciate your help and understand the position you're in."

"No problem." He gave her a polite hug, and then they all walked toward the front door.

As he went down their front steps, Joe turned back and said, "I'm real sorry for you folks to have to go through this. Unfortunately it's all too common nowadays. But you have that little boy to think of. I know you'll make the right decision."

As they closed the front door, David and Shelley turned to one another, their eyes questioning, their hearts leaden. Joe Slade was right. The question was, were they prepared to do it this way?

*****

Not knowing what else to do with the Ziploc bag of drug supplies, David flushed the crystal meth and the pills down the toilet while Shelley threw the rest of the things into the garbage, emptied a bunch of old leftovers from the fridge on top of it, then tied up the bag and brought it to the outside can.

They felt like criminals, and the ugliness of it hadn't been lost on her when she'd dumped the stuff into the trash and noticed that the glass pipe had landed on top of a Dora the Explorer yogurt from Patrick's before-bed snack, the cute monkey on the container looking grotesquely misshapen through the toxic glass.

With Patrick sleeping upstairs, the older kids at work, and Alexandra having disappeared since the previous afternoon when she'd said she was walking to the shopping center to look for a job, they were able to sit in the living room and talk.

"I don't really see what other option we have," she began.

"So you think I should turn in my own daughter to the police!" David was instantly defensive.

Shelley sighed, immediately weary of placating him and his insecurities about his kids and hers. Sick of being careful not to stress the "anxiety patient," or worry that he secretly wanted a divorce.

"I think that *our* daughter has such an extreme problem, it's become clear that our efforts are not resolving it," she said firmly. "I also think that *our* other kids and *our* grandson are being exposed to things we would never allow our family to be exposed to."

Surprise registered on David's face, as he surely never expected her to be so strong on this position. Or truthfully, *any* position, being that she'd been so weepy and careful around him over the past months.

"I don't know, Shell," he muttered, running both hands up his face and into his hair.

"It's hard. For all of us. And if it weren't for the warrant, I might think there are other ways to handle it, but Joe is right: Alexandra is going to have to face up to that at some point either way. To me, I'd rather see her go into a court-appointed drug program now, when she needs it, than to try and help her get her life together in other ways, only to eventually end up in jail anyway."

He just looked at her, mortified. She couldn't blame him; it was horrifying, and verbalizing it made it even more real. Trying to reconcile the idea of a family member being in a prison drug program—to accept that she actually *belonged* there—was nearly unfathomable. Yet here they were.

Suddenly, her mind clicked on the understanding that David was going to be unable to make this decision. That she would have to be the strong one and lead them through this particular episode in their life.

After a few more minutes of discussion, during which she laid out her idea for a plan that she thought would be the least awful of the options, the conversation came to a close. David, still uncertain, conceded with some reservations, but agreed that neither of them could come up with a better idea. He looked emotionally wrung out which was exactly how she felt.

As they sat there, she reached for David, trying to find comfort in one another the way they always had. He pulled away, almost imperceptibly, but enough to make her feel as though she'd been slapped.

Determined not to let him destroy her heart any further, she stood, her spine straight as a dancer's, and walked up the stairs to their bedroom, silently tiptoeing past Patrick sleeping in his crib and going straight into the master bath. She turned the radio on low volume and let the tub begin filling, then lay on the floor crying tears she didn't even know she had left inside her.

Chapter 34

The next afternoon, David was at work and Shelley was home with Patrick, sitting at the kitchen table with coloring books and crayons, teaching him the colors and the shapes. They were filling in a red square when Alexandra strode through the front door, looking exactly like the junkie she'd become; her hair was so filthy and stringy, Shelley couldn't venture to guess how it could have gotten like that in two days.

Standing in the foyer, she glared at them, expecting Shelley to lay into her for disappearing again, but Shelley didn't even bother. She just looked at her with disgust and flicked her chin, indicating that she should go upstairs. Without saying a word, Alexandra turned and walked up the steps, and Shelley heard the shower turn on a few minutes later.

Not wanting to miss the opportunity to put her plan into action, she gave Patrick two more shapes to color while she snuck upstairs into Alexandra's room. Quickly locating her jacket, she checked the pockets, then went through her pocketbook, fighting the urge to go get her gardening gloves before sticking her hands in there.

Confident that she'd located any contraband and forcing herself not to focus on the question that always went through her mind: *Where does she get the money to keep buying these things?* Shelley went back downstairs and flushed the drugs, once again throwing the other things into the kitchen trash and then emptying the small bathroom wastebasket on top.

With her nerves buzzing she sat with Patrick, praising him for coloring the blue triangle and the yellow circle, trying to behave normally in his presence. Considering the unimaginable things he'd likely been through, he was doing amazingly well with integrating back into their family and had begun smiling more and talking more, the sparkle returned to his eyes once again. Although it usually disappeared again around Alexandra.

The minute she heard the shower turn off Shelley zipped upstairs, knocked on the bathroom door, and told Alexandra that she needed her to go to the store.

"I don't have any money," she shouted through the door.

"That's all right, I have some," she responded, knowing that if she gave her money—in any amount, for any reason—she would go right back out again.

"Okay. Lemme get dressed and I'll go."

*****

The moment of truth arrived and Shelley tried to set aside her guilty feelings, reminding herself that awful though it was, this had to be done.

Just as she anticipated, Alexandra was dressed and ready in record time to head out the door with Shelley's money. Also according to plan, she obviously hadn't taken the time to check her pocketbook and notice that her stuff was missing.

"See you in a few!" Alexandra called happily, breaking Shelley's heart once again at how she could lie so blatantly when it was her full intention to go buy drugs and most likely not come home for days.

Pulling her iPhone out, she texted Joe Slade, her finger hovering above the Send button for an extra beat before going ahead with it: *Alexandra Johansen is walking up the street right now and there is a warrant for her arrest.*

Dragging in a deep breath, trying to regulate her breathing that sounded ragged even to her own ears, she turned back to Patrick who was excited, yelling "Maymaw, Maymaw! I wanna do geen!"

Picking up the green crayon with the knowledge that there was no turning back now, there was nothing left to do but color. And wait.

*****

Shelley didn't know what she expected to happen. Sirens screaming? The phone ringing? Some sort of dramatic scene that would transpire on the front lawn?

Nothing happened. Hours went by with no phone call, no signal that anything was amiss whatsoever.

Patrick had his afternoon nap during which she prepared the chicken pieces that they would have for dinner, did a load of laundry, and checked her e-mail many times to see if there was anything from David, who she figured may have received a call at work. There was nothing.

Later, claustrophobic and figuring that even though the February afternoon was chilly it would be good to get out of the house, she pulled Patrick's wagon out of the garage, put Tiny on his leash, and went for a brisk walk around the neighborhood.

When she returned there was a message on the machine from the dentist's office saying that it was time to schedule a cleaning, but that was it. Nothing from David, the police, Alexandra, or anyone else.

Grateful that both Grace and Rose were planning to be home for dinner, she distracted herself by cutting up the vegetables and seasoning the rice that would go with their chicken. Patrick, oblivious that anything was going on, ran around and around the circular track of their house with Tiny—through the living room, up the hallway, through the kitchen, into the dining room, back through the living room, and so on—with both of them squeaking Tiny's toys and Patrick screaming and giggling about the dog "chasing" him.

Despite herself, they did bring a smile to her face. Goofballs. Even the high-pitched sound of the squeaky toys was welcome, compared to the monotony of just waiting all day.

Seven o'clock came, with Rose and Grace both zooming in at the last minute after having said they'd be home. David, who would normally have arrived home by six, was nowhere to be seen. She tried calling his cell but there was no answer. She double-checked her text messages; even if he were stuck in a meeting, he would always at least text to let her know if he was going to be late.

Finally, after waiting another fifteen minutes, they went ahead and ate, as Rose had plans to go out with friends and Shelley didn't want the chicken to dry out.

By eight o'clock, when they had the table cleared and the dishes done, she was starting to become more than just a little worried. In their entire eleven-year marriage, David had never just not shown up without calling or texting. Grace, seeing that she was preoccupied, offered to give Patrick his bath and tuck him in, which she gratefully accepted.

She tried calling David's phone again but there was still no answer. She sent several texts, saying that she was worried and asking if he was okay but never received a reply.

The evening went on and as it got later and later she started really freaking out. Maybe he was in an accident? Should she start calling hospitals? Could he be at the police station? But if he was, why wouldn't he call to let her know? Should she call Joe The Cop? Just wait? Her imagination ran wild with every possible scenario, including entirely implausible ones.

By ten-thirty she was just about to start calling hospitals when a text came through on her phone: *Don't worry, David is with Brian.* It was from Claire. She replied: *Where are they?* Several long minutes passed (clearly Claire was no more skilled at texting than she) before she received: *I don't know. Out for drinks. Brian is driving.*

What are we, in high school? Why is she texting me instead of just calling? Understanding that she must be uncomfortable and probably wasn't supposed to tell her anything at all, Shelley just replied, *Thanks.*

*****

Shelley sat up waiting until around midnight, then finally went up to the bedroom to try and sleep. It wasn't until around one fifteen that she heard shuffling and flew downstairs to see if it was David.

It was. It was David, smashed like she'd never seen him, being walked into the house by Brian, who was practically holding him upright and had a very apologetic look on his face.

"I'm sorry Shelley. I tried to tell him to slow down but he was on quite a tear tonight."

"It's okay." What else was she going to say?

"His car is at the Ale House. I thought we were just meeting for a couple of beers after work."

"Okay. We'll get it tomorrow. Thanks."

"Why're you two tho serious?" David slurred. "Like a buncha fuddy-duddies," he laughed, ricocheting down the hall on his way into the kitchen.

Brian stood by the door, looking understandably exhausted after what was surely a long day and night for him. "Do you need me to stay?" he asked wearily. "I can help you get him up to bed if you want."

"I can hear you!" David shouted. "I'm not goin' ta bed. I'm having a snack."

"No, I'll be fine," she said to Brian. "Thanks anyway. Get home safely."

"Okay." He shook his head. "Sorry Shelley."

She nodded, shut the door behind him, then returned to the kitchen where David was standing in front of the open refrigerator doors.

"Would you like me to make you some toast with apple butter?" she asked.

"Toast! Wiss apple butter!" he slammed the doors closed and leaned on the kitchen counter. "Dass what I used ta eat when I was dating my wife!"

"I know, David. It's what we always eat together at night. Do you want some?"

"I don't wan no fuckin' apple toast!" His voice was loud. Really loud.

"Try to keep your voice down!" she stage whispered. "Patrick and the girls are sleeping upstairs."

Suddenly he looked at her as if just now noticing she was there.

"You! You're like a trader. I mean tray-tor. Traitor. That's it."

My God! How much did he drink? She'd never seen David like this. She popped some bread into the toaster, figuring it would be good to get any sort of bread into him, apple butter or not.

"Aren't you even gonna say anything? You! The traitor!"

She sighed. "Look David. Obviously you've had a lot to drink. You're being very loud and I'm sure you're saying things you don't mean." She refrained from pointing out that this was something he'd recently begun doing even when he wasn't drunk. "Let's just get you a snack and to bed before you end up saying something you'll regret."

"Regret," he laughed bitterly-slash-drunkenly. "That's a word."

She tried not to let what he was saying hurt her. She understood that he must have received some type of communication from either the police or Alexandra or both. It was a very trying day for all of them. But it hurt. It still hurt.

"Here's your toast," she said, sliding the two pieces onto a paper plate.

"Toast."

"You're welcome," she said sarcastically.

"I'd like ta make a toast!" David shouted, holding the piece of bread up in the air. "To my wife, whose kids are so fucking perfect and sends mine to jail!"

"David…" she tried to remain rational, "we discussed this and both agreed that there was nothing else we could do!"

"Daavid," he mimicked. Then, "Yeah, yeah. Nothing else ta do."

Was he truly agreeing with her or being sarcastic? At this point, it really didn't matter, Shelley decided.

Her ear caught a sound coming from upstairs and she listened carefully. It was Patrick, calling her. "Maay-maaw! Maymaw!"

"You woke up the baby in the middle of the night!" she admonished. "And I can't believe you're turning against me and making it seem like *I'm* the problem person in all of this!"

She walked to the steps and ascended the first two when she heard Rose's voice, "I got him Mom."

"Okay, thanks sweetie."

Anger welled inside her at the knowledge that not only was David treating her like this, but that the kids overheard it too. She went back to the kitchen where David was eating his second piece of toast and said, "This is unacceptable, David. Completely unacceptable."

She saw a flicker of recognition in his eyes, the knowledge that he'd pushed things too far. Holding his stare, she didn't flinch or even blink. Finally, he looked away and said, "I'm gonna go lie down."

Shelley spent a couple of minutes straightening up the kitchen, wiping up the crumbs and throwing out the paper plate. By the time she walked into the living room, he was passed out on the couch, his arm hanging over the side at a contorted angle.

She walked over, placed his arm across his stomach, and covered him with a blanket. Then she went to the garage and got a bucket, set it next to the couch, and shut the lights.

There was nothing else she could do but go to sleep, thankful that the horrible "day of betrayal" was over.

Chapter 35

Over the next several months, things returned to normal. Or more accurately, their new normal.

Alexandra was sentenced to a four-month court-appointed drug treatment program, which, much to their dismay, was not paid for by the court but was mandatory in order to avoid jail time. At a cost of seven thousand dollars per month, with only a small portion covered by their insurance, all of their Bora Bora money ended up being spent on the program.

Lovely. Just what they always dreamed about.

Alexandra also had to sign paperwork giving permission for David and Shelley to be Patrick's guardians in her absence. Which was a good thing because it turned out that David had been bluffing when he'd told her that he was already an authorized foster.

With the school year over, Russell, Grace, and Rose were all home and back in the throes of summer activities. Everyone was getting excited for Michael and Lanie's upcoming wedding; it was going to be a medium-sized affair with about seventy-five guests at the Carolina Inn, an upscale catering hall with an elegant historic flair. Annabelle and Patrick, who would both be two, were designated as the flower girl and ring bearer. Michael and Shelley had fun taking them shopping and picking out Annabelle's frilly little dress and Patrick's tiny tuxedo with the little cummerbund and hankie to match the dress color.

In an interesting turn of events, Patrick and Shelley spent quite a bit of time with Michael and Annabelle, meeting at the park or the library for play dates several times per week. The two adults found themselves bonding over being the "outsiders." Shelley, who was often the lone Grandma, and Michael, as a stay-at-home fiancée, connected in a way they never had before.

One afternoon each week Michael took Patrick for the day to give her a break, and vice versa. Spending so much time together, the toddlers became more like siblings who played nicely together most of the time, even developing their own little language, and occasionally fighting over a coveted toy or book.

There was a rhythm to their lives and while it was certainly not what she would have imagined things would be like when her children were nineteen and older, it was a life.

Her life.

*****

Things between David and Shelley became less strained over time. After a raging hangover and a day of him apologizing, she'd decided that it was pointless to keep taking issue with his drunken outburst. They both recognized that reporting Alexandra was something he had been unable to do himself, and he would just have to learn to live with his discomfort over Shelley having to be the leader in that scenario.

Once Alexandra was settled in at her treatment program and was no longer held at the jail, David's anxiety waned significantly. The program allowed for visitation once every two weeks, and he felt optimistic after visiting her and seeing that—at least physically—she seemed healthier, with the pockmarks gone from her face and having gained a little weight.

At Alexandra's request, he'd gone alone for the visits and had participated in some counseling sessions during which she admitted that she was extremely overwhelmed with being such a young mother and losing her own mother. She confided that she didn't feel any better equipped to go back to doing it, and while alarming, it was at least the truth, and David and Shelley agreed that her honesty was a step in the right direction.

For David, the sessions facilitated a new type of relationship between him and Alexandra. For the first time since she'd joined their family, the two weren't as strained or angry toward one another. Sure, there was the issue that she was in the program, but David felt hopeful that at least something was finally going in the right direction with his new daughter.

Unfortunately, she still continued to place blame for her drug problem on others whenever possible. Concerned, David had discussed this privately with her counselor who said that it was completely normal for a recovering addict to hold on to these excuses, and reassured David that, as a court-appointed program, she wouldn't be allowed to leave until they felt she really had come to terms with everything.

After the several traumatic months that David and Shelley had gone through, they were both making a concerted effort to try and get their marriage back on track. Now that Patrick had returned, they didn't have their leisurely morning coffee together, but they did have a lunch date once a week. When Michael had Patrick for the day, David would come home for lunch and they would often skip eating, spending the time making love in their bedroom instead. Grinning like teenagers, David would kiss her goodbye and head back to work with his sandwich wrapped in a paper towel to eat in the car along the way.

Shelley still fought with herself daily to try and get back to trusting in their love, repeating the mantra she'd gotten from Claire to keep herself on track: *I will continue to love him for all the good things that have made up our entire marriage, rather than hating him for the small time we had a problem.* Whenever she felt herself pulling away, she'd remind herself that he hadn't cheated on her, beat her, or put them into financial ruin with some sort of secret gambling problem. Worse things could have happened, and daily life was so good between them that she'd come to believe that at this point, if what he'd done ruined the marriage permanently, it would be her own fault for not letting it go.

*****

"What's everyone doing next year?" Michael asked. They were all sitting around the dining room table one Saturday afternoon, eating roast beef sandwiches and potato salad.

"I decided to stay and do my Master's at Colorado State," Russell said. "I got an apartment with two buddies in Old Town and I'm working on lining up a job that starts in August."

"So you really like it there, I guess," Grace piped in.

Russell rolled his eyes at her. "Yeah. Obviously."

"It just seems like it would be so cold. Isn't it, like, really cold there?"

"Yeah, it's cold. But it's fine."

"The Old Town area is really nice," Shelley interjected. "Dad and I had a great time there with all the restaurants and art galleries when we visited."

"What about you, Rose?" Michael asked. "Are you going back to campus or staying here this year?"

"I'm planning on going back to campus. Last year was fine and everything, but it got to be a bit much driving forty minutes each way every day."

They all nodded in agreement, then Rose glanced at David and said guiltily. "I mean, don't get me wrong, I *appreciated* being able to go to Europe and live at home the rest of the year, but…"

He laughed, waving her off. "It's fine, Rose. We understand."

"So then it looks like only Grace will still be home this year," Russell said.

"Actually…" Grace began, looking nervously between Shelley and David. "I've been planning to talk to you guys about that, but since it came up…"

"What?" David asked.

"I've been thinking. I know State's not that far, but it is still a twenty-minute drive and I'd kind of like to get out on my own. I've been talking to some girlfriends and Cassie wants in too because we wouldn't be very far from Meredith where she goes."

"So you're thinking you may want to get an apartment this year?"

"Yeah. I mean, I know it will cost more than living at home, but it wouldn't be more than the dorm fees would be, because I'll have three roommates. And we'll be right downtown so I could just walk or take the bus to classes."

"Oh, you've already looked at apartments?" Shelley asked, surprised.

"Well, we weren't really planning on it yet but Cassie's friend Lindsay already has this place and two of her roommates moved out so she's looking for two more. Cassie and I would have to share a room but it's pretty big and would only cost two hundred fifty dollars a month each. And it's really cool because it has, like, this huge living room and a kitchen with all the pots and stuff already, so I wouldn't really need any furniture or anything."

Shelley flushed with internal pleasure, understanding the excitement of being a young girl about to head out on her own for the first time. David and she looked at each other, silently knowing what the other was thinking: *Two fifty a month? Not bad compared to the others!*

"I don't think that would be a problem," David said. "You did well last year with your grades and responsibilities, so if you think you're ready I think it's fine as long as your mom agrees."

Shelley nodded. "I think it's fine too. Just remember, we'll be giving you money for food that's equal to what a meal plan would cost, so you'll still need your job for spending money."

"Of course! I'd never stop working at City Styles. I love it there!"

Rose laughed. "Of course! Without the employee discount you could never afford those jeans you're wearing!"

Everyone chuckled, all too familiar with Grace's penchant for ridiculously expensive jeans, then paused a few minutes, taking bites of their sandwiches and refilling their glasses of pink lemonade.

"So does this mean you guys will be putting the house on the market?" Michael asked.

Surprised, Shelley looked at David and saw that he was no more prepared for this question than she was.

"I don't know," she said. "We didn't know until just this minute that all of you guys would be off on your own. Why?"

"Just wondering. You've always said that as soon as we're all out you're selling the house, that's all."

Everyone chuckled lightly, as this was something they'd teased the kids about for years—that the minute they all moved out, they would sell the house and get a tiny apartment so no one could move back in with them.

"That's true," Shelley said. "But we haven't had a chance to talk about it and I'm not sure what to do because of Patrick and things being so uncertain with Alexandra."

"Why? You want to buy a house?" David joked.

"Actually, Lanie and I have talked about getting a bigger place after the wedding."

"Really?" This was news to them. "Why do you want a bigger house?"

"We just both think it would be nice. Now that she's a partner and works from home a lot, she'd prefer to have an office that's a bit more separate, plus, as Annabelle gets older, it would be nice to have a half bath so guests wouldn't have to go into the messy 'kid bathroom.' That kind of thing."

"I see," David said. "Makes sense, as long as you can afford it."

"We can," Michael said. Then impressed them by going on, "We've been saving all the money from not having to pay Annabelle's daycare anymore. At first we were going to pay off the school loans in full but since they have such low interest rates we thought it would be better to save a bigger down payment for another house first. Plus, Lanie's expecting a big bonus check next month from a huge commercial project she's closing on, and there was the signing bonus from when she became partner last month."

"Wow, it sounds like you've really planned this out. I'm proud of you, Son."

"Me too." Shelley said.

Russell made a gagging noise. "Well, now that we've all had our mushy moment, I'm off to meet up with my buddies." He grabbed his plate and cup. "See you later!"

Everyone else started shuffling around too, lunch finished and time to get on with their day. Soon, David and Shelley, and Patrick in his booster seat, were the only ones left at the table, all of it cleaned up around them as they looked into each other's eyes and had another of their silent conversations: *These kids are turning out pretty good after all!*

Chapter 36

Who am I? That was the question Shelley became preoccupied with that summer, during which she had quite a bit of free time even though most of the kids were home. They all helped with Patrick and the rest of the time they were rarely around

It was free time that afforded her the opportunity to reflect on the question that had become enormous to her: *Who am I?*

Patrick's grandmother?

David's ass-kissing wife?

Rose and Grace's mother?

Russell and Michael's stepmother?

A drug addict's family member?

Lanie's future mother-in-law?

Tiny and Frick's pet mommy?

They were all accurate descriptions but for some reason didn't feel like *enough.* All were tied in with other people and it felt like there was no actual Her.

Not to mention that some of them—being David's *ass-kissing* wife in particular—felt completely unnatural altogether. It still seemed surreal that she had put up with so much crap from him in the past year.

An amateur photographer? An occasional bubble bath taker? A bird house painter? A reader of books?

Those were true too, and did bring more of a sense of her as a separate person, unrelated to others, although they also didn't feel like enough.

Well, what did you expect to be? she admonished herself. *The curer of cancer? A Nobel Prize winner?*

She would stand in her master bathroom and look at herself in the mirror, almost surprised to see that there was any reflection there at all. It was as if she expected to be invisible, the way she felt. Or ugly, which is how she'd been feeling throughout what she internally referred to as The Big Terrible Incident With David.

Yet in reality, she actually looked kind of... the same.

She'd been through a similar thing before, in her thirties, when she'd felt like she'd disappeared in the throes of Momnesia. Back then, she'd taken active steps to try and rediscover who she was, or who she even wanted to be.

She rewound in her mind, thinking of what she'd done back then. What had made her feel happy and complete. (Aside from ending the miserable marriage she was in at the time.) She'd started going out dancing with friends. Stopped interacting with phony people who really didn't enhance her life in any way. Listened to music she enjoyed. Exercised.

All of which she'd stopped doing again. *Why did I stop? And would I still enjoy those things now?*

She realized that she stopped doing them because she got involved with David. When they fell in love it was all-consuming, and the most special thing that had ever happened to her. Until recently, she'd been blissfully happy, fully believing that the poor, deprived rest of the world was unaware that such a level of connected love was within the realm of possibility. Just like *she* hadn't known before either.

Looking back, she comprehended that as their relationship developed and they'd gotten married, she'd become consumed with a new version of Momnesia: trying to make their combined family work throughout those first years of dramatic teenage turmoil, complete with fender benders, gothic makeup, and secret tattoo-getting.

David was financially stable enough to support their family, and once they married she was in the enviable position—for the first time in her life—of not having to work if she didn't want to. She'd sold her very successful business, Flawless Floors, which she already had when they met, not knowing that within months, his gold digger of an ex-wife would implement unexpected strategies that would put them close to financial ruin.

Once things settled down, there had been a few years that were not so filled with angst—before Alexandra, Patrick, and Tiny came along, during which she'd accumulated her nice wardrobe, spent time with people who were pleasant acquaintances, volunteered with the Women's Club, and so forth. Every other week, all four of their kids spent the weekend with their other parents, and she and David had two days to just be a couple together, reconnecting as adults.

Looking back now she asked herself, *What was it that made me so happy during that time?* She hadn't been going out dancing, or doing most of the things she enjoyed before she met David. Lord knew she wasn't receiving such personal satisfaction from interacting with phony acquaintances.

Shelley pondered this for weeks, unable to come to a conclusion as to exactly what it was that had made her so happy during that time. Frustrated, she'd think and think, ultimately feeling even more discontented about not being able to figure it out. But although her mind was not forthcoming, she knew that her heart needed the answer to bring her happiness back.

Then, one afternoon while planting flats of impatiens in the shady areas of the yard with Patrick, it all became clear: It was her friendship with David that had made her so happy. It was feeling loved and cherished, wholly and completely, that had made her feel full and satisfied. It was feeling safe—in every way possible that a person can feel safe—that had allowed her to enjoy life in a way she never had before. It was being "David's Wife," mind, body, soul, and with every fiber of her being.

With a sinking heart she realized that she didn't feel that way anymore. She wanted to believe that David still felt that strongly about her. He said that he did and he acted like he did. *She* was the problem. She was just so hurt that it seemed nothing could make her feel whole again.

*****

Coming to terms with this led her to realize that she was going to have to take active steps to seek her own happiness, regardless of her relationship with David. She'd always believed that it was healthier for people to create their own individual happiness anyway, rather than circulating it around others, and so she'd promised herself that she'd focus on "walking the walk," so to speak.

Michael and Lanie's wedding was approaching and she needed to shop for a dress. A Stepmother of The Groom dress. She wanted something elegant, sexy, appropriate. Form-fitting but not slutty.

Something that would allow her to run after Patrick when necessary without feeling like she looked like a mess within five minutes.

She decided to go to a dress boutique in downtown Raleigh that was known for having a wide selection of elegant off-the-rack evening wear, supported by their reputation for doing professional alterations without the need to custom-order. While Rose watched Patrick at home, Shelley went by herself, determined to find pleasure in spending an afternoon doing something just for her.

After stopping at a nearby cafe for a leisurely cup of coffee and a few chapters of her book, Shelley walked into the boutique in a good mood, ready to tackle the fabrics and styles with flair. It was a quiet afternoon and although she didn't hear anything buzz, a woman immediately came out of the back office to greet her.

"Good afternoon!" she said, her rich Southern accent bringing immediate visions of sweet tea on a plantation patio.

"Good afternoon," Shelley replied, in her finely-honed neutral accent that still had a tinge of New Yorker no matter how hard she tried.

"I'm Donna Lee. And who might you be?" the woman inquired warmly.

"Shelley Morsony," she said. "Nice to meet you."

"Nice to meet you too. Is it okay if I call you Shelley? We're kind of informal around here. That's why I only told you my first name, Donna Lee, even though really it's Donna Lee Clayton-Carpenter."

Shelley smiled and nodded, and then the woman continued, dramatically placing her hand over her heart, "Oh my! Isn't that just like silly ole me, saying we're informal when we're in a formalwear store!"

Shelley laughed and said, "It's okay, I knew what you meant."

"See, I just knew we'd hit it off right from the start. The very minute I saw you!" She put her arm around Shelley's shoulders and said, "Now, what are you looking for today, love?"

"An evening gown for my stepson's wedding."

"A weddin'! Well isn't that so fun! I just love weddings!"

"Yes, it's a very exciting time," she said, trying to sound anywhere near as enthusiastic as Donna Lee. Although she doubted she could ever be quite that bubbly, short of winning the lottery. "It's at the Carolina Inn on a Saturday evening, so I'm going to need a floor-length gown."

"Mmm. The Carolina Inn," she mused, clasping her hands together and gazing dreamily up at the ceiling. "One of the very best places in the area, if I don't say."

Shelley nodded, and did *not* say, *You just said.*

"Now honey, let me ask you a personal question, if you don't mind. I mean, it's just us girls anyway." She laughed and looked around as if to confirm that they were the only ones within earshot. Then she unnecessarily lowered her voice and went on, "I think we need to find you somethin' that shows off that young wife figure you've got. Don't *tell* me your husband's not older 'cause I just know there's no way you're old enough to be the mother of a boy who's getting married!"

Shelley chuckled, agreeing, "Yes, my husband is about eight years older, but I don't think that's quite enough to make me a trophy wife or anything."

Donna Lee laughed, a rich, Southern sound, "Honey, *every* wife is a trophy wife—if you're doing it right!" With a smart wink, she straightened the hem of her elegant, grass-green silk blouse and strutted off toward the floor-length gowns. "Now, I'm sure we can find you something just perfect!"

Lanie, being perhaps the most laid-back bride Shelley had ever heard of, hadn't set any guidelines for dress colors or styles, saying that as long as everyone chose a solid rather than a pattern, they'd all look wonderful in the photos anyway. Nonetheless, knowing that Lanie's mom, Jackie, had chosen a red gown, Shelley carefully steered away from anything green that would make it look like a Christmas wedding, or other shades of red that could cause them to look mismatched.

She tried on numerous dresses in earth tones, as well as a black one and one in a rich navy blue. Donna Lee brought gown after gown to the dressing room, trying to guide her toward ones that were more formfitting and strapless, while Shelley leaned more toward something with at least a spaghetti strap. Finally, she told Donna Lee, "I do have a two-year-old grandson who I'll be keeping an eye on, so I'd really like to stick with dresses that have some type of strap."

She stopped a moment, losing her momentum, then conspiratorially said, "I see. Is that why they're getting married? These young 'uns today. In my day, my daddy would have killed me if I'd done such a thing!"

"No, no!" Shelley said, for some reason rushing to explain. "It's not their baby. No, my grandson is our other daughter's child." She left out the fact that actually, the bride did have a baby. But that was beside the point.

"Well then," Donna Lee said, back to business. "His own mama will be the one runnin' after him at the wedding, not you!"

Feeling no need to explain any further, she asserted, "I'd really prefer a gown with straps, either way."

After a few more try-ons, Shelley kept returning to the navy blue one. Even though it was a darker color, it was a very sheer fabric, had half-inch shoulder straps, and was adorned with just a little bit of elegant beadwork along the *décolletage* and bodice.

Donna Lee went to return the other dresses to their racks as Shelley slipped into the more extravagant underthings she'd brought with her, impressing herself at having had the foresight to bring them and the shoes she planned to wear, in case she needed a fitting.

Within minutes she was standing on top of a small hemming podium while Donna Lee, on the floor with pins in her mouth, worked on finding the right length for the gown.

When they were satisfied that it was pinned just right—determined not only by their visual estimation but also Donna Lee's insistence that Shelley walk around, sit in a chair, and so forth, she said, "Now, let me take a look at this waist area."

Shelley stood there while she nipped and tucked, scampering around her like the mice from Cinderella. She chattered the whole time, telling her about the dresses she'd worn to her own children's weddings, and talking about how she and her husband had started getting more involved in dog shows with their two standard poodles, whom she loved because they were "frou frou," and her husband loved because they're good watch dogs.

"What about you, sweetheart," she asked. "Do you have a dog?"

"Yes. I have one dog and one cat."

"Oh my! A dog *and* a cat! I've never been one for cats. But do tell me about your dog. What's its name?"

"Tiny."

"Tiny! Oh, he must be just the sweetest little thing. Do you have a picture?"

"Sure," Shelley laughed to herself, stepping off the podium and walking toward the dressing room to change back into her normal clothes. For some reason she was particularly tickled over the shock value that was sure to occur when Donna Lee saw a photo of Tiny.

Stepping out of the gown, careful not to displace any of the pins, she felt herself smiling, and thought how silly it was that she was having so much fun talking about her dog and other miscellany with a perfect stranger. Then sadness fell over her as she asked herself for the millionth time, *Is this it? Is this what my life has become—having so little in my life that my greatest pleasure is an inane conversation with a saleswoman?*

Navigating to the photo on her phone, she shrugged to herself and walked back over to where Donna Lee was carefully arranging the dress back onto a hanger. She handed her the phone so she could see the photo, which depicted Tiny wearing his Thomas the Train bandana, with Frick sitting right in front of him. It was a perfect shot that showed the full scale of just how tiny Tiny wasn't, and she recalled having used her phone to capture the moment quickly, as it looked like a posed shot, even though they had just been sitting around as normal... Frick following Tiny around like a kitten follows a mama cat.

"Oh my!" Donna Lee said, placing her hand over her heart. "This is Tiny? Bless his heart, he is just enormous!"

"Yes, it's pretty ironic that his name is Tiny," Shelley smiled.

"Well aren't you just so clever! I don't know that I could ever think of such a perfect name for an animal."

"Thanks," she said, as she slid the phone back into her purse.

Writing up her order form, Donna Lee glanced up and said, "So love, tell me more about yourself."

Silent, Shelley couldn't think of a thing to say. *Who am I?* She couldn't even answer the question herself, never mind tell someone else.

As she hesitated, Donna Lee paused in her writing and looked up at her with a wisdom in her eyes that allowed Shelley to see more than the exterior Southern charm she'd been presenting thus far.

"You know, like, what do you spend your time doing?"

"Oh, you know," she mumbled. "Married life. I have five grown children and a grandson we're raising." She felt so pathetic. She *sounded* so pathetic.

Donna Lee clasped her hands under her chin and with true joy exclaimed, "Oh! So you're a mom and a grammy! And a wife!"

She sounded so excited that Shelley felt guilty for having felt pathetic a moment earlier.

With a laugh, Donna Lee added, "A *trophy* wife!"

Shelley couldn't help but laugh along with her.

Finished with the paperwork, Donna Lee busied herself tamping some other piles of papers on her desk and carefully said, "I remember when I was your age, just a few years ago. I just felt like everything I did wasn't *enough!*" She glanced up at Shelley, likely wondering whether she was crossing a line talking about this with a customer. Shelley nodded in reassurance. "But more recently I realized that's what life *is*. It's all the little things we women do every day. All the things we put into raising our families that seem small at the time but add up to be *a life*. Our lives. Their *childhoods.*"

Like a lightbulb during a brown-out, only half-lit and flickering a bit, Shelley felt a small part of herself consider what she said. *Is that really the answer? That who we actually are is the sum of all the little things we do?* Promising herself that she'd give it some more consideration at another time, she thanked her again for helping her with the gown and Donna Lee came around the desk to give her a warm Southern hug.

"It has been such a pleasure getting to *know* you Shelley!" she exclaimed, then backed off a bit when she noticed that she was making her uncomfortable. "And I just can't wait to see you in that weddin' gown once I've got it all fixed up for you!"

"Thanks, Donna Lee. I'll see you in a few weeks."

Chapter 37

A whirlwind of activity preceded Michael and Lanie's wedding: Flowers and music were selected, fittings were finalized, and Shelley and David were hosting a rehearsal dinner. But of course, all of the wedding preparations didn't prevent other things from sprouting up along the way.

Alexandra, still in her drug treatment program for longer than the initial four month court-appointed stint, finally took ownership of the fact that it was not *their* fault she was in there, but her own fault for getting into drugs and trouble with the law in the first place.

David had been attending every other Sunday for family day, when they would have a private session with her therapist, as well as attending several group counseling sessions and some "fun, team-building activities," such as playing family volleyball or horseshoes. Each time he came home, he would give Shelley a brief update on how it went, clearly struggling between wanting to keep her posted and feeling obligated to preserve the confidentiality of their sessions. Shelley, uncomfortable with the situation and preoccupied with other things, didn't push it. She was just glad both David and Alexandra seemed to be healing.

One Saturday evening, after a long day of chasing after Patrick, doing housework, and running many errands, the couple were in bed early, trying to unwind with a little television. As they sat there, each propped up against their pile of pillows with Frick in the middle and Tiny lying across their feet at the foot of the bed, David broached the subject of Alexandra and her treatment.

"So, tomorrow is family day again," he said casually, reaching for her hand and holding it in his.

"Yup," she replied, already knowing, since it would be Sunday and he'd attended every other Sunday for the last several months.

"Alex is hoping you'll come this time," he said, surprising her.

"Really?" she reached for the remote control and lowered the volume, then turned to him. "When did she tell you this?"

"Last visit."

"You knew *for two weeks* that she wanted me to go but you waited until now to tell me?"

"I know, I know, I should have said something sooner," he shook his head sheepishly, "but you have so much going on and I didn't want you to have the extra stress of thinking about it."

Unreasonably angry, she tried to squelch her tone a bit. "You make it sound like I'm so unstable that I can't know about an appointment until the last minute!"

"I didn't say you were unstable."

"But you implied it!" she objected. "Did it ever occur to you that if I'd known ahead of time I might have gotten some other things done that I thought I'd be doing tomorrow?"

"What do you have to do that's so important?" he asked, first with confusion, and then his expression quickly changing to anger. "What could you possibly have to do that's more important than this?"

As if her life was just filled with trivial nonsense!

"It's just that it would have been nice to know beforehand, David. I know you think my life is unimportant compared to the *all-consuming* Alexandra problem, but I'm doing my best with the baby, the rehearsal dinner, the wedding, and everything else around here!"

He shook his head, once again expressing disappointment.

She didn't care.

"Plus, it would have been nice to be able to mentally prepare myself for it too!"

He looked at her. She looked at him. Neither had anything else to say.

Shelley sighed. "What time are we leaving?"

"Nine."

"Great. I'll set my *alarm,*" she said snidely. He knew she hated getting up early on weekends. "Oh wait, let me get out of bed now so I can call Michael to see if he can watch Patrick *at the last minute* while we go. I *assume* she doesn't want us to bring *her son?*"

Finally looking appropriately regretful, David muttered, "Yeah. Sorry."

*****

As David drove, navigating through the Sunday morning downtown church traffic to get to the highway, he contemplated what would be the wisest way to handle things. He'd thought he was doing the right thing by not telling Shelley until last night that they would be going, but clearly that was a mistake. Should he tell her now that he suspected Alexandra might have a bombshell to announce at today's session?

He didn't know for sure; it might just be a normal session. But he'd been developing a niggling suspicion that Alexandra may be planning something other than coming home and being a responsible mom in just a few weeks. There was a lot of talk about how she never had a "normal" childhood. Or rather, normal teenaged years. At the program, the entire focus was on the "client," and what's best for them… regardless of how it could affect other people. He'd speculated to himself more than once that she might plan on extending her stay or attending an additional program. Or something.

He had mixed feelings about it. On one hand, he agreed that the most important thing was for her to stay off drugs and if coming home to their house right away was going to "make her" (how ridiculous!) turn back into a drug addict, then that was probably not the best option. On the other hand, *she* was Patrick's mother and to not start being responsible for him just seemed, well, irresponsible.

Pain throbbed in his gut as he realized that in the past—before he *ruined* their marriage—he never would have hesitated to discuss this with Shelley. He wouldn't have worried that she'd freak out or they'd get into a fight about it. They would have dissected all the pros and cons together, both of them understanding that it was pure conjecture until they actually had the meeting.

Now, he wasn't sure. It felt like everything turned into a problem lately. Like they were on opposite teams instead of the same one.

Unable to stand it any longer, David felt the threat of tears and saliva pooling in his throat. He gulped it down, along with some of his male pride. This was more important. *Shelley* was more important. He pulled over to the side of the road.

"What are you doing?" Shelley asked.

"I *need* you, Shelley." He shifted the car into park.

Turning to her, he placed his hands on each side of her face, hoping, praying that his emotions would reach her through the wall that had been erected between them. His eyes bore straight into hers—and, he hoped, into her soul—beseeching. "I *need* you. I need *us*. Please, Shelley. *Please* tell me that we can be again all that I know we can be. All that we were before."

Breathless, she felt like the air had been sucked out of her lungs. The car. Her world. She could feel all of the tension that had been held inside her boiling up like a rumble of thunder growing closer when a storm is on its way. Trying to suppress it would be like trying to prevent leaves from falling on a windy autumn day. She couldn't.

One word sobbed through her lips: "David!" Her mind reeled, *My* David. *My* David!

As he drew her into his arms, wrapping her tightly against him, her face automatically went into the crook of his neck where they'd always agreed they were shaped like matching puzzle pieces. They clicked into place. Not just their bodies, where they clung to one another like two who were just rescued from a desert island, but their souls, which had painfully missed one another and were finally reunited.

"I need you back, my Sweet Shelley Bean. *All* of you." He stroked her hair, his arms around her not loosening.

"I need you too, Mr. My Love. All of *you.*"

Chapter 38

During the remainder of the drive, David filled her in on some of his suspicions about what Alexandra might have to say and also reminded her—apologizing profusely—that this was a *jail* drug treatment program. They would be patted down and searched.

They parked, walked across the lot hand-in-hand, and entered the building. After putting her handbag through the scanning device (the male attendant holding up an item in his gloved hand and inquiring, brow raised, "Is this a *personal* massage device?" "Um, no, it's a pen shaped like a lipstick," she'd replied, much to his disappointment), they were escorted to the family visitation area.

Having braced herself for a prisonlike environment, once they were inside Shelley was surprised to find that it was very similar to the other drug treatment programs they'd visited the previous summer. The walls were painted in soothing colors, there were inspirational posters on the walls, and there was one of those little rock fountains plugged into an outlet at a table that also offered coffee, tea, and all the fixings.

With a guilty pang, she realized that she really hadn't asked, that's why she didn't know. Of course, she had asked David each week upon his return, "How was it?" but that was pretty much it. She hadn't asked for details and he hadn't offered any, "Fine, thanks," he would reply. And she had left it at that.

After waiting only a few minutes, a young woman came to join them. She sported a jet-black, super short pixie hairdo and a stud in her nose, her low-rise jeans revealing a strip of smooth, young stomach below a black tee-shirt that depicted some band or another. Which is why Shelley found it so shocking when she extended her hand and said, "Hi, you must be Shelley. I'm Dr. Berry, but you can call me Dr. Betsy."

This is the doctor? Shelley thought. *She looks like a kid! And her name is Betsy Berry?* She felt an inappropriate giggle swelling up inside her. Squelching it, she smiled and shook her hand.

"Don't worry, you're not the first parent to think I look more like a client than a therapist," Dr. Berry—um, Betsy—said, causing Shelley to blush at having had her thoughts read so aptly. "And no, I've never been a drug addict, but yes, I do dress like this normally, not only so I can fit in… it's one of the benefits of working here." She laughed warmly.

Continuing to take the lead, she sat down and said, "I thought we'd spend a few minutes getting to know one another and then Alexandra will join us in a bit."

Shelley nodded, she and David sitting in two of the four chairs that seemed oddly close together in such a large room.

"This is one of the rooms we use for our group sessions as well as family visits," Dr. Betsy explained, again disconcertingly reading Shelley's mind.

"Okay."

"So why don't you tell me a bit about what's been going on with you at home?"

Shelley glanced at David and he nodded, encouraging.

"Well," Shelley began hesitantly, "I've been doing my best with Patrick, Alexandra's son."

Dr. Betsy nodded, allowing her to continue.

"He's a great baby. Actually, becoming more of a little boy now. He's very sweet." *Why do I sound like I'm defending him?* "And smart," she added.

Again, Dr. Betsy nodded but didn't say anything more. Turning to David for help, Shelley said, "David? Do you have anything to add?"

"Not really. We've already talked at length about my thoughts and what I've been going through."

Again, it struck Shelley that she hadn't really been there for David. Hadn't *delved into* the emotions he was experiencing with his daughter—his newfound daughter—being in a jail drug treatment program. The emotions *he* might have about raising his—surprise!—grandson.

"And Alexandra?" the counselor prompted. "How do you feel about her?"

Cornered, Shelley didn't know what to say. *She's an ungrateful little snot? I feel sorry for her that her mother died? I feel sorry for myself because now I have to raise a baby, but I want the best for her?* All were true, yet none seemed right to voice out loud.

"Shelley," Dr. Betsy said, reaching out and placing a hand on her arm. Shelley had to fight the urge to correct, *It's* Mrs. *Morsony, young lady!* "It's perfectly understandable to have mixed feelings. Alexandra and the baby had to be quite a surprise for you to accept."

It's Patrick. His name is Patrick! she suppressed. "Yes, it has been," Shelley said aloud.

"Has it been easier or more difficult with Alexandra not there?" she asked.

"Easier or more difficult?" Shelley parroted, disbelieving. "It's certainly easier than when she was living at home and being a drug addict, but that doesn't mean it's a good thing either. I'm looking forward to her coming home, living a responsible and happy life, and being a good mother to her son."

Did the young doctor look a bit alarmed, or was it just Shelley's imagination?

"Okay, well, we're just about out of time. I'm going invite Alexandra in and we can continue from there."

*****

Arriving back at home, Shelley was exhausted. She felt as if she'd been run over by a steamroller. In fact, *steamrolled* would be a perfect description for exactly what had occurred once Alexandra joined them in the meeting. In her opinion, anyway.

What's with these freakin' twelve step people, anyway? was all she could think. She couldn't accept the concept that as long as you *apologized* for your abhorrent behavior, it was *okay* to do whatever you wanted, *regardless* of what was the responsible thing to do!

And this didn't apply only to past transgressions. Oh no! According to *Doctor* Betsy (crunchy granola, liberal squirt!), simply *recognizing* your limitations made it okay to shirk your responsibilities in the future too!

Alexandra had come into the room—thankfully looking a lot more like a normal girl her age, complete with a little meat on her bones, clean hair, and a healthy appearance—and after an uncomfortably loose hug, launched right into apologizing for all the terrible things she'd done.

Apparently, this was Step 9: Making Amends to Those You Have Wronged. It was supposed to "allow the client to shed the weight of guilt, remorse, and shame," Dr. Betsy had explained.

Okay, fine... good for Alex! Shelley thought. Watching David's expression, she understood that this was not the first time he was hearing this.

But then Alexandra had continued and with the help of Dr. Betsy, went on to explain that during the process of Understanding Her Own Limitations (Step 10, which Shelley assumed was supposed to make it acceptable), she had come to a realization: She didn't want to be a mother just yet. She *wasn't ready.* (*No shit!* Shelley thought.) Instead, when she was released from the program in two weeks, she planned to move into another program, a voluntary independent living program, where she would reside with other recovering drug addicts and would go on mission trips to help others. (Step 12, they were informed: Helping Others.)

Oh! And let's not leave out the fact that the independent living place was in New Mexico. Hours away from where they lived. With *her son!*

Stupefied, both Shelley and David sat there mutely.

Alexandra, evidently having expected them to jump for joy that she *knew her limitations* and wanted to *help others,* appeared to be disappointed at their lack of reaction.

Dr. Betsy had jumped in. "For a young girl who has been through a trauma like Alexandra has, we feel she has made excellent progress in our program."

"A trauma?" Shelley said.

"Yes. Being raped?" Dr. Betsy said with barely disguised disdain.

"Raped! Oh my God! Alexandra, when were you raped? Why didn't you tell us?" Shelley exclaimed, genuine concern banging at her heart.

"Well, um, you know. Like, in Mexico. When I got pregnant."

"What? That wasn't rape. You slept with the guy. On purpose. He didn't *force* you. At least that's what you told us."

"Mrs. Morsony," Dr. Betsy said (now using her proper name like you would when scolding a child), "By the letter of the law, any time a man has sex with a girl who is sixteen years old, it is considered rape. Statuatory rape."

"Oh please!" Shelley said before she could stop herself.

Alexandra was looking at her shoes. David was looking at Dr. Betsy like a deer caught in headlights. Dr. Betsy was looking at Shelley like she was a serial killer.

Shelley, pushed beyond the limits of her own self-discipline went on. "I know it's not the politically correct thing to say. And I'm not saying that statuatory rape doesn't exist. But that was not the case! No one tricked her into doing anything. She *voluntarily* slept with a man and, in my opinion since she didn't use a condom, *voluntarily* got pregnant!"

"Well, by law, Mrs. Morsony, that's still rape since an adult is supposed to know better. Unfortunately, he can't be found and convicted. But that doesn't mean that it's healthy for Alexandra to have her young life ruined and be forced to raise a rapist's child if that's not something she feels is within her own personal limitations."

Shelley decided not to argue about the rape angle for now and give it more thought later. *Should* she consider it a trauma? *Was* Alexandra the victim of a child predator? For the moment, she felt it was more imperative to focus on the issue of her abdicating her role as Patrick's mother.

"Limitations! What about *my* limitations? What about *Patrick's* limitations? It was Alexandra's choice to bring a baby into this world and he is *her* responsibility. And personally, I think it's very irresponsible for you, as a therapist, to counsel her that abandoning her child would be an acceptable thing to do."

"We recognize and accept that those are your feelings, Mrs. Morsony," the doctor said with finality.

Well then, I suppose that just settles things, doesn't it?

David finally spoke. "Okay, so this is the information you brought us here to share," he said, his counseling speak making Shelley want to gag. "With that said, what do you have in mind for Patrick's upbringing?" He was looking at Alexandra, directing the question at her.

"Well, um, I don't know." She was still looking at her feet.

"You don't know!..." Shelley began.

Dr. Betsy interrupted, "Alexandra and I have examined the options both during our private counseling sessions and during group work." She looked from Shelley to David to make sure she had their full attention, then continued, "And it is not her intention to make the baby your responsibility. She just knows that she herself can't continue to do it at this time."

"At this time?" David started, "Does that mean..."

"No, she is not saying she only needs a temporary break. She has come to terms with the fact that the best option is for her to give Patrick up for adoption permanently. To make a fresh start."

"A fresh start!" Shelley objected, her voice at a fevered pitch. "A fresh start for whom?! Certainly not Patrick!"

"Yes, for Patrick too," said Dr. Betsy, calmly. "It can't be good for him to be raised by a mother who is not able, can it?" Her tone imparted that they were being difficult, that they should understand this. Agree even!

"I don't see how this can be good for anyone," David said. Then added, "Including Alexandra. People have to learn to face up to their responsibilities in life."

"Yes, but to what extent, Mr. Morsony? You have other children, right? Haven't they made mistakes that you forgot and forgave so they could move on with a fresh start?"

"Of course! But there's a big difference between getting grounded because you keep losing your phone and then eventually being trusted with a new one, versus abandoning a child. A huge difference! There are some things in life that you just don't get an all-out 'do over' on!"

"I disagree," Dr. Betsy said. "Here at the program, our main focus is on helping addicts live their life a new way. And whatever it takes to ensure that they don't return to a life of drugs and crime is our ultimate goal."

Silence descended upon them, having arrived at this impasse. It was so quiet for a moment that all you could hear was the bubbling sound of the little fake waterfall tumbling over the miniature rock fountain.

Finally David said, "Alexandra, are you absolutely certain this is what you want?"

For the first time all session, she raised her eyes right to his and said, "Yes."

Chapter 39

Shelley and David were given some documents as they left the facility; they had to file them within a week if they wanted to adopt Patrick, otherwise they would be considered temporary guardians while the system searched for a "permanent family." A week! It seemed like a breathtakingly short time to come to terms with the idea that they'd be raising Patrick for life.

Not that they weren't happy about adopting Patrick. They loved him with a ferocity that can only be felt for a family member. Their love was perhaps even more intense with the understanding that they had saved him from a life with either a mother who didn't want him or being shuffled through the foster care system.

He was wanted. Maybe not planned, but definitely wanted. So, with their own love and communication renewed, the two set about envisioning their future differently. Many hours were spent brainstorming what would be the best way to alleviate some of their stress, while also ensuring Patrick the best future.

They made lists. What were the things they'd planned on spending their time doing once the kids were off on their own? Which of those things might they still do, even with raising Patrick? What had to be crossed off... for the next sixteen years?

One decision that was not very difficult to make was selling the house. With just two adults and a toddler, they didn't feel it was necessary to keep the two-story colonial that had a big yard and required so much upkeep. They started looking into townhouses, with an eye out for one that had their master downstairs and was in a good school district. They were used to taking Tiny for leash walks anyway, and they found the idea of not having any lawn or exterior maintenance very appealing.

With their search underway, largely in the hands of their Realtor, Marion, they started de-cluttering their house, getting it ready to sell. This turned out to be more of a quandary than they'd anticipated:

Michael was the only one who was permanently housed elsewhere, and they didn't know what to do with all the rest of the kids' stuff. Rose, Grace, and Russell, all living temporarily in college environments, would still need their furniture and belongings eventually, but would have nowhere to keep all of it right now. Plus, should the kids ever need only some of their stuff, they wanted them to have access to it, which pretty much eliminated the idea of a storage facility.

They decided to use the extra bedroom at their new place (wherever that may be) as if it were a storage room, then they asked all of the kids to come by and go through their things so they could take whatever they needed and condense everything else for now.

They bought several cases of cardboard boxes, a few rolls of packing tape and some Sharpies, and made a bit of an event out of it. Patrick spent the day with Lanie and Annabelle, while Michael, Rose, and Grace came over to organize their stuff and help with Russell's, since he was so far away.

David ordered a bunch of pizzas and turned on the family playlist of music as everyone scattered throughout the house, throwing out drawers full of old pens, squealing over found childhood stuffed animals, and teasing one another about things like kindergarten-aged soccer trophies. ("Woo, you were really quite an athlete!")

Shelley headed into Alexandra's room to pack up her things, which David would bring during his final visit the following week. She didn't need to do much for Patrick, since she was the one who kept track of his things and had been donating his baby clothes and infant toys as he grew out of them.

Opening the first drawer of Alexandra's dresser, she sighed at the reminder that—like all teenager's drawers—all of the clothes were rumpled in there like balls, rather than folded. Methodically, she began folding and stacking, surprising herself at how quickly she made it through three drawers full of clothing, placing them neatly into the old suitcase of Alexandra's that they'd pulled down from the attic.

When she got to the bottom drawer, she came across other stuff, too. It was that drawer that everyone has… the one with all sorts of miscellany that there really is no other place for. Feeling guilty about going through her personal things, but having no other option, Shelley began pulling items out: An old, ratty baby blankie that she assumed must have been Alexandra's when she was little; a tiny Girl Scout vest that had Brownie-level patches; a folded-up note written in adolescent handwriting about how boring math class is, and so on.

Pulling out a larger item, Shelley walked over and sat down on the bed. The photo album was cheaply made, with a faded pink cover and worn corners, as though it had been thumbed through many, many times. Opening the cover, the first pages revealed snapshots of a woman who must have been a younger Patty, with newborn Alexandra in her arms. The baby had the requisite pink and white striped hospital hat on, and Patty had the look of an exhausted but excited new mom.

Leafing through, it was evident that a lot of love had been put into this book—and their life. Like traveling through a timeline of Alexandra's existence, there were photos of mother and daughter in the traditional poses, such as in front of their Christmas tree, and one of a pigtailed six-year-old Alexandra with the Easter bunny. Interspersed were hand-written notes documenting her first words, first steps, first day of school, first period. Candid images also appeared: baking cookies, digging in the garden, Tiny as a puppy with his adoption papers.

Emotions washed over Shelley like waves at the beach. Initial relief that Alexandra had been raised by an apparently doting, involved mother, was followed by a ripple of resentment at Patty having denied David the opportunity to know his child. She experienced a surge of camaraderie when she came across photos of Patty volunteering at school, doing some sort of planting project—dirt everywhere, smiling children—followed by a crushing longing on Alexandra's behalf at having lost her caring mother so young.

Was I really *there for her as much as she needed me to be?* Shelley contemplated. When Alexandra had first arrived, it had been such a shock. The house had been overrun with kids and activities in the first place, and then Patrick had come along so shortly after. *Is any amount of support ever enough to make up for losing one's mother?*

Thinking back to that time—really thinking, forcing herself to be objective—Shelley realized that no, she had not fully been there for her the way she really needed. Sure, she had provided her with a place to live, took care of her dog, signed her up for mom-to-be classes, drove her there. But emotionally, Shelley conceded now, she had remained mostly detached, focusing more on logistics.

Her throat tightening with the threat of tears, she tried to give herself credit for all she *had* done. Yet it still didn't change the core comprehension that Alexandra had needed more. It was so obvious now but at the time it was as if she was so busy just trying to keep her own head above water, the full impact of the emotional side hadn't occurred to her.

With regret burning her stomach, Shelley stood to place the photo album into a box. Deciding that it would be less likely to be damaged if it were standing up, she turned it and a sheaf of papers fell out from the back cover. She bent to pick up the small stack of loose leaf, immediately recognizing Alexandra's handwriting. It was a poem, and while she did feel guilty of invading her privacy by reading it, she couldn't help wanting to understand her better, to possibly learn how she really felt.

Why?

Why do only some birds fly at night?
And where do they go, it doesn't seem right.
Why do we lose and just lose, lose, lose, lose,
our mothers, our homes, and even our shoes?
We all make mistakes
but they're never forgotten.
"Yes they are" people say,
but they still think I'm rotten.
I must be ungrateful,
though that's not what they say,
I just know they must think it day after day.
Are they nice? Oh yeah sure,
but I know they don't mean it,
'cause I've done what they wouldn't,
even the blind should have seen it.
I just want to forget,
to be numb for a while,
to look at my dog,
and his big goofy smile.
It doesn't really matter,
there's no way to undo it.
So for now all I can do,
is to say fuckin' screw it!

*****

Thirty minutes later, Shelley was still sitting on the floor in Alexandra's room when David came looking for her.

"Hey, Sweet Shelley Be..." he began. Then, "What's wrong, babe?"

She showed him the poem, watching his facial expression reflect her same feelings as he read it.

"Wow."

"I know."

"I mean, I thought we were doing pretty well by her."

"So did I. But think about it. Between normal teenage drama, her mother dying, having a baby, and moving in with a new family, were we really there for her emotionally? From this, it sounds like surely not."

"I don't know, Shell," he exhaled heavily. "We reorganized our entire life. Did all the things we could think of. I'm not sure what else we could have done."

"I don't know exactly either, but I feel like maybe I should have talked to her more. Or cut her more slack. Or *something.*"

"More slack? I don't see how any more slack could be cut. We've been raising Patrick with almost no help from her, we hardly gave her any household chores. I think we've done everything we could."

"I know what you mean, but think about it: If she didn't have the baby, don't you think we would have felt the need to give more *emotional* support about her mom dying and moving in with us? I feel like I just got so busy with Patrick that I kind of forgot about Alexandra."

"I think you're being too hard on yourself, Shelley Bean." He drew her into his arms. "I think you've worked your ass off for everyone in this family and no matter how much you do, they as kids will never feel like it's enough. That's the nature of kids. Everything is about them."

Shelley turned her face, enjoying the comfort of nestling it against his chest as he held her. "I know, but I see now that Alexandra as a child herself obviously needed more."

With nothing he could say, knowing he wouldn't change her mind anyway, David continued to hold her a while, then said, "Come on down. Pizza's ready."

Chapter 40

"So," Michael began in what David and Shelley had come to recognize as his I'm a Man With a Family Now voice. "There's something Lanie and I would like to discuss with you."

It was evening, and after the exhausting day of cleaning out and condensing, Rose and Grace each headed back to their respective colleges, while Lanie was kind enough to bring Patrick home so they wouldn't have to come out and get him.

"Okay," David said, immediately giving his full attention.

"Lanie and I have been talking about what we want to do after the wedding," Michael began. "You know, house-wise."

David and Shelley both nodded.

"And we are thinking that we would like to buy this house from you."

"Hmm. Really?" David began. "I know you mentioned something a while back, but we thought you were just kidding."

"I kind of was. I mean, I wasn't sure whether we could afford it, or how Lanie would feel about moving into my parents' house, or whatever. But now that we've had time to discuss it, we both think it would be a great idea."

"Wow, that's really nice!" Shelley interjected. "That you would want to live here, I mean."

"Well, it was a nice place to grow up, it's a great neighborhood, and we think it would be good for Annabelle."

"You're right, it probably would."

"So, we thought we'd talk to you guys about, you know, a price and stuff," Michael went on, now nervous. They could tell he was trying to be very manly about it, but it was inevitable that he'd feel somewhat apprehensive, as this was likely one of the first financial discussions he'd ever had, and with his father, to boot! Glancing at one another, the couple shared a moment of pride.

"As you know, we've already met with Marion to discuss fair market value but we've been waiting to do the formal listing until we're finished with shaping things up," David explained.

"We know," Lanie said. "That's why we wanted to talk with you now, even though we're so busy with the wedding next week and everything. We figure we can all save some money by just doing a direct sale, so we wanted to see if we could arrange things before you had the obligation to pay a Realtor."

"Great idea. I'm impressed!" David said.

Shelley nodded in agreement.

"Another thing is, you could just leave Patrick's room the way it is and not have to repaint it and stuff."

"Well," Shelley began. "We would still put on fresh paint. It's got all the trains stenciled on and his name on the wall. I would want you to have it just as clean and fresh as any other buyer."

"That's not what I meant. We were thinking, you know, for when Patrick spends time over here with us."

"Well, that's very nice, but he doesn't need a whole room just to come over for play dates!"

Lanie jumped in. "Actually, we were hoping that you might let us keep him with us sometimes." At Shelley's expression of shock she added, "Not all the time, but you know, for weekends or when you guys want to travel or something."

David stiffened, his tone instantly more formal. "That's very nice, you two. But you have your own family to worry about. Patrick is our responsibility and we'll be just fine."

"Dad," Michael cajoled. "That's not how we mean it. Remember when you were our age? Having more little ones around was no big deal! We just figured it would be fun to have him around more, plus, he and Annabelle are crazy about each other. And this way you guys can have some free weekends to go and do… whatever it is you do." He rolled his eyes comically, in keeping with the kids' habit of teasing them about their "old people romance."

"I think that would be lovely," Shelley said.

"Great. It's all settled then," Michael said, taking the lead again. "I mean, we can sort out the details after the wedding but we wanted to talk to you before you did the listing."

David, clearly struggling with the entire scenario in which his son was suddenly behaving like a grown man, was further dismayed when Michael stood, reached out, and shook his hand. Quite firmly.

Chapter 41

The wedding was absolutely perfect.

Donna Lee had performed the alterations to Shelley's navy blue dress, and when she went to pick it up was sure to reassert, "Now you just go be the hot trophy wife you *are* at that weddin', ya hear?" Shelley couldn't help hearing that sugary reminder in her head all throughout the evening.

The simple ceremony was beautiful, focused more on the couple's love for one another than on tradition. Of course, Patrick and Annabelle as ring bearer and flower girl drew oohs and aahs from the small crowd as they toddled their way down the aisle.

The food was excellent, the weather was comfortable, the band was talented. Shelley enjoyed every moment being held in David's arms as they danced, the first of their kids married and happy. Something big to celebrate.

Thankful that she'd insisted on the dress with the straps, she'd carried Patrick around to visit all of the tables. He had shed his tiny tuxedo jacket and rolled up his sleeves just like the "big boys" did the minute the formal photographs were over. For the first time, she felt relaxed introducing herself as his grandmother. Didn't feel the need to explain where his mother was. Just accepted, enjoyed, and appreciated him for the adorable little human being that he was. Another branch on the tree of their unusual family.

She even felt good about Alexandra. Having had more time to think about her decision, and with her new perspective of just how traumatic the past several years had been for her, she was truly okay with it. She didn't agree with her giving Patrick up, but she understood it. Shelley was glad that Alexandra was off drugs and seemed happy. That she was going to do something with her life that was meaningful to her, and that she might even make a difference in other people's lives too.

She knew that David felt better too. That at least knowing where she was, not wondering whether she was dead or alive, and not feeling like he'd failed her, was helping him come to terms with things as well. It was as if once they made their custody of Patrick permanent, having another child to raise was not the biggest issue anymore. It left him more able to focus on the actual father-daughter relationship, rather than what was right or wrong.

With everything in place, it felt like there was no need to "fix" anything anymore.

Well, maybe there was one more thing.

*****

The morning after the wedding, Shelley and David zipped along in the car with Patrick, Tiny, and all of Alexandra's belongings. It would be the last time they would see her before she left for New Mexico, and so with some apprehension, they'd opted to bring everyone she might want to say goodbye to.

David had arranged with Dr. Betsy for a staff member to keep an eye on Patrick for a short while, which was something they were accustomed to, since many of their clients had children who occasionally came for visitation.

Tiny, ears and lips flapping joyfully in the wind as he rode with his head out the window, would be fine for a short time in the car, as the weather was mild and they could leave the windows open.

The couple chatted as they grew closer to the facility, each feeling confident about the things they'd agreed to talk about. With David's hand threaded through hers, resting on the middle console, Shelley felt content in her heart, secure in their decision.

Once again parking and going through security (Shelley *tried* to warn the guy that sticking your hands inside toddler pockets is never a good idea), the three entered the family visiting area where they were greeted by Dr. Betsy and an intern.

"Oh. My. God!" the intern squealed. "Isn't he just the cutest thing in the whole entire world! Come this way, cutie, want to play in the toy room?"

Relieved to see that the toy room was connected to the room they were in, Shelley walked Patrick by the hand and helped him get settled playing with the young girl. Once he saw the miniature ball pit, he forgot all about his grandparents and was fine when Shelley kissed his cheek and said that she'd be right back.

When she returned to the large room, Alexandra was already there, looking even healthier than before, albeit nervous. After quick hugs, they all sat down and Dr. Betsy began speaking.

"So, this will be our last meeting. Alexandra has really excelled in our program and I have every confidence that she will go on to lead a happy, productive, and *clean* life."

Alexandra nodded. "Thank you."

Silence ensued, prompting Shelley to notice that the rock fountain wasn't making any noise. She glanced over and noted that it had been replaced by a candelabra.

"Clients were complaining that it made them feel like they had to pee," Dr. Betsy said.

Wow, that girl really is a mind reader! Shelley thought. Then, *Well, here goes!*

"Alexandra," Shelley began. She tried to steady her voice, overwhelmed by her emotions already. "I wanted to let you know that I appreciate all of the hard work you've had to do in this program and I accept the apologies you made last time."

With a surprised expression, Alexandra nodded, then looked down.

"I also want to let you know that *I'm* sorry." Alexandra's head whipped up, her face revealing confusion.

"I've realized that, as much as I've tried to help you with the baby, I haven't really been there for you as much as you needed." As Alexandra began to object, Shelley held a hand up. "Let me finish. I know I was overwhelmed but still, with your mom dying and never knowing your dad, and everything else, I wish I had been there for *you* more. Emotionally, rather than just physically."

"You did what you could. What you thought was right," Alexandra said.

"That's true, but I still want you to know that I wish I'd been there for you more. That we'd talked more."

"Thank you."

There was silence for a moment.

David spoke. "We would also like to talk with you about how we will handle Patrick's upbringing."

Fearfully, Alexandra said, "What do you mean?"

"What I mean is, we consider you part of our family, Alex. You're my daughter." He looked at Shelley. "*Our* daughter. You may go and live in New Mexico, but family is family and we're hoping you will still be a part of ours."

Facilitating the conversation, Dr. Betsy prompted, "Can you tell us more about what you mean, David?"

"Well, we're hoping Alexandra may come and visit. That we can speak on the phone. Maybe even exchange letters or pictures once in a while."

Alexandra, tears streaming, said, "I would like that."

"We also would like to get your input on how you want us to handle things with Patrick," Shelley said. "We think it would be nice for him to know that you're his mother and we are his grandparents. That we're raising him because you were too young and not ready, but that you do still love him, even if you're not personally raising him on a daily basis."

Stunned, Alexandra appeared frozen. David quickly inserted, "We're not saying we *have to* do that. We just thought it might be a nice way to handle things. That maybe you could still be, at least, *known* to him."

Sobbing now, Alexandra leapt from the chair and threw herself into David's arms. She was crying so hard that her speech was incoherent, so he just held her, his hand soothing down the back of her head, smoothing her hair, stroking like one would a baby. His baby.

Dr. Betsy got up and went to grab a box of tissues from a side table, trying to inconspicuously dab at her own eyes as she returned. Alexandra whipped a few from the box and wiped her nose, laughing a little and saying, "I think I got boogers on your shirt."

"Wouldn't be the first time and I hope it's not the last," David said.

Epilogue

Two years later, Shelley found herself enjoying Christmas in a way she never had before. In other words, she didn't feel like a slave, wasn't personally cooking for twenty people, and hadn't spent the last three months agonizing over what gifts would ensure eternal happiness for each family member.

With adult kids, cash was king, and with only Patrick and Annabelle to buy toys for, it was easy as pie. Oh, and speaking of pie, Shelley did make one. *One!* It was like a miracle!

Shelley took her time as she helped by setting the table at Michael and Lanie's house—her old house. The guys had the big, flat screen TV on in the living room and she could hear them all: David, Michael, Russell, and Keith, arguing good-naturedly over some sports statistics or another.

Her and David's relief had been palpable upon meeting Keith, Alexandra's boyfriend. They had met while on a mission trip, and they'd been pretty concerned about her getting into a relationship with a former drug addict. Although Alexandra had said on the phone that he was a good guy with a decent job as a service manager for a car dealership, they couldn't help worrying… particularly when she mentioned that he had a Harley.

Fortunately, when Alexandra and this new boyfriend arrived for their visit, all visions of a Tyler replica went right out the window. He was a clean-cut, nice guy who enjoyed his motorcycle more as a "weekend warrior" for scenic road trips, rather than as a lifestyle. He had no snake tattoos (not that they could see anyhow, which was fine with them), and appeared to have not only all of his teeth, but a decent manner of speaking and—most importantly—easily made Alexandra smile.

As Shelley continued to place the silverware carefully in their places, she treated herself to the indulgence of what she and David privately called a "family accounting," in which they went over each of the family members and how they were doing.

Not only were things going well with Alexandra's love life, but her overall life seemed to be going well too. True to what they'd discussed before she left, they stayed in touch with weekly phone calls and regular e-mails. They even Skyped sometimes, so Patrick could actually see his mom and Alexandra could see him growing up.

She was taking courses in social work with the plan to advance her career and help more addicts with recovery, and had sent photos of her small apartment, which she enjoyed decorating with pieces she'd find at garage sales and then refinish into shabby chic décor.

They were proud of her. Genuinely proud. With no forced brightness, no underlying second meaning, no "buts" providing exceptions. She was doing well and so were they.

A thunderous yet high-pitched sound approached and Shelley jumped aside just in time to avoid being trampled by Patrick, Annabelle, and Tiny, who were running the circular track of the house, Tiny with a rope toy in his mouth and the two kids squeezing his squeakies. Goofballs. *Some things never change,* she thought affectionately.

Lanie came waddling out of the kitchen, yelling, "Hey you guys, slow it down!" as she wiped her hands on a towel. Her belly was round with pregnancy, now in her third trimester... she and Michael were expecting their second baby—their first together—in just two more months.

Shelley chuckled to herself and called to Rose, asking her to help with serving. She was engrossed in a debate with Russell about who was likely to make more money: Rose majoring in information technology, or Russell who would have his MBA. She was trying to make the point that it was important to be happy at your job too, while Russell was asserting that having lots of money does make you happy.

They both make good points, Shelley laughed to herself.

Grace, also overhearing their conversation, called out to chime in, "It won't matter anyway because your sister is going to be a famous fashion designer!"

The two rolled their eyes, likely thinking about how Grace would always find a way to wear expensive jeans.

With Lanie now herding everyone toward the table, Shelley found her seat next to David. She could see that his face was flushed with pleasure—and probably from wine too—enjoying that the family was all together.

Once they were all seated, Keith surprised everyone by asking if they would mind him saying a blessing before they ate.

"Of course," David said. Although they weren't a religious family, saying grace before a meal, especially on Christmas, would be nice.

Everyone closed their eyes—except Annabelle and Patrick, Shelley was sure—and they all joined hands around the table.

Keith spoke: "God, we thank you for the many ways you have blessed us this day. We ask you to bless us, and our food, and to bless those we love who are not here with us. We pray for the souls who are lost in their journey of life, that they may find their way, and we pray for the continued health and happiness that we at this table are enjoying today. We bless you and give thanks in your Spirit on Christmas Day and every day. Amen."

"Amen," they all said collectively.

"What men, Mommy?" Patrick asked, directing his question toward Alexandra.

Everyone laughed, then waited, tongue-in-cheek, to see how she would answer. Was she going to try and explain God and Jesus, all in one sitting, here at the table?

"We didn't say 'men,' honey. We said 'amen,' which just means that we agree."

There was a pause while Patrick contemplated this, then David broke the silence by saying, "Let's eat."

"A man!" shouted Patrick.

And again, not for the first time and not for the last that evening, everyone laughed together.

The End

Acknowledgments

As I arrive at the publication of *Unexpecting*, I owe the greatest appreciation to my readers. It is because of your support, encouragement, and letting me know about your enjoyment of my books, that I continue writing for the public rather than only for my personal pleasure.

I would also like to thank my husband, Mark, for being understanding when I've been angry at him for no logical reason, due to frustrations in the lives of my fictional characters.

To the many, many teenagers in my life, as well as all of the nice, mean, quirky, friendly, and unfriendly people whose personalities I've stolen from to develop the characters, I thank you for your existence.

I can't forget to mention my cat Indy, who is kind of old and was my inspiration for Frick. He is a pain in the neck, constantly insisting on being on my lap and desk while I'm writing, but I love him anyway. And a special thanks to my friend Randy's dog, Otto, who is in heaven, but now lives forever in the likeness of Tiny. To see photos of Otto/Tiny, I invite you to visit his special page: www.LoriTheAuthor.com/Tiny.

About the Author

Lori Verni-Fogarsi has been an author, speaker, and small business consultant since 1995. She has been featured in major media including *Lifetime Women's Network*, the *My Carolina Today Show*, and *Boston Globe Forums Live.* Her public speaking has occurred at many prestigious venues including *North Carolina State University, Nassau Community College,* and many more.

She has received two awards for her novel, *Momnesia*, and her nonfiction, *Everything You Need to Know About House Training Puppies and Adult Dogs,* continues to be one of the most highly recommended in its genre since 2005.

Lori is a happy married mom of two, stepmom of two more, and has two cats, both rotten. She is very excited to bring you *Unexpecting*, and enjoys getting to know her readers via social media and in person. She invites you to get to know her, and learn about past and future projects at **www.LoriTheAuthor.com**.

Unexpecting

Reader's Discussion Guide

1. What did you think of the way Shelley and David handled Alexandra's early integration into their family? Do you think you would have handled things similarly or differently?

2. What about Alexandra's behavior, as well as the other kids'? Did they behave the way you might have expected, or were you surprised at their reactions?

3. How did you feel about Shelley and David's parenting style? With Alexandra? With Patrick? With the other kids? Did you feel like they did too much, too little, or that you would have done about the same?

4. Did you get the sense that Shelley and David's relationship was solid (prior to the Big Terrible Incident)? Or did you suspect that something might go amiss?

5. When Claire comes over to talk to Shelley, she says, "I realized that I could either hate him for the one extremely horrible thing he did, or I could love him for all of the many wonderful things he's always done."

   What was your reaction to this perspective? Do you think that, like Claire and Shelley, you might be able to heal through this mantra, or do you feel it would be impossible? Has anything ever occurred in your life that was similar? Discuss.

6. How did you feel about the way David and Shelley handled Alexandra's drug problem? Did you feel that they over or underreacted? In the same circumstances, do you think you would have turned her in to Joe The Cop, or done something different?

7. Shelley fluctuates with her sense of Self throughout the story. She becomes more attached to Patrick than she would have expected, while at the same time resenting the overall situation. When he's gone, she both misses him and relishes her free time. How do you think you might feel in similar circumstances? Discuss.

8. At times, things get a little hectic with all of the kids: Michael moving home, Rose wanting to go on an exchange program, etc. Did you feel overwhelmed at all, reading about the pace of life they were trying to keep up? How does this compare to your household?

9. Regarding Alexandra's taking care of Patrick: Did you feel like Shelley and David expected too much of her? Not enough? What do you think you might have done differently or the same?

10. Toward the end, Alexandra decides to go on with her own life and not continue parenting Patrick. Were you surprised at her decision? What are your thoughts on this?

11. What did you think of the therapist referring to Alexandra's pregnancy as having been a rape? Is this something that occurred to you earlier in the story? Either way, did you agree or disagree with the suggestion that she was a victim?

12. Shelley comes to a point where she feels regret at not having been there more for Alexandra on an emotional level, regarding the loss of her mother and the other changes. Did you agree or disagree with her feeling this way? How did you feel about her apologizing to Alexandra and accepting her decision to give up Patrick?

13. What did you think about David and Alexandra's relationship? Although David wasn't featured as strongly throughout the story, did you get the sense that it was important to him? Why or why not? Why do you think the author chose to write it this way?

14. What did you think of Shelley and David's decision to encourage Alexandra to still be a part of their family and known to Patrick as his mother even though they would be raising him?

If you enjoyed *Unexpecting,* you might also enjoy *Momnesia,* by Lori Verni-Fogarsi!

Momnesia includes many of the same characters from *Unexpecting,* except that it takes place ten years earlier. David and Shelley don't even know one another yet! *Momnesia* is Shelley's story as she divorces her first husband and struggles with trying to find balance between her responsibilities to her young children, while also taking care of her Self. She sets about finessing balance between her "momminess" and her "sexiness!" (Warning for those with very delicate sensibilities: There is a bit more of a "spice factor" with language/content in *Momnesia!*)

Sneak peek! Enjoy the first chapter of *Momnesia!*

Chapter 1

I was in my car in the parking lot of the supermarket. That I was certain about. What I was not sure about was… well, everything else.

For example, did I just come into the car with the groceries or had I yet to go into the store? Should I get divorced? (The question I'd been pining about for more than two years.) Or continue along in my unhappy marriage?

You know that your life has become far too miserable when you can't even recall what you're doing versus what you've already done. As I sat there watching shoppers going in and out of the store, shepherding children and loading up their cars, I told myself, *This is ridiculous! Of course I can remember. Just think!*

I recalled waking the kids—a task no easier on camp mornings than on school days. Cleaning the waffle iron—the direct result of my guilt over their customary cereal. Walking them to the neighbor's, thankful that it wasn't my turn to drive, the syrupy air dotted with mosquitoes almost as irritating as the girls' litany of complaints (the counselors are mean, they don't like the pizza). The sour taste of resentment at having to do everything while Paul, apparently having an "up" day, would saunter by and do things like tickle them—always ready to usurp but never to help.

I'd returned home, showered and dressed, then gathered my things.

Turning toward the passenger seat, my errand supplies were still there: the bank deposit, some library books, and a proposal to drop off at a client's showroom. Somewhat relieved, I recalled carrying those things to the car. Walking out to my driveway, the heat had been wriggling up from the pavement in a mirage of waves. I'd opened the car door and the scalding interior air had slapped me, causing my teeth to throb as if I'd bitten into an ice cream.

That's it. That was all I could remember. I had no recollection of driving to the store or parking the car, both of which I had obviously done. With rising panic, I tried to convince myself that it was one of those situations where it's such a familiar task that your car simply "knows" the way.

On the other hand, to have absolutely no idea of whether or not I'd gone *into* the store was so farfetched that the misery I carried with me became oppressively apparent as far more than a preoccupation. Clearly, my indecisiveness about my marriage had intensified to a debilitating level.

Look at what I've become. This can't go on any longer.

An understanding hovered just outside my reach—like when a word is on the tip of your tongue but you can't get it to come out. I blinked, nauseous, tiny black spots zigzagging like sperm in my periphery.

Digging through my purse, I pulled out a cigarette and lit it, exhaling a plume of smoke just in time to notice two PTA acquaintances walking by, averting their eyes and talking behind their hands. *Greeaat.*

I cracked the window and chills rippled over me, causing goose bumps to rise along my arms. Which I'm sure would have been an alarming sensation at any time, but on that day held even more weight being that I was, thankfully, still cognizant enough to realize that it was a sweltering August day in North Carolina and that the temperature had to be over one hundred degrees.

As if on autopilot, my arm reached out to hit a button and a rush of cool air blasted onto my neck where the perspiration was streaming down and pooling along my collarbone.

My anxiety continued to rise, knowing that I had to turn around and see if there were bags in the back of the car, but feeling paralyzed, unable to turn my head. Postponing the inevitable, I contemplated the little vehicle that steers twenty shopping carts—or more specifically, the teenager whose machismo expression failed to fully conceal his grin as he drove it. *Why are we so afraid to let our real selves be seen?*

Images began flashing through my mind like one of those slideshows presented at the end of kindergarten year, filled with heart-pulling images: Paul doing a lemonade stand with the kids, their giggles shining brighter than their lime-green and turquoise pitchers. Rusty bringing his Frisbee to me, his hopeful brown eyes filled with unconditional canine adoration.

Who will keep the cats? Can I deal with cutting the lawn? Did I go in the damn store? This is fucking crazy!

Finally, impatient with the situation—and in fact, my entire life—I forced myself to look.

They were there. The groceries. And to make matters worse, it was obvious this had been no small shopping trip either. There were about nine bags, which to my practiced eye amounted to around $127. worth of food shopping.

Returning to forward-facing, my eyes skimmed past the rest of the interior: two booster seats in the back and miscellaneous litter that included crumpled napkins, empty juice boxes, and a Wiggles CD. Absurdly, I thought, *This place is a pigsty. I've really got to clean that up.*

Another emotion washed over me: relief. And I don't mean relief from the heat, the dissipating shock, or even the fact that I could check the grocery shopping off of my to-do list. No, this was an all-consuming relief, like when it's Christmas night and your kids are happy, everyone's been fed, and the annual holiday slavery is behind you.

I was relieved because it was over. My "Should I? Shouldn't I? Dilemma" had finally come to an end. There was no further question, nothing else to pine over. Without the tiniest smidgen of doubt, it was time to get divorced.

*****

I realize that, although serious, this one incident might sound like a frivolous way to make such a critical decision. But the truth is, it wasn't so much the one incident as much as it was the *final* incident—the proverbial straw that broke the camel's back, breaking me out of the cognitive dissonance that had gone on for so long regarding my marriage. And besides, I think anyone would agree that when you find yourself so emotionally disoriented that you entirely lose large chunks of time out of your life, things have gone way too far.

Not to mention my conversation just a week earlier with my gynecologist during which she asked, "So, I see that you're physically healthy. And how are *you* doing?" While I did not pour my heart out with all the details of my unhappy marriage, I did end up disclosing enough information about my current state of unhappiness for her to suggest, "I can prescribe something that will make you feel a whole lot better. Many women at your stage of life are taking antidepressants."

This threw me back to a memory from about twelve years prior when my friend Faith, (who is twenty-five years older) told me, "Wait and see. Once you have kids and get to be around forty you'll be taking Buspar just like the rest of us." We were sitting around a campfire, passing a bottle of cherry brandy amongst a group of women that included her sister, best friend, mother, and cousin. All of whom were nodding enthusiastically and agreeing, "Yup, it's the best. A real life saver!"

I remember thinking at the time that those women were crazy. And I didn't mean crazy in the sense of actually being a person with a mental disorder that requires medication. I meant crazy metaphorically, as in how could it be possible that *all* of them were so miserable that they have resorted to medicating themselves just to get through life?

Back then, I was thinking that they needed therapy, not drugs. And that day, sitting in my car in the parking lot of the supermarket, I realized that what I needed was also not a prescription, but a divorce. And maybe some therapy too.

*****

Heading home, knowing I'd be telling Paul that "this was it," I dreaded the discussion. Honestly, not so much because he'd be distraught. He doesn't get distraught. (Except for when he does.) Selfishly, I was dreading it because I knew he would act shocked and that it was going to drive me crazy.

After all, how could he be shocked when all I'd been talking about with him for more than two years was the fact that we were unhappy and I thought we should consider a divorce? I'd spoken to him about it in person, on the phone, in writing, and via e-mail. We went to marriage counseling for a year. We did the date night thing, the creative conversations, the discussing with mutual friends. We tried all the things people try when they don't want to tear apart their family and ruin the lives of their two young daughters.

Nonetheless, I knew he'd be shocked. And the reason I knew that was because after ten years of marriage, I knew that he was surprised about almost everything.

For example, "Oh, we're leaving now?" he'd cry, dismayed that it was time to leave despite the fact that I'd been running around for the previous three hours, bathing two children, getting them dressed, packing their snacks, walking the dog, hollering for everyone to get coats on, warming up the car, and making sure the business answering machine was set. "I didn't know we were leaving," he'd grumble, as he'd head into the bathroom for a nice long one while the kids and I would sit in the car and wait.

I also knew that he'd be shocked because he didn't really think anything was wrong in the first place. Of course, he knew *I* was unhappy. But the reality is, he could have continued in the marriage—with all of its dysfunctional idiosyncrasies—forever. Pleasantly cohabiting like roommates with me facilitating every aspect of his and the children's lives, running our family business, and taking care of every detail, while he would simply come and go to and from work and cut the grass once a week. Well, that's not entirely true: sometimes he wouldn't even cut the grass because he "wasn't feeling up to it," while other times he'd compulsively implement household projects—projects which inevitably became my responsibility when he'd lose steam.

You're probably thinking this sounds bitter on my part. However, I really don't think it should be described as bitterness so much as disgust: with myself for having let it go on for so long, with him for not being different than he was, and with both of us for making such a poor choice of spouse in the first place.

If you'd like to read more, please visit www.LoriTheAuthor.com, find *Momnesia* on Amazon or other websites, or ask at your local bookstore.